THE
ARTIFACT

LINDA S. GLEASON

Paperback-Press
an imprint of A & S Publishing
A & S Holmes, Inc.

.

ISBN-13: 978-1-945669-56-9

DEDICATION

This book is dedicated to our ancestors who still live within our hearts and who someday will again walk with us into the future.

ACKNOWLEDGMENTS

First and foremost, I would like to express my gratitude to Publishing Coordinator Sharon Kizziah-Holmes at Paperback-Press, Editor Wanda Fittro and Copy Editor Shirley McCann and Cindy Brady, for their help and guidance in publishing my book.

A special thanks to my good friend Barbara Steelman who believed and understood what this book was all about. My thanks also to Jaime Cole, a Beta Reader from the Springfield Writers Guild for her input.

My gratitude to Candy Simonson for her assistance in the design of the book cover. A special acknowledgment to the Cahokia Mounds State Historic site and the painting of Cahokia as it may have appeared c. AD 1150; painted by Michael Hampshire (britanica.com).

For the research of the novel, I would like to acknowledge The Field Museum of Chicago, Illinois. The Cahokia Mounds State Historic site and the Interpretive Center near Collinsville, Illinois. Web site, Ancient Origins.

Background information from James Tyberonn on the Lemurians from his article "The Blue Beings of Inner Earth and the Crystalline Shift," Sedona Journal.

Background information on the Society of Jesus from web site, society-of-jesus.brainsip.com. Father Eusebio Francisco Kino and the Duchess of Aveiro y Arcos, of Madrid taken from "Rim of Christendom" and "Kino's Historical Memoir of Pimeria Alta" by Herbert E. Bolton. The Jesuits, Father Kino and the Duchess of Aveiro y Arcos were real historic people from the past that the author built a story of fiction around.

FACTS

The Cahokia Mounds State Historic Site with more than 2200 acres is the most sophisticated prehistoric civilization north of Mexico. Once was home to around 20,000 people, flourishing between the 11th and 12th century, boasted over 120 mounds including the ten-story earthen pyramid known as Monk's Mound. A place where Native Americans made pilgrimages for special rituals linked to the origin of the cosmos.

The technology for Space Archaeology Satellite Imaging does exist. Space Satellite Archaeology – NASA satellite imaging. https://www.age-of-the-sage.org/

The UFO sighting event of 2000 was real--A triangular shaped craft, as long as a football field was chased by multiple police officers over several small towns in Southern Illinois. This is viewed as one of the most substantial UFO sightings in the history of the phenomenon with their in-depth testimonies fully documented by investigators. – Documentary Review – "Seeing is Believing: The Truth About UFO's" by Peter Jennings, ABC-TV, 2-24-2005

The Knights of Malta--A European Society formed in c.1049, is one of the oldest institutions of western and Christian civilization formed with its hospital roots. The society still exist today with its over 120,000 members now in the charity business in 120 countries. A lay religious order of the Catholic Church since 1113.
www.orderofmalta.int/sovereign-order-of-malta

CHAPTER 1

Pimeria Alta of New Spain – June, 1767

Near midday, the Jesuit priests arrived with their final loads of gold and silver at their destination, the Guadalupe Mine. The high mountaintop formed two peaks, with three hundred-foot cliffs on two sides, which ensured a rugged drop to the box canyons below.

The entrance to the mine near the top of the south peak had a backdrop of jagged solid granite rock that resembled the crown of thorns worn by Our Lord Jesus Christ. The abandoned mine's tunnels, now stripped and depleted, held a large volume of pure silver and gold that the Jesuits had processed into bars and hoarded away deep within her caverns.

The priests, wearing their long black robes, stood close to a ledge and looked down into the Santa Cruz Valley. In the far distance, they could barely make out the white dome atop the Tumacacori Mission. They were saddened as they realized that this might be the last time all of them would be here together, and distressed that they were being forced to leave this new country they had come to love. Yet, they held out that small flicker of hope that God would see their safe return, to be part of the New Order.

Father Giovanni Vega had already placed the crate that housed the 'Spiritual Artifact' deep within the mine, hiding it as instructed, when he assumed the guardianship from his mentor, Father Kino.

The Jesuits brought their diaries, records and maps of all the other secretly stored mines of Pimeria Alta, to be stored away. The mine now held a far greater wealth and treasure, with God overseeing and awaiting the proper time for the owners to reclaim.

The Pima Indians were busy unloading the treasure over five hundred feet under the surface, with a Jesuit supervising the operation, hurrying them, as they needed to quickly return to their Missions before the soldiers arrived. The time passed and the father pulled his time piece from his robe, noting it was five-fifty-five. He signaled to the others it was time. All the Indians were accounted for below ground.

Father Vega approached the young padre Bentz, handing him a box covered with an Agnus Dei, impressed with crosses and lambs, kissed by the Pope. The young assassin unwrapped the explosive, his body trembled, his hands quivered. Father Vega stepped up encouraging him, "Be virtuous, faithful, and trust in God. He will instill in you all the strength thy hands will need to do what thou must."

The other priests bowed their heads in prayer while Father Vega called upon the highest of the Angels, "Come most powerful, blessed Angels of the Heavens. Come Cherubim! Come Seraphim! Come forth Angels of Charity! Come now and fill God's holy servant with his power and glory!"

The overcast grey sky suddenly changed before their eyes, as black thunder heads rolled in above them. They heard a loud cracking sound, as a lightning spear streaked from the heavens downward piercing the earth. The priests, cloaked in fear, carried on their ritual. The young dutiful Jesuit did as he was told.

Soon there came a deafening explosion and an excruciating rumbling of the earth, as waves of energy rolled and overturned soil and rocks, knocking everyone to the ground. A blanket of brown earth covered up the entrance of the mine. Then it eventually settled into quietness. They detected an energy flowing among them, the holy presence of The Angel of Death. Soon, he would be showing the twenty-one souls their pathway to heaven. They took one last moment to look upon their now sealed and hidden treasure site. To their surprise, new markings were made on the granite rocks above where the mine entrance had been, in the form of a cross.

CHAPTER 2

Chicago, Illinois – Present Time

Laurel Robertson awoke with a startle. She sensed adrenaline moving through her body, a feeling of cold, electrical energy.

"What was that?" She uttered, while still in a very drowsy state. "What was that noise?" She questioned again, as she rolled over. A loud rumbling sound permeated her memory as she became more awake. Laurel realized she must be dreaming again. Yet, she had these faint pictures left in her mind of big boulders and rocks flying in the air. And a feeling of sadness.

She moved her head towards the bed-side clock, grudgingly opening her eyes. Her view coming into focus, she saw three numbers, all the same, 5:55. "There it is again," she shrieked, and partially rose from her warm bed. It was like she felt the numbers. They had an eerie charge. This was the third time she had seen three fives on a digital read-out in the past few weeks. "What does it all mean?" She tried to reason it out, with no results. Giving up on the puzzle she rolled over and tried to sleep again. Her restless body refused to cooperate. "All right, you win!"

With reluctance, she left her bed, and the cold early morning air quickly engulfed her partially nude body, giving her muscles a temporary shock. She slipped on some sweats, stepped into her warm, fur-lined moccasins, and made her way to the kitchen, where she put a kettle on for some hot tea. She could not function well until after that first cup. Taking a sip of the warm green tea, laced with honey, her thoughts returned to the strange dream she awakened to. What's with this five, five, five? It's like someone, or something is deliberately drawing my attention to those particular numbers–but why?

Laurel was still contemplating the dream, when she put on the heavy robe lying on the foot stool by the atrium door of her apartment and stepped out on the terrace. The morning air was a bit nippy but was to be expected for Chicago's March weather. Thankfully, the hot Brazilian tea was warming her from the inside out.

She turned the cushion over on the wicker chair, dumping the recent lake effect snow and wrapped herself in a heavy warm quilt she brought from inside. She sat and listened to the peaceful, tranquil setting. It was times like this that reminded her why she loved Chicago. The early morning darkness still surrounded her, with the moon shinning across the branches of the large potted evergreen, highlighting the white patches of snow that glistened in shades of blue and gold. The short life span of tranquility would soon dwindle, as the bountiful sounds of the Windy City would soon be fully awake.

As first light slowly began to appear, she gazed out across the park-like area, which had now exposed a wonderful view of the lakefront. While her eyes were fixed on the water; her thoughts went deeper as she tried to remember the dream. She could almost hear her Grams voice, explaining, "Laurel, many times those dreams are not actually what they appear to be." She drifted deeper into her memory, recalling more of what Grams had to say.

"Mostly we dream in symbols. Everyone in the dream is usually the dreamer, even though there are different characters playing out the dream." Her grandmother then stressed to her, "These same rules even apply to the precognitive dream."

Laurel tried to reason the dream out. There was this very loud noise. Could it have been an explosion? There was a loud rumbling noise too, the sounds of a storm maybe, or something crashing into another object? She felt a great sadness, one that sank clear to her core. This was puzzling. Why did she always end up with this sad, desolate feeling?

What if this was a precognitive dream. Could this mean sometime soon, I'm going to be involved in this? Her thoughts shifted and she smiled. Probably subconsciously, I'm making a mountain out of a mole hill. All this procrastinating about which project to do this summer rattling around in my head.

Laurel, confused about the whole thing, thought it might be outside her field of knowledge, and decided she needed to talk to her grandmother. She made a mental note to call her in the evening, with the hope that she could sort it out. Or maybe one of the practitioners at the

Metaphysical Center could help. She missed seeing Grams. Taking the position with The Field Museum of Natural History kept them apart more than she had wished.

Laurel's craving for another cup of tea prompted her to take leave of her private winter haven. Her friends and colleagues were right when they said she was lucky to have found this spacious singles apartment. They often joked that her place was like walking through one of the museum's exotic South American exhibits, with tropical trees and artifacts displayed about. Her taste and style of furniture was unique for a Missouri girl. Unique but very comfortable.

Glancing at the clock. she realized it was getting late. She couldn't be tardy, today of all days. She was about to meet her new boss, or should she say, her ex-lover.

CHAPTER 3

Laurel checked the time as she pulled onto Lake Shore Drive, and hurriedly maneuvered around some tour busses waiting to park at the Museum. She would not have guessed that fate would slam her back into a work situation, all too soon, with Dr. Alex Zuckerman, the newly appointed Director of Archaeology and Anthropology–and her ex-lover. She needed to keep it that way, and not fall under his spell again.

She quickly parked her FJ Cruiser in the reserved area for the Archaeology Department and entered the museum through the Grand Stanley Field Hall. She stopped briefly to check her appearance in the huge mirror next to the elevators. Using her fingertips, she whisked out the layers of her shoulder length ash blond hair and wasn't happy that the winter months had taken its toll on her natural highlights. As she brushed her bangs aside, the reflection of her blue-green eyes showed its tiredness from a lack of sleep. Off to the side she caught sight of one of the security guards, approaching her with a smile on his face.

"Good morn, Professor Robertson. You're lookin' mighty sharp! Got an important meeting today?"

Laurel smiled back at him in the mirror, "Yes George." She nodded her head while checking her makeup. "Don't see me in a skirt every day, do you?" Laurel, at thirty-two, was happy to have the occasion to dress up and show some leg. It was a welcome change from the pants and t-shirt she usually wore. She hurriedly straightened her light blue scarf draped over her navy jacket and smoothed down her skirt that stopped just above her knees. Ole' George has been standing guard over the exhibit of Sue, the world's most famous T. Rex, long before she started working with the museum.

"How's your mother doing, now that she's out of the hospital?"

"She doing really good, Professor, it's so nice of you to ask."

"I think you shared with me your mom was around seventy-six. That's the same age as my grandma." Laurel checked the time and walked toward the elevator.

"You got it right. She even asked me to stop and get her one of those special 'Chicago pizzas' after my shift today."

"My goodness, I'm glad to hear she is getting along so well. Give her my best." Laurel waved bye, stepped into the elevator, and took the short ride to the basement. She quickly keyed in a code at her office door and picked up her folder for the meeting.

"Good morning Laurel. Hope you're rested and ready for our meeting with Director Zuckerman."

"Hey, Steph, I wish I could say I had enough sleep, but I awoke early to that same dream again."

Stephanie gave her a compassionate smile as she tried to assure her. "You'll get to the bottom of it, just give it some time. You're pretty good at solving puzzles. Don't push, it will come to you."

They entered a room already full of people, with the hum of multiple conversations against a background of classical music. *It had to be Alex that set the tone for this meeting.*

Looking around the room she noticed some familiar faces visiting with one another. While others, obvious first timers, anxiously looked around, slowly wandering from group to group, trying to feel a connection to where they might fit in.

Laurel's attention was captured when she heard laughter in the far corner, she turned her head and there he was, looking as handsome and distinguished as ever. She felt her heart beat faster. Not a reaction she thought she would have. Yes, this was him, The Great Alex Zuckerman. She noticed he sported a little gray on the sides of his hair now–very becoming!

Her thoughts took her back to when she was one of his students at the University, and how she became infatuated with this man's knowledge and experience, and of course, his good looks. It wasn't long before he became physically attracted to her, and a relationship began. After a few years in the field working on her Master's Degree, she was appointed to his team. They spent a lot of time together on and off the job. As time passed, she felt the relationship lacked the emotional fulfillment she needed, although she was still physically attracted to him.

He taught her some of the real heart of Archaeology, even though he could be a real asshole sometimes. He was like any one of those professional men at the top of his field, always in a state of high anxiety, for fear of someone taking his authority away from him. She tried not to let him get to her. Laurel was smart and worked hard to earn her awards. She felt accomplished and worthy of being in this line of work.

Laurel began to see another side of Alex, he was turning into an egotistical powerhouse and she needed to distance herself. As a result, she resigned from his team and searched for a new position. After several months of interviews, she was happy to acquire a position with the McMelton Corporation, which contracted with The Field Museum.

She would not have guessed they both would be working at the same place again. *It's like fate is playing nasty tricks with me*, she whined to herself. But, Laurel had to admit, she'd missed him.

There was a surge of loud laughter that brought Laurel's full attention back into the room. A large group had gathered around Alex, and by the sound of things, he was entertaining them with his usual stories about his latest adventures. Laurel smiled inwardly. *She hoped* he didn't bring along his pictures, which he usually projected overhead.

She moved toward a table where some of her team members had gathered, making a point of staying clear of where Alex was standing. Stephanie motioned for her to take the seat she saved next to the aisle. Before she sat she turned and looked over to where he was, just as he looked up. He gave her that handsome sexy smile that she hadn't seen for a long while, making her knees grow weak, and she nearly missed her chair.

"Hey girl," Stephanie voiced as she grabbed her arm to help steady her. "What's going on with you?"

"Just lost my balance, is all."

CHAPTER 4

A mature, petite woman with platinum hair, dressed in an expensive light blue business suit, entered the room and walked down the aisle toward the podium. When she noticed Laurel, she smiled and paused briefly to speak to her. "Laurel, I'm hearing wonderful things about the research you're doing in your lab. Keep up the good work."

Laurel felt pleased and honored, as this was the official who hired her. She was most anxious to have another talk with her about the funding she applied for, but this was not the time or place. She hoped to catch her later.

The official continued to the front and called the meeting to order, banging the hammer on the podium.

"Welcome everyone!" She banged the hammer again. "Welcome! Would everyone please take a seat now?" The official may have appeared small and petite, but as some of the older members in the room could attest, she bore enormous weight in this corporation.

"My name is Joann Maury. As Vice President of the McMelton Corporation, I am honored to introduce your new Director of the Anthropology/Archaeology Department here at The Field Museum. Some of you are already acquainted with the fine academic skills Dr. Zuckerman taught at the University of Illinois. He later advanced to become the Director of the entire Anthropology/Archaeology Department at that University. He headed the Research Laboratory…"

Dr. Zuckerman, you may not be considered muscular and a hunk, like some of the other younger teachers back at the University, Laurel's thoughts overrode the words of the introduction. *But, I see your physique of thirty-eight is still holding up nicely, and you look even more distinguished with the mustache.* She caught herself scanning his body from top to bottom, a body she had not seen in two years. *Not many know that once when you were a younger teacher you were 'The Poster Guy' for 'Guess Jeans' in an ad campaign that ran four consecutive years. Choosing you, not only for your physique, but your mature, outdoorsman features. And, now your academics have put you at the top of our field.*

Laurel's consciousness filtered back to the room with Mrs. Maury's long introduction still in process.

"He specialized in Historical Archaeology, conducted field research in South America, Mexico, the Caribbean, and published papers on these. He now has three published books and…"

Alex Zuckerman rose from his seat prematurely and walked towards Mrs. Maury. "Thank you very much, Mrs. Maury." He reached out to shake her hand and continued to thank her for the wonderful introduction, making it seem like she was finished. He turned to the audience and humbly remarked, "We could be here all day with that long list of achievements she has compiled."

The room resounded with laughter. Then he appealed to the members in the room. "Give Mrs. Maury a grateful hand of applause for the wonderful introduction, I appreciate it very much." He led the clapping and the room joined in.

He now singularly stood at the podium and with a big smile he announced, "I'm Alex Zuckerman, and I'm proud to be your new Director." Everyone applauded again.

Laurel's thoughts drifted back again to her college days. He always had a way of putting his students at ease, but on the opposite end of the spectrum, he demanded respect. And, he had an irresistible attraction, which was accented by his baritone speaking voice. *All the female students were mesmerized by his tone, including me.*

Laurel's thoughts returned to the meeting and noticed Alex seemed to be looking around the room. Then she had a stark realization. *He's not just looking around as he talks, but I think he's looking for me. Of course, he is. He has the roster of team leaders, as well as the entire list of members.*

She felt a flush of nervous energy surge throughout her body. Her reaction was automatic, with the need to look her best. Laurel began to change her body composure, raising her chin, while she took her hand and brushed her hair back from her eyes. At the same time, she comfortably crossed her legs, showing off some curvature. Unconsciously, she propped her right elbow on the table, and touched her fingers to her lower lip, accenting her new posture with an attentive look on her face. She didn't mind watching what Dr. Alex Zuckerman's reactions would be to seeing her again.

After the preliminaries were done, the meeting progressed to the summer projects. Laurel's thoughts went almost into panic. *What will I say? I haven't decided yet. I don't know why I keep procrastinating about this. Surely, he won't call on me first. I'll go over the pro's and con's while he talks and make my decision.*

Alex looked up from his papers. Peering over the top of his readers, he called out, "Where is Laurel...Laurel Robertson?"

Laurel felt an icy streak of adrenaline run through her body. So much for thinking that he wouldn't call on her first.

He continued, while stretching to see her better. "Are you ready to go back to the Cahokia site, over by St Louis? We still have several mounds to process, and more questions that need answering about this ancient Mississippian culture. I feel since you've already spent a lot of time there, and it's reported you have great leadership managing a team, you may be ready to add this summer to your findings and publish a new paper. Or," he paused, still checking his chart. When he looked back up at Laurel, he sported a warmhearted smile, and enthusiastically said, "Better yet. Why not join my team in Arizona, down by the Saguaro National Park?"

Laurel reflected on this information, as she had thought about going to Arizona many times. This was close to where her mom and grandmother's dig site was, before her mom's fatal accident. She had only a few actual memories of her mother, that of being loving and warm. She often felt her mom was still with her in spirit. She recalled one photo when she was only four years old, sitting in a playpen at the site. Her mom, Grams, and their crew were all in the background.

Her mother was a very beautiful woman. Everyone told Laurel she looked just like her. Being the third generation in this field of work, how could she not follow in their footsteps?"

"Laurel!" Professor Zuckerman's baritone voice became louder. Hearing her name brought her immediately back to the present.

"I'm told they found quantities of rare pieces of pottery and other interesting samples in the Saguaro Caves that need to be processed. This could be right up your alley, Laurel. You might get lucky with that fancy electronic device of yours and find a buried treasure inside one of the caves. What was the manufacture name on it?"

Everyone laughed along at Zuckerman's teasing remarks toward Laurel's early passion in life. People that knew Laurel and her early history with metal detectors, knew she was a competitive contender, winning lots of awards. If there was any treasure to be found, they all would put their money on Laurel finding it.

Laurel's dad was co-owner of Electronics Distributer Company, specializing in high end metal detectors. When she was nine through fourteen years of age, she would go out with her dad, his partner, and his two boys on some of the treasure hunts sponsored by various clubs and dealerships. She really enjoyed their trips and the challenge of the competition. Most of her reward items, artifacts, and some of the winning trophies were displayed in her apartment.

She had fond memories of her dad. He had been a major influence in her life, until his fatal plane crash, when she was fourteen years old.

Laurel noticed everyone staring at her and felt a warm flush of emotion streak across her face. Instinctively she put on a smile and waved her arm in the air, indicating she was a good sport with the tease. Inwardly she thought, I know you Alex Zuckerman, you always did like to tease me, but you're up to something. I'm just not sure what it is yet.

"Think about it. I'll get back to you with this. I'm sure we can work something out position wise, which would be agreeable to you. Perhaps we can talk more about it tomorrow."

She wondered if Alex knew about her application for more funding with her projects on the Ancient Cahokia site. She applied last October, with Mrs. Maury, who indicated at that time, it probably would be approved by the board, with her recommendation. But now it was March, and she had not received any response.

No more procrastinating. She must make a choice before these meetings are over, and there are now even more choices on the table–if only she knew whether the board was going to accept or decline her applications.

Laurel's thoughts went back to what Alex said earlier, "Join my team." Is he planning on heading a team in Arizona, as well as being the Director over all the projects of the entire Archaeology/Anthropology department? That's not even possible. Laurel felt an inward smile as she had a faint visual of her ex-boyfriend darting in a closet, ripping his shirt open to reveal his superhero suit. *Well, Professor, you may think you are a Superhero, but I haven't seen any phone booths out in the field sites lately.* She chuckled to herself.

Decision making was usually one of Laurel's strong suits, but lately, for some strange reason, she was procrastinating until the last possible minute.

The meeting was progressing long into the afternoon when the new director was given a message to read from the Corporation. He smiled as he proceeded to get everyone's attention. Waving the invitation high in the air he exclaimed, "Oh, you'll not want to miss this get-together!"

CHAPTER 5

"Listen up! Everyone is invited to a cocktail party this evening, put on by the McMelton Corporation–food, drinks, live music. Did I mention food and drinks? It's being held at the Leo Burnett Building, on the top floor with a bird's eye view of tonight's televised live performance of the famous tightrope walker, Nick Wallenda! Maybe some of you may have heard about this guy?"

Conversations erupted throughout the large room, with echoes of partial phrases; 'Grand Canyon', 'unbelievable', 'Daredevil', 'The Falls'! The group's reaction brought shouts of cheer and pleasure, drowning out the director until he let out a shrill whistle and raised his arms in a quieting motion.

"He will start his walk at a height of 588 feet and will walk across the Chicago River to the Marina City West Tower. And then," the Director continued, "If that's not enough, he will continue his walk from the West Tower to the East Tower blindfolded!"

The new Director dismissed the meeting for the day declaring with a smile, "See you at the party."

Laurel felt happy to be back in her apartment again, even though it was only for a short while. She plopped herself down on the large oversized chair in the living room, and kicked off her heels, sinking her feet down in the plush cushion on the ottoman. She was just acclimating to the peaceful atmosphere, sipping some green tea and munching on a piece of Ghirardelli dark mint-chocolate, when her phone rang. She checked the I.D. answering, "Hello Grams, you've got perfect timing. I just got home."

Her grandmother must have picked up on the stress in her voice, regardless of Laurel's attempt to sound cheerful. "Are you all right, Laurel?"

"Yes Grams." She sighed. "I'm fine, it's just been a long, stressful day, that's all, and the day's not even over yet. I've got a corporate cocktail party yet to go."

"I'm worried about you Laurel, are you getting enough rest? I bet you're not eating well either."

"Laurel knew she couldn't hide anything from her grandmother. "Those strange dreams have started up again, along with those-five-five-five's, I keep seeing on a digital read out."

"Do you remember anything of the dreams?"

"Well, yes and no. It's bits and pieces, and it makes no sense to me. I wake up with an overwhelming feeling of sadness. Then I look at the clock, and its five- five- five. It's like someone, or something, is trying to get a message to me, and I'm just not getting it."

"Laurel, they teach a process over at the Metaphysical Center, next to our property. They have good results with it. Do you have a few minutes?"

"Yes, I'm open to just about anything right now."

"This exercise might sound a little simple, but it does produce positive results so here's what I want you to do while we talk. Get a notebook, attach a pen to it, and lay it by your bedside table. Now this evening. . ." Her Grandmother went on explaining the exercise.

"Yes Grams, I get your point, it's important to record the first thing I remember; what I saw, a word, a sound, or what I felt. So what if nothing comes forth?"

"It may take several tries, so continue to do this every night."

"Grams, I always appreciate your input on these matters. By the way, you'll probably never guess in a million years who our new Director turned out to be."

"I haven't a clue."

"Well it turns out to be, the one and only Dr. Alex Zuckerman. He managed to tease and embarrass me in front of one hundred fifteen corporate employees, and it happened not long after the meeting was underway."

"Oh Laurel, I'm so sorry he has turned up in your life again. I thought you were doing so nicely there in Chicago, not being around him, and giving yourself opportunities for a different relationship."

"I know Grams. It was a shock to see him. He asked me if I wanted to continue heading a team at the Cahokia site, but before I could answer, he offered other options for my consideration. I admit, the Saguaro National Park option did sound appealing to me. Isn't this close to where you and mom were before the accident?"

"Very close, but Laurel, you don't want to be in that area, there is not much left to discover there. You were doing great work at the Cahokia site, and got some published work done. You need this summer to finish up your findings and get the new results down on paper. This is making a name for you. You don't want to mess up by going to a different place and starting all over. You'd be letting someone else swoop in, taking up where you left off and garnering all the credit and honor for themselves."

"I know. He said we would talk more with the details tomorrow. For now, I've got to get ready for the party. I'll call you in a few days, when I have more information. Love you, Grams."

Laurel was concerned about her grandmother's comments. Even though part of what she said was true, it was the tone she used. It was if she was steering her away from Arizona. This had happened all too much in the past, and she just let it slide. Now, more than ever, Laurel needed to know why. She closed her eyes to try and block out everything, to rest just a few minutes before getting ready for the party–dosing off.

CHAPTER 6

Laurel opened her eyes, at first not recognizing where she was. She felt like she was still in a dream state. She closed her eyes again and felt numbness all over her body. Then a thought managed to seep through – *The cocktail party!*

She jumped up out of her chair, blurting "What time is it?" She checked her watch. I must of fell asleep–but, I can still make it.

Laurel stepped into the shower as bits and pieces of the dream state continued to come forth. She briefly saw a figure dressed in black and a small horse loaded down with something bulky. It was just a flash and then it was gone. It made no sense to her.

While sitting at her makeup mirror she felt a cool breeze gently blow across her face. Looking toward the window, she saw it was closed. *What made that breeze across my face? What is that faint earthy smell?* She looked around the room and saw a white mist forming before her that began to swirl around, transforming into a person wearing a black robe with a wide brim hat. He was bent down by a spring, drinking fresh cool water in his cupped hands. Then the visual was gone, disappearing instantly, leaving the taste of fresh spring water in her mouth. *Who was that? I thought it was me– but it couldn't be. This figure was a man, wearing a black robe–a priest maybe? It seemed so real; even tasting the water. What is going on with me?*

Laurel had a sudden thirst and made her way to the kitchen. She took a good drink . The filtered water didn't hold a candle to the spring water in her vision. She walked toward the patio window and noticed the full moon just coming up. She tried to recall more of the dream while gazing out at the moon but found nothing was going to manifest. She gave up and decided to get ready for the party.

She used the curling iron for a frilly party look, reapplied her makeup then opened the closet door and reached in for her new dress. She slipped into it and stood in front of her full-length mirror. The dress was made of black silky material, with deep magenta orchids print splashed about, like an artist's rendition. The sleeveless top had hand-beaded sparkle detail around the low-cut bodice and again across the hips for a flattering fit. She loved the flirty asymmetrical hemline.

To compliment the look, she added a sparkly necklace and earrings in silver tones. then slipped on a pair of black strapped heals. She put some essentials in a small black clutch bag, and reached into her closet for her wool coat, adding a magenta scarf.

Laurel stepped off the shuttle and was making her way toward the entry of the Burnett building when she caught a glimpse of a man standing in the crowd, wearing a blue stocking cap and gray parka. She could have sworn this was the same man at the museum where she parked her cruiser earlier. She turned to get a better look, but then he was gone, lost in the moving crowd. A moment later, she felt someone grab hold of her arm. She spun around ready to strike the predator.

"Wait up, Ms. Laurel. I'm so sorry, I didn't mean to startle you. I just wanted to walk up with you."

"Hey, Rosie, it's okay." She let out the breath she had been holding. "I've just been a little jumpy lately."

Rosie was a nickname Usher wore proudly since college basketball. His lengthy six feet three African American athletic frame was still in great shape. He was a fun-loving guy who kept everyone around him feeling alive and happy. He was also smart and dependable. Because of this, Laurel elected him to her team for the last two years.

"Ms. Laurel, may I ask you what your intentions are about the job sites?"

"I haven't met with Director Zuckerman yet to hear his proposals. It depends on what he has to say."

"I just want you to know, be it the Cahokia, or the Arizona site, or where ever, I want to stay on your team. I feel I am gaining so much knowledge and experience from your instructions and guidance. I want to continue, wherever it takes me,"

"Thank you, Rosie, that means a lot to me. I will tell you this, one of my preconditions is I will retain my same team as before and you will be my first choice. I appreciate your candor, and I will let you know as soon as I make my decision."

The elevator door opened to a hallway busy with people. Laurel and Rosie maneuvered their way to stand in line for the security check. They soon were allowed into the conference hall, which was filled with not only corporate members, but other invited guests. Laurel noticed a steady flow of people on the right side of the room. Television crew members, camera technicians, and numerous others made their way through to an adjacent room where they were setting up for the big live production of Wallenda's performance.

Rosie proclaimed, "Excuse me Ms. Laurel, I see a spread of food with my name on it. May I bring you something Ms. Laurel?"

"No thank you, but you go on ahead. Enjoy!"

Laurel made her way through the large group of people over to the window, and watched the crew checking the cables, making sure they were properly stabilized for the tight rope performance. It was a cold and windy evening and she became anxious about his safety. She heard rumors that the city didn't require him to wear a harness. When he crossed Niagara Falls, he was required to use a tethering device. She turned away, wanting to change her thoughts. She was glad it was warm inside and felt comfortable in her sleeveless dress and loved the way the hem line moved across her thighs and calves as she made her way over to the drink table.

Laurel managed to get up to the table, even though it was crowded, and got a freshly chilled Margarita. Just as she turned to leave, she felt a stern bump to her elbow and a shove.

"Hah! That was cooold."

"Oh! I'm so sorry," she said to the man, now squeezed up firm against her. "Did I get much on you?" Laurel looked down at his clothing as they separated.

He shivered as he looked down at his pants. Looking back at Laurel with a strange expression on his face, he broke out in laughter saying, "You did good Ms.–it landed just enough off to the side, not to be embarrassing." Laurel couldn't help herself, she had to laugh at his humor.

"How about you, I hope you didn't get any on that pretty dress."

Laurel checked. "I'm good here."

She noticed he also was checking her dress out. His hazel eyes met up with her blue-green eyes and in that instant, she knew he had been checking her out, and not for Margarita spills.

His brows lifted over his rolling eyes, and his shoulders shrugged. Then came that little school boy expression with a half-smile, like he had just been caught with his hand in the cookie jar.

Laurel smiled at his gestures and they broke out in laughter again. He placed his hand over her grip on the empty glass.

"Here, allow me to get you another drink." His personality shifted to a gentlemanly fashion, lifting her glass from her hand, and turned to the drink table.

She liked his appearance; he looked sharp in his dark blue sports jacket, with a logo on the pocket. She surmised he was about her age, and he wore a five o'clock shadow that matched his dark brown wavy hair. But, most of all, he had a million-dollar smile.

They walked away from the crowded table and he handed her the fresh drink, along with an introduction, "I'm Nicholas Kenyon, with the World Wonders & Mystery Television Network. Everyone calls me Nick."

CHAPTER 7

"Thanks Nick, for the fresh drink. I'm Laurel Robertson." She sipped the drink, enjoying the taste of the margarita.

Laurel motioned to the logo on his jacket. "Did you have anything to do with this evening's entertainment?"

"Well actually, in the initial contact, I had something to do with getting his interest up. We know each other. One day shortly after I moved to Chicago, I asked him how he would feel about walking among the world's first skyscraper in 'The Big Windy City'? So, it was launched from there. This is part of my work as Production Manager."

"I heard a rumor that he is doing the walk without a harness."

"That would be correct, the legal team didn't require him to wear one. He wanted it that way, so they said yes to his request."

He leaned into her a bit to read her name tag and asked, "What do you do for the McMelton Corporation? Are you a Board Member? A secretary? Office Manager? Or…"

Laurel intervened, stepping up to the plate, before he got too lost in his guessing game. "I'm a contract professional with The Field Museum, here in Chicago. I have a Masters in Historical Archaeology and Anthropology." It was obvious from the surprised look on his face, he didn't expect her position to be professional.

His expression changed to a more serious one as he straightened his posture. "That's interesting. What are you working on?"

"Well, Mr. Kenyon, for the past several years I've been studying the Ancient Cahokia Civilization. You may have heard of them. Their main capital was home to many hundreds to thousands of people. It's pretty close to here, on the edge of the Mississippi, by East St. Louis."

"I believe I might have. Didn't that come out in the news a few years back about some drilling in one of those huge piles of dirt? Something happened, but I don't remember the details."

"Yes, they were installing some drains on the west slump of one of those huge 'piles of dirt', as you termed it. But, it does have a name, it's called Monks Mound. While boring for the fifth drain, they hit something. As they attempted to retract the drill, the bit broke off in this stone mass, or whatever it was. So, there is a $5000 bit with an electronic sensor that is now a new artifact buried in the Ancient Monks Mound. Maybe a thousand years from now Archaeologists will come across this and think it to be an ancient artifact too."

"Wow, that's astonishing. Can't they do more drilling, maybe at different angles?"

"That drilling company refused to do more, because of the high cost of the bits, and the funding for the project was very low at that time, so they didn't try another drill company."

"It sounds like the mound is pretty big."

Laurel nodded. "It's like a ten-story earthen colossus. This giant is the largest prehistoric earthwork in all the Americas."

"That's very interesting," he replied.

"It's the largest of the other 120 mounds, scattered around the same area," she added.

"I didn't realize there were so many," he remarked.

"It was home to around 20,000 people at its peak," she continued, "unfortunately, relentless development of the 20th century took its own toll on the Cahokia ruins."

"Yes, I image so," he added. "There was an interstate that was built, and a gambling hall!"

Laurel interjected, "Before that, mounds were flatted for farming, small towns, and subdivisions were built."

"There is somewhat of a mystery concerning the rocks, or whatever material the drill hit!" she exclaimed. "So far, there have been NO rocks found in any of the other mounds and these Mississippians would have had to travel ten to fifteen miles away to get these stones, as there are none like this in the area. Thus, they must have had some significant reason, or perhaps some ceremonial purposes for their use. We can't dig down deep enough on the west side, to reach the stones, or whatever this material is, without jeopardizing the safety of the whole mound."

He intervened, "Do you suppose this material of sorts, was already there, and the Ancient's built right over the top of it, for whatever reason?"

"Excuse me, I don't mean to intrude, but I couldn't help from overhearing your conversation." Rosie interjected.

"It's fine, Rosie." Laurel welcomed him with a pat on his arm. She introduced the two men and explained Rosie grew up around St Louis. "His family's history goes back decades, living in the area around the Cahokia Mounds. I think Rosie could add some interesting insights."

"It is a great possibility they built over the top of something already there," Rosie stated. "Another factor you may find interesting since you are with the Wonders & Mystery Network, is the fact that these mounds are also near St. Louis and Scott Air Force Base. All of these surrounding areas are in the midst of a periodical UFO hot-spot."

"Are you saying they are seeing a lot of UFO activity there?" Nick asked.

"Yes," Rosie continued. "One of the largest UFO sightings in recorded history took place right there in 2000. Multiple police officers, and several residents from the area spotted a massive triangular flying object, zipping from one town to the next, then mysteriously disappearing."

Laurel looked to Nick, and said, "Do you think the *real reason* these strange flying machines were here, was because of the Air Force Base? Or could the *real reason* they keep coming back to this same area be some attraction, or perhaps some unfinished business relating to these mysterious and ancient structures. just a few miles away from the base?"

"Wow!" Nick replied. "I had no idea all that activity was happening around St. Louis."

Rosie explained, "My uncle was one of the officers that saw the UFO's, and he said it was spectacular and frightening at the same time. There has been speculation for years that something incredibly strange is hidden beneath the Cahokia Mounds. Some even suggest the mounds were built to cover up an ancient artifact that was hidden there centuries before."

Nick asked, "What kind of instruments have they used, like-electronics, radar, and other types?"

"Yes," Laurel replied, "Those have been tried and magnetic as well. None of these can penetrate deep enough to provide significant clues. Therefore, I have applied for funding for the Space Satellite Imaging Technology."

"This sounds like NASA Technology!" Nick declared.

"You're right!" she affirmed. "This technology is different than all the other types. It will go deep enough and show us, to some degree, the size, and the shape, of this mysterious mass under Monks Mound. However, it will not tell us exactly what it is; but hopefully, this will give us better clues, as to what is there. Maybe we can see how to get the drainage done to save this Ancient historical monstrosity."

He looked at Laurel. "I would be interested in talking more about this project of yours. It might be something we could use on Wonders & Mystery. Could we get together in a few days to discuss this further?" He handed her his card and asked for hers. His commutator beeped and he stepped aside to answer.

"Well, it seems I am needed elsewhere by the team." Nick shook Rosie's hand, thanking him for sharing his story. Rosie left to go back for more food. As Nick reached out his hand to shake Laurel's, he stared adamantly into her eyes. "It has been a real pleasure to meet you Ms. Robertson, so glad you bumped into me. It's been a very interesting conversation on the Monks Mound Project. I'll call you later."

Laurel watched him walk away, eventually blending with the other guests. She had a warm feeling about this guy. She smiled as she visualized his face, along with his humorous mannerisms. All too soon, her new visual was intruded upon, when she heard a familiar baritone voice, with a southern accent behind her.

"Good evening, Laurel. Are you enjoying the party?" Her vision of Nick Kenyon's face quickly vanished and was replaced with Alex Zuckerman's. She felt apprehensive being alone with Alex, even though there were people around. Laurel put on a pleasant smile and replied. "Good evening Alex. I'm having a good time, they've put on an extravagant party here, with indelible entertainment. How are you doing?"

"Doing great! Thank you for asking." Alex moved closer to Laurel. "Since we all left early this afternoon, there were no handouts for the schedule of appointments for tomorrow. So, I'm just telling the first four listed when I see them around tonight. Laurel, your time was set at 9:00 a.m., hope this is okay, being short notice and all?"

"That's fine. I'm staying for the tightrope walk, then leaving."

"Laurel, I just wanted to say, I hope you were not offended in any way over my teasing and having a little fun with the group this morning. I wanted to bring some humor to an otherwise dry meeting. If you were offended, I apologize most heartedly. I want you to know I would never do anything to harm you."

His familiar apologetic charm was breaking through her defenses. She managed to pull up a half smile. "I can take a little teasing, as you know, but times have changed. I'm a Team Leader now, we have to hold it down, so I receive the respect I deserve."

"I understand." Laurel felt his tone changed, like he really meant it. He smiled. "May I add you are looking well and more beautiful than ever. How long has it been, six months, maybe a year?"

"Almost two years." She laughed. "And you are handsome as ever, with a little gray showing on the sides. I like that look. It becomes you."

"Laurel, I hoped to have this conversation with you before now, but the timing just didn't fall right." He turned, looked directly at her face, and spoke in a softer, more sincere tone. "I want you to understand I knew you had acquired a position with the Museum, and I am very proud of you and your achievements. You have advanced very nicely, as I knew you would. How else could you not–under my teachings." He laughed, then continued. "But seriously, when I was approached with this position for Director, I debated, because of you. I don't have a problem working together, and I hoped you didn't either."

"Alex, I will certainly give it my best. With both of us working toward a strong business relationship, it should turn out to everyone's benefit." *I really wished you not be employed here at all.*

Laurel felt the sincerity in Alex's little dissertation to her. Alex had always been above board and fair in his dealings with her, but she was in a relationship with him at that time. What would he do now that there are no loving feelings? She had witnessed too many wrong doings toward others who dared to go against him.

One of the staff members announced the Wallenda walk was soon to start and motioned for everyone to come closer to the viewing windows.

"I'm going to get something to drink, may I get you something, Laurel?"

Alex's eyes met hers and she thought she saw desire and longing. It was enough for Laurel to take notice and she felt his magnetic energy surging into her personal boundary. She pulled her eyes away from his. "I'll take the usual, thank you."

Laurel was anxious to see if he remembered her drink. How many drink preferences has he got stored in that vast and keen memory anyway? He seemed to be here alone, but how many girlfriends had he gone through since her?

It wasn't long before Alex returned with the drinks. "Here you go, a Margarita iced, no salt on the rim. Enjoy!" He clinked his Scotch against her glass.

Laurel was impressed he remembered, but still wondered if there was a woman in his life. *Why do I even care?*

Wallenda didn't disappoint. His performance brought ooh's and ahh's to the assembled group. At one point, a sudden wind gust caused him great struggle to stay upright, and Laurel unconsciously grabbed Alex's arm in anticipation until he regained his balance. Discovering what she did, she released her hold and stepped away. His performance was breathtaking and exciting. Towards the end of his walk he put on a blindfold and walked several feet on the stretch cable over the busy streets below. Everyone held their breath as more gusts of wind blew, jeopardizing his balance until he made it to the end. The Windy City was certainly being kind to him. A round of applause and cheers broke out when he reached the end.

Laurel turned to Alex stating, "That was the most exciting performance I've ever witnessed!"

Alex stepped closer to her, reaching for her arm, pulling her next to him like he was going to kiss her.

She pushed away saying, "I've got to go now, I'll see you at nine o'clock."

The band was just getting started for the second part of the evening's entertainment, as Laurel walked by the dance floor heading for the exit. She noticed Nick talking to a couple on the other side of the dance floor. About that time, he looked up and saw her and vigorously waved his arms trying to gain her attention. He made his way over to where she stood.

"Ms. Robertson," he tenderly spoke her name as he reached for her hand. "May I have this dance? His hazel eyes gazed deeply into hers, as if saying *you can trust me.*

She placed her hand in his and out on the floor they went. He was a strong and smooth leader, swirling and turning her swiftly about, making the asymmetrical hemline of her dress wrap high against her thighs, then swirling down against her calves, all in rhythm of their movements. It wasn't long before the other dancers moved back, giving them the floor.

Laurel felt dancing with him was so natural, as if she had known him forever and they had danced together many times before. She enjoyed every passing second.

Eventually the music came to an end and Nick put on an appreciative smile, took a formal bow and as he straightened his flirtatious eyes met with hers. "Thank you very much for the dance, Ms. Robertson."

She returned the formal gesture, by pulling up the lower part of her dress and dipping into a low curtsey. Smiling, she replied, "It was all my pleasure, Mr. Kenyon."

Applause came from all around the dance floor. People converged saying how much they enjoyed watching them and asked how long had they been dancing together. After a while of conversing with the crowd, Laurel whispered to Nick a reminder about her early appointment, and her need to leave. Although, she was enjoying herself and wished she could stay all night.

They thanked everyone and he escorted her to the coat room, talking and laughing on the way down to the shuttle about the crowd thinking they were seasoned dance partners.

"Good night, Mr. Kenyon, I had a wonderful evening." Laurel felt her heart beating faster.

He brought her hand to his lips, kissing her gently saying, "I enjoyed our dancing, we'll have to do this again some time. Good night, have a safe trip home."

Laurel was still dancing in her mind. *I like this new guy. Maybe he is interested in my project and will call me; regardless I would like to see him again!*

CHAPTER 8

Laurel entered her building's parking garage still buzzing from the music and dance. She thought about Nick and how their dancing seemed natural as the elevator glided up to the seventh floor. The door opened and she stepped out into the corridor, smiling at how humorous he had been this evening. As she got closer to her apartment she saw a sliver of light spilling out into the hallway. *Did my door not shut tight when I left earlier? Of course, it did–it always fastens and locks.* She stood still, as a cold adrenaline swept through her body.

She reached in her purse for the small canister of 'Lightning Bolt'. *I've had this canister a long time–will it still work?* She felt apprehensive about using it. The cold continued to flow through her as she took a deep breath. Placing her finger on top of the spray nozzle, she acknowledged to herself, *I'm now armed and ready as I'll ever be!*

With a firm shove of the door, it swung open exposing a lighted living room full of chaos. She stood momentary in shock. *Am I in the right apartment?* Her eyes scanned the debris thrown about. *Yes, it's my stuff alright.* She stepped inside, maneuvering around the items, being careful not to break anything. She felt intense hurt swelling up inside, seeing her possessions so mistreated, some even ruined.

The more damage she saw, the hurt shifted to anger. *Who did this?* She heard a crunching sound come from the back of the apartment. *Was the intruder still inside?* Her anger changed to fear. *Is he going to come back in here and see the door open? I could hide quickly behind the sofa and spray him when he gets close? But he might have a gun. Bullets are faster than my spray.* Her instincts told her to retreat to the outside hall.

She hid around the corner behind a tall planter and called 911. Laurel peeked through the leaves of the plant, watching adamantly toward her front door.

In a few minutes, the Chicago Police and the building security both arrived, and Laurel stepped out from behind her camouflage.

"I'm the one who called," Laurel proclaimed. "My door was ajar with the lights on, so I pulled my canister of mace and stepped inside. When I heard a noise in the back bedroom, I left and called you guys. I've been watching, so they're still in there."

The officers cautioned her to get back while they went in. After what seemed like a long duration, the officers walked back out.

"We did a thorough search Ms. Robertson, we found no one in the apartment. We did find the door to the patio not completely closed. Apparently, they left by that door."

Laurel blurted out in disbelief, "But where did they go? Seven floors up in a nine-floor building?"

One of the officers spoke. "You'll need to do an inventory but it doesn't look like the usual theft items, like electronics or jewelry have been taken. It appears they were looking for something, Ms. Robertson. Do you have any idea what that was?"

"No, I can't think of what they would be after. . .But wait, I do have a small safe in the bedroom closet." Laurel and the officer made their way back to the closet. She found the safe opened, with the contents including her passport, other important papers and an envelope of money, tossed aside on the closet floor.

"Well, it appears they didn't want what you had in the safe. . . not even the cash." The officer declared. "Even more reason they were looking for specific items. Continue checking to see if anything is missing, and call us, Ms. Robertson." He handed her his card.

"But Officer," Laurel said. "You still haven't explained how the intruder got out of my apartment. If they left by the balcony, those side privacy walls are ten feet high, with a steel balcony guard across the front."

"They may have opened the balcony door to see how hard it was to escape, then left by the front door, and you missed seeing them. Or, it could be they exited by the balcony. We've called for backup to check those apartments."

One officer stayed by her balcony to make sure they didn't return. After a thorough search of the adjoining apartments, no intruder was found and no dead body lay on the ground below.

"We will get that lock fixed within a couple of hours and in the meantime, we have posted a security guard out in the hall, next to your door," the Super assured her before he left.

Laurel was now alone, standing in the middle of the debris. It was obvious the officers were right. It looks like they were searching for something, but what?

She felt exhausted. Making her way to the bedroom, she locked the door behind her. She changed into her t-shirt and pajama pants, sprawled her body across the covers, clutched her pillow with one hand and snatched the quilt with the other, encapsulating her body for the night. *Relax and let go of the mystery of what they were looking for. You need sleep for now. . . just relax. . .*

CHAPTER 9

Laurel awakened from her short night's sleep. She had tossed and turned most of the night. She rolled over in bed, with her eyes still closed, visualizing a small horse carrying numerous bulky sacks on its back. Her consciousness felt foggy, not knowing where she was. Slowly she opened her eyes. Shapes and shadows were coming into focus, launched by the moonlight shining through the window. Across from her stood a dresser with a mirror that seemed familiar. Rising on one arm she looked around seeing her belongings strewed about the room. Her memory had rebooted to its fullness with the apartment brake-in.

Then she remembered something else. Her appointment! Laurel looked toward the night stand to check the time, but there was no clock. *My phone–It will have the time.* It had just enough charge to register the time before going dark. *Where is my charging station?* She shuffled through the mess, retrieving it under a heap of towels and set it up. She hurried through her shower and made herself presentable for the meeting. *God, I'm so glad the museum is close by.*

"Well, good morning, Laurel. I trust you had a good time at the party last night?" Dr. Zuckerman inquired.

"Morning. Yes, I enjoyed the party very much. The Corporation really knows how to put on an event." Laurel couldn't help but notice how sharp he appeared.

"I hear you and a guy from the Wonders and Mystery Network put on quite an exposition on the dance floor. I'm sorry I missed it." he proclaimed with a smile.

"Oh. . . we were just having some fun. Apparently, the crowd liked it." She shrugged, trying to indicate it wasn't a big deal.

"I saw you talking to him earlier, along with one of our team members, who I haven't met yet." Laurel felt like Alex was fishing for her dance partner's name, but she evaded giving him the information. She wanted to keep it quiet, hoping the funding would come soon and direct to her, since it was in the works before the new director was hired.

"Yes, that was Usher Sanders, everyone calls him Rosie." Alex checked his roster for Usher's information.

Laurel interjected, "He has been on my team since I came here and he does exemplar work. He indicated to me his desire to stay on my team. You said yesterday you wanted to offer me other choices of which team to head up. I would be interested in hearing about those."

"The other choices include another mound site, with a different tribe, farther north on the Mississippi River. We'll call that job site, number two. Some digs have been done there, but not enough. The job site number three, that I spoke of yesterday, is at Saguaro National. As you know the Director's duty is to ride 'ramrod' over all the teams. As a result, my position as a Team Leader at this site will have to be shared by another leader professed in his work, as I will not be able to be there full time.

"I have considered you, Laurel, as you are qualified and a proven leader. Both our names would be on any discoveries, papers written, and all work done as a joint venture. But, here is the sweet part, the pay will be the same as a single Team Leader position. So this could turn out to be a good deal for you. You have wanted to be in that area, where your grandmother and mom had their camp. You could decide to continue staying in the Cahokia area, where you will be experiencing more of the same boring findings, or spread your wings out to a new horizon. What do you think?"

"Has this museum ever sent a team down to Saguaro National?"

"I believe it was back in '91', with a team led by a Richard, or Ronald Wright. His findings are on record here. You can check them out."

"With there being three different job sites up for offer, I would like to take a short break to make my decision, if you don't mind. I promise to be quick, as I know you have appointments booked throughout the day."

"I do have more appointments, but I can spare some time for you, Laurel. How about meeting me back here in two hours. Will that give you enough time?"

"Thank you, I believe it will."

"Great, maybe then we can get things started with your new position." He smiled.

Laurel left his office feeling like 'ole Alex Zuckerman' was up to his old way of doing business. She recalled Zuckerman's offer. Everything would have his name on it, as well as hers. Even if she did all the work, his name would be first on the finds, or any written publications. She knew what that would mean. He would take all the credit and glory, and she would be a nobody. Just an assistant to him.

She checked out Richard Wright's findings, reading his latest published papers. The findings failed to inspire her. The board could rule on the funding applications any time now. It's best to wait it out. Even if they don't come through, it's wise to continue with Cahokia, at least for one more year. I've already prepared a lot toward more publications, and this will be all in my name.

Two hours later, Laurel returned to Zuckerman's office, greeting another archaeologist that was leaving. Alex motioned her to come inside and take a seat. He smiled. "Tell me what you have decided."

"Alex, I have given the proposals much thought and although I wanted to go to the South West, this area is about one to two years too early for me. I want to stay at Cahokia, finish my work, and publish my findings. I also am requesting the same team members as last year." Laurel handed him the list. "If there are any extra workers, I could use them."

She knew Alex would be disappointed with her decision, and right on que his smile faded. Moments passed and he said nothing, looking down at the papers on his desk.

"All right. I realize this is important for you and your career and good for the Museum. You may have the same members as last year; and any leftover workers we can spare." He reached out to shake her hand in a most professional manner and affirmed, "It's good to be working with you again, Laurel."

She could feel his disappointment with the tone of his voice. Laurel thanked him again for the opportunity to complete her work, and they went over some of the business details and plans, then quite abruptly he said, "Oh, you were going to tell me about 'Mr. Wonders and Mystery' man."

"Well–w–ell?" Laurel stammered, trying to think of how to explain her connection with Nick.

"Sorry, if that's a personal matter."

Laurel summarized this might be the out she needed right now and quickly replied, "Really nothing to tell. How about you, Alex–is there someone special in your life?"

"There you go, still answering a question with a question." Alex turned his head upward, looking around the open space in the room, as he normally did when he was constructing what he was about to say. "Well, there was this girl, shrugging his shoulders, but I let her get away. It wasn't until after she had gone, I realized just how special she was to me."

Laurel felt a lump in her throat. *Was he referring to our relationship?* She needed to steer him away from that conversation.

"Oh, I forgot to tell you. My apartment was broken into during the party last night."

"That's horrible. Are you okay?"

"I'm fine. I think they were still there when I arrived and was walking around the chaos in the living room when I heard a noise in the back. The only thing I had for protection was my canister of mace."

"Don't tell me you went after them!"

"I considered hiding and spraying them when they came by me, but I wasn't sure the mace was still good, so I darted to the hall and called the police. I still don't know if anything was taken, until I finish picking things up. The officer pointed out that the usual things a robber goes after–electronics, jewelry and cash–were not taken."

"What about some of your personal artifacts, did you keep those in your apartment?"

"Yes, some are kept there, with the rest at the Crawford Estate in Springfield. Of course, no specimen from work was ever brought home. I haven't had time to go through things yet. I plan on going straight back to the apartment after our meeting to take inventory."

"What about your research work on your laptop, or actual papers?"

"Yes, my research is kept on my laptop. I can't think it so important that it would warrant someone to steal it?" She stood. "I'll let my team know we are still good to go on Cahokia, then I plan on going back to my apartment to check things out."

"All right, Laurel. I'm glad you were not hurt, but promise me this– no more chasing after bad guys with only a small mace canister– all right? Also, report back to me about your research data," he exclaimed, as she hurried out the office door.

CHAPTER 10

Laurel met with her team and informed them of the Director's decision to base them again at the Cahokia site. Everyone was pleased with the decision and relieved they were not held in limbo for weeks not knowing where they would be working. Laurel scheduled an educational class at the museum for tomorrow. Stephanie was already in Laurel's office working on one of the databases. She volunteered to go home with her to help pick up the mess and do inventory. They loaded up in Laurel's car and within a few minutes they were standing outside her apartment door.

As Laurel turned the key in the new lock, she looked at Stephanie warning her, "Don't faint from the initial shock." She pushed the door open revealing an unbelievable cyclone of a mess.

Stephanie never took her eyes off the cluttered piles of stuff scattered over the living room. "Is the whole apartment like this?"

"Pretty much. I cleared off the bed early this morning, so I could lie across it to rest. I fell asleep instead, waking up just in time to go to my meeting. I told Alex about the break-in and he wanted me to check my laptop to see if it had been tampered with. Also, I did have a file of facts and figures relating to my research, in a dark blue folder, we need to be on the lookout for."

Stephanie started cleaning up the turned over plants, sweeping up the potting soil. Some of the plants had to be repotted. "Why such reckless havoc?"

Laurel found her laptop on the kitchen table underneath some dish towels. After checking it out, she commented, "Everything seems to be all right with my laptop– no entries were made while I was gone."

"Were they looking for something buried in these pots? Some of these plants were pulled out by their roots–not just knocked over."

"The officers said it appeared they were looking for something particular. They didn't want the cash in the safe, or any electronics, these are usual theft items. They weren't even gathered up to be taken."

The girls worked hard for three hours and the apartment slowly returned to its normal, organized appearance, with nothing missing that Laurel could discern. She thanked Stephanie for all the hard work, giving her a most grateful hug, then remarked, "I bet you are as hungry as I am." They decided to stop for lunch on the way back to the Museum.

While in route Laurel stopped at a traffic light and looked up to a nearby billboard depicting an ad about a new western movie, showing a man on horseback with a few mules loaded down, following him. Bells went off in her head. *Where have I seen this before?* She was still contemplating the billboard when Stephanie reached over and started shaking her shoulder.

"Laurel. Laurel! The light has changed. People behind us are getting anxious."

By now, horns were blaring and the constant blasts of noise snapped Laurel back from the mesmerizing trance. She slowly drove down the street, turning into a restaurant drive and parked.

"Wow!" Stephanie exclaimed. "Where were you? It's like you were in another place. Your face even turned pale. Your eyes were blank, like you were in a daze."

"It was really strange Steph. I looked up at the billboard back there at the light and something triggered within me. I saw these mules with bulky sacks on their backs. It was like I was right there with them."

"Does this have to do with your dreams?"

Laurel nodded. "My grandmother told me about a self-hypnosis process they taught at the Spiritual Healing Center, and I have been using it."

"That sounds like an interesting place, one that I would like to check out."

"Grams and my step grandfather, Lawrence Crawford, donated a few acres to the Spiritual Center of the Ozarks, and built two buildings for them to hold their classes and sessions. I'm going to Springfield on Easter break, and Grams wanted me to invite several of the team members to come with me. She would love to have the whole team, it would be like old times to her, since she was an Archaeologist also."

"Sounds great. I would love to come! My parents are going to Arizona to visit my sister and their new baby, so they won't be home this Easter. How many do they have room for?"

"Actually, all those that want to come. They have over 11,000 sq. ft. in the main house, with four guest rooms. And there is a log cabin, over a hundred years old, that sleeps four, all sitting on 12 acres on the edge of Springfield Lake."

During lunch, Laurel told Stephanie about Alex pushing for her to explain who the guy was she was talking to last night. "He's labeled him 'Mr. Wonders and Mystery Man'. He thought he was my boyfriend," Laurel grinned. "So I just let him continue to think he was. Then I asked if he has someone special in his life. He starting telling about this girl that he once knew, and how special she was to him, not realizing this until he let her get away. Oh God, Stephanie, he was talking about me."

"Laurel, that put you in a terrible spot! What did you do after he said that?"

"I changed the tone of the conversation by telling him about my break-in last night."

"Laurel, I saw the two of you at the party, you were in a deep conversation. I almost stopped to say hello, but decided it was not the best time. I could tell he still cares deeply for you."

"I am beginning to find that out, first last night, then this morning. But it's over. We have to remain purely professional now." She glanced at the time. "We best be getting back to the Museum, I've got to make arrangements for the class tomorrow."

Laurel's thoughts kept returning to Alex. *Is he trying to worm his way back into another relationship with me?*

CHAPTER 11

Laurel made sure the food and drinks for the class brunch had been delivered. She moved some of the tables and chairs around, sitting up for her first education class of the new season. She went upstairs to the Ancient Cahokia Display to partially rope off the area in the visitor's gallery, where she would be bringing her class for further education.

The class room was filling up by the time Laurel returned, and she was glad to see the sign she'd placed on the table reading, "Eat–Drink–Get Acquainted worked. This was great. She wanted them to mingle and talk to each other while partaking of the delicious food she had catered. Laurel got some tea and walked around saying hello, being friendly, allowing everyone time to enjoy themselves.

After a while Laurel went to the drum that sat by her desk, and beat with the wrapped sticks, a short Indian rhythm, her way to let the team know that class was about to start.

"Would everyone please take a seat," Laurel announced in a friendly, but authoritative voice, as she stood in front of her desk, facing the small group.

"First, I would like to welcome back those members from last year returning to the group and a special welcome to our new members. This will be their first paying job!" Cheers and applause vibrated amongst them. Laurel continued. "At the same time, this is on the job, advanced training, entirely different than your collage days."

"We are striving to be more aware of our interpretations of our finds here with the Cahokia excavations. Merely digging up old remains, symbols, inscriptions and writings is just where our job begins. True archaeology is the reading of these symbols and writings when found. The mound builders' symbols before they are read, are nothing but artistic pieces and neat designs. They don't mean anything yet. But when read, and I mean read correctly, it tells a true story of the early history of North America. These relics are in fact telling us and all of humankind that a mysterious race, which we named Cahokia, resided in the so-called 'American Bottom' along the Mississippi shore in Illinois."

A new member, Christina Carter asked, "It appears these Ancient's were intelligent beings."

Laurel leaned against her desk. "Yes, Christina, these mound builders were a highly civilized and enlightened people, with a knowledge of the cosmic forces and how it worked. This showed us that they had a scientific wisdom greater than we have acquired today."

Laurel continued her lecture for a short time, then she led the group upstairs to the Ancient Mound Builders area, where there was on display a scale model of Cahokia's Capital City. The group stood in awe around a raised platform that displayed an artist's renditions in miniature form of the vast Ancient Capital of a now forgotten human race.

Laurel pointed out, "In the back part of the plaza stands the 100-ft. giant colossus, Monks Mound, with the Chieftain house on top."

Gideon Rothermel, one of the new members asked, "How long did it take them to build this particular one?"

"Aha. . . that's a great question!" Laurel remarked. "Archaeologist in the past determined various dates from their findings, that put the age span of 250 years. But new evidence, including our work," she smiled, "has now determined that Monks Mound was in fact, built in only a few decades, more like twenty to forty years. Also, the work was continuous, around the clock."

"The Grand Plaza was built at the same time as the Monks Mound, as well as the small 'ridge-top' Mound 49 in the middle of the Plaza. Inside the vast plaza were eight other mounds of various sizes, all with hut houses and thatched roofs, where civic and political leaders lived. The City was laid out in a horseshoe fashion with a stockade fence built around it. There were numerous residential houses in the city and vast neighborhoods scattered outwards from the fenced area."

A man from the visitors' section spoke, "When was this large of a city built? It, no doubt, took a very long time."

"Well," Laurel replied, "originally this started with a village of only 1000 souls. Then shortly after 1050 A.D. everything at and around this old village started changing. It is clear from Archaeological discoveries, that over a very short period, some group or, it could have been just a single person, redesigned Cahokia from a village into a vast city! So the height of the growth of the city peaked around A.D. 1150."

"I heard they just up and left, all of them!" another visitor remarked.

Laurel affirmed the remark. "They abandoned the city around 1200's, and by 1400 CE the civilization was completely deserted!" The visitor responded, "But why did they leave?" Where did they go?"

Laurel explained, "There were many hypotheses on why they left, such as climate changes, and crop depletion. It is believed they most likely moved south. My team and I are still doing research on that very question."

"Good morning, Laurel." Joann Maury spoke in her cheerful manner. "I see you're drawing in some interesting questions."

Laurel returned the greeting and re-introduced the class to the Vice President of the McMelton Corporation. While they were all busy visiting about the model, Mrs. Maury directed Laurel off to the side. "Can you come to my office this afternoon, after you finish up with your class? I have some important things I need to discuss with you."

Laurel replied, "Of course, I will be through with my class around two. May I ask what this is about?"

"I'll discuss the matter later in my office."

"Oh, does it have anything to do with my applications for the project funding?"

"No more questions. You may return to your class now, I will see you in my office at 2:00 o'clock."

Laurel continued with the class, but it was hard to keep her concentration on the subject at hand as she wondered, *is this good news or bad?* She led them back to the office for some more work and then broke for a late lunch. The class then journeyed down to the basement lab where she gave instructions on analyzing some specimens. After thirty minutes Laurel whispered to Rosie, "I have a meeting with Mrs. Maury and I will be gone for a while, so I'm leaving you personally in charge."

"No problem, Ms. Laurel, I've got it covered."

Laurel hurried out of the lab with the intention of stopping off at her office to gather up her files of the funding projects. When she arrived outside Mrs. Maury door, she hesitated. *What is this dismal feeling sweeping over me?* Checking her watch, she discovered she had a few moments to spare so she took a deep breath. . .then another, as she programmed positive thoughts for the meeting, hoping the universe would pull them toward her.

CHAPTER 12

Laurel knocked on Mrs. Maury open door, and she replied, "Come in, Laurel, and have a seat." Mrs. Maury looked up from her papers she was shuffling. "The board met last night and voted on some of the funding applications before them." Mrs. Maury smiled when she added, "I am pleased to tell you, one of your two applications passed."

Laurel couldn't contain her excitement. "That's wonderful. Which one did they pass?"

"They unanimously passed #107SASIT, The Space Archaeology Satellite Imaging Technology. You can re-submit the other application after this project is finished. I was at the meeting and they consulted with me on both projects and asked my opinion. I expressed the Satellite Imaging project would indeed be of great benefit to the museum." She paused. "Laurel, there is another issue that we need to deal with."

"Yes Mrs. Maury…,"

she interrupted her. "Please call me Joann."

"Certainly, Joann. Is there a problem?"

"There is an issue that needs to be dealt with. I spoke with our new Director, Dr. Zuckerman this morning, and through our conversation I discovered he knew nothing about your applications for any funding. Why didn't you discuss this with him at your meeting yesterday?" The tone in Mrs. Maury voice had gone from proud to disappointment. Laurel felt she had to explain herself and their history.

"Mrs. Maury. . . I mean, Joann. I don't know if when Dr. Zuckerman was hired for this position, he disclosed that he and I had a past relationship, or if this even mattered with the hiring board?"

"What kind of relationship was it, you working on the same team, like a work situation, or a dating type relationship?"

"It was all the above. We were working together and living together. I thought it was a serious love relationship but then we had problems. I quit my job with the University and applied to several places. This was the best of my three interviews. It has been around two years since I walked out on him.

"But there was another reason I didn't tell him. When we were back at the University, anyone applying for funding for a project turned in the application to Director Zukerman. I was aware of projects being scrubbed because he attached his note to the application stating the project was not worthy of the funds being spent prior to presenting them before the board. I was afraid our break-up, or even his past way of judging applications, would spoil my chances with the board. Therefore, I stalled about telling him." By this time, Laurel had become emotional and a tear ran down her cheek. Joann came over to comfort her.

"First off," Joann imparted, "Your project is worthy, I put my stamp of approval on it myself. Now you and our New Director have a problem that you are going to have to work out. Both of you are extremely talented archaeologists, and you, Laurel, are showing a promising future, with your instinct and resourcefulness. Didn't you tell me, both your mother and grandmother were in this field? So no wonder you're talented– it's in your genes." Joann walked back behind her desk.

"Laurel, may I have permission to ask you a personal question? If you don't want to answer, you don't have to." Laurel nodded for her to continue. "This relationship and the break-up barely two years ago–how do you feel about him? Are you still in love with him?"

Laurel looked down, pausing before answering, then she looked up and replied, "Yes and no. I suppose I needed some actual physical distance apart from him to search my heart for my true feelings. From the resent conversations I've had with him the last two days, I think he might be trying to win me back. It's been very subtle. I'm not sure what to do about it. So far I've managed to change the subject."

"Is it your wish to keep it professional until you know for certain how you feel?"

"Yes," Laurel nodded.

"All right. The Director's duties are to oversee all divisions of the Archaeology-Anthropology Department. Your duties are to let him know about any funding projects and to work with him on these. Now Laurel, do you think you can do that?"

"Yes Joann, I can be professional, if he will conduct himself strictly in a professional way."

"Laurel, I will sit down with him and see if I can straighten things out. I promise I won't tell him everything you told me."

"Thank you."

"Now that the Board sees this project of yours as a go, are you ready to take the lead and start making plans to carry it out?"

"Yes, Joann, I am."

"Then after my talk with Director Zuckerman, you will have to let him know you had a project that was approved by the Board last night. Go over it with him so he can see what has been approved. Do you think you can do this?" A concerned look came over Laurel's face and she hesitated.

"I could be present when you tell the Director about the funding, "Joann imparted. " Let's all meet here tomorrow at 10:00 o'clock."

CHAPTER 13

Laurel left Joann Maury's office and walked briskly down the hall to the women's restroom. She wore a smile on her face as she checked out all the booths to make sure she was alone. Certain no one was around, she cut loose with several jumps high in the air, letting out cheers of joy! She stood tall and proud in front of the mirror, smiling and speaking to herself. "Congratulations Ms. Laurel Robertson! You have just been awarded your first project! YEA! YEA!"

Before she could finish with her congratulatory statement the bathroom door swung open and a girl entered the room. She laughed as she greeted Laurel.

"Yea, congratulations! Let me be the second one to congratulate you. That's quite a feat Ms. Robertson. I would be cheering too." The girl walked past her to the other end of the mirror area.

"Thank you," Laurel replied, still too excited to be embarrassed.

It was getting late in the afternoon when Laurel pushed through the double doors to the lab. She strolled down the long hallway of paneled partitions on each side, dividing the teams into their own individual spaces. The mild aroma of cleaning agents filled the air, along with the humming sounds of the overhead exhaust fans, which partially drowned the chatter of conversations as she passed by each section. She walked on to the end of the first hall where the door straight in front of her bore a plaque titled 'Ancient Cahokia Civilization', and underneath was her name as Team Leader.

Laurel opened the door and walked to where Rosie was sitting. "How's it going Rosie?" she inquired, as she peered over his shoulder.

"We're doing great here, Ms. Laurel. I showed the new guys what we discovered by using the new cleaning technique on the specimens from last summer's dig."

Pleased they were excited about using some new techniques which allowed them to make new discoveries that otherwise would have remained hidden, she moved about the room checking on each one's work. Laurel wore a smile and a glow about her that was hard to contain. But she had to, for it was too early to tell the team about the wonderful news, at least not until after tomorrow's meeting with Director Alex. *I'm thankful Joann will be there for support. Just what am I going to say to him? I'll work it out–I've got to.*

She welcomed the end of the work day and whispered in Stephanie's ear, "I've got something exciting and important to tell you, if you have time to meet over at the Club after we finish here."

Laurel went upstairs to her office. While sitting at her desk contemplating what had transpired throughout the day, something strange started happening. A mist formed in front of her, then she saw an apparition of Mother Mary. *Such a wonderful Spiritual essence I'm feeling –it's emanating over to me.* It lasted for a few seconds, then slowly vanished. She tried to get into that same state of mind, but it was no use. She wondered why she saw the blessed Mother now. She hadn't been a very good Catholic, straying from the Catholic Church just after her dad's plane crash. *Is she trying to tell me something?* Laurel remained in a quiet meditated state for a while, but nothing else came to her.

Stephanie arrived at the club first and parked her yellow and white jeep on the west parking lot where Laurel could see it and went inside to find a table. "The Pier 22', being a member only Club, was a popular meeting spot for a lot of business and professional people who worked in this area of Chicago. She was delighted that the Corporation supplied a membership for the team leaders, plus one additional member on each team.

Laurel scanned across the room looking for her friend. She put on a boastful, happy smile and made her way to Stephanie's table.

"What happened at the meeting with Mrs. Maury?"

Laurel became excited all over again, as she related the joyful news of receiving funds for her project; then the downward spiral of how she would have to explain to the Director why she didn't tell him about her applications.

Stephanie reached over and placed her hand on top of Laurel's and with a compassionate tone said, "Laurel, you have every right to be excited since this is your first awarding of funds for your project. I am so happy for you! Laurel, know that tomorrow is another day, the sun will rise and shine its glory all around you and your meeting, with new positive energy that will be yours to receive."

"Stephanie, I don't know where you get those burst of 'wisdom quotes', but I appreciate it and I thank you deeply for your support."

"Let's be happy about the award." She squealed with delight and rising up out of her seat she wrapped both of her long arms around Laurel hugging her tight."

The server soon brought drinks to their table and stated, "Two Margaritas for the pretty ladies compliments of the nice-looking guy at the bar." Laurel's thoughts immediately turned to Alex. *Was he the one that sent the drinks? There are not that many guys who know my drink preference.* She sure didn't want to deal with him before tomorrow.

"Can you tell me which one at the bar sent the drinks?" Laurel politely asked the server.

"It's the nice looking fellow standing talking to the guy sitting on the third stool from the wall," she replied.

Laurel rose up slightly to see who it was, then with relief that radiated across her face she replied, "Please tell the nice-looking person thanks for the drinks and come join us." She turned to Stephanie, "That's the guy I met at the party the other night."

Stephanie's brow furrowed. "What do you think Professor Zuckerman's reaction will be when he finds out you withheld information from him?"

"Well Steph, he's not going to like it. I'm sure glad that Joann Maury will be there when I tell him. I'm not sure what to expect from him–hurt–anger?"

"Good evening, Ms. Robertson." Laurel looked up to see Nick Kenyon and another man standing by the table.

"Mr. Kenyon, thank you for the drinks. Would you and you friend like to join us?"

Nick introduced his associate, Nigel Stewart to both. "Nigel is also a production manager at World Wonders and Mystery. Did we hear some cheering coming from this table a few minutes ago?"

"Yes, we are excited." Laurel remarked.

Stephanie chimed in. "We are extremely happy. Laurel has been awarded funding for a great new project."

"Is this about your NASA Satellite Imaging project?" Nick inquired.

"Yes. I'm a bit overjoyed about the news. I just found out this afternoon."

Nick gave her a big smile as he reached out to shake her hand. "Congratulations, Laurel." Laurel could sense his gentlemanly charm as he placed his other hand on her forearm. She felt a special energy swirling from his hands to her.

Nigel speaking with his British accent expressed, "Best Wishes to You." He reached over to shake her hand. Nigel turned to Stephanie. "Do you work on the same team as Laurel?"

"Yes, I certainly do. I'm as excited about all of this as she is."

Nick turned to Laurel. "I took the liberty of sharing your story about the Ancient Cahokia and the mounds, along with the input your associate Rosie shared about UFO's being in the area. Nigel here, feels the same as I do. Filming the NASA Satellite Imaging and showing the results to the public would make a great documentary."

Nigel spoke up, "There hasn't been any documentary show about the Ancient Indians and the Cahokia Mounds, thus it would be North America's equivalent to the pyramids of Egypt and Mexico. We, as representatives of the World Wonders and Mystery Network, would like to be the first to produce this. What say you?"

Laurel was overwhelmed with the possibilities this could bring, not only with their dig site and what might be disclosed and uncovered, but this could be a personal advancement in their field of Archaeology and Anthropology.

"Thank you for suggesting this. We will need to meet with the Corporation officials that are contracted with the Field Museum. They will need to get permission. Then there is the Board over the State Historic Park. We will need their permission also."

Nick explained, "Both Nigel and I will be working on this together. Do you know how much money has been allotted for your project?"

"The amount funded was the proposed bid from Dr. Emily A. Weston, at Columbia University," Laurel disclosed. "I haven't had a chance to go over all the figures yet, but I do know it is for the area immediately around Monks Mound."

Nick nodded. "So how far out will the satellite imaging go?"

"I'm not sure what the distance of the scan will be," Laurel replied. "I'll need to consult with Dr. Weston. I have a meeting tomorrow with two top officials. One of which was just hired a few days ago, Director, Alex Zuckerman. It's a delicate situation as he knows nothing of my application for funding yet, so I would appreciate your discretion."

Nigel conveyed, "We understand and will say nothing until you set up a meeting with the officials."

Laurel and Stephanie stayed and talked with the two producers for a while then Laurel announced she had some work to do and needed to leave.

Nick asked, "May I walk you to your vehicle?"

"Thank you, Mr. Kenyon, I would like that."

"I admire your choice in vehicles." He moved closer to where she stood. Looking into her eyes, he said, "This speaks a lot about you, Ms. Laurel."

"Yes, Mr. Kenyon. . . and what would that be?" Laurel smiled, anticipating what he might say next.

"Well. . .it tells me, Ms. Laurel, you are a sporty, fun loving person. Also, very precise and serious in your work, which might carry over into your personal life and relationships."

She felt drawn to him, finding herself anticipating his kiss. All too soon he backed away saying, "Good evening, Ms. Laurel. Slide on up there. I'll stay here and watch you leave."

As Laurel pulled out the drive, she looked up in the rearview mirror to see him wave good-by, then he turned and walked back inside the club.

CHAPTER 14

Laurel went to bed with thoughts on how to deal with Alex. Finally drifting off to sleep, sinking deeply into a dream state, she experienced a box being lowered into a deep hole in the ground. When she awoke, the dream was still hanging around. She recalled seeing flashes of symbols, then they were gone.

When she awoke, her chest and head were hurting. The dream still was hanging around. She recalled seeing flashes, she had felt the hot sun beat down on her, then there were cold-cold nights. She saw a large spotted wildcat, a most beautiful animal, with Spiritual overtones. What did all this mean? She contemplated the dream for a while longer, then another thought rushed in. *The Meeting! What am I going to say to the new director. . . a.k.a. my ex-boyfriend?*

She felt her face, arms, and her chest– *why am I so blasted hot?* Looking in the bathroom mirror she saw redness spread over her body. It felt and even looked like she was sunburned.

Then she recalled parts of the dream again, the part where the hot sun beat down upon *him,* while he laid on the ground. There were flashes of a male body, then back to her female body. She was becoming confused. . *.it must have been me, as my skin is sunburned. But how can this be? This was a dream–you can't carry things from your dreams into this reality. There must be some other explanation for this.* No matter how hard she tried she couldn't explain it.

Laurel's thoughts switched back to her concern about the meeting. At the same time, she was excited about the satellite imaging, plus a potential TV documentary. She selected a top that would cover up most of the sunburn, took extra care with her make-up and hair, thinking she needed all the help she could get.

"Good morning, Ms. Laurel," Rosie greeted. "You're looking extra special today, got another important meeting?"

"A very important meeting. I will need for you to mind the team while I'm gone." Laurel headed for the door and noticed Stephanie look toward her with a silent *Good Luck* formed on her lips. Laurel smiled back as she left the lab. Still not knowing what she would say at the meeting, she managed to find a quiet place away from everyone, to contemplate her notes and to bring herself into alignment.

Laurel entered the office to find Alex and Joann Maury sitting at the work table drinking coffee. "Good morning," Laurel greeted.

"Help yourself to something to drink, we just sat down ourselves." Joann Maury turned to Alex. "Dr. Zuckerman, I called this meeting to align you, Laurel, and myself on the same page, so to speak. Since you have only been here a few days, I need to catch you up on several projects and funding applications that were already in process. Two nights ago, the board met and voted on a few of these projects that had been before them for several months. I am pleased that one of Laurel's projects was approved."

Alex looked surprised, his face giving way to a forced smile. "Well congratulations, Laurel! Why didn't you tell me about the funding apps? What kind of a project did you require extra money for?" He fired one question after another, not giving her enough time for any answers.

Laurel spoke up, commanding her place in the conversation. "My project is the space archaeology satellite imaging of the Cahokia Monks Mound area."

"Really. I have heard of satellite imaging. And the Board. . . approved your proposal? I believed this type of imaging to be very costly. Could I see a copy of your proposal and the dollar amount for this project?" Alex spoke with an authoritive tone. Laurel handed him the estimated proposal from Dr. Emily G. Weston.

Alex briefly scanned the proposal. "Why on earth would we want to spend this much money on such high-tech science?"

Joann interjected, "I looked over the original proposal and helped her with it, mainly because I also saw the need under the current circumstances. After she made some changes that we talked about, I felt it was a worthy project proposal and put my approval on the final draft. It was submitted last October. Laurel, why don't you catch Dr. Zuckerman up on the activities at the Cahokia site?"

Laurel proceeded to explain the problems that had been developing over the years at Monks Mound, and all the other solutions that were tried, with no successful outcome. She explained in detail each process that was used and why it was becoming critical that they find other solutions to repair the third largest ancient pyramid in the Americas.

"Oh, I see." Dr. Zuckerman replied. "I'm most pleased, Laurel, with your detailed presentation on the status of Monks Mound. In this case, I can see some higher technology needs to be utilized. It is time that an organization such as ours should be leading the action. I take it you checked out the credentials of this satellite imaging company?"

"Of course." Laurel was happy Joann didn't let him belittle her project and was pleased she had convinced Alex of the immense need for this technology. She began placing the plans out on the table, and was about to explain the documentary proposal, when Mrs. Maury excused herself from the room for a few minutes.

Alex came very close to her side, to view the papers she spread out. Laurel felt his energy, one she once endeared so much. That same feeling was now easing its way through her body.

What is happening? She moved away a few steps, turned, and faced him. He was looking at her with that longing in his eyes she knew too well.

Laurel realized she still had some of those feelings for him. *What am I going to do?*

He reached out with a light touch easing her closer to him as he gazed purposely into her eyes. She felt the message he was sending; *her mind wandered back to an island of balmy breezes, where their love was only surpassed by their sexual appetite for each other.*

Wake up–You stupid girl! she shouted to herself. Can't you see what's happening? You're being pulled into his fantasy. Laurel managed to pull away from him and made an excuse to go to the rest room.

Getting away from the energy he was sending out to her was a relief. She took a deep breath, rebalancing herself, then placed a wad of moist paper towels on the back of her neck. Then Laurel remembered she had not yet explained the documentary. A wonderful bonus to her whole project.

She re-entered the room, grateful Mrs. Maury had returned. "Before we go further, I need to tell you both about a very important development I only learned about last evening. I have been approached by the production managers of the World Wonders & Mystery TV Network. They are very interested in making an exclusive documentary about the Ancient Cahokia Civilization and want to include the filming of the Space Archaeology satellite imaging and the results."

"That sounds very interesting," Alex remarked.

"There is more. They realize my funding was submitted and voted on with only the Monks Mound Area, but for their documentary they would like to expand further out to include more of this vast Ancient Indian settlement. They asked if we are willing to have the satellite scan renegotiated to scan out further, with most of the extra expense taken care of by their sponsors. This could benefit our organization as well as theirs."

"Laurel, this is a fantastic proposal! To be part of a World Documentary, and it would be great exposure for the Museum," Joann said.

"It certainly is," Alex remarked. "You said they want to scan more of Cahokia area? We need an expanded perimeter diagram from the satellite imaging company and what that cost would entail."

"I think the Board will be interested in the publicity from this documentary." Joann reflected excitement in her voice.

"I will be consulting with Dr. Weston to get those perimeters; in the meantime, the TV producers are waiting for a call to meet with us for a formal presentation of what they will be doing in conjunction with the Museum," Laurel announced.

"Let's go ahead and make that call to set a meeting with them." Joann walked to her desk and picked up her appointment book. "I'm free Friday morning."

CHAPTER 15

Laurel was pleased that the meeting went well and that she could finally tell her team members the exciting news. On a problematic note, she must see to it her shields stay up when around Alex, making sure he doesn't try to reel her in, as he tried this morning.

She called the group together to make the announcement. Everyone was elated about the project, anxious to help anyway they could. "We have one week to start working on the preparations before we take our Easter Break. After ten days, we'll return here to finalize our part of what they may want for the satellite imaging, and the Documentary."

Laurel shuffled through her notes, trying to decipher what she needed to do first. "Oh, I almost forgot. I will be going home to my grandparents, in Missouri, for the Easter Break, and they extended an invitation to any of you to come and stay at their home. There is plenty of room in the main house, along with a second home and a Log Cabin. There is always good food prepared, and I guarantee you will not go hungry. There are plenty of things to do in the area, some of which is bound to peak your interest. As some of you know, my grandmother was in Archaeology and now dabbles in antiques. My grandfather is a retired attorney and his hobby is rare books. He has a massive two-story library that rivals many public and private libraries."

Stephanie added, "I'm going to check out the Metaphysical community that adjoins their property. I hear it is one of the best."

Everyone tried to return to their various tasks, but it was difficult at first because of all the news and excitement. Laurel returned to her office where she phoned Dr. Emily Weston to explain the new developments with the World Wonders & Mystery TV Network and the documentary they would be doing.

"They need your permission Dr. Weston, to film your technology results, and interview you. We need to include a greater amount of the Cahokia area, so we will need a new proposal with the exact perimeters of the scan and the additional cost."

"That's wonderful they want to do a documentary on the Cahokia civilization. I'll work up a new proposal, and since I would be getting advertisement for my company, I am sure we could come to an agreement on the cost."

Laurel explained when they would be meeting with the production managers and arranged for a conference call.

She was glad to be home in her apartment once again. It had been a busy day, working her main job duties, plus the new project preparations on top of it all. She settled on the sofa with her favorite cup of Yerba Mate` tea and brought back to mind all that took place in the meeting with Alex. *Why do I let him get to me?* It's going to be harder than she imagined to keep things professional.

Her thoughts shifted to Nick Kenyon. She liked this guy. He is funny, a gentleman, fun to be around, a good dancer, and nice looking. Laurel had been around him several times, but not really on a date. It could be the TV Company has a rule against fraternization. Or maybe he is just not that much into her, other than being a friend and a client. Since they would be working together, maybe it's for the best...

Laurel picked up her phone and clicked on her grandmother's number. After she answered, Laurel politely asked, "How are you?"

"I'm fine, Laurel, been waiting to hear from you."

I've been meaning to call you for days. I just wanted you to know I've invited everyone to come to Springfield for the Easter break, as you asked. I will have a head count on Friday."

"Wonderful! Lawrence and I are looking forward to having the company."

Laurel told her grandmother the great news about her project being approved and the strong possibility that a major TV Network would be doing a documentary. "That's fantastic, Laurel! When do you think they will do it?"

"It will be after Easter, as we are still in the planning stage. I'm sure it will be soon though. According to Dr. Weston, she wants to do the satellite imaging in the moist weeks of spring for the best results. We have a meeting tomorrow afternoon to go over the plans with the production managers of the TV Network and will be speaking with Dr. Weston again."

Laurel double checked with her grandmother, "Are you sure you and Lawrence are feeling well enough to have a bunch of young budding Archeologist as house guests?"

"Don't you worry about it, I'm still pretty active for my age and Lawrence's knee surgery is healing well. He goes most everywhere with his cane for now."

"It's a comfort to know you guys have a lot of help with that oversized mansion! "

"Would you like for me to make an appointment for a session over at The Center while you're here?"

"Yes, go ahead, maybe they can make some sense out of all these strange dreams."

"Laurel, since the invite was to anyone on your team, does this include Alex?"

"I don't think he will be coming. I made the announcement to the team while in the lab and he wasn't there. But there is always that possibility that he could hear about it from someone. Well Grams, I haven't eaten yet and need to try and find some food. I'll say good-by until Friday."

CHAPTER 16

Laurel's grandmother had just hung up the phone when she received a call from her friend in Tucson. "Barbara, this is Nina June. I've been trying to reach you. The museum here in Tucson has received a purchase order from Phoenix University for the purchase of the excess archived pottery shards stored in #SP section."

Barbara was stunned by the news. "I should have known this day would come. How long before you have to move on it?"

"Only three days. When do you think you can get here?"

"I need two days driving my car. I can't drive straight through any more at my age."

"What about Lawrence helping with the drive?"

"No, that's out of the question. He's just now over the long recovery period from his knee surgery. Even though he is doing great, it might be too much of a strain for him to drive. Besides, I don't want to involve him."

"Ok Barbara, I understand your dilemma. I'll hold off the transfer one more day until you get here. Do you have any idea where you will move the artifacts to?"

Barbara thought for a moment. "Burying it in the back yard is out of the question. Issie and Lizzie would probably dig it up. I can't think of any secure place to move it to with this short notice."

"Barbara, my brother who has the antique shop in Phoenix, told me about one of his clients storing some of his valuables at a vault facility there in Phoenix. He said it is a public storage with private vaults, not connected with the financial industry. So the Bank Secrecy Act, nor the

Treasury Department, has any jurisdiction to govern or regulate their business. He also said they have a state of the art security system with armed security guards."

"That sounds like the answer to my problem. Can you get me their phone number?"

"I don't have their number but check online. The name has something to do with a mountain in Phoenix. I'm sure there's not that many vault facilities in the area."

"Drive safely. I'll talk to you later."

Barbara hung up and checked the computer for the web site. She mulled over the information as she read; *a private safe deposit vault embedded in a mountain, surrounded by tons of steel, concrete and rock– 12-inch steel reinforced walls and floor, 6,000-pound steel vault door– humidity temperature controlled–various size boxes, or rooms! Owner guarantees untraceable privacy. State of the Art Security system with armed Guards!* This is an answer to my prayers.

After Barbara called and secured the rental of her vault, she went looking for Lawrence to tell him about the sudden trip she was about to take. She loved Lawrence and had never lied to him in all their twenty-six years of marriage. But this was different. She had to keep this from him. Lawrence knew Nina was a dear friend of Barbara's since college and their early Archaeology days. They kept in close touch, often going on antique trips together. He also knew she was searching for a particular Tiffany lamp. She decided to use that as her excuse. At least it was believable.

"You what? Can't you go after Easter? Don't you have Laurel and all her bunch arriving soon?"

"It will be fine. Maria and Ralph have been preparing for days and everything is practically ready for their arrival no matter how many show up. Besides, I'll be back the day they get here, hopefully with my original Tiffany." Barbara put her arms around Lawrence and gave him a lingering hug. "You'll be okay with this won't you?"

"Yes, I will be fine, but I'll miss you."

"Issie and Lizzie will keep you company till I get back," Barbara declared giving him a smile. "I'm going to bed early so I can get an early start tomorrow." She hugged him and said good night.

The next morning, she woke up earlier than usual and packed an overnight bag and some snacks for the trip. She added a large bakery shopping bag to use for camouflaging the artifacts during transport. Lawrence got up and started putting his things in an overnight bag also. "I changed my mind. I'm going with you," he announced. "I fueled your

Highlander last night and checked everything over, so we're ready to go."

Barbara was surprised, "You're going with me? This won't be a fun trip for you, I'm worried about your knee, besides you'll probably be bored to death."

"I'm going along to keep you company and alert. I'm your relief driver. No more arguments. That is that!"

They drove away from the Crawford Estate before sunrise. "I called Ralph and Maria last night to let them know both of us were going to Tucson for three or four days, so don't worry, everything is covered." Lawrence smiled.

Barbara had some time to think on the drive south. She was thankful Nina told her about the vault facility in Phoenix. It will be very secure there and she won't have the cylinder-artifact, the Aztec map, and articles of clothing and jewelry hidden on our property. Barbara's thoughts turned to Lawrence. She knew he would question bringing a sack full of stuff out of the Tucson Museum and storing it at the Phoenix vault facility. Barbara didn't think she could keep this secret from him any longer. "You're awful quiet over there. What are you thinking about?" Lawrence asked, "I can almost hear your wheels turning."

"Well, I'm contemplating something. . .something I should have shared with you before now." Barbara tried to control her emotions and keep her voice steady.

"Are you having an affair?"

"What? No!" She didn't know if he was serious or not, she glanced over at him, "Stop teasing me. You know I love you too much for that. This has to do with the time Madelene and I worked a site in Arizona. The wreck we were in twenty-eight years ago was no accident. After my Jeep Wagoneer missed the curve and crashed down into a steep ravine, I was unconscious for a while. When I came to, my eyes were still closed and I could hear two men talking. They were going through everything we had packed. After a while they left. I managed to move enough to check on Madelene. She had been thrown from the driver's seat." Tears welled up in Barbara's eyes. She couldn't see to drive any longer and pulled the SUV over to the side of the road. Just telling him about this was very painful.

Lawrence put his arm around her. After a while he took over the driving. "Do you know what these men were looking for?"

"Not really. Both Madelene and I were working at a dig site with a special permit. We had rented a small house in a little village on the western side of Tubac. Our food supplies needed to be replenished, so I gathered up little four-year old Laurel and went into the village market place while Madelene went back to the site with our two local Mexican-Indian guides that we hired to help us."

"You said the wreck was not an accident?" Lawrence inquired.

"Keep your shirt on, I'm getting to that. Madelene said she found an opening between some rocks that tunneled into a small cave. The two helpers waited outside, they were superstitious and would not go in. There was a drawing/painting on the cave wall that Madelene said was not your typical hieroglyphics."

"What did it show?"

"Well, she said the painting told a story like most hieroglyphics, but it seemed to be a map also. It had what looked like three triangle stars, with flames trailing behind."

"This sounds like comets, or space ships," Lawrence remarked.

"Madelene said the stars looked like they were landing at different sites. The third one landed by a group of Pyramids or large mounds next to a very long river that emptied into a massive body of water far below the site."

"The Mounds by the long river sounds like the Ancient Cahokia Mounds on the Mississippi, where Laurel has been working," Lawrence proclaimed.

"I know," Barbara remarked with a worried look as she turned to Lawrence. "They are making plans to have the NASA satellite imaging scan the Monk's Mound area. This new type of imaging technology could pick up this ship, or remains of whatever it was, if it is still there."

"This Satellite imaging will soon take place just weeks from now. Don't you think you should tell Laurel what her mother saw in the cave?"

"There is more to this story. Madelene wanted to go back to the cave the next day to see if there was more inside."

"So, did Madelene find anything else?" Lawrence asked.

Barbara hesitated not wanting to say what was found in the cave, other than the hieroglyphics. "Well, first Madelene went to the house where the two helpers lived, as she always did before going out to the site. They were not anywhere around. She spent time looking for them, but no one had seen them. Finally, she gave up and went to the site by herself. When she got to the area, everything looked different. The cave entrance had been blown up! She could tell by how the rocks laid and the smell of explosives still lingering in the air. It became clear to her somebody didn't want her back in that cave. She looked around, knowing the perpetrators could still be in the area, and decided to leave before they saw her.

Lawrence asked, "Was it the superstitious Indians in the area who did this?"

"It's possible. She couldn't believe they would have done this. They had been reliable guides and helpers for the duration of their stay. But she never located them." It was getting late, when Lawrence pulled into an Amarillo motel for the evening. They were both very tired. Even though Lawrence wanted to hear more of her mysterious story, they put it on hold until the next day.

Barbara called her friend Nina June and explained Lawrence was with her and her decision to share the bizarre story that took place twenty-eight years ago.

"Have you told him everything–even why you are making this trip?" Nina inquired.

Barbara lowered her voice when Lawrence came out of the bathroom.

"Not yet," Barbara replied, as she headed toward the bathroom, shutting the door and turning on the water. "I've not mentioned the Artifact or the clothing, just that she saw the Hieroglyphics drawing and painting, and it was not the typical kind."

"Barbara, I know you can't talk freely right now, so don't say anything, just hear me out. You and I have been through everything together, both hell and high water. I love you and you know you can trust me to always look out for your best interest. I know you love Lawrence with all your heart, and he makes a good companion for you. But, Barbara, the rest of the information you are about to tell him could be a real game changer.

"Think long and hard before you tell him everything. Make damn well sure you can trust him. Time itself, changes things and people. Remember who you are, Barb. Remember what the readers at the Center have told you, and what you intuitively know about yourself. You did not parish in that wreck because it was your spiritual hierarchy in the ascension process–to be the next Guardian of the 'Spiritual Artifact'.

"You also remained to help raise your granddaughter, Laurel. You are the Guardian now, don't forget what your duties entail, you must keep the Artifact out of hands that would do harm to Earth and humans."

"I know." Barbara sighed.

"Promise me you will meditate on telling Lawrence or anyone else this secret."

"All right Nina, I hear you. I will meditate on it and call you tomorrow."

CHAPTER 17

The next morning, Barbara took the first driving shift and was deep in thought about the conversation she had with Nina. *I don't have to involve Lawrence, just because he chose to help with the long drive. This Guardianship I chose to accept is my responsibility and mine alone, for all my life, until I pass it on to another responsible person of ascension standing. I must do all I can to protect 'the Artifact' along with the Aztec items. They will be kept safe in the cave vault in Phoenix, until the enlighten one comes to activate it.* Her thoughts dissolved rapidly when Lawrence leaned over to her. "Are you ready to talk more about your mysterious secret?"

"Hmm. . . well, where was I?"

"The wreck wasn't an accident," Lawrence reminded her.

"Right. Madelene's husband, John and I were told by the sheriff's department that the brakes had been tampered with, which caused the wreck. They never caught the men I heard going through our belongings, and after twenty-eight years, I don't have much hope they ever will. We kept checking with the Highway Patrol but nothing's ever turned up. I think the men that tampered with our brakes and went through our Jeep have something to do with that cave and what Madelene saw."

Both maintained a period of silence as she continued driving. Lawrence opened his book and started reading and Barbara's thoughts led her to the break-in they had three weeks previously. She was certain it was somebody looking for the 'Artifact'. Hopefully they were satisfied it was not at their estate. They took nothing, so it was not a typical robbery, *they probably knew all along I was still alive. They might be watching me. Nina and I will need to be extra careful tomorrow.*

Barbara and Lawrence made it into Tucson by evening and she placed a call to Nina to let her know they were in town. They talked briefly, then she added, "What time do you want Lawrence to drop me off tomorrow?"

"What do you mean drop you off?" Lawrence questioned her when the call ended.

"Lawrence, I love you dearly and you are the best companion any lady could ever ask for, but Nina and I planned to spend some girl time and do some intense antiquing in some unique shops. She needs to make a delivery in Phoenix, so she is taking the van. So you will have my car to go check out some book dealers, or something that interests you."

"I guess some girl time will do you good. It's hard to keep up with you two anyway."

Lawrence dropped Barbara off at the Museum and went on in search of a book dealer. Barbara went through the employee entrance and asked for her friend Nina. Nina soon appeared with a guest badge, placing it on her jacket. She gave her a warm welcoming hug. "Are you by yourself?"

"I am and anxious to get started."

"Great, I've got my order loaded in the van, all we need to do is add yours." They walked down to a lower level storage where numerous shelving was full of items stored in bins then on to another area where locked bins appeared. Nina stopped at the bin number on her card, asking Barbara for her key. Barbara inserted her key and the lock released. "Check the package to see that everything is there, then we can place another wrapper around it and tape it closed." Barbara carefully unwrapped the different pieces and spent some time inspecting each, not knowing when the next time she would be able to study them.

"Everything is here. Nina, I think my SUV may have been followed. I noticed a dark van that turned after us the last two turns. They may have seen Lawrence drop me off and are waiting for me to leave by the same door, or they may be watching all outlets. In any case, we will have to be cautious."

Nina pulled her van close to the exit and Barbara laid down in the front seat while Nina drove the van out of the enclosed museum parking garage. She remained hidden for several blocks.

"I think you can raise up now," Nina remarked. "Let's deliver yours first. Are they expecting you?"

"I'll phone them now, letting them know my approximate arrival time and the vehicle I'm in."

When they arrived at the mountain facility, they were stopped at the security gate by armed guards who searched the van. Barbara held her breath as the guard waved the wand over her bundle of items. They soon were cleared and the steel door opened, allowing them to pull inside, the door shutting quickly behind them. Once inside they were met by more guards and an agent who showed Nina to a plush waiting area next to her van and took Barbara to a desk where she completed her lease requirements.

The attendant gave instructions, "You need to choose a signature name for your leased area, any name, or even a pseudonym-such as 'Mickey Mouse or Donald Duck', then you'll be given a key. The signature name is compared to that on record, if it matches vault access is granted, and your key opens your vault."

Laurel wondered what name should she put down. What about the pets, Issie and Lizzie? No, that's too easy. Maybe their name sakes, Queen Isabella and Elizabeth? She entered the names on the card. Next, she had to decide the number of years to lease for. "Before I choose, what happens if I parish?"

"You may name a beneficiary. If none is named, the vault contents are held in place for a period of two years. Then if no one signs the name on record, and produces the key, it becomes the property of AVF Mountain Vault."

Do I want to name someone? I don't know who I trust to be the next guardian. "I will leave the beneficiary blank for now. I'll contact you later when I've decided."

She completed the lease and was escorted down the elevator deep within the bowels of mother earth. She then walked to her personal vault, where she placed the very powerful Artifact in the most secure place she could find. She locked her vault, and an armed guard took her back to the surface where she was united with her friend Nina. They boarded the van and awaited clearance for the steel gate to rise. They finally were on their way to the University of Phoenix, their last stop, before going to some quaint antique shops. Barbara took a deep breath releasing a great deal of stress.

"I bet you're glad that's taken care of. We could not have left it much longer in the museum anyway with my retirement coming up," Nina remarked.

"Most of my worries are over, except I will have to name a beneficiary before long, in case something happens to me."

"I know you were still doing some research on the artifact device." Have you learned anything new?"

"My research in the beginning was basically reading what other prominent researchers have written. It led to the Templers that were privy to a secret connecting with the origins of Christianity. There also is a connection to Wolfram von Eschenbach, who maintained nearly eight centuries ago that the Templers were guardians of the Holy Grail - whatever the Holy Grail really is."

"I thought that was the cup that held Jesus's blood," Nina remarked.

"I did too, until I read several hypotheses. One turned out to be about his blood line. After the crucifixion, the Magdalene was with child. She was smuggled to Gaul, where the Jewish community already existed. All of this came out in a book and later a block buster movie. Then there was another clue in Wolfram's story that caught my attention debunking the bloodline theory."

"What was in his writings?"

"According to Wolfram, the Grail is a stone, not a bloodline. There was a phrase, 'Lapsit exillis'. Scholars have suggested a few interpretations; stone from the heavens, or it fell from heaven, or a stone fallen from heaven, or of 'lapis elixir–the Philosopher's Stone of alchemy'. This kept gnawing at me, this stone thing, Nina. I saw that Artifact and held it in my hands. It is a very hard material, like a stone, even the end had a capstone. In a way, it's as if it did fall from heaven."

"That story is very interesting, and he referenced the stone as being the Grail coming from heaven?" Nina smiled as she continued listening.

"Nina, I tried a different approach to this mystery, by standing back and looking at the cave map. It clearly depicted these star ships appearing to come from Heaven and landing in three different places on earth–but I believe it is the stones that accompany the ships that are 'the Grail coming from Heaven'! My guess there is probably at least one in each ship. This ship depicted as landing on the left side of the map near the Islamic Temple, with the Artifact that came from it, could have been what the Templers discovered after taking residence over the foundations of King Solomon's temple," Barbara explained.

Nina imparted, "In theory King Solomon did a lot of mining–he could have found that starship and took the device or stone artifact from it. They said he had a lot of power and wealth and was connected to God in his leadership with his regime. It's possible he was able to use this Artifact, which helped him acquire this power and wealth!"

"All of those ships appeared to have descended from the same place, and they were all drawn alike, in a sort of triangle design, with what looked like fire trailing behind them or some lines to show movement."

"What do you think that device was used for?" Nina questioned.

"Maybe a communication tool, or a scientific device for analyzing something here on Earth? Or something necessary with their ships navigation or repair? All speculation on my part."

"When they find that ship in the Cahokia area, and that could be very soon, the device may or may not still be there!" Barbara voiced, wondering if it was.

"I hear what you're saying! These Ancient Indians, if they could have entered the ship –they probably took it with them when they left!" Nina remarked.

Nina pulled around to the loading dock at the University and keyed in the number for delivery.

They were on their way to the quaint antique district where Nina's brother had his shop, when Nina asked, "You said you had a feeling someone was watching you again? Do you think it is the same group that rummaged through your Jeep, twenty some years ago? And why would they leave you alone for that long then suddenly start looking to you again?"

"It's very possible they thought I was dead too, or just ruled me out as having the Artifact and started searching somewhere else."

Nina parked the van in the lot behind the store. They both visited with Nina's brother Sam for a while before Barbara stated she wanted to see the Tiffany he saved for her. Nina announced she had forgotten the package she was bringing for Sam's birthday and headed to the back door. She came rushing back. "Oh God, there are men breaking into my van. Call 911."

"The three wore dark sweats with hoods. They searched mainly under the seats and had nothing in their hands when they left," Nina told the police.

"Did they leave on foot, or vehicle?" the officer questioned.

"They ran to a black van with a driver waiting for them."

"Were there any markings on the van?"

"No, it was solid black, looked like a new one, maybe?" After the police left, Sam's maintenance man repaired the seats enough for them to make the drive back to Tucson.

"It's clear their attention is back on me. They must have followed us when we left the museum. They had no way of knowing what we left at the Vault facility. It's obvious they are looking for the Artifact."

CHAPTER 18

Laurel and her team kept busy preparing for the Space Satellite NASA imaging. Friday rolled around before they knew it and those that wanted to go on the trip met at the museum parking lot. It worked out well with a total of eight.

The three girls elected to go with Laurel, with the guys loading up in Rosie's Jeep- Rubicon. The weather was nice and sunny and the group traveled together, staying in touch by cell, coordinating lunch, breaks, and driver switches.

Stephanie asked, "Do you think your grandmother could call ahead and make an appointment for me at the Center, like she did for you?"

"Sure," Laurel replied. "Anyone else before I call?"

Laurel placed the call and Lawrence answered.

"Morning Laurel, we are in the car. Your grandmother is driving. I'm putting the phone on speaker."

"Hi! We just got underway–all eight of us and we wanted to phone ahead and make some more appointments with the Center. We need their number if you have it with you."

"I've got it in my address book in my purse. Lawrence, will you look it up for her."

"Grams, where are you guys?"

"We're on our way home from Arizona. Made a quick trip to see my friend Nina and picked up a beautiful antique Tiffany. You know, the one I have been looking for." Lawrence gave Laurel the number she wanted and they continued talking.

"What time do you plan on getting home?" Laurel asked.

"I estimate you guys will probably get there long before us," Lawrence answered. "But don't you worry, all preparations have been made for your group's arrival. Ralph and Maria are expecting you and they'll show you the sleeping arrangements. We will see you when we arrive. Also, there will be plenty of food in the kitchen, if anyone is hungry. Have fun!"

"Okay. Tell them there will be four guys, with three girls, besides myself."

Laurel was quiet for a while after they hung up. She couldn't believe Grams took off on an antiquing trip with all this company arriving. She's not even going to be there when we arrive. It isn't like her at all! Something is going on that she's not saying. . . and Laurel aimed to find out!

It was late and all were tired when Laurel pulled up to the gate and keyed in the speaker. "Hello Laurel, I see you guys made it," Ralph commented.

"Hi there Ralph, we have two cars to pull in." Rosie drove in behind Laurel and the security gate promptly closed behind them. Laurel led the way to the parking behind the house. Outside lighting lit up the back entry along with the massive outdoor living area.

Laurel's pets howled and barked loudly. They were overly excited wagging their bushy tails and jumping up on the fence. Laurel rushed over to the pen to greet them. "How's my good girls–it's been a long time since I saw you!" She reached through the fence with both hands grabbing hold of their long beautiful white and silver coats, giving them some rough play with her hands and they reciprocated with lots of licking, dancing and whining. They ran around the pen and back for more petting.

"Come and meet Issie and Lizzie, my pet wolves. But just one person at a time. They are friendly and have been trained just as a regular dog. Put you hand near the opening and let them smell you first, saying 'Good Girl!' Then slowly ease in to pet the one who smelled you." The guys were taken with them, but two of the girls Gabi and Christine were hesitant and stayed back. "Tomorrow we can let them out, they love to run and play in the back. It's all fenced in, so they can't get out and run the neighborhood. We were afraid someone might shoot them, not knowing they were domesticated."

"Can I help with the bags?" Ralph asked.

"Sure thing." Laurel patted him on the back. "Everyone, meet Ralph." They all introduced themselves while unloading their bags. Ralph led the way through the rear entry hall that opened into the vast center foyer.

"You fellas can sit your bags down here for the moment while I take the ladies bags up to their bedrooms." A woman stepped through the kitchen door. "Maria, how are you doing!" Laurel hugged her then turned to the group. "Meet Maria, Ralph's lovely wife and the best cook in the Ozarks!"

Maria gave a modest smile. "I knew you might be hungry so I prepared a snack. Go on in and help yourselves." She then turned back to Laurel. "I can't wait to hear about any new discovery you may have found at your dig site." Laurel began to fill her in while they both followed Ralph and the girls as they made their way up the vast circular staircase. Maria showed the three girls their rooms and inquired if they needed anything.

After everyone enjoyed the midnight snack, Ralph asked the guys if they were ready to find their quarters.

"Oh, I bet you guys will like this," Laurel remarked. "Ralph is putting you up in the log cabin. It's well over a hundred years old and it's had some refurbishing." He flipped the switch inside the back entry illuminating a path winding through the forest. Even the girls tagged along to see it. Laurel explained her grandparents added some modern conveniences while keeping the old atmosphere.

The cabin had two beds in the loft, with another two beds on the lower level, a sitting area, bath and a kitchenette. It worked out well for the guys. Ralph pointed out the features, "It's equipped with a PVA, meaning a Pro Visual-Audio distribution panel, security cameras, closed circuit T.V., and high-speed internet."

Laurel announced, "I know everybody must be tired so I'll show you the rest of the place tomorrow before I go over to the Center for my appointment." She asked Ralph and Maria if they had heard from her grandparents lately. "I'm concerned. I've not heard a thing this evening and it's now 12:30 A.M."

Laurel keyed in her Grams phone, it rang and rang finally going to voice mail. Laurel left a message for them to return the call. "They may have stopped at a motel, but it's not like them not to call one of us." Laurel went to her room and got ready for bed, hoping to hear back soon.

CHAPTER 19

Laurel was in a deep sleep, then became restless, tossing and turning, and throwing off her covers. She became partially awake, recalling a dream; *a stormy day, dark clouds moving overhead, there was lightning and thunder–then a loud burst! Rocks flying and tumbling–feeling of sadness. . .* Then swiftly she was totally awake. Laurel looked at the clock on the dresser. it was 5-5-5! What's going on with all the five lining up?

"Grams! Why hasn't one of them called me?" Laurel reached for her phone to place another call, just as it rang.

"Hello Grams, where are you?"

"Hello Sweetie. Did you sleep well in your big Olé Poster bed?"

"I had more dreams. I'll tell you when I see you. I was very worried about the two of you when you didn't come home last night. I got the impression when I spoke to Lawrence that you guys were closer to Springfield."

"We got tired and stopped at a motel here in Amarillo to get some sleep. It was so late I thought you probably were asleep and I didn't want to wake you. Laurel, we had some problems early this morning. We're at the Amarillo Police precinct. We are okay. Don't worry." Grams voice quivered. "A group of men searched through my car, even taking some seats apart, looking for something. They tried to break into our room. Lawrence warned them he had a gun, but they kept on coming. When the door opened enough, Lawrence shot one of them, maybe more, we don't know. They put the injured man into the van, we couldn't tell if more than one caught a bullet. There were blood droppings on the sidewalk."

"My word Grams! What a terrible ordeal for you both. I'm thankful you're all right! Is the man dead that he shot?"

"We don't know and the police haven't located them yet. Laurel, don't forget your appointments over at the Center. And have your friends check the board in the kitchen. There is a reminder list of all the things to do in the Springfield area."

"Grams, there you go worrying about us when you guys are the ones with problems."

"We'll be okay. Lawrence's firm contacted an attorney here and Lawrence is in there talking with him now. When we get released from here we will have to get a mechanic to come out and put the seats back like they should be before we can drive back. I've got to go now. The investigator wants to take my statement. I'll call you later." Laurel was glad they were not hurt but she was still worried about them. She knew Lawrence, being an attorney, knew what to expect, and she was glad he had a Texas attorney to advise him.

Her thoughts drifted to the dreams for a while, trying to recall more detail. She needed to write as much as she could remember down so she could go over it with the dream analyst this morning and maybe get to the bottom of this.

Stephanie stopped by Laurel's room to confirm their appointments. "Since they are about the same time, we can walk over together, I always take the short cut," Laurel told her. Gabi and Christine knocked on the door, sticking their heads inside. "Good morning, come on in and join us," Laurel said, in a cherry tone.

Christine remarked, "Your antique bed is a work of art!" She walked around the room admiring it.

Gabi added, "The mirror is so sharp and clear, not like the way the older ones fog up."

"I always admired this Spanish four poster bed. It has been in my grandmother's side of the family since the 1770's. My junior year in high school I wanted to change my room, so I asked if I could have it. For my sixteenth birthday, my grandmother had the mirror restored. then we went shopping for all new furnishings."

Maria appeared at the door to tell them there was a bunch of hungry guys requesting permission to eat breakfast, with or without the girls. This brought a round of laughter. "Miss Laurel, I'm so glad you're back. You always bring so much joy to this home." Maria smiled.

"Thanks Maria, tell them we are on our way down."

Laurel announced at breakfast that her grandparents would be detained for a while and they both said hello and were anxious to meet everyone. Laurel felt she should keep quiet about their problems until she heard more details.

"I would like to show everyone around the place before Stephanie and I go to the Center for our appointments." Laurel stood up from the table. "You're already where we gather the most, the kitchen and family room. Also, Grams posted an area attraction list on the board in the family room you can read later." She led them back to the massive tiled foyer and stood in front of the large antique table. "My grandparents had the mansion built in 2000. It is approximately 11,000 square feet." She pointed over to the formal dining room divided by pillars and arches, then pointed to another area where a matching arch and pillars opened to the formal living room, full of antique furnishings. There were lots of comments of grandeur from the group.

"Trust me, this may look amazing, but these furnishings are the most uncomfortable in the whole house." She lifted her arm to the curved stairs and explained it led to the east wing with four bedrooms. "The balcony that wraps above the foyer leads over to the west wing, housing my grandparents master suite, study and a spiral staircase, connecting to the library." She pointed out the elevator cage on the west wing balcony that goes from the loft down to the walk-out basement.

"I like that see through, steel design on the front. It reminds me of one I saw in a film at a fancy hotel in Paris," Stephanie remarked.

"There is a main hallway to the library just off this foyer." She led them down two wide steps into the massive, two story library.

"Wow! Are you kidding me!" Aaron exclaimed.

"You said he had a rather large collection of books," Justin added. "This is larger than the library back in my home town."

Laurel called their attention to an area of books on Archaeology and Anthropology, even some journals written by her grandmother, and other prominent people. She pointed upstairs. "You may note there is a smaller room with a glass front, this is where Lawrence keeps his rare book collection, it is humidity and temperature controlled for preservation. The door is kept locked and this is one area you are restricted from entering." Laurel checked her watch and noted her time was running short. "I'm running out of time with this tour, but you can check out the walk-out basement later. There is an Antique Saloon Bar, an exercise room, an old-time theater room, plus other points of interest.

She led them outside to the stepped patio. They could see a lot more now that it was daylight. "I need to caution you about the dogs again. Do not let them out without me being present. Even though there is three and a half acres of zoo quality fence for them to run and play in, it's better to be safe than sorry. I will leave my car keys on the kitchen table for anyone to use. I have changed the key code for the gates, while we are here to Arch1, so you can come and go anytime. Maria will prepare lunch and dinner and there is always food on the cabinet, or in the 'fridge' for whenever you get hungry – Just help yourselves."

CHAPTER 20

Stephanie seemed anxious on the walk over to the Center, asking numerous questions about her upcoming appointment.

"They probably will interview you first, a sort of get acquainted," Laurel explained. "Then they might have you lie on the table for a Reiki session."

"Is that the same thing you used on me last summer when I hurt my shoulder?" Stephanie inquired.

"The energy system I used was similar to this, it's called Reiki Tummo. What I did is call up a specific healing energy."

"What you did was wonderful and amazing, it healed so fast. Did they teach you how to do that at the Center?"

"No, I went with Grams to an ashram in Indonesia when I was sixteen. She wanted to learn from a Master. I went along with her just to see the country. Needless to say, I became interested in this technique also."

Laurel keyed in the code at the gate and they walked a short distance to the front entry. "Since we are splitting up, let's plan on meeting back here in the reception area after we are finished, then we can walk back together."

Laurel was introduced to the new dream specialist. *This is good. It is best that she does not know me, or my history.* Soft music played in the background, with a mild aroma of white sage filtering through the air. The middle age lady listened attentively as Laurel described what she remembered of the dreams and visions. Looking over her notes for a few minutes, she put them aside, placed her hands over Laurel's and closed her eyes. The specialist seemed to be in meditation. Then she began to speak, "This one who is the dreamer suffers from guilt."

"What?" Laurel questioned.

"Guilt. You are going through some kind of 'spiritual guilt'. There is a pattern here. Your dreams are telling me you are going through a spiritual dilemma. The black clouds are brewing a storm within you; visuals of men in black robes, indicate a form of religion, a type of priest. The lowering of the box in the ground, is you hiding away your most powerful possession. While the Blessed Mother Mary watches over you and what you have buried. The spotted cat, the mighty Jaguar, typically found in the far south part of the Americas, has come to protect you. It's the kind of spiritual crisis that has to be resolved, or you will never find peace."

"What is this repetition of the 5-5-5 I keep seeing when I look at a digital clock?"

"I believe this is a time for you to be aware of, as your attention keeps being directed to this. They are not telling me if this is past, present, or future. If it has been an occurrence that took place in the past, then it is up to you to find out what it was. You continue to see it, so it is very, very important for you to solve. But if this is a time something is going to happen in the future, you need to watch out for this and be prepared."

"What can I do? Meditate more?"

"No, for a great many this would be the answer, but my intuition tells me you have to do more than that." The dream specialist suddenly went silent, closing her eyes, seemingly lost in thought again. A moment later she looked at Laurel and continued.

"You have to re-examine your roots. This is where your problem lies. You have to find out who and what you really are."

"I don't understand."

"Laurel, everyone has a path in life, a path that is solely their own. Yours may be a special one. To find out for certain, you must learn more about your roots. I believe the problem you are experiencing can be solved once and for all, but you need to apply more time to it."

"Do you think I should talk to my Catholic priest? However, he may not know me, for I haven't been to church in ages."

"Well, you could do that, but it is my belief that you have to do more. Much more. I don't think your dreams are Makyo. I think they might be actual visions of things to happen soon in your future, if they are not occurrences that have already taken place. If I am correct and they are visions, then you must resolve this, or you will not get any peace of mind. Again, I cannot discern if this is a past or a future occurrence. I'll ask them again." She closed her eyes, then after a few moments, shook her head. "No, they will not tell me."

"Do you mean I should quit my job and apply all my time into seeking out my roots? The museum I work for recently granted me funds to help solve a serious problem in the ancient Cahokia mounds before one side of it slides apart causing the whole pyramid to collapse. This is going to require my full attention in the upcoming weeks. I can't just up and quit before this is done."

"You need to search within your soul, Laurel. What's more important to you? Taking pictures of an ancient civilization's very tall pile of dirt and learning how to fix its problem so it doesn't fall apart? Or, solving the torment of what these dreams are doing to you. Putting this to rest, so you can go on with your life in peace and harmony."

"I get your point, and I do appreciate your taking the time to help me." Laurel politely thanked her again before leaving and going back to the empty reception room to wait on Stephanie. Laurel was glad a CD was made of the session so she could listen later to see if she missed anything. She sat on the padded bench by the front window alone, as the receptionist had left for a lunch break. Her thoughts were accompanied by the gentle melody of a few rain drops that steadily increased, blossoming into a deluge of hard, steady rain. The momentum soothed her mind and she began to reflect on another level of what the dream analyst told her. *She said I was experiencing guilt, spiritual guilt. Well she could be right. I might be unconsciously experiencing these feelings by my not continuing with the religious faith I was brought up with. Maybe this is why I keep seeing Mother Mary? I always held a special place in my heart for her.* Stephanie walked into the reception room sporting a big happy grin on her face. "Did you get the session I thought you would?" Laurel inquired.

"It was much like you said, plus she gave some valuable input while she was working on certain areas, also we were given a big surprise," she said, motioning toward the window. "Where did all this rain come from?"

"It wasn't in the forecast or we could have brought some rain gear. It's coming down lighter now, but we still need to borrow some umbrellas." Laurel went to the back and returned with only one small umbrella. "Let's go by the street back to the house. We won't get so muddy that way."

"Tell me what she said about your dreams."

"She addressed most of the things I told her about. She thinks it is serious and urgent that I get to the bottom of it."

CHAPTER 21

The girls were struggling to stay dry sharing the one small umbrella, weaving around the puddles in the road, when a black Jeep drove up beside them. A man rolled his window down. "Hey you two gorgeous ducks–out puddle jumping today? How about me giving you a ride?"

Stephanie, being closest one to the Jeep, moved Laurel further to the side of the road. "He could be a pervert. Just ignore him. Laurel thought his voice sounded familiar and strained to see around Stephanie.

"Chris, is that you?"

"It is I, your old partner. Hop in, I'm going to your place."

"It's okay, Stephanie. I know this good-looking guy. I'll sit up front, you get in the back."

"I was talking to Lawrence one-day last week, he said you would be coming home for several days. I was in the neighborhood and hoped to see you, but not looking like a wet duck."

Stephanie laughed. Laurel introduced the two explaining, "Chris's family moved to the Springfield area when he was seven and we shared all our school days. Our dads were in the electronics business together and we went on many treasure hunts as a group. Be careful. Chris will keep you in stitches if you let him."

"You know what they say." Chris looked to Stephanie. "If it waddles like a duck, quacks like a duck, then it probably is a duck."

"Ha! Ha!" Stephanie cackled in his ear. "I guess that makes me just another duck from the same flock. I'm just as wet."

"Very good," Chris replied. "I think I like your friend, Laurel. She will fit right in."

"Stephanie, would you roll down your window and put in the new code." Laurel leaned over and ran her hand across his close beard. "How many days growth have we got here? It looks good on you."

"Thanks, it is about three weeks."

"It's so nice to see you again, I was just thinking about you last night."

"I hope it was good thoughts," he affectionately smiled at her. "I wonder if this would be a good time for a visit with our kids, being you have some company here. How many are staying?"

"There are four guys and three girls. Both cars are gone, but that doesn't tell me much. I'll go inside and see who stayed behind."

Stephanie asked Chris, "I think I am missing something here. Were you two married?"

"Well, Laurel has always been the love of my life. And I have asked her to marry me, not once, but twice, since we have two kids together, twins to be exact. But she turned me down both times."

"Oh, I'm so sorry, I didn't know. She and I have been good friends since I started working with her team but she never told me she had kids."

Chris walked over to the pen where the two wolfs were and they reacted the same way they had with Laurel the night before.

"It's okay to have them in the family room, we are the only ones here." She joined him at the pen, keyed in the code, and let the wolves out.

"Look girls, look who's here!" Laurel threw Chris a big towel and they both wrestled and dried them off. Both dogs were ready for play. After the excitement of their little reunion calmed down, Issie walked over to Stephanie, who was standing on the side lines, joyfully watching the play. Issie calmly put her head under Stephanie's hand and bumped it upwards.

Stephanie's green eyes and Issie's blue eyes were fixated, neither of them blinked or moved. Then Stephanie spoke in her soft voice. "You are the most beautiful creature I have ever seen." She let Issie smell her hands and then she started petting her, all the while talking to her like they were long lost friends. Chris came over to pet Issie stating, "You are a natural with her. I bet you come from a dog family."

"My dad raised English Setters for bird hunting, I used to play with the pups till they got old enough to train." They were soon joined by Lizzie who wanted in on the petting.

Laurel came over. "Stephanie, I see you have made a hit with our twins!" Stephanie turned to Chris with a bewildered look. Chris smiled, "I was just pulling your leg."

When the play quieted down, Laurel explained that they were in South Dakota on a company sponsored treasure hunt with their dads. "Chris and I were off by ourselves working our electronic devices with me being closer to the base of the mountain when I heard whining and crying. Thinking the protective mother would be near, I got the heck away, telling Chris what I heard. We both left the area. Then we came across the mother wolf. She was right in our path, dead from a gunshot wound. So we doubled back to where I heard the crying and found her den. Out of a litter of five, these two survived. We were referred to a retired vet in the area who checked them over and made a formula for them to nurse on."

"It was a full-time job with both of us feeding them around the clock," Chris added.

"When we got back home, Grams and Lawrence helped us out while we were in school. It wasn't long until they were a couple of healthy, thriving animals. We all fell in love with them."

Chris remarked, "For a long time the pups thought we were their mom and dad." They all laughed. "It was Lawrence who sought out professional training for them."

"Anybody hungry as I am? Laurel questioned. "Let's see what Maria left in the 'fridge' for lunch. Look Chris, your favorite berry cobbler. I bet you called over here and talked to Maria, didn't you.?" The three gathered around the table enjoying their lunch. Chris explained he went to the electronics show in Vegas. "I saw a new metal detector prototype on display that looked promising, so I had them ship one. They claimed it was better, with several improvements, over the current ones used by archaeologist. It arrived yesterday with a CD and other literature." He got up and headed for his jeep, when he met Maria in the foyer.

"Maria, my sweetheart," giving her a big hug. "You have the key to my heart. I enjoyed the berry cobbler immensely."

"Just keeping my favorite guy happy."

He brought the detector into the family room. They started inspecting the new device, when Laurel got a call from her grandmother. Excusing herself, she left the room, walked out past the foyer and down the steps leading to the library where she could talk more freely. After a while she returned to the family room explaining the problem her grandparents had.

"They are all right but will be delayed by a day." Laurel went on to tell the frightening events her Grams and Lawrence had gone through.

"Boy, it sounds like they wanted something very badly that they thought your grandparents had," Chris remarked.

Grams said, "They took nothing, even left her prized antique lamp sitting in the parking lot, undamaged. They did some damage on the seats and pried up the cargo area. Apparently, they thought something was hidden underneath."

"Did they get a look at the men?" Chris asked.

"She didn't say. I'm sure they will give us more details when they get here."

"That sounds familiar," Stephanie uttered. "The break-in at your apartment, they made one hell of a mess and didn't take anything there either."

"What? They ransacked your apartment?" Chris shook his head giving Laurel a concerned look. Laurel just shrugged it off.

The three of them went back to examining the new electronic device. "It looks like it quit raining, let's give her a try out back," Laurel remarked.

"I was hoping you would say that." Chris whistled for Iissie and Lizzie to go outside with them. Laurel entered the code in the back gate and the three of them tracked across the tree covered acreage heavy with the fragrance of wet pines and lush foliage from the spring rain. Tall mature oak trees filled the wooded area. Reaching the back of the enclosed property stood another locked gate. The three of them passed through, leaving the dogs behind inside their pen. From here they walked another fifty yards to a cliff that dropped to the edge of Springfield Lake.

"It's nice to have a lake in your back yard," Stephanie laughed. Chris turned the new prototype on and began its operation. He gave it a basic trial and found it running properly, then passed it on to Laurel so she could get a feel for it. She fine-tuned it and ran it over the ground then passed the detector to Stephanie.

"See what you can detect," Laurel said.

The new proto beeped, then beeped again. Laurel came and looked at the blank screen. She switched one of the buttons and it brought up a graph.

"Looks like you found something, Stephanie. It's showing an object– three feet down and it's depicting the size too."

"Whoopie!" The guys don't know what they're missing."

"A true test would be to take it back with us to Cahokia." Laura looked at Chris. "What kind of price tag are we looking at?"

"If this new prototype works for you, old partner, then I'm easy."

"I think I'm liking your old partner more and more," Stephanie declared while giving him her look of approval.

Chris stayed to meet the guys and they all hung out in the recreation room for the evening.

CHAPTER 22

Laurel awoke to Robin's singing just outside her window. She loved the nature sanctuary built just beyond the bedroom deck with a background of cedars and pines, perfect for wild birds. Their music was interrupted by a gentle knock on her door.

"Laurel are you awake yet?"

"Grams! Come in, I'm awake." The door opened and her grandmother entered wearing her pajamas and a mid-length house coat. "We took turns driving and got here around two this morning," she explained while bending down to give Laurel a kiss.

"You two went through a scary ordeal on that trip to visit Nina June. I bet you're still shook up some." Laurel moved from the bed to the sitting area, motioning her grandmother to come and sit.

"I'm doing okay, I've had more sleep than Lawrence. He drove last so I left him still asleep in our bed."

"Did Lawrence have a problem with the police for shooting that man?"

"I'm glad the law firm here took care of getting him an attorney there in Amarillo. That certainly helped in dealing with the police. I hope that intruder is still alive and they catch him as well as the others."

"Grams, the way you described them searching the SUV, even going through the box the lamp was packed in, shows they were looking for a particular item. Doesn't this sound all too familiar? First it was your house, then my apartment, and nothing was taken, because they haven't found what their looking for yet. And now Grams, their attention is back to you."

"Wait! You said they searched your apartment?"

"It was while I was gone, the night of the cocktail party. Grams, focus back to your Amarillo break-in–they could have killed both of you. You know I love you, but you need to talk to me. Are you in some sort of trouble?"

"No, of course not! It's probably just a case of mistaken identity. You'll see when they catch these guys, when one or more show up at the hospital, or clinic with bullet wounds. Don't you worry. Now tell me about your session with the dream specialist. I'm anxious to find out what they told you."

Laurel knew her grandmother was hiding something. But since Grams remained closed mouth for now, she would just have to try other tactics later.

"I'll let you hear the CD while I go downstairs and get us some coffee." Laurel set up her computer for play, then left the room, returning shortly with a tray of coffee, tea and blueberry muffins.

"My goodness, she didn't mess around, she thinks your dreams are actual visions," Barbara commented. "What do you think about what she said?"

"She doesn't know if this is something that happened in the past, or to happen in the future. She started out by saying I was suffering from spiritual guilt. I don't feel like that."

"Laurel, you started breaking away from church around the time of your dad's plane accident. Maybe you suffer guilt straying from your faith? You're dreaming about men in black robes and Mother Mary. They are symbolic of the Catholic religion."

"There are some things about my faith that have changed, some things I no longer hold to be true, I still believe in a supreme being. She also said I must find out who and what I really am, I could be on a special path. To accomplish this, I have to learn more about my roots."

"What do you want to know?"

"To start with, were there any people of religion in the family, like a priest that wore black robes?" Before Grams could answer, they heard a playful knock at the door. Laurel reluctantly put their conversation on hold, opening her door to find the three girls. "We thought we would check to see what your plans were for the day," Stephanie said.

"Come on in and meet my grandmother, Barbara. We were having an early morning pajama party. They got here around two this morning." Laurel introduced her team mates.

Barbara announced, "We are going to have a special birthday party this evening for Laurel, so if you go somewhere be back by 6:30."

"Wow!" Gabi blurted. "The Easter Bunny brought you." Her comment brought laughter to the room.

"That's very close to being the truth," Barbara remarked. "Madelene, which is Laurel's mother, and I were busy making desserts, when she went into labor. Her delivery date wasn't until several more weeks. We rushed her to St. Johns. They couldn't slow things down, Apparently, Laurel was anxious to join our world. She was born just after eleven, keeping her birth on the eve before Easter."

"So, Grams, I hope you didn't invite the whole town. . .or did you? Tell me you didn't."

"You'll see, just a few of your friends, and a few of ours, plus all of your archaeology buddies,"

"Don't forget to invite Chris," Stephanie blushed.

"We need to tell the guys before they take out on some adventure," Laurel said as she approached the intercom and buzzed the cabin.

"Good morning," Rosie answered.

"You guys coming over for some breakfast anytime soon?"

"Just getting ready to go out the door."

"We're all pretty hungry!" Somebody yelled in the background.

They got ready and met in the kitchen-family room. Maria's Spanish scrambled eggs were a big hit with everyone.

Lawrence walked into the room growling, "What's all the excitement about down here?"

"I'm so glad you're all right!" Laurel said as she rushed to give him a hug, then turned and introduced him to their house guests. Lawrence being professional, walked over and shook each person's hand as he got their name. The group was most eager to hear more about the traumatic experience they went through. "Mr. Crawford," Justin said. "We heard you shot one of the guys breaking into your room. Did you shoot through the door?"

"You may all call me Lawrence. I considered shooting through it, but not knowing if the bullets would go through that heavy metal door, or ricochet back on us, I decided against it. I yelled at them, telling them I had a gun, then fired a warning shot, but they didn't stop. By that time, they had pried the door enough for me to get a direct shot at them. I emptied a round. It all happened so fast. A van drove up and the group pulled one man in the sliding door. Then the van spun around the corner of our building. I don't know if there was more than one that caught my bullets or not."

"Did you get a good look at them, sir?" Aaron questioned.

"Well, not good enough. They all were wearing black hoodies, except for two of them at the door. They were both white and bald. There must have been four or five plus the driver of the van."

"Barbara, where were you while all this was going on?" Gabi inquired.

"After I called the front desk, and they called the police, Lawrence wanted me to go in the bathroom and lock the door. Instead, I went to the suitcase and got another clip ready to hand him, if needed."

"Grams!" Laurel shook her head. "Sounds just like you."

Maria served breakfast to Mr. C. and everyone talked among themselves, making plans for the day.

CHAPTER 23

It was late afternoon and the girls were back at the Crawford Estate cleaning up and trying on some of Laurel's dresses she had stored in her closet. Stephanie checked on the guys. They had just arrived at the cabin and planned to be over at the set time.

Laurel received an unexpected phone call from Alex. Thoughts rushed through her mind as to whether this was business related or personal. Nervous energy crept in, as she excused herself. Why was he calling her on spring break? She stepped out into the hall, shutting the door behind her. "Hello, this is Laurel."

"Good Evening Laurel. I'm here in your beautiful 'Queen City' as they call it and want to come by to wish you a happy birthday!" His voice almost sang the words.

"Alex. What on earth are you doing in Springfield?" Laurel walked away from the bedroom door toward the balcony to continue the conversation.

"I'm on my way to my aunt's farm in Oklahoma and swung through Springfield this afternoon. I spoke with Rosie last week, so I knew some of the team would be here. I haven't seen or talked to your grandparents in a few years–I would love to visit with them also, if that's all right?"

"That will be fine, Alex. Grams put together a party for this evening. I have no idea what she has planned. We've been away from the house most of the day and just got back. She's been very secretive. She did tell the guys that it's casual dress and there will be lots of food, drinks, and such. I don't know how many are coming. You know Grams, she might invite everyone she knows." Laurel laughed.

"It's good to hear your laughter again. I miss that about you." He paused. "So, I guess I'll come over this evening. See you later."

Laurel couldn't believe her ears. I *must have forgotten he had an aunt in Oklahoma, or does he?* This was typical of Alex. She didn't know why she was so surprised. Laurel had to wonder if he was just using that as an excuse to come over and see her. She turned and faced outward on the balcony still thinking about Alex when suddenly, her attention was drawn to the activity below her. A group of people were busy setting up and decorating the vast entry hall with Grams giving instructions about the walkout basement and patio area. Laurel stepped backward hugging the wall, hoping they didn't notice her. She didn't want to spoil her grandmother's surprise.

Back inside the room, the girls were busy trying on some of Laurel's dresses. Gabi and Christine managed to find a dress. Fortunately, they were about the same size. But 'long tall sally' Stephanie, was still searching through the rack for a dress long enough.

Laurel dressed in her pale blue dress, with three-quarter sleeves, embellished in light blue sparkle around the low neckline. It was form fitting and mid-length.

Christine whispered in her ear, "Better watch out, some handsome guy will fall in love with you wearing that number."

Stephanie was getting to the panicky state when Laurel walked over and pulled out two of the long dresses. "Will one of these work for you if we shorten it?" Stephanie put on an enormous smile and chose the pale teal-green. Everyone pitched in and before long Stephanie stood looking at herself in the full-length mirror. The other three applauded and said in unison, "You look great."

Laurel left her room again and walked around the balcony over to her grandmother and Lawrence's suite and knocked on their door. Lawrence answered with the comment, "You're looking pretty as ever Miss Birthday Girl."

"Thank you. I wanted to give you guys a heads-up about a call I just received. Is Grams here?"

"Not yet, she's still downstairs. What's wrong?"

"Alex called, he's here in Springfield, saying he was on his way to his aunt's farm in Oklahoma and he wanted to drop by to wish me a happy birthday. And say hello to you and Grams and everyone this evening. I told him about the party."

"Don't worry, there will be enough people here for him to talk with. You just have a good time this evening. We'll manage him. I was just getting ready to find Barbara, so I'll tell her about his call. I'm sure she has lost track of the time. She needs to get up here and get dressed."

Lawrence walked over to the PVA panel and found her in the basement level. After numerous attempts, he couldn't get her attention. "I'll just go down and get her."

Laurel left Lawrence as he entered the elevator just outside their suite. She walked around the balcony where she could see Lawrence in the cage dropping past the foyer which was beautifully decorated in large masks. As she scanned around the room she saw large elegant sequined masquerade masks on the walls. Her birthday party had a theme. Velvet ribbons in purple, green, blue, and golden colors covered the entrance, pillars, and the staircase. The dining table was set up with a beautiful vase full of yellow roses in the center. Heating elements awaited the food. Then she noticed Maria pushing a cart carrying a large layered birthday cake across the foyer to another table and placed it in the center, where several other cakes with different color icings were already positioned. *Boy, Grams has out done herself this time.*

CHAPTER 24

The girls, all decked out and ready, decided it was time to join the party. The four of them descended the stairs, making their grand entrance. They received their colorful masks with Laurel being the last one in line. The attendant briefly glanced at a photo, then back to her. With a smile she asked, "You are Laurel Robertson, aren't you?"

"Yes, I am the birthday girl." The attendant expressed how beautiful she looked and helped her with the special see-through silver mask, trimmed in glitter around the edges, and embellished with white feathers on one side. Then she placed a beautiful silver tiara imbedded with Swarovski Diamonds on top of her head.

The four of them stayed together, easing their way among the many guests until they spied the other four teammates, off to the far side of the room, gathered around someone. When they walked up and joined them, Laurel was not surprised to discover their new director, Alex Zuckerman.

Alex stopped in the middle of his sentence, when Laurel joined them. Putting on a great smile, he reached out for her hand, and with his unique baritone voice he greeted, "Happy Birthday Laurel. You look stunning, as always."

"Thank you, Alex. I think my grandmother has outdone herself this time." Laurel wanted to take her focus away from Alex, so she turned her head to scan the room, smiling at all the new surprises she discovered on this side. "Has anyone seen what's happening downstairs?"

Aaron spoke up, "Justin and I went down. They had an assortment of gaming tables set up with dealers at each of them, plus a bartender and a snack table."

"I looked out on the patio," Justin remarked. "They had seating around a large fire pit and hanging lanterns with lights like these," he pointed up to the colorful paper accordion lanterns strung across the room.

"Laurel, can I get you something from the bar?" Alex asked.

"Thank you, I guess I could use a drink," Laurel replied. *I may need a relaxer to get through this evening.* The others began to disburse to either the drink or the food tables, leaving Laurel alone with her thoughts. *I'll be polite and have this one drink with him, then slip away–mingle around. Alex looked nice this evening, even the mask complimented his personage. The ladies were fascinated by him. I sometimes wonder why I ever left him. Maybe I should have tried harder since it appears he is still hung up on me.*

Soon Alex returned with the drinks and she noticed he was going out of his way to be extra attentive. "It's nice to be working with you again, Laurel. I've missed not seeing you around the last few days."

This was the old Alex she liked, the Alex she was attracted to. Laurel realized she still had an urge to be around him, to make love to him. She felt a blush form on her cheeks. Thankfully, Lawrence walked up before her thoughts went any further.

"Sorry to interrupt, but I would like to introduce you to one of my distinguished book clients, Professor Matthew Vaughn, with Missouri State University. This is my granddaughter, Laurel Robertson."

He removed his mask and shook her hand. "So nice to meet you, Laurel. I've heard many nice things about you. Happy Birthday!" Laurel was taken with his southern accent, trying to place just where he might be from.

Lawrence added, "Laurel is one of the team leaders in Archaeology and Anthropology at the Chicago Museum. Her associate, Dr. Alex Zuckerman, is director of this large department." They all were engrossed in conversation for a while, then Lawrence excused himself and went to find Barbara.

Lawrence made numerous clangs on a glass to get everyone's attention and handed Barbara the microphone. Laurel excused herself and moved to where her grandmother stood. "Welcome everyone to our home and the Gala Masquerade Event in honor of Laurel's birthday!" Piano music played an upbeat birthday melody as Maria lit the single candle on top of the multi-tiered cake. Applauding and cheers bestowed Laurel as she blew it out, then Maria served her the first piece.

Laurel took the mic. "Everyone, this cake is my favorite, Italian Coconut Cream. Oh, it is sooo good! Maria may be Spanish, but she makes this luscious cake better than any Italian. No offense to any

Italians here." Laughter and cheering echoed throughout. "Step on up, there is plenty of cake to go around, she baked some dark chocolate too, for the chocoholics."

Barbara took the mic and announced, "We are honored to have with us this evening a large group of archaeologists who are Laurel's associates from the Field Museum in Chicago." Another round of applause and cheers erupted. "There will be several games played tonight, so please keep your masks on until they are over. There will be prizes! All proceeds at the gaming tables on the lower level will be going to the Archaeology scholarship fund." The loudest and longest cheering and applause of the evening came from all the archaeologists present. "So go on down and enjoy yourselves!" Then the music started up again.

Laurel watched her old friend Chris as he danced with Stephanie, thinking they made a cute couple. As she headed towards the stairs to see what was set up, someone from behind her said, "Wait up, I'll walk with you." Laurel turned around to see it was the southern speaking professor Lawrence introduced to her earlier.

"Professor Vaughn, are you enjoying yourself?"

"Boy, your grandparents sure know how to throw a party," he replied.

"I'm trying to place your accent. Where did you say you were from?"

"Originally from South Carolina, but I ended up getting my Ph.D. at Princeton University."

"I thought I picked up some Carolina in there." She smiled, as she looked up to meet his blue-gray eyes. "I know a better, uncrowded route to the lower level. Come with me." She guided him to the back entry and out onto the upper patio. From here they overlooked the outside living area below that had plush seating around a large lighted fire pit. The Professor removed his jacket, placing it around Laurel's shoulders and they descended the steps to a garden landing of statues and urns awaiting spring plants. Another set of steps placed them on a walking path leading around the large fountain with a statue of a woman pouring water from a jug into the pool below. He paused briefly to read the inscription on the base of the fountain *"In the spring time came the promise of God's blessings as water poured forth into the valley below, nourishing and enhancing all life."* The path took them to the inviting fire pit, just outside the lower level entry, where they sat down and continued their conversation.

"What is it you teach?" Laurel inquired.

"Philosophy. My main interest is in theory of meaning, Metaphysics and Philosophy of Psychology. Then I have a wide background in Religious History that I sometimes teach."

"That's very interesting. I've studied Metaphysics also." As they talked, she admired his appearance. The man was neat, had a light shadow of a beard, with the hint of a mustache forming across his upper lip. His dark brown hair, brushed back from his high forehead, was curly on the back half, covering his long neck for a medium-long length. When he turned his head, the reflection of the dancing fire shined against his dark hair.

He definitely spoke with his eyes. Laurel surmised he was a happy person, for he smiled a lot. She could listen to him talk all night, with his deep voice, carrying those southern Carolina tones with an up-lift. The night air was cooling down, so she proposed they go inside and rejoin the party.

The professor opened the door for Laurel to a busy group of gaming tables that were now full, while other guests stood around watching and talking. Laurel stopped to visit with a few people as they made their way to the poker room at the far end of the lower level. Peeking inside, they noticed two open chairs. "Come on in," the dealer said. Laurel looked to the professor and he nodded yes. They played for a while then opted out so others waiting could try their luck. They weaved through the guests making their way to the 'Old Western Bar' where Laurel nudged herself up between two people, with Professor Vaughn standing behind her.

"Well, hi there–Ms. Birthday Girl! I've been looking around for you. It appears instead you found me." Laughter rang with Alex's remarks.

"Alex, Professor Vaughn and I just left the poker room."

"Hello again, Professor! Have any luck with the cards?"

"Yes, we almost cleaned the house out," Matthew Vaughn proclaimed with a smile.

"You two want something to drink?" Alex winked at Laurel. "I have an in with Sam, the bartender," he joked.

The three of them were getting along well, having a good conversation and joking around, Matthew and Alex seemed to like each other, having similar teaching professions. Soon another old friend of Laurel's came and joined them, "I'd like you to meet a good friend of mine, my old college roommate, Kourtney Reed. She is with Green County CID Division. She's a detective, and a damn good one, so better watch your P's and Q's."

"Laurel, don't scare them off from me, it's not often I meet two handsome guys in the same night." The two introduced themselves and Kourtney joined in the conversation. Kourtney was a tall attractive woman, half American Indian with long black hair, and an athletic figure.

Laurel was smiling, and she kept looking at Kourtney.

"What's with you? What are you smiling about?" Kourtney asked.

"Yes, we want to know too," Matthew urged.

"I was just remembering the time Kourtney and I enrolled in karate back when the college was called SMSU. We both enrolled in a self-defense class and it was the first day. The instructor called on Kourtney to assist him by playing the victim of an assault. She was supposed to just stand there. He approached her and she immediately took him down. I laughed so hard, tears were flowing." They all laughed, then wanted to know if she previously had the training? Kourtney kept smiling, never answering the question.

"Laurel, be careful of those stories back in our college days. I might let loose a few on you."

"I wouldn't mind hearing a few of those stories," Alex remarked.

"I bet you get a lot of teasing from this guy since you two are working together," Matthew said.

"He tries, but sometimes it backfires," she laughed.

Kourtney uttered, "I remember one-time Laurel. . ."

"Please, don't tell any of my old stories. Be nice, it's my birthday," Laurel pleaded. Just then Lawrence walked up and asked if he could borrow Dr. Zuckerman for a few minutes, promising to bring him back. After excusing themselves, Lawrence led the way over to the elevator. Laurel watched them walk away together and was concerned, wondering what this was all about.

CHAPTER 25

"Come on over," Barbara announced when the two men arrived in the library. "Lawrence and I have not seen or spoken with you in a couple of years. We all need to catch- up. How have you been?"

"I am fine, thank you for asking. I hope the both of you have been well." Alex wiped his hands along his trousers, not wanting his nervousness to show.

"I finally got my knee surgery behind me, but it still gives me trouble at times," Lawrence admitted.

Barbara played along with the catch-up until just the right moment, then she moved to the more serious aspect of their reunion.

"Alex, you have known me for a while and you know I try to be a good and fair person and I don't mingle in other people's lives. You know that I practically raised Laurel, and she is the finest granddaughter anyone could ask for. Ever since Laurel has become an adult, I have tried to stay out of her relationships, until now."

"I don't understand, is there a problem?" Alex questioned.

Lawrence spoke up, "Alex we think you are a great teacher and a fine Director of Archaeology, but here's the thing. Laurel tells us she broke up with you, that she doesn't love you any longer, and she explained she told you this."

Barbara joined in, "She moved away two years ago. Now you have followed her to her work place and you're using every opportunity to be with her. We suspect it's to win her back, which she doesn't want."

"It may appear to you that I am following her around, but with this new position, my duties include working closely with each team leader, to advise and help meet their goals. Laurel has landed a large project with the Space Archaeology satellite imaging, plus the T.V. Documentary will require a lot of work. Please understand I have the upmost, highest regards for Laurel and her welfare."

"We understand that you need to advise her, but you are using that as an excuse." Lawrence remarked.

Barbara rose to her feet, staring him down, she asserted, "Laurel has shared with me about how you have misused your position on several occasions. Now Alex, I am here to tell you, I will not stand by and let you to do this any longer. You may think that Laurel won't risk turning you in on a sexual harassment charge. But I am warning you Alex. It is me you need to take seriously." Barbara became louder and angrier as she preceded.

"Don't forget, I was very prominent in your field once. I still know some of the major players. If you do not heed what I am saying, you will wake up some day with your world shattered so badly that your days in the Archaeology field will look like ancient history. All your success and accomplishments will be for nothing."

Alex stood up. "Barbara, I am certain you misunderstood Laurel's comments she has made concerning our relationship. As you know there are always two sides of the story. I am so sorry it has gotten to this broad misunderstanding."

"Professor, there is no misunderstanding on our end," Lawrence remarked. "Enough has been said. Our little reunion is over. Come on Alex, I promised to return you to the place you were at, so let's take the elevator back down."

Barbara watched as they left the room, wondering if Alex took her seriously. Just outside the library opening she touched the code on the security panel, lowering the steel gate, keeping out any unwanted guest for the night.

No more words were spoken between Lawrence and Alex as they descended to an array of voices and laughter coming from the party crowd with dance music playing in the background. Lawrence opened the gate and said, "You may stay for the rest of the evening."

Alex walked back to the bar where he left the group, but they were no longer there. He scouted around the busy room but didn't see any of them. He walked back to the bar and squeezed in to catch Sam's attention, "I'll have another Johnny Walker-black label please." Alex was not pleased that he had been threatened and it was beginning to wear on him. He downed the scotch and got up from the bar and looked around again, still fuming from his recent conversation and the frustration over not finding Laurel and her friends. The music spilling over from the upper level was becoming louder and he decided to go up and check it out.

The current upbeat dance number came to an end, replaced by slow moving, romantic music. Matthew asked Laurel for the dance. She liked the way he held her, close but not too tight. He was tall enough that he had to look down to see her face. Their eyes met, and Laurel smiled. "Do you know your eyes are talking?"

He laughed and smiled back. "What are they saying?" he asked, drawling out his Carolina accent.

"They asked me a question." Laurel liked teasing him.

"That's interesting." He kept a steady gaze into her eyes. "I was thinking something, but I was unaware that my eyes actually spoke anything." He swung her around then back again, pulling her even closer, pressing the lower part of his body up against hers. They kept teasing each other back and forth until Laurel said, "Yes." Her eyes now focused on his lips.

"Yes what?" He moved his lips closer to hers making sure they didn't touch.

"Yes, that would be nice," Laurel answered, moistening her lips in anticipation. Then she felt the vibration from the firm tapping on Matthew's shoulder.

"May I cut in?" Alex asked in a dark tone not sounding like a request, but a stern demand. Matthew looked to Laurel, as if asking what she wanted? Reluctantly, Laurel said, "Yes." He then released Laurel into the arms of her colleague.

Laurel felt there was something wrong. She wondered if Alex witnessed their display of affection on the dance floor? Was he jealous? Or could there be something else? What happened when he left with Lawrence? As he held her in his arms she could feel the tenseness of his muscles. Was he angry? There was a hardened look on Alex's face. Laurel had to find out what the problem was.

"Alex, is there something wrong?"

"Why don't you ask your grandparents." He released her. "I'm not very good company, maybe I had better say goodnight and go on back to the motel." He walked off the dance floor. Laurel just stood there for a moment watching him walk away, toward the front entry.

Matthew hurried after him. There was an exchange of words on the front porch. Laurel caught up just in time to witness Alex deliver a punch to Matthew, hard enough to send him tumbling backwards, sprawling into the potted Juniper. Alex swiftly took off toward the parking area.

"Professor, I am so sorry." Laurel blurted, as she bent down to see if he was hurt. Then she rose up to see where Alex went. "Alex wait up! I need to talk with you. Don't leave!"

Alex stopped and turned around. When Laurel got close enough to him, she reached out for his hand. He grabbed her by the shoulders, squeezing hard he pulled her closer to him, staring into her face. Laurel trembled, not knowing what he might do. They had some bad arguments before, but he had never physically harmed her. Within minutes, Kourtney and Chris caught up to them.

"Take your hands off her. Now!" Kourtney shouted.

Alex released his hold on Laurel saying, "I'm upset and hurting, but you know I would never hurt you–don't you?"

Laurel hesitated. "Yes, I know you wouldn't." She turned to Chris and Kourtney. "It's all right. I need to briefly talk to Alex before he leaves. I'll be back to the house in a few minutes." Kourtney motioned for Chris to walk back just enough to give them some privacy. Laurel adopted a softer, tone, "Are you upset because of what you saw with Matthew and me?"

"Laurel, I'm trying hard to let you go, but your display of affection for another man, right in front of my eyes–I guess I was not ready for that. Plus, having a horrific argument with your grandparents–it was just too much. Then when Vaughn tried to tell me it wasn't your fault, he didn't know we were a couple. I lost it."

"But Alex, it's been two years. Did you think I should have joined a convent, just so you would never see me with another man?" Laurel touched his arm. "Alex, I have been trying to tell you it's over between us. You're the one that invited yourself to this party. Didn't it ever occur to you I might be dancing with someone?"

"It wasn't just a dance, Laurel. You two were practically having sex right on the dance floor."

"Well, I guess I might have got carried away in the moment, no thanks to those damn Margaritas."

"Laurel, I've been trying to tell you I have been blind and stupid in the past when we were together. That I took you for granted, not thinking about your needs, only mine. Please forgive me. I miss you like crazy. I need you Laurel and want you back in my life. I still love you." He reached out to her, giving her a passionate kiss.

She stepped back away from him saying, "Alex–don't, I don't want to restart our relationship again. Tell me what happened with my grandparents? What was the argument about?"

"It's best you ask them. I've got to go. Tell Vaughn I'm sorry."

"Alex, talk to me. What did they say to you that got you all worked up?"

"It will be all right. Go back to the house."

Laurel watched him as he hurriedly got into his silver Hummer and pealed out, leaving behind his displeasure with deep cuts in the Crawford's well-kept manicured lawn.

Kourtney and Chris walked down to where she stood. "You can do no more out here in the cold. Come back to the house with us," Kourtney said in a compassionate tone. They found Stephanie and Matthew in the family room, where she had just placed an ice pack on his left eye.

"Matthew, I am so sorry! Alex is gone now, but I did talk to him before he left. He said to tell you he should not have hit you, and to tell you he is sorry."

"Man, you are going to have a whopper of a shiner tomorrow," Chris blurted out.

"Oh no! Mr. Crawford invited me to come over tomorrow for Easter Dinner."

"I would just as soon no one else know Alex decked you. No one besides the four of us saw this, did they?" Laurel asked. They all shook their heads. "You could put a bandage patch over it and make up some excuse. Or I could give you some concealer for you to use tomorrow, if that would work."

"I don't know if your concealer will be dark enough, he has darker skin than you, Laurel," Stephanie remarked.

"All right, let's go upstairs. I will mix some liquid makeup until we get it right." Matthew followed Laurel up the stairs into her room. "Wow," he related as he eyed the beautiful antique bed. "Is this your bedroom?"

"It is. The bed was from my grandmother's side of the family. Have a seat in front of the make-up mirror." She motioned him towards the bench.

"I don't know. What if Mr. Crawford catches me in here alone with you?"

"Relax, professor, this will only take a few moments."

"So your friend Stephanie tells me you and the director used to an item. Or, are you still dating?"

"We are definitely not dating. He told me tonight he wished we had never broken up." Laurel mixed some colors then dabbed some on his face. "No, not right–need to add just a bit darker tone." She kept mixing until finally she said, "That's it–Perfect." She handed him the mixture in a small container.

Matthew rose to his feet and whispered close to her ear, "You, my friend, are the perfect one. I would never walk away from you."

Laurel smiled. "But you hardly know me, Professor Vaughn."

"I've asked you to call me Matthew, at least twice, and I've been trying real hard to know you better all evening. I almost stole a sweet kiss, but instead got a black eye." They both laughed at his joke. The laughter stretched and pulled at Matthew's swollen eye, causing him to moan with pain, covering his assaulted area with his hand.

"Maybe you could use something to ease the pain."

"That would be nice." He removed his hand from his face and lowered his head anticipating a kiss. Instead, Laurel turned and opened a drawer where she kept some over the counter pain medicines.

"Can you take Tylenol?" Laurel asked. Suddenly there was a knock at the door.

"Laurel, are you in there?" her grandmother yelled, while she tried to turn the locked door knob.

"Yes, Grams, just a moment!" She motioned for Matthew to get in the closet, then she walked to her bedroom door and opened it, flicking the light switch off. "I was just leaving to go back downstairs after refreshing my make-up." She stepped out in the hall, shutting the door promptly behind her. "Is there something you wanted me for?" Laurel pleasantly asked, guiding her grandmother down the hall toward the stairs.

"I was wondering if you had seen Professor Vaughn. I wanted to be sure he knew he's welcome for dinner tomorrow evening."

"He mentioned he would be coming when I spoke with him earlier."

"Also, I wanted to invite you and any of your crew to go to the Easter Mass in the morning, so please spread the word."

Laurel separated from her grandmother to find Stephanie and Chris to go rescue Matthew out of her closet and escort him out of the house while Laurel made sure no one saw them leave. The party continued until midnight, then the staff cleaned up, making ready for the large Easter event tomorrow evening.

Laurel went upstairs to her bedroom and threw herself across her bed. *I am so glad this party is over! How could something so grand, end up so badly? Everything seems to go wrong with every relationship, every good looking, nice guy that I meet; Matthew Vaughn, here in Springfield, a hunk of a man getting punched by my ex; then there is Nick Kenyon, the producer in Chicago, who just seems to want a work relationship; even Alex walked off and left me. Not to mention all the other relationships I've had since college days that went nowhere. Am I destined to be alone the rest of my life?*

CHAPTER 26

Laurel experienced a rough night, awakening, then back to a restless sleep, until she just flat gave up. "What's the use", she proclaimed, opening her eyes to the sunlight streaming between the gap in the drapes. Her mind was filled with a memory of a cross on a rock. She tried to remember more but was interrupted by whining and pawing at her door.

She opened the door to two overjoyed canines ready to give her lots of love and licks. They were always excited when Laurel came home, still playful even in their older age. When it was just family in the house, they would follow Laurel around, not letting her out of sight. But with all the guests coming and going, she would have to keep them close by her, so they wouldn't have any sudden surprises.

There was a gentle knock on the door. "Laurel? It's Stephanie. Is it all right if I come in?"

"Just a moment." Giving her pets instructions; "Sit–it's okay," Laurel spoke to her dogs before opening the door with a cheery tone, "Come on in Stephanie, just say hello to the girls. Remember to let them smell your hand again. Let's see if they remember you from the other day."

"Sure they do." Stephanie let them sniff and lick her long fingers. "Your grandmother had some company with her when she left to go to Mass. Gabi, Christine, and Gideon climbed into her SUV. Did she give you any more static about going?"

"No, she just reminded me late last night when she came up to my room asking if I had seen Professor Vaughn." She smiled.

"Laurel, you and Matthew were getting a little romantic on the dance floor. I must say you guys did make a nice couple. I take it that's why

Alex interrupted you two. I almost feel for the guy I didn't realize how much he still loved you."

"I know Stephanie, but I couldn't tell him no you can't come over when he knew there were seven team members here already. I did find out there was more to the story than just me and Matthew that fueled his anger. He admitted a bad argument occurred with my grandparents just before he witnessed us on the dance floor."

"What did he say happened?"

"I asked him repeatedly to tell me, but he wouldn't. I know Grams wasn't pleased that he's working as Director at the Museum. I shared with her that I felt he was trying to win me back. I shared too much and suspect that may have been the fuel for the argument. I shouldn't have said anything to her at all."

"Are you going to ask them what happened?"

"I'm going to talk with both, there are a lot of things I'm curious about."

Laurel showered and did her hair, finishing before Grams returned. Maybe I'll go ahead and talk with Lawrence. Finding him in his study, she politely knocked outside his door.

"Laurel, come on in. You didn't go to Mass with the rest of them?"

"No, I just wasn't up for it. Are you busy? Could I talk to you about something?"

"Any time, Laurel. What's bothering you?"

"It's about last night. I mean, the party was wonderful! I had a good time and everyone seemed to enjoy themselves. Your friend, Professor Vaughn and I became better acquainted and were joined by Alex, Kourtney, Stephanie and Chris. Alex was doing fine, with no problem. Both he and Matthew seemed to respect and like each other. We were all laughing and joking around and then you borrowed Alex and went somewhere. Sometime later he caught up with us. I could tell something was really bothering him."

"Yes, your grandmother wanted to speak with Alex and asked me to round him up and bring him to the library where we could talk. I'm sorry, Laurel, I'm afraid our little reunion did not go very well."

"What did Grams say to him?"

"The conversation started out all right, but soon escalated. Barbara told him to back off from making unwanted advances at work, or she threatened to use her influence to ruin his career."

"It's all my fault. I should not have shared my feelings with Grams."

"So, what did Alex say happened?" Lawrence inquired.

"He found all of us on the dance floor. I could tell there was something wrong from the expression on his face and his actions. He was hurt and angry. Things did not go well. He left shortly afterwards. "Is Grams all right?"

"She managed to shake it off. You know Barbara, she can get very protective when it comes to her only grandchild. I've been concerned somewhat about her. She's been acting mysteriously even before going on this last trip to Arizona."

"I thought it strange that Grams would up and leave to go on a shopping trip, as far away as Arizona when she knew a lot of company was coming for Easter break."

"Not only that, but she didn't want me to go with her. I insisted, but when we got there she conned me into letting her letting her go off by herself."

"But she told me she went with Nina June antiquing and found the lamp she had been wanting."

"That's right, but there were these secretive talks on the phone. There is something suspicious about the whole trip. Nina told she caught three men searching the Museum van and partially removing their seats while they were in her brother's antique store. That's in Phoenix, not Tucson. Then you add the break-in at the motel on top of that."

"Wasn't this in Amarillo, on your return trip back to Springfield?"

"That's right. They were not counting on an old man having a 9 MM automatic."

"So the men were dressed the same and searched under the seats in both vehicles. Whatever they were looking for must have been small enough to fit under the seating, possibly a compartment under the seat, or in the floor?"

"With the way your grandmother has been acting, I think she has gotten herself into a mass of trouble. –And she's not telling us what it is."

Talking and laughter floated up from the rear of the foyer as the group returning from the church made their way toward the kitchen-family room. Lawrence suggested, "Lets join them for now and later when everything settles down, say early-afternoon, we can meet in our sitting room and talk with Barbara in private."

"Sounds good. I would like to get to the bottom of this before we leave tomorrow. I'm really worried about her."

The family room was filling up with everyone. Barbara helped Maria prepare and arrange the brunch. Laurel stepped in to help. "Missed you this morning, Laurel. You would have liked the service. It was a special one. I saw Professor Vaughn, and on the way out, I talked to your old roommate, Kourtney. She has turned out to be a radiant woman and I hear a smart detective too."

Laurel's thoughts were of Matthew's eye. She hoped the make-up was enough to camouflage the shiner. "Are they both coming over this evening for dinner?"

I didn't talk to the Professor this morning, but he sat across the aisle from us. He had with him a young girl, so pretty and well behaved. I think it must have been his daughter. I'll have to ask Lawrence if he has a family. As for Kourtney, she must go in to work for part of the day but hoped she could make it for dinner."

"Chris will be here also," Laurel noted. "Grams, since we must head back to Chicago tomorrow, we need to block off some personal time this afternoon, before the guests get here. How about we meet in the sitting area off your bedroom, that way we won't be interrupted."

CHAPTER 27

It was early in the afternoon when Lawrence whispered to Laurel that Barbara went upstairs. "I'll give you two a few minutes alone before I come up."

Laurel knocked on her door. "Grams are you in there?"

"Come on in, Laurel. I'm brewing some tea for us. Oh, I just can't believe you're going back to Chicago tomorrow. Your vacation has just been too short. It seems you just got here. We've not had enough time to ourselves."

Laurel held her thoughts in check. *Had you not spent most of my vacation time off in Arizona, we would have had more time.*

"Come, let's sit over here with the tea. Grams, I shouldn't have let you assume I couldn't manage Alex in our personal relationship, because the argument you had with him last night, has done more harm than good. I wish you had not said anything at all to him. We must work on this project together. There can be no hostile tension between us, or this project will fail. I can handle Alex. Grams, I really need for you to call him and apologize."

"What! You want me to apologize to him? Laurel, you are lacking somewhat in your self-confidence. You don't need Alex. You're more than able to do this on your own. I have observed you in the past, every time you are pressed, or in a tight squeeze, you manage to excel if left to your own initiatives."

"I know Grams, but with the Satellite Imaging project coming up, there is an enormous amount of work that needs to be done. There is a deadline that we must meet and so little time to do it. I can delegate some to the team, but it takes me, the Director, even Joann Maury, the Vice President of the Corporation, to do certain official things. I have enough problems, without adding this to the list. Laurel picked up Barbara's phone keying in his number then placed it in her hands. "I listed his phone number in your contacts under Alex. Just touch his name, it will ring him."

Barbara mused something under her breath while shaking her head back and forth. Laurel stood up, turning her back to her grandmother and walked over to the large picture window. While sipping her tea, she stared out to the stillness of the lake, watching the ducks bask in the warm afternoon sun. It was unseasonably warm for this time of the year. There was no conversation, the room fell in silence, still as the waters below. *Only if my life was as calm and simple as those waterfowl, just floating around down there.* Then she heard her grandmother pressing the keys. Then the faint ringing and more ringing, until the voice mail came on. She left a message for him to call her back.

"Thank you for calling him, I know it was hard for you to do Grams." Laurel wrapped her arms around her, giving her a loving hug. "It means the world to me. Please let me know when he calls back."

Right on cue, Lawrence entered the room asking, "Am I interrupting anything?"

"We just finished talking about my project at work. But please, come join us. We need to talk more about what we discussed earlier."

"Now, what have the two of you been up to this fine, beautiful day?" Barbara questioned.

"Grams, you know both Lawrence and I love you very much and there isn't anything that we wouldn't do for you."

"Yes, and I for each of you."

Lawrence spoke up, "Both of us are concerned that due to the recent situations, mainly the Arizona trip, that you are in trouble, that you are keeping secrets from us."

"Well, what makes you think what happened in Arizona has to do with me?"

"Barbara, during our conversation on the trip down to Arizona, you told me the accident that involved you and Madelene was no accident, that the brakes were tampered with. Then these men went through your vehicle looking for the items Madelene found in a cave."

"Wait a minute! Grams, is this true? Why have you been keeping this from me?"

"Both your father and I thought you would be better off, not knowing any of the details of this terrible, appalling occurrence so long ago."

Barbara turned to Lawrence staring, squinting her eyes and frowning with displeasure.

"Barbara, Laurel is no longer a child. You should have told her the truth. She deserves to know. Also, there is the Phoenix break-in of Nina's van. Then on the way home, another break-in at the motel in Amarillo. Which almost got us killed! If all of this is connected back to those cave items and those men have picked up their search again, we are not out of the woods yet."

"Grams, the break in here in this house, not long ago–they probably were looking for these so-called cave items. My apartment break-in shortly after that. They were still inside when I came home. To think I almost confronted them with my small mace canister. Also, I saw a man standing in the museum parking, close to my car. Then that same man again downtown watching me as I was getting ready to enter the building where the party was held that night. I'm sure of it. That's the night of the break-in at my apartment, I hadn't put it all together until now."

"They have widened their search, but why?" Lawrence questioned. "After all these years of not bothering you, they suddenly started searching again. Barbara, can't you see these men are dangerous. Think back. What did Madelene do with the cave items?"

"I'm not sure. It has been twenty-eight years and my long-term memory is fuzzy."

"All right, let's all calm down." Taking her grandmother's hands in her own she patted them gently. "Grams, take a few breaths and relax." Laurel placed some pillows on the back of the chaise lounge, asking her grandmother to lie back. "Let's use the regressive hypnosis technique to help you relax and remember. Is this all right with you, Grams?" Laurel could tell she was in deep thought about her answer. She also knew if her grandmother, while under a hypnotic trance, didn't want to truthfully give up a secret, she would not.

Finally, Barbara replied, "That will be fine. I need to relax, save my energy for tonight." Barbara stretched out on the lounge, making herself comfortable.

Laurel asked her if Lawrence could stay. Barbara thought for a minute, then said he could stay, if he said nothing. Laurel spoke to Lawrence explaining the process, and why it was necessary that he remain quiet, as she handed him a pen and paper to put his questions on.

CHAPTER 28

Laurel started the process by talking her down in a calm voice. "Close your eyes Barbara and relax. . .release all of the tension. . .take another deep breath, continuing to relax. . ." Laurel knew her grandmother was an easy subject and would go deep into a hypnotic state, if she allowed herself to. Lawrence sat very quietly in his chair, observing the procedure while Laurel kept repeating the relaxing process until she became deep enough to begin.

"Barbara, I want you to go back to what happened after Madelene found the cave items. I'm sure she showed them to you. Go back to this time and focus. Tell me what happened next."

Barbara slowly began talking "John came down to Phoenix. . .business. . .drove to our camp. He's. . .not seen Madelene or. . .little Laurel in weeks."

Laurel reached for her cell phone and switched on the recorder. "Where was this camp site, Barbara?" With her eyes still closed, she moved her head slightly back and forth, as if searching for the location. "The area was near Tubac. . . on the edge of Presidio State Historic Park." Barbara soon began talking more freely the deeper she went.

"Rented a small house, in a little village—western side of Tubac. Three students, helping us had left, gone back to the University. Our food supplies needed replenishing. I gathered up Laurel, went into Tubac. Madelene went back to the site with our two local Mexican-Indian guides we hired to help us.

"Madelene said she found an opening between some rocks. Shinning her light into it, she saw something. She made the opening larger with the aid of the two Indian helpers. She crawled in, the two helpers waited outside–superstitious."

"I entered the opening by crawling on hands and knees." Barbara was recalling her daughter's own words as she described what she saw.

*"By shinning my flashlight, I could see there was a wider opening ahead– just a few more feet to go. I smelled the pungent aroma as I passed through the cloistered environment. Finally, I was through the crawl space and could now stand up inside the cave–maybe the first human in hundreds, or thousands of years to see this! I shined the light around. There was a drawing on the wall– it was distinct, with the colors well preserved. I continued to shine the light down a little to what appeared to be a natural shelf-like projection – with items on it. Walking up to it– taking the brush from my tool belt, I dusted off what appeared to be a leather pouch. Opening it I carefully pulled out a cylinder-shaped object. Brushing off some dust, revealed a shiny nubby surface with a circular knob-like head on one end, with raised sym*bols."

Laurel asked, "Did you recognize those symbols?" Laurel wasn't sure whether Barbara was recalling what her daughter told her or if she was channeling Madelene.

"None were familiar to me. I placed it back in the pouch and put it in the bag hanging from my waist. My attention went to the bundle of items wrapped in a blanket. The blanket has Aztec designs on it. Unrolling it exposed clothing for two young people. A boy's garment, larger than the girl's. There was jewelry, arm bands, bracelets, head gear. This was not the common tribal   clothing and jewelry but looked to be Royal items. There also was an unusual medallion disk. I don't think it was an Aztec design? Why did they leave this behind?"

Laurel became emotional hearing her own mother's words. She fought back the tears, for she had more questions. Laurel asked, "You say there was an unusual medallion disk, did you recognize the design?"

"I do not recognize it."

"Could you describe it for me?" Laurel asked.

"I can try. It is circular, about four inches wide. One side has a pattern going around the outside circle, laid out in small broken rectangle patterns, which looks to have several symbols inside each of these. There are more designs laid out in the center, too detailed to describe."

"That's all right. Could you tell what material it is made from?"

"I think it is bronze. But there is color to it also. It has medium blue painted background areas. The lines are bright white, the rectangular boxes are mostly gold and dark blue. The other side is like a mirror with a few of those bright white lines overlaid on top."

Laurel said, "That is good, what else did you see in the cave?"

"*I continued to shine the light around, noticing where they had built a fire. From the looks of things, maybe staying a short while? From the foot prints and other containers, I could tell there were around four other heavier people with the children. Going back to the drawing, I could tell it was Aztec also. Pulling out my notebook, I sketched the drawing in detail. It was getting late–the sun would be going down soon, I decided to leave–taking the collection back to the house–to examine and study in better light. I crawled out the way I came. The two helpers I left standing guard were gone.*"

The dialect of Madelene's voice changed back to Barbara's again.

"All right, what did you do next?"

"That evening we were expecting John for dinner–he had spent the day in Phoenix–a buying trip for his electronics business. He wanted to see Madelene and little Laurel, before going back to Springfield. Madelene was overjoyed with her finds in the cave, along with seeing John. We cleared the table, laid out a clean inspection cloth and put on gloves. Madelene pulled items from her sack, placing them on table. John placed Laurel in a highchair, out of reach.

"My attention was drawn to the leather like pouch. I assessed it was made from some sort of treated animal hide. I pulled out the metal-like cylinder object and examined it. I didn't recognize any of the raised symbols on the rounded head. Maybe I have a book at home that would help. Madelene began depressing one symbol after another. Nothing happened. She continued pressing very fast. Suddenly it lit up, emitting a high pitch sound that startled all of us.

"Then the noise started again. Madelene's flash light would light up, on its own. Then intermittently, both the flash light and overhead kitchen lights went off and on. At the same time, different high pitch tones, coming from the artifact, shrieked in our ears." Barbara placed her hands over her ears, as if she was hearing this as she did twenty-eight years in the past. "This is painful. It's scary!" Barbara's voice started to crack.

"It is all right," Laurel said. "I want you to move ahead to the time when the noise has stopped. You are safe now. What are you doing now?"

"We moved away from it and the noise became less harsh. Thinking the artifact might be radio-active, John grabbed Laurel and took her outside, putting her in his truck. Madelene tried to place the cap back on– and the shirking sounds died down. Oh! It suddenly moved from her hands, and the cap swiftly slammed shut. With a loud click, it securely locked itself. John returned with one of his Geiger meters and held it over the Artifact. There was no dial movement, no clicking sounds. We surmised whatever it was must not be radioactive. She placed it back in the leather pouch.

Lawrence handed Laurel the paper with a question. "Barbara, where did you get the term Artifact?'

She thought, for a moment, then replied, "It was the men going through the wreckage, one of them said, "Keep looking, they must have the 'Spiritual Artifact' here with them."

"Did they say what the purpose was of this 'Spiritual Artifact? Why they wanted it?"

Barbara replied, "I'm listening. They're talking to each other." There was a long silence.

"Go ahead. Listen to what the men are saying," Laurel replied.

"It seemed that it took a long time, we had so much packed in that Jeep. I must have been unconscious for a while. I lay there listening. I'm not moving. I don't think I can move. My face is laying on something. I can only see with one eye. They wore dark clothes. Don't know how many? More than two. Then one said, 'It's not here. Maybe the man has it. Maybe they hid it somewhere, before leaving.' He spoke with an accent.

"One said, don't bother with the two women. I have already checked them. They are both dead."

"Maybe that's why I can't move? I'm dead? But, I heard them talking. I saw them move past me. I heard them leave in the van."

"Madelene! Madelene! They said we were both dead. . ."

CHAPTER 29

"If we were dead, wouldn't our spirits be raised up, floating around above our lifeless bodies?" Barbara leaned forward a little on the lounge, looking down, with eyes still closed, as if trying to see below her. "They must be wrong. I feel like I'm in my body, I just can't move. Why can't I move? I have no pain. But it's so quiet now. Madelene. . .I don't hear anything from her, not even a moan. I must go see about her! God, I can't be dead! Got to force this body to move."

Then both Laurel and Lawrence watched her struggling movement on the lounge chair. Her arms slapped against her legs. Her hands grabbing the air, then clawing at the chase lounge, like she was finally able to move her body, all the while calling out to Madelene with tears flowing down her cheeks. Soon she became hysterical! She screamed out, "Almighty God and the Blessed Mother. . .Help Me!"

Lawrence grabbed Laurel's arm, shaking her. She read his lips. *"Do Something! Pull her out. Now!"*

"All right, Barbara. You are detaching yourself from this scene emotionally. You are all right. You are moving above this scene, letting go of all the emotion. You are calm and relaxed now." Laurel continued with the process of bringing her out of the hypnotic state, but not without tears of her own. She was fighting her own emotions. Laurel turned off the recording, placing the phone back in her pocket. She wiped the tears from her face before her grandmother opened her eyes.

"How do you feel, Grams?" Laurel managed to ask in an upbeat tone, with a smile on her face. Barbara stretched and moved about. "I feel fine, really rested. Did I sleep? I hope I didn't snore. Oh, my goodness! I can't believe the time. I must have been under a lot longer than anticipated."

Lawrence remarked, "You were in the trance process for around two hours. Do you remember any of it?"

Barbara stood up. "Some of it. It's getting so late; the guest will be arriving soon. I've got things to do, to prepare for the dinner. We can get together later. For now, you guys move out of here, so I can change." Barbara made a shooing motion with her arms. "Love you both, but it's good-bye for now!" Barbara's voice had a merry, musical tone.

They walked down the hall, away from hearing distance of the closed bedroom door. Lawrence stopped and complimented Laurel. "You did a great job back there with that regression. Are you all right? I know that must have been difficult for you, hearing about your mother, and then when Barbara spoke in your mother's own words."

"It was very difficult in places, but I cherish the part of my mom, describing the cave and what she saw inside. I wish she had been with me longer."

"Laurel, there is more to the story that she didn't describe! While on the drive down to Arizona, Barbara told me about the Hieroglyphics on the cave wall, describing it in detail. This is something you must hear in Barbara's own words, because I probably won't get it right if I attempted to tell you. So, we need to get back with her before you leave tomorrow."

"What was it?"

"Let's just say, if I am right, it could involve you and your archaeology site at Cahokia. Wait and let her tell you." Lawrence turned and headed toward the elevator, closing the steel gate. It soon lowered out of sight, as Laurel stood to ponder his words.

Back in her bedroom, Laurel pulled out her cell phone and checked to see if the recording was there, listening again to the segment where her mother spoke. Tears streamed down her face until she finally turned it off. She walked over to the photo on her dresser. Picking it up, she held it close to her heart, while she slumped into the oversized chair in her sitting room.

Her emotions rose the more she thought about what her grandmother kept from her all these years. "Why?" she cried out. She was hurt that the person she loved, who helped raise her along with her dad, kept this from her. It's understandable why they would delay telling me until I got older, but good God, I'm thirty-two. There is no excuse for this!

The more Laurel thought about the regression, the more she experienced mixed feelings. The tears started drying up and anger seeped into her being. Anger mixed with surprise. The description of what my mother found–this 'Spiritual Artifact'–it's astonishing! She wasn't afraid of it, she kept on pressing the symbols until it opened. After hearing her speak, she realized who she took after.

There was a knock at the door, "Laurel, its Stephanie have you got a minute?"

"Are you alone?" Laurel asked, grabbing more tissue.

"Yes Laurel, do you have a minute?"

"Come in Stephanie, I'm over here by the windows."

"What have you been up to? Haven't seen you for hours." After glancing at her face, she said, "Oh my gosh, you've been crying. What happened?"

"I've had my cry. Now, I'm just flat-out angry." Stephanie put her arms around her and with a consoling tone, she said, "What has got you all worked up? It's Alex again, isn't it?"

Laurel wiped her tears. "No, he's not to blame this time. Stephanie, you are a good friend, and some of the things I am about to say must be held in the strictest of confidence."

"I can zip it up." In a jester she ran her fingers across her lips. "You know you can trust me."

"As you know, I've been concerned that my grandmother was keeping secrets about this recent trip to Arizona, and several other things, including steering me away from working down around the Tubac area. Lawrence and I both thought she might be in trouble. So we held a meeting with her after brunch. We asked her point blank if she was in trouble and didn't want to tell us. It was Lawrence who gave up one of grandmother's secrets and she got real upset about it too."

"And that would be what?"

"The accident that took my mother's life was no accident. The brakes were tampered with to kill them both. She led me to believe it was an accident my whole life. So did my father."

"Why on this good earth would they harbor such a secret?"

"Well the reason these guys wanted to cause the Jeep to wreck, was they thought Grams and my mom had the items taken from a cave my mom uncovered. They were determined to get it. I have it all on the recording."

"Where did you get all this info?"

"Sorry, I got ahead of myself. She couldn't answer some of our questions, claiming she couldn't remember. I asked her if we could do a hypnotic regression to relax her enough so she could remember. She consented." Laurel went on explaining to Stephanie what her grandmother disclosed in the two-hour session.

"This is partly why I was crying. This is the only recording I have of my mom's own words, describing what was in the cave."

"Laurel, that is awesome! Thank God you recorded it. So the items she took out of the cave must have been ancient or valuable for those men wanting to steal it, at all cost."

"Steph–I was there. I saw it– but I was only four years old when this happened."

"What did they do with this so called 'Spiritual Artifact'?"

"She said the men that caused the wreck called it 'the Spiritual Artifact'. She became so emotional, I had to pull her out of the regression before she could tell us what they did with the Artifacts. Steph, there is something more weird and astonishing that she described."

"What could that be?"

"The men said both my mom and my grandma were dead, but Grams described what went on, while the men were searching through the wreckage. She couldn't move but could see with one eye and could hear. The way she described it, and the movement of her body, while she was lying on the lounge–I believe that at one point she was in fact, dead. Then through her prayers and affirmations she managed to bring her consciousness back inside her physical body to the Earth plane."

Tears were now flowing from Stephanie's eyes, as well as Laurel. Stephanie raised up from her chair, putting her arms around her friend, comforting her the best that she could.

"It's getting late, and we both need to change and redo our make-up, before everyone arrives. Thank you, Steph, for being a good listener." Laurel knew she had to put the situation with her grandmother on hold long enough to get through the traditional dinner party this evening.

CHAPTER 30

Easter dinner at the Crawford's was a tradition, this being the twenty-sixth year, carried over from Barbara's side of the family. Some of the guests were already arriving and mingling about in the vast foyer and living room when Laurel descended the staircase. Some of the guests she only saw once a year, and it was nice to catch up. Laurel mingled around trying to make her way over to the drink refreshment table when she spotted Chris, and Stephanie standing close by.

"Hello Miss Laurel. Have you seen the professor yet this evening?" Chris inquired, keeping his voice low.

"Good evening to the both of you." Laurel leaned into them whispering, "Have you seen him up close? Is he wearing the makeup I mixed for him?"

Stephanie smiled, shaking her head slowly. "No. Neither of us have been that close. I did encourage him to keep the ice pack on last night. He has been over there talking to the Bishop for quite some time now."

Laurel didn't see her grandmother out in the foyer. She was concerned about her and went looking in the kitchen. She found her in the family room giving Lawrence a rough time.

"Come on Grams, let's put all our differences on hold for a few hours. What do you say? There's a house full of people here to join in on this special occasion. I even saw the new Bishop out there talking to Professor Vaughn. You should go out and welcome him to your home. It is such an honor for him to be here. Come Grams, I'll even go with you, if you like."

"Oh Laurel, I would love for you to go with me." She took Laurel's hand and politely weaved through the guests with a promise to return and visit. When Professor Vaughn observed them approaching he smiled and invited them over.

Barbara extended her greeting. "Welcome Bishop Marin to our home. I am Barbara Crawford. My husband, Lawrence, will be joining us shortly. I see you have already met Professor Vaughn. I would like for you to meet my granddaughter, Laurel Robertson."

The Bishop moved toward Laurel and placed his arms around her giving her a loving hug. Stepping back, he gazed intensely into her eyes. "There is a light that surrounds you, my lovely child of God. You are indeed an old soul. Your path is one of great challenges. You have traveled many incarnations, through other worlds and many universes, for a single purpose." The Bishop paused, tilted his head as if listening to another voice, then started speaking again. "You Laurel, are helping to bring forth the fruits of humankind's labor into a New Birth. Please be consciously aware of this, my child." He moved his hand in the sign of the cross. "Be one with Jesus." Leaning toward her again, he kissed her cheek, then bowed. "I am here to serve you."

"Oh, gracious, Mother Mary!" Barbara sighed.

Professor Vaughn reached for her arm, and spying a nearby chair he asked, "Would you like to sit a spell right here by us." She nodded and he helped sit her next to another lady before returning to the Bishop and Laurel.

Laurel was deep in thought for a few moments, contemplating the Bishop's words to her. "It is with a loving and grateful heart, I thank you Father, for awakening my spiritual remembrance. But I must return to Chicago, as I am working on an important project."

"And what has taken all your attention my child? What could possibly be more pressing for you to detour off your path?"

"I am an archaeologist, by profession, working through the Field Museum of Natural History. My project is in the Ancient Cahokia State Park." The Bishop was from the St Louis area and knew about the mounds. So Laurel filled him in on her research.

Mathew listened attentively to their conversation then his thoughts drifted back to what the Bishop previously said to Laurel, how it surprised him, yet it shouldn't have. He had just met Laurel yesterday, but he felt like he had known her before. He, too, had picked up something special about her. It was more than her outward beauty, more than his testosterone that went into overload that kept him thinking about her all last night. She seemed to have an air of mystery and secrets—something that attracted him to her. What was I expecting last night with that strong of an attraction towards her? A wonderful dance partner? A passionate kiss? A little love making perhaps? And where did it get me? A knock on my ass, with a big ole' shiner! That's what it got me. He chuckled under his breath at his own humorous thoughts.

The Bishop turned his attention back to the professor. "You mentioned earlier you taught classes on Religious History. How did you get interested in this?"

"My education had its beginning in South Carolina, with the Jesuit curriculum all the way through high school. After that, my Mother encouraged me to go into the Seminary, which I attended in Saint Louis at the Kinrick-Glennon Seminary."

"That's where I served as Auxiliary Bishop. You were right under my wings."

"I know, but there were so many students. I couldn't expect you to have known of me, as I was in the undergraduate instructional program. Part of my studies were of Religious History, not just Catholics, but others as well. I left the seminary because I felt I could help others by going into the Philosophy field. I attended Princeton University, where I earned my Ph.D. and found my passion with Metaphysics and the Philosophy of Science."

Bishop Marin remarked, "You have a great amount of spiritual background and therefore, can be of exceptional support to your students."

"Thank you, Father. I believe I can help make a difference in their lives." Another member of the clergy approached asking if he could speak with the Bishop, so Laurel and the Professor excused themselves. Laurel looked to the chair where her grandmother was sitting, but, she was gone.

"I must find her and see if she is all right," she stated to Matthew.

"When I left her, she was physically all right, still a bit dazed from the Bishop's words, but she was cognitive, talking and answering my questions." They began by searching the foyer first. It was becoming more crowded now and difficult to see, so they went up the stairs to scan the area but didn't find her.

"Let's look in the family room and kitchen." She took his hand leading the way. Maria was busy in the kitchen, she had not seen her either. "She is usually here, helping with last minute touches. The dinner is scheduled to start in fifteen minutes."

"Maria, please delay the dinner until we find her."

Laurel went to the PVA panel on the wall. After punching in a code, she scanned the entire house and the surroundings outside. They did take notice that Lawrence was in the foyer, but still, nothing of Barbara.

Laurel ran it again, but there was no sign of her. "There are some areas the camera is not aimed at."

Where are those areas?" Matthew asked.

"Mostly the bathrooms and closets."

"I'll let you search those." Matthew grinned. He asked her to scan again and this time she noticed something strange in one of the rooms.

"Matthew, look at this frame, its blanked out. Nothing but a little static."

"What room is that?"

Laurel slowly ran the scan again until she saw the blank static frame, then backed up one more remarking, "It's a view of the entire library hall. The camera shot after the blank one is the view looking through the library entrance, then after this are various shots inside the library. So, backing up. . . there has to be another camera in that hall."

"Let's check it out," Matthew suggested. When they went down the wide steps leading into the hall, they looked to the left, toward the front of the house, finding the camera that took the hall shot just before the blank frame. Next, they made notice of the camera pointing toward the library entrance. Looking around they could not see any extra cameras which would have shown the blank static frame. Laurel pointed to the closet door at the end of the hall. She tried to open the door. "The knob starts to turn like it's going to open, but it feels like it's stuck."

"Here let me try." Matthew put his muscles to work, giving it his all. "I don't think it's stuck, but it could be half-way locked." He kept trying, then hearing a grind, he felt something release, and turned the knob. He opened the door, stopping half-way.

"What's wrong?" Laurel asked. He backed away. Turning around, he faced Laurel with a very surprised expression on his face.

CHAPTER 31

"Why did you stop? What's there?" She couldn't see until he moved to her left, giving her a full view.

"What the heck?" She blurted out, as she opened the door all the way. She stood staring at a pair of steel doors. Matthew motioned up high on the left to the camera they were looking for. Laurel nodded her head, acknowledging there was no red light. Viewing the security code panel, she punched in some familiar codes, trying to gain access. Nothing happened.

"Do you think your grandmother is in there? Laurel, this appears to be a panic room or better known in today's world, as a safe room. I believe that camera is controlled from inside that room."

"She might be inside and not able to get out. She would never run late for a dinner celebration. I think it is time to get Lawrence over here. He'll know the code. Hurry, let's go find him," Laurel declared.

They found him running a search on the PVA panel.

"We've been searching for Grams for a while too," Laurel said. "I noticed a blank static frame on the panel, and we tracked it down."

"What frame are you talking about? I didn't notice that when I checked."

"The one off the hall, close by the library entrance camera. You know, the one where you open a hall closet and there is a pair of steel doors greeting you in the face."

"You two found the safe room? I'll have to talk to our security people about this camera glitch."

"We think Mrs. Crawford could be in there. She was emotionally overcome and left the foyer and disappeared."

Laurel adding, "I punched in the only codes I knew, but it didn't open. You must have a special code for this room. I'm worried about her. And when did you put in a safe room?"

"A few months ago, after the break-in. Let's check it out." The three of them headed for the library hall, finding the closet door just as they left it. Lawrence punched the code in and the steel panels slid open.

They found Barbara sitting in a comfortable upholstered chair, off to the side of a small, beautiful sanctuary.

"Barbara, we have been looking everywhere for you!" Lawrence proclaimed, breathing a sigh of relief.

Barbara awakened, stretching her arms. "Oh my. I'm glad you woke me. I came in here to meditate and I must have dozed off. What time is it?" She looked down at her watch. "I didn't realize it was so late, we need to see if Maria and her helpers have the food ready."

"Grams, you had us worried sick. You really should have told us you were leaving."

She touched Laurel's arm. "I'm sorry. I really didn't plan on being gone this long. Now, come Laurel, you can help us with the final preparations."

After dinner, Laurel found her team downstairs and informed them she needed to stay one more day in Springfield to take care of some unforeseen family business.

"You guys can stay and do some activities available, or if Aaron wants to return, you could hitch a ride back with him.

Laurel knew she would have to approach her grandmother about the hieroglyphics tomorrow. It would not be easy, now that her emotions were already under stress. *As for myself, I have been through a lot too. I need to relax and sooth my own emotions. I need to chill out.* She poured herself a glass of wine.

"I could use a glass of that myself," a soft, manly voice came from behind her.

"Sure thing. One more coming up," Laurel replied with a friendly smile as she poured Matthew a glass.

"Let's go out by the fire pit. I would like to talk with you for a while." Mathew confiscated the bottle, heading for the door. Laurel, wondering what he wanted to discuss, picked up the ponchos and blankets hanging on the rack by the door. They made themselves comfortable sitting quietly, for a few moments. Matthew commented, "The wine is very good, it tastes like a blend of several.". He read the label, "Chateauneuf du Pape."

"It's a blended wine from Phone, France. I enjoy it when staying here. Lawrence keeps it for his private stock and shares it with me when I come home." "You know Matthew, there is some history concerning this wine that you might be interested in. The first vines in Chateauneuf were planted by the ancient Romans in the Southern Rhone Valley. One of the best preserved ancient amphitheaters built by the Romans in all of Europe is not far from Chateauneuf."

"No wonder it tastes so good, it goes back a long way."

"The du Pape added to the name, translates "The Pope's New Castle." This is when Pope Clement V moved to Avignon in 1309."

"I know this story and why it happened. There were deep issues between King Phillip of France and the Papacy. The King wanted to rid his country of the Knights Templers and he also had his eyes set to acquire the rich land to the south of him which was owned by the wealthy Cathars and where a large membership of the Knights Templers resided. The King owed the order money and had no control over them. He engineered the kidnapping and death of one Pope Boniface Vlll and quite possibly the murder by poison of Benedict Xl. Then in 1305, Philippe managed to secure the election of his own candidate, the archbishop of Bordeaux to the vacant papal throne. He took the name of Clement V and was now indebted to Philippe's demands. After this is when the surprise arrest of the Templers started, they were imprisoned and tortured."

They continued sipping the wine, staring into the dancing flames, following the little red sparks as they drifted up slowly into the night sky, then propelling like tiny rockets, going back home.

"I can almost hear your wheels turning." Matthew teased. "Would you like to talk about what happened today? I'm more than a good dancer. I've been told, I'm a good listener too." He smiled and refreshed their drinks.

"I believe you're qualified after hearing what you told the Bishop about your background." She returned his smile.

"The Bishop's words for you, Laurel, came from deep within his heart. Did you resonate with what he revealed for you?"

Laurel liked to hear him talk. His southern accent was music to her ears. "I've barely had time to reflect on it. The search for my grandmother kept us busy right up to dinner, then I visited with the guests the rest of the evening."

"Bishop Marin lectured once when I attended Saint Louis University. The following day one of my teachers committed on the Bishop's history, explaining that he was known to deliver 'Soul Readings' on occasion, when crossing the path of another special person. He even is known to recite prophesy. So, Ms. Robertson, you can believe there is great truth in his words he spoke to you this evening."

She listened intensely while Matthew explained his knowledge of the Bishop's past. She reflected in her mind some of the phrases he said to her, while struggling to remember his exact words. She starred into the red and blue flames in the fire pit, deep into the molecules of their existence.

"Laurel, how do you feel about what he said to you?" Matthew asked again.

"I remember some of the phrases. I am trying to understand what he meant by them. Do you remember what he said to me?"

"Well, he greeted you with a hug. He stepped back and looked intensely into your eyes. I believe he was reading your soul. I remember he said a light surrounds you."

"Yes, then he spoke about my path having great challenges. He said I have an old soul as if to tell me I have been through many incarnations, other worlds, and other universes. I resonate with that. I have these dreams about events I haven't experienced. They are sometimes very intense."

"I recall him saying you would help bring forth the fruits of humankind's labor into new birth. What are your feelings about this?" Matthew pressed her further.

"I don't really know how I feel about this remark. I probably could make a guess. Humankind's labor into new births could simply mean a single person each incarnation is reborn on earth for his experiences and learning, then one day the whole human race will be reborn as a group into a New Birth, a New Reality, a New World?"

"See how easily you arrived at the meaning of the Bishop's words."

Laurel held her glass out for a bit more wine. "But Matthew, we are all doing this. He made it sound like I was mostly responsible for this taking place."

"You may be the special child of God that will lead the way to this mass rebirth of Humankind. This is my take of his comments to you. Your grandmother was quite taken with the Bishop's words."

"My grandmother might have understood more than I did. Mathew, earlier today, I found out some secrets she has been keeping from me all my life."

"Why would she do that? Is this something you can share with me?"

"My grandmother, as well as my mother, was in archaeology when I was a baby." Laurel explained what she learned while her grandmother was under the hypnosis.

"It sounds like while your grandmother's physical body was lying dead in the wreckage, her spirit was on the other side. She knew her daughter; your mother, was in spirit also. But, it was your grandmother that had special abilities to see her granddaughter was a special soul. She came back for you, Laurel, knowing you would need spiritual guidance. She probably felt a profound need to protect the cave items found by your mother."

"To protect the cave items? Matthew, I asked her where my mother hid them. She said she didn't know."

"She possibly may still be trying to protect you, Laurel. You mentioned you are staying another day because of something that Lawrence said."

"Even though my project needs my attention back in Chicago, Lawrence claims I need to hear what the hieroglyphics looked like from my grandmother. He thought it involved the Ancient Cahokia site. I can't even think this is possible."

"Why not? Could there not have been an Aztec priest that could have foretold the past and the future? I think you made a wise choice to stay longer so she could describe the story they left on the wall."

Laurel proceeded to pour more wine into their glasses and found the bottle empty. "Stay right here, I'll go inside for another bottle."

It was late in the evening and her team members and some other guests were in the theater with a good movie. The night was unseasonably warm and the fire pit was theirs alone. Laurel flipped off the overhead party lights, and the beautiful night sky shown even brighter with a natural display of stars. Matthew opened the bottle and filled their glasses. "My grandmother mentioned a young girl was sitting next to you at the early morning Mass."

"That would be my seven-year-old daughter, Sophia. I picked her up before the service and returned her back to her mother this afternoon. Her mother and I were married in South Carolina, not long after I came out of the seminary. After eighteen months we mutually dissolved it. She taught in the elementary system there and when a teaching position came open in Nixa, I helped her with the move, so Sophia and I could be closer."

"That is great that you see her more often. Grams said she was quite a little lady, so well behaved. I would like to meet her sometime."

"Perhaps on one of your next visits. How often do you come to Springfield?"

"I usually come home often, but since I took the archaeology position with the Field Museum, it hasn't been as often as I would like." They talked into the early hours of the morning. Laurel's friendship with

Matthew was growing stronger, and she felt he was more than interested in her, too. Just sitting next to him, she began to feel something. A swirling of cool, dry energy, flowing and circling inside her. It felt good. Laurel turned and gazed at Matthew with a growing desire in her heart.

Matthew took his eyes off the fire, looked to Laurel, and reached for her hands. "I enjoyed our dance last night, at least until we were interrupted."

Laurel responded with an affectionate smile, and passion filled her heart. He gently moved his hands to her arms, pulling her closer. His eyes seemed to be asking her for the kiss he didn't receive last time. Placing his long fingertips on her soft check, he stared into her eyes.

"Have you any idea," he whispered, "how irresistibly attractive you are this evening? Even more than last night." The words he spoke, combined with the deep compelling timbre of his voice, had the seductive impact Laurel hoped his kiss would have.

She placed her hand on the nape of his long neck, feeling the waves of his hair wrapping through her fingers. He slid his fingertips very slowly down to the corner of her mouth, and her lips opened slightly, as if an invitation had been issued. With her other hand, she placed her fingertips on his short-bearded jaw. He pulled her tighter to him, her breast rubbing on his chest.

"Laurel. . ." He slowly removed his finger from her lips, backing his body, ever so slowly, away from their closeness, still gazing into her eyes.

"For a moment, it looked as though, I was gazing into the eyes of an Angel." Matthew said softly. He seemed confused. He didn't move, or even speak for a few moments. Laurel's lips quivered, she could almost taste the contours of his lips joining with hers. She didn't understand his reluctance. Laurel was trying to read his eyes. They appeared as if he had discovered something new and different. Then he backed away, as if changing his mind about kissing her.

Laurel was disappointed, but in an effort not to let it show, she moved away and started gathering the wine bottle and glasses to take inside.

"It's getting late, or to be more precise, it's getting early in the morning." He laughed a little, while smiling at her. "I better say good-night, before Mr. Crawford comes out and runs me off." He gave her a soft kiss on her temple, thanked her for the wonderful evening, and asked her to call him before she left.

By now the wonderful energy she felt twenty minutes ago had dissipated. *What just happened back there?* She tried to analyze Matthew's actions. *We were about to kiss, and my body was sending shivers of primitive sensations all over. I wanted him to make mad passionate love to me.* She wondered why he would get her all worked up. . .then wane out?

The movie was over and the attendees were pouring forth from the home theater into the rec room, expressing their views on the production when Laurel entered the room.

Rosie asked, "When we get back to Chicago, do you want us to do anything in preparation for the upcoming reports you'll be taking before the Board?"

"Yes, thank you. Start with the list on my bulletin board. That will be a big help. What time will you be leaving?"

"We are all packed. We're going to the cabin to get some shut-eye till five, then we're headed out."

"Maria will fix you a quick breakfast." Laurel shook his hand, and stated, "If I don't see you before you leave–drive safely. The girls and I will join you in one more day."

Laurel was anxious to crawl under the sheets, putting this day behind her. Her thoughts kept returning to Matthew. Tossing and turning, she couldn't fall asleep. Why did she care so much about him? *He was becoming a good friend and I was sexually attracted to him. Why did he get me all worked up–then take off? He seemed to be afraid of me for some strange reason. Maybe we took it too far, or could it be–he is just like that? I'm pretty sure this is just another relationship in ruins. . .*

CHAPTER 32

It was after eight when Laurel awoke. Her one goal for today, try and get her Grams to describe in detail what the cave hieroglyphics looked like.

She found her grandmother and Lawrence sitting in the kitchen. "Good morning you two."

"Morning, Laurel," they both replied. "Did you sleep well?" her grandmother inquired. We slept in ourselves since we stayed up late talking to everyone. Had some good visits."

"Saw you and Matthew out by the fire pit last night, did those flames provide enough heat for you?" Lawrence inquired, with a teasing smile on his face.

"The ponchos and lap blankets someone left by the back door, plus your wonderful Chateauneuf du Pape, kept us nice and toasty, thank you." Laurel felt a slight blush rise to her checks.

"Aren't you glad Lawrence asked him to your birthday party? Did you find out about the little girl I saw him with Sunday morning?"

Laurel kept her grandmother talking, trying to discern her feelings, while she scrambled an egg for her English muffin. "Grams, I only caught a glimpse of your new meditation room and alter. I would love to see it this morning."

"I would love to show it to you after breakfast."

The three of them went to the spacious new room with Barbara leading the way over to the Meditation area.

"Where did you find such a beautiful piece?" Laurel stood admiring the detail of the elaborate Spanish altar.

"It was advertised under one of the church auctions. It came from an estate of a lady from Phoenix and was in her family since the mid seventeen hundreds. The large Immaculate Heart of Mary Statue was in that same sale block, and it is authentic from Spain. Both are in excellent condition. I feel blessed to have acquired them."

"I know some time back you mentioned you wanted a specific place for a sanctuary, your own special meditation area. This provides a nice quiet, peaceful atmosphere." Laurel walked closer to the statue to check the detail. Coming within four feet, she was compelled to stop. *What is this energy I feel? It's coming from the Mary statue.*

"When we built the safe room a couple of months ago, Barbara decided the room could double as a meditation area also." Lawrence directed her attention to the other side of the room. "Over here are cabinets full of food provisions; everything needed to weather a disaster, including its own portable toilet room. Stocked in the other cabinets are guns and ammunition, vests, and extra phones. Over here are cots and bedding."

"I'm sorry," her grandmother said. "I know I neglected to tell you about it. Every time I spoke with you, after hanging up, I realized I forgot to tell you once again."

Lawrence added, "I decided to limit the knowledge of its existence to a very few. Of course, we didn't mean to exclude you. I'm sure you understand some of the principals of having a safe room."

"That's all right. We are all so busy lately." She stepped back from statue of Mary and the energy stopped flowing from it. Lawrence and Barbara started to leave the room, when Barbara asked Laurel, "Would you like to stay longer? She is mesmerizing."

Laurel turned to her grandmother, "Would you come over here and stand, and tell me what you feel?"

"Are you sensing something?" Barbara walked to the statue. She turned and looked at Laurel, then shook her head from side to side, "I don't feel anything. You were always the most sensitive one in the family. What did you pick up?"

"Oh, just a little energy. Probably some remaining subtle energy from your meditating. Grams, how about we go up to the copula and look through your old photos?" After some time went by, looking through many old pictures, Grams was returning to her old self. They were having fun, even laughing and joking about some of the dresses the subjects were wearing. She looked up from the stack of memorabilia, with a more serious tone in her voice.

"Laurel, I must apologize for not confiding in you about the truth surrounding the wreck when you became old enough. I thought I could shield and protect you, but now it looks like the past is catching up to me. I need to be more cautious. This group, whomever they are, have homed in on me. With all the break-ins and searches in the vehicles that have recently occurred, it's plain they have stepped up their search for this device they call the "Spiritual Artifact". Even you, Laurel, should be more aware of your surroundings."

"Grams, Lawrence said you told him about the drawing/painting my mother saw on the cave wall. He was concerned that part of your description sounded like it could be the area of the Ancient Cahokia? I would like very much to hear or see that description."

Her grandmother hesitated for moment, then she said, "Let's go down to my desk where I can draw on paper."

Laurel watched her grandmother as she sketched a very basic drawing of what her mother saw on the cave wall. Devoid of much of the details, it appeared to be a history of past events or even a map.

"What's your take on this drawing, Grams?"

"I can tell you this, that Artifact device was very powerful. You be extremely careful, if you do find one in that park. You could get burned badly or even killed. Aside from telling your team, or any other workers, the truth of what could or might be uncovered, make something up, so they don't try to use it or make it work. You might just save their life."

Laurel assured her she would be cautious and make some plans to protect her team. "It will be of great help when we get back the results of the satellite imaging. Maybe it will show whether it is still there. I am especially glad the documentary people wanted to span out from Monks Mound, maybe this will help pick up on it."

"I knew this would be better, to draw it out on paper for you. Keep this safe. Don't let it lie around where others can see it." She handed the drawing over to Laurel.

"Thanks Grams. Maybe they can program the scan to watch for this."

"I hope they discover what the Monks Mound problem is and show an avenue to repair it. It would be disastrous to lose the largest prehistoric earthwork pyramid in all the Americas. I am so proud of you Laurel, for setting your goal to help save it."

"Speaking of work, did Alex call you back?"

"He has not contacted me yet."

"That's strange. This doesn't sound like him. Why don't you call again?"

Barbara dialed his number, moments later she whispered, "It went to voice mail again, I'll leave another message."

Laurel left her grandmother and continued to reflect on the information she provided, or perhaps, didn't provide. This was disappointing, especially coming from an accomplished archaeologist, trained to watch for detail. Even though Grams was not inside the cave, you can bet she examined the notebook drawing her daughter made. She felt Grams was still hiding things from her. Laurel knew the Aztec usually gave a lot of detail in their hieroglyphics, but it has been twenty-eight years. she could have forgotten some of the specifics. *I sense in my heart, she knows where mom's drawing is. And maybe the Artifact and the other cave items.*

CHAPTER 33

The morning was almost gone when Laurel put the finishing touches on her packing. She previously planned with the girls to leave close to noon and she wanted to play with the twins before heading out, knowing it would be a long time before she could make it back home.

"Hey Issie–go get it!" Laurel yelled, as she popped a ball with the tennis racket up high into the depths of the massive back yard. Everyone cheered when Issie retrieved the ball, dropping it at her feet, anxious for more play. She hit another ball, "Go get it Lizzie!" Not to be outdone, Lizzie leaped high in the air, catching her ball, Even more cheering came from the growing group of spectators.

Chris arrived just in time to join in the fun. Then much to her surprise, Matthew came around from the front parking, casually dressed in jeans, white shirt with unbuttoned collar and dark blazer. Laurel kept on with her play a while longer. She wasn't at all pleased with the way things were left between them last night, so she didn't come out from the fenced area until she was finished. She gave Stephanie the nod to come and relieve her.

"Well, hello, Professor. Didn't expect to see you today," Laurel said. "I was giving the twins a bit of a workout before we left."

"They are an exquisite pair of beauties, especially the one that leaped so high in the air." Matthew observed with a smile.

"That one is Lizzie, she's the stronger of the two."

Matthew noticed Ralph carrying bags out and placing them beside the FJ cruiser. "I see you're getting ready to pack her up. I thought you were staying one whole day more, leaving tomorrow morning."

"I finished with my business early." She walked over to the side of her vehicle to load some of her baggage in the upper storage box.

"Here, let me help," Matthew offered.

"Why thanks. Your tall stature is kind of handy to have around."

"Hand me your phone."

"What?" She questioned, but then she caught on. Reaching in her back pocket, she pulled it out, and after entering her code, she placed it into his hands.

"Now, how were you going to call me if you didn't have my number?" he growled, shaking his head.

"And if I don't call you?"

"Oh, I'm sorry." he declared, slapping the palm of his hand to his forehead. I had something for you and forgot and left it back in my car. I'm running a little late for a meeting with one of my students. Would you be kind enough to walk me back to get it?"

"I guess I could," she replied. "What did you say you had?" Laurel questioned, trying to remember if he mentioned wanting to give her, or loan her something?

When they reached his vehicle, Matthew turned to her and said, "I've been trying to give this to you, but I was reluctant for fear you would steal my heart." Looking into her eyes, he reached out and touched her, sliding his fingers through her hair. Holding the side of her head in one hand, he gently lifted her chin. He moistened his lips with his tongue, slightly pressing his lips to hers. Laurel was getting aroused just like last night, when a voice inside her said, *this is act two of the same play as last night.* Then he delivered the kiss he had promised.

Laurel eased back. "Well, Professor Vaughn. . .you indeed are handy to have around."

"Thank you, Ms. Robinson, for the wonderful kiss. I hope it was as good for you as it was for me." He caressed the back of her neck. "I'm sorry I have to leave, but I'll only be gone for a couple of hours, as opposed to a few weeks, or months."

"Why Professor, if I didn't know better, one might think you were trying to entice me to stay over."

Matthew stepped closer, again with his hand gently caressing her neck, and the other sliding across her breast.

He softly asked, "How's it working?" Touching her lips with his fingers, he asked her, "Would you like to have more?"

Laurel looked around, checking to see if anyone was close by. "Careful Professor. I think you've overestimated..." she touched her moist lips in light kisses along his neck. "...the dynamics of your kiss," she whispered then kissed his lips with a melting hunger.

She pressed herself against his hard body, tantalizing and teasing him then leaned away from him and smiled as she gazed into his blue eyes. "Sorry it's time for me to go. Good luck with your appointment."

She walked twelve feet away and turned around to catch his expression. It was one of pure agony. *Serves him right. He wants to play the game of teasing, then leave-em. . .well Professor, I'm a good student.*

Laurel swiftly walked toward the back, feeling the heat on her face and then her whole body. It was hard for her to leave him. She definitely was feeling something for him and wishing they could continue their little 'morning delight'. *Think about something else,* she told herself.

She went straight inside, up to her room and soaked a hand towel in some cool water, then held it to her face. Her revenge for his horse-play got Laurel as well! *Why did he have to be so hot?* She moved the cool towel to her neck.

Stephanie came rushing in the room. "What happened with you and Matthew? Why is your face so red? Oh! Was there a little hanky-panky going on?" Stephanie laughed.

"I got my fill of him. Teasing and arousing me, then leaving. So, I turned the table on him. But that guy is so hot. He reminds me of that actor– what's his name. . .Matthew McConaughey. He even has his first name. I almost didn't stop with the teasing,"

"Well, he sure got you going. I know he digs you Laurel, after talking with him yesterday. I can even tell by the way he looks at you. Are you sure you didn't misread his intentions?"

"I guess it's possible. He confuses me. Regardless, I bet he thinks I'm a pretty bad girl by now. I didn't intend to carry on, to be so passionate, especially out in the open. However, I did check our surroundings. We were alone. Regardless it was so out of character for me. I will never be able to look him in the face again. It's a good thing I'm going back to Chicago."

"Now, it can't be all that bad." Stephanie patted her arm. "You know, looking at this from my viewpoint, you two are both attractive and successful. It's no wonder you're attracted to one another. Maybe we need to put you two in a hotel suite, lock the door and throw away the key. I bet the two of you might find some answers to your problems." Stephanie laughed.

"Ha! Ha! If that happens, one or both of us may need the paramedics." They both laughed so hard tears ran down their cheeks.

They were finally underway, with Laurel at the helm and Stephanie as co-pilot. Christina, in the back, was keeping time to the music coming through her ear buds, while Gabi was actively surfing on her cell. They passed around the sandwiches that Maria packed. Traveling always seemed to bring out the hunger in everyone.

It was sad leaving Springfield this visit, saying goodbye to her grandparents was harder to do this time. So much had transpired and not enough questions were answered. The time seemed to pass, but not as quickly as Laurel had hoped it would. The humming of the FJ engine soon took Laurel's thoughts back to the scene she would just as soon forget about, her and Matthew's final goodbye. How could she have done such an out of character deed? *I burned that bridge and there's no way to fix it–ever!*

She forced her thoughts to move away from that blunder onto her grandmother's description of what her mother saw on the cave wall. *Ships landing on the surface of Earth? Was it true? Was there any physical proof of one being found?* She decided to spend the travel time more productively.

"Stephanie, according to the cave drawings, three ships came from the heavens and landed on Earth."

"Yes, I'm following you."

"The Aztec priest took one of those devices, called the Spiritual Artifact, that was aboard that ship. He traveled north, taking the Artifact with him, along with two small children, and some guards. He left it, the clothing, and the drawing on the wall in a cave. This was the cave my mother found. So would you check to see if anything unexplained or unusual was found in that Aztec area? Check archaeology news first, then go into the archives. See how far back it will take us."

After a long search Stephanie said, "Not finding a good answer. As far as any part of a ship goes–nothing. Maybe those ET's got their business over with and went on their merry way, leaving the Artifact behind."

"That Artifact was what those men were trying to find, searching the wreckage that killed my mother. Thinking my grandmother may have it, is why they started searching the houses and vehicles again."

"Why do they want it so badly?"

"I'm not certain, other than the fact it is ancient, the materials were not found on earth, so it is an extraterrestrial device, and it can cause lights to go on and off.""Sounds to me like it's pretty powerful. I wonder what all it can do?" Stephanie questioned.

"Grams said it could be putting out harmful radiation, so approach it with caution, and use a meter on it."

"So, these men, how did they know your mom took it out of the cave?"

"My guess is their guides or some others may have been watching. Wait a minute. She said they took it somewhere to be tested, maybe its whereabouts were leaked out from that facility."

Stephanie had a puzzled look. "The men that looked through the wreckage didn't find the Artifact, so where did they take it? Who did they leave it with?"

"So far, Grams hasn't told me. She claims she doesn't know. I'm going to have to keep on her until she answers that question."

It made for a long day when Gabi pulled the FJ into the museum parking lot just before midnight. They had taken turns with the driving, so a fresh driver was behind the wheel most of the way. "Everyone, get some good sleep, and come in around ten in the morning," Laurel instructed as they all transferred their belongings over into their vehicles.

CHAPTER 34

The alarm on the clock rang out in Laurel's apartment, but she paid no attention, as the bells blended in with the action adventure taking place on another level of her consciousness. She tossed and rolled, acting and participating in her dream world. Suddenly she opened her eyes staring at the dresser on the other wall, asking herself, *where am I? What is that noise?*

Slowly she became more awake and realized her alarm clock was going off. Reaching out to shut it off, she felt a strange sensation. One of being in two places at the same time. It felt like she was being pulled to be in one place, then yanked back to another. Flashes of visions came and went. One of men, then both men and women. Angry protesting, pacing back and forth. She heard guns firing and saw the men and women running for cover. Then the flashes stopped. She sat quietly on her bed, willing her mind to go back to that same place, hoping to get them back. She waited another five minutes, but it was no use, they were gone. She gave up on the dreams and got ready to go to the office.

Laurel arrived at the same time as Christina and they talked as they went down to the offices discussing their schedule for the morning. Entering, they found Rosie and Aaron working on the list she had left.

"Well, look at the night owls dragging into the office." Aaron remarked, with a laugh. "Did you guys get any sleep?"

"Yes, thank you. I got close to five hours, counting the cat naps in the car before we got back. What about you Christina?"

"Close to the same. I'm so thankful we slept in, otherwise I would have been close to zombie state." They all laughed as Christina imitated zombie moves.

Aaron commented, "Rosie and I were the only ones from any of the Archaeology or Anthropology offices that showed up yesterday. We went down to the lab to get the results of our scan we ran before we left for Springfield. We kept hearing noises we never heard before. We were anxious to get the analysis and get the hell out of there. It was truly like the movie 'Night at The Museum'."

"We both kept looking over our shoulder, even when we returned to this room," Rosie said. "We started playing some music to break-up the eerie silence and drown out the sudden knocks and pings."

"You could have beat on my drum over by my desk. I bet it would have run off those bad spirits running amuck," Laurel teased.

"Spirits? Did I hear you say they were running off spirits?" Stephanie questioned as she entered the office-class room.

"The guys thought they heard ghosts. The museum was open, with an overabundance of visitors. That probably explains it." Laurel's phone rang. "Good morning, Laurel, this is Dr. Weston. How are thing's going with your project?"

"Good morning to you! I just got back to the office from a short Easter holiday. We are hard at work this morning on the board's proposals. Getting this approved by the two boards will be the hardest of all the tasks, mainly because of time involved. Dr. Weston, I was planning on calling you anyway today." Laurel left the room to get to an area where she could talk in private. "I have some new facts I just learned while on my visit in Springfield. Well, Dr. Weston this might sound a little crazy but. . ."

"Go ahead. I have done some unorthodox things, with a lot of people calling me crazy, before I finally developed this satellite imaging program. So, I am not surprised by anything."

"I have to ask that what I am about to tell you be keep in the strictest confidence. Can you do this?"

"Laurel, you have my word."

"I might have mentioned that I come from a third generation of archaeology. While visiting with my grandmother, who mostly raised me, she finally let me in on a secret she had kept from me for twenty-eight years. My mom found some items in an Aztec cave with some well-preserved hieroglyphics on the wall. It showed three ships falling from the sky." Laurel went on explaining what they found.

"I believe I already know your question. You want to know if the program will detect an extraterrestrial ship?"

"That. . . plus there is more. She discovered the Aztec priest had rescued two royal children away from the palace, so the Spaniards would not capture them. They left their royal clothing and jewelry behind, as well as an Artifact, a powerful devise of some sort, in a leather case. They had the Artifact tested and results showed it is not made from any material found on Earth. I believe it was something used in conjunction with that ship. There probably is at least one of these devices on each of those ships. Meaning, there could be at least one like it in the grounds at Cahokia. There has not been any record of a discovery of a ship, any part of a ship, or even the strange device ever being discovered in the surrounding area of the Cahokia civilization. If the ship didn't fly back out and the hieroglyphics didn't show that it did, it's still there."

"So, the Artifact and the ship's material make-up are foreign to Earth. Hold on a minute. . ." Laurel heard Dr. Weston mumbling in the background. "Dr. Weston. . . Dr. Weston are you there?"

"I'm here, Laurel. I'm just working out some equations."

"I need to tell you, when the endcap is opened on the metal cylinder device and the content is extended out of the container, it reads high on a radio-active meter. But when it retracted inside the metal case, with the end cap closed, there was a safe reading on the meter."

"I understand. The radio-active part is not relevant to my scans, but the material of the ship and the artifact is. How large is this Artifact?"

"It's a cylinder shape, maybe six to ten inches long."

"I've got some time to work on this while you get your approvals. I'll see what I can do. Give me a call when they are finalized."

The five were kept busy all morning working and compiling their facts and information, plus the information needed for the production managers. Things were going smooth now that Alex was still away. . .She wondered when he would come back and if he had returned Grams call yet. The group worked until six and the guys were starting to moan with hunger pains, for they had depleted all the snacks. "Ok! I hear you," Laurel announced. "You guys worked extremely hard, especially you two coming in yesterday. I thank you very much. This is going to be something we all can be proud of. Let's all leave now. Try to get some rest tonight. I will return back at seven in the morning, for all those that would like to join me."

Laurel and Stephanie stopped by Pier 22 for a relaxer before heading home. "Laurel, this place is hopping, what's going on?"

"Beat's me, you would think it would be quiet since a lot of the professionals and business people are still out on break. Let's try and find a table." After scouting around Stephanie got Laurel's attention up at the bar.

"This is a heck of a note. Work hard all day, then stand on our feet some more, to belly-up to a bar." One could almost see steam flowing from Stephanie's neck.

"Careful, your red hair is starting to glow," a man said, standing on the other side of Stephanie. She turned and glared at him.

"Sorry Madam, I was only teasing." He said, along with a big smile. "I'm Charlie, may I purchase something cool for you and your friend?"

She accessed the situation and Laurel noticed her friend relax a little. "I'm Stephanie, I'll take a Strawberry Daiquiri, my friend will have a Margarita on the rocks, no rim salt please." He immediately got the bartender's attention, ordering the drinks.

"What's happing here? I've not seen this big of a crowd, ever," Stephanie said.

"They brought in entertainment. Cleared out a partition in the back part of the building, giving them room for a band and a dance floor."

"Come Stephanie, I see a table about to be ours." The table was close by and Laurel maneuvered her way in to stake her claim but, just as she got there, a man cut in front of her causing her to miss getting there first. "Well, of all the nerve." She murmured as she returned to the bar. The man next to Stephanie spied another table where the people were about to leave and alerted Stephanie.

"Red, go grab that one." He pointed to show her where it was. "Show them how it's done." Stephanie laid her hand on the back of a chair and turned to get Laurel's attention. While turning back to the table, she saw a man had slid into one of the other chairs, his body turned away from her.

"Now look here, Mister. I was here first. This is my table!" Stephanie asserted. He turned his head toward her. She raised her hand to her face. "I know you. You're the British guy with the TV Channel."

Nigel replied, "And you're the archaeologist with the Cahokia Mounds."

Laurel overheard the exchange as she and the man from the bar arrived at the table. "I see you have already met Charlie, our lead camera tech," Nick announced as he joined them.

"Well sort of. We didn't know Charlie was with your group," Laurel replied.

"Ladies, I would formally like to introduce our famed director of photography, Charlie Sorkin," Nick announced as he pulled out a chair for Laurel. "So, how's the project coming along?" he inquired.

"Really good. I feel we accomplished a great deal today. We returned from Missouri around midnight, got a few hours of sleep and went right to work. Tomorrow we should complete the proposals. We'll just need the vice president's approval. Many of the museum's people and the corporation officers are still on Easter break, so we may have to wait for their return. Did you take any break for Easter?"

"Oh yes, I hid eggs for my son–three times," Nick replied. "He loved finding them."

"I bet you had just as much fun hiding them, too." Laurel took a sip of her drink. "I should finish up on the facts and interesting points about the Cahokia Civilization for your commentator and director by tomorrow. Shall I call you when it is completed?"

"Most certainly. They can begin working on this as soon as they get your information," Nick replied. Nigel leaned in to interject the outlines for the filming, stating they would go over the protocols when meeting tomorrow. The band was all set-up and started playing.

"They sound pretty good," Charlie remarked.

"This is a nice improvement, they should draw in a nice crowd," Nigel replied.

Laurel and Stephanie stayed awhile listening to the band and visiting with the group, then left the club after the entertainment's first set.

CHAPTER 35

Laurel was first to arrive at her office and commenced working on the Cahokia history and points of interest. She had just finished when Joann Maury knocked on the frame of her open door. "Good morning, I see you are hard at work early."

Laurel smiled. "I'm so glad to see you. My four teammates and I have most of the preliminary work finished. One completed just this minute. The history and points of interest of the Cahokia Civilization, the commentator will require to write his documentary. This, of course, will need your approval before I hand it off to the producers. They wanted to start working on this part today, if possible. Even before getting the Board's approval. I should have the other proposals completed for your approval later today."

"Laurel, did you even take your Easter Break?"

"Yes, along with seven of my team, we all went to my grandparents place in Missouri. We had a wonderful time. They threw a big masquerade party for my birthday, a band for dancing, with a casino set up on the lower level, and lots of food and drinks. She went on telling about the other activities and events. This is my second full day back. Rosie and Aaron came in a day ahead of me, doing some work on this."

"I'm glad everyone got a break. Now then, did you double check all dates and facts that went into this compilation? And the correct terminology of the words you want presented?" Joann asked.

"Yes ma'am, and two others checked after I wrote it. Have you heard anything from Director Zuckerman?"

"He called from Oklahoma and said he would be late returning back to his office. His aunt was in the hospital for surgery."

The other work on the Board proposals kept Laurel busy, but her thoughts kept returning to Alex. His story of going to his aunt's farm in Oklahoma for Easter was probably true. She thought he just made that up as an excuse! Stephanie and Christina came in, with Rosie and Aaron directly following. "Got it all done yet?" Stephanie inquired.

"Real close. Should have the rest of it ready for Joann Maury's hands before the day is over. She came in earlier and left with the part I had completed."

"What have you got for us to do this morning, Miss Laurel?" Rosie sounded eager to get to work.

"I need you guys to prepare some maps, please. One set for the TV Producers, another for Dr. Weston. Print them and lay them out on the work table so I can make my marks. And get a transport tube ready for each. The TV producer or a rep will come by later to pick theirs up. The other one, we will overnight to Dr. Weston."

"Stephanie, I need you to find out if the board members on our project committee are back yet. If not, find out when they will return. That list is in my blue notebook on my desk. Check with Ms. Grainger, if she isn't in charge of this, then she can direct you to the right office."

Laurel faxed Dr. Weston requesting her revised cost figures, along with the perimeters she planned on using for the Space Archaeology Imaging proposal. She was hoping to get a low cost on the revised figure. . .all she could do now was wait.

Stephanie returned from her assignment and slumped in the chair next to Laurel. "I didn't get all of the members located, and I couldn't get any information when they would return." Stephanie sighed in exhaustion. Just then Joann Maury walked into the office carrying the folder Laurel had previously given her.

"Maybe Joann can help with obtaining their whereabouts," Laurel replied. They explained the latest problem to her, and she stated she could help. Sitting down at the big table, she opened the folder of the facts and information on the Cahokia and explained the few changes needed. She wanted to see a written transcript, signed by the producers, of the actual commentary they were going to use in the documentary.

"I want no surprises when I view their documentary over the air. This is serious business." She thumped her index finger on top of the folder. "This has to be approved by me or else we open ourselves up to lawsuits. A lot of people's jobs are on the line. This could have a domino effect."

Tension enveloped the room as she spoke. Laurel was glad she had Rosie and Stephanie check the facts and information sheet before passing it on to Joann.

"Now Stephanie, get your list and come with me," Joann remarked.

After making the revisions on her computer she made the call to Nick Kenyon. Laurel asked Christina to design a software program for the Cahokia facts and information as laid out, so when they presented any future papers regarding this, it would tell us if something was wrong, misspelled, left out or added too, without spending precious time going over any future documents.

"Hello there!" Nick greeted as he, Nigel and Charlie walked into the office.

"Welcome to my office/classroom." Laurel smiled, happy to see them.

"Wow!" Nick voiced, looking around the room at all the computers, whiteboards, books, instruments, and other numerous teaching tools. Then Nigel eyed the maps spread out on the long tables and walked over to get a better view.

"First, I need to explain the file I put together for your narrator of the documentary to use as a guide. It is full of information and facts he will need. I have just been told by the Vice President of the Corporation, Mrs. Joann Maury, that she must see and approve the written commentary that will be used in actual broadcast, prior to the broadcast. Or, the deal is off."

The two producers nodded their heads and smiled. "This is a normal practice of ours, anyway. No problem."

Laurel gave them everything they would need from her office explaining they may want to film the model display of an artist rendition of the Capital City, upstairs in the Ancient Americans section, along with some of the artifacts. "This is great, just what we need," Charlie remarked.

"Also, a large assortment of artifacts can be found on display at the Cahokia museum on site. We are trying to get all of this done, so Dr. Weston can scan while the grounds are still moist. Just as soon as we get the board's approval and your written commentary is approved, we are set to go."

"Can we get a few shots of your lab while we are here?" Nick asked.

"Sure, just follow me." They passed by different groups of archaeology teams before they got to Laurel's lab. They followed her into an all equipped high-tech lab stocked with computers, magnifiers, carbon dating equipment, trays of specimens soaking in cleaning materials, etc.

"Listen-up everyone, I'm showing the TV Producers our lab, you may go ahead with your work," Laurel announced.

"This is impressive!" Nick remarked.

"It certainly is," Nigel added while he scanned everything over.

Laurel explained, "They are busy processing the finds from last summer's dig. We do it all, from documenting and extracting at the dig site, to cleaning, analyzing, dating, and cataloging. We get it ready for display or storing. Some of our work here has produced artifacts not only for the Field Museum and the Park Museum, but we also have a nice display at the Smithsonian." Nick pointed to an instrument that was attached to a computer. "Hum. . .this looks interesting. What's it used for?"

"This system helps us analyze the composition of specimens."

"Is it okay for Charlie to get a few shots of this for the Doc?"

Laurel gave permission for him to film and noticed Nick was glancing at her with a gleam in his eye. Could he be feeling something for her after all? She kept thinking about how hot Matthew was, and how she wished she could change what happened between them.

"I am finished here," Charlie declared.

"Great, let's go back upstairs," Laurel said.

"Laurel, I don't think you realize how long it takes to make a documentary of this caliber." Nick proceeded to explain the long process.

"I now understand completely," she said. "We need to back your documentary out of the other proposal with Dr. Weston's. That will give you sufficient time to make your documentary, and by that time she will have her approval to do her imaging. Then you'll include her results in the filming. It will work out fine."

CHAPTER 36

The following day, Laurel was on her way to Joann Maury's office before going over to the conference room to present the revised proposal to the six-member board.

"Wait up, Laurel." The deep baritone voice caught her by surprise. She forced a smile before turning around. "Hello, Alex. Welcome back! I heard your aunt was in the hospital. Is she doing all right?" Laurel held the folders tight against her chest.

"Yes, thank you for asking. She is doing much better, expecting to go home tomorrow. Her daughter lives nearby and will care for her. I'm headed to Joann's office, too. I'm anxious to see your proposals. Did Dr. Weston give you a good deal?"

"I think it's very reasonable," Laurel replied, still holding the folders tightly, not volunteering anything, until she presented them to Joann Maury. Laurel kept her quick pace right on into Joann's office, with Alex following. After some preliminary talk, Joann stated, "All right, Laurel, let's see what you've got."

Laurel placed a large map of Cahokia on an easel and gave them both a folder. Pointing to the displayed map she explained, "Dr. Weston increased the perimeters to expand outwards in all directions from Monks Mound, taking in the outer residential areas beyond the central precinct. This will give us a wider view of what is already discovered and all of what the satellite imaging will disclose underground that is yet to be discovered.

"The Wonders and Mystery proposal had to be backed out from this proposal because of the time involved to prepare the narration and the film. Once we get both boards' approval for Dr. Weston's proposal, then she can do her work while the ground is still moist. This is crucial. Notice the original perimeters vs the expanded new perimeters, then the original cost vs the new low cost."

"There is not a big difference in the expense. Could this be a mistake?" Alex interrupted.

"Below you will notice an explanation to your question," Laurel read aloud. "The World Wonders and Mystery TV Network sponsors are paying for the extra technical and filming expenses for the expanded perimeters. Dr. Weston's company has discounted her service fees for the expansion."

Joann rose from her seat, remarking, "I think it will fly. What do you think Dr. Zuckerman?"

"What would happen if the Documentary does not air? Could she then come back and sue for more money, claiming this expansion cost was based on the Documentary airing with the sponsors picking up the cost difference?"

"I will make a call to our legal department. You two hang around till we get an answer."

Laurel walked to the coffee station pouring a cup of hot water to douse her tea bag. Alex came closer to where she stood and complimented her on putting the proposal together adding, "Remember Laurel, it's always prudent to think ahead about all the negatives and what could go wrong, when working with proposals and contracts."

"Thanks for the reminder, Alex. I need to speak to you privately after we finish here if you have time."

"I'll check my schedule." He pulled out his cell replying, "How about two this afternoon?"

"I believe that will work for me."

"Joann hung up her phone explaining, "You need to add a clause to take care of this." She handed her the statement the legal department advised. "Then fax to Dr. Weston for her signature, with a new third page added to all the proposals."

Time was of the essence and Laurel immediately dialed Dr. Weston. She turned back to the two explaining, "Dr. Weston's secretary said she was scanning with the Satellite imaging and gave instructions that she could not stop or be bothered for a least one more hour."

Alex asked her to hand him the phone. "I'm Director Alex Zuckerman with the Cahokia Project. This is an urgent matter. Can you slip her a note? "Write these words on the note. *Emergency Fax awaits your signature–added clause to proposal–no other changes–signed, Laurel and Director Dr. Zuckerman -Cahokia Project.* We are sending the fax now. Please, make sure she gets this ASAP, as our Board of Directors meets at 11:00 AM this morning." Alex handed the phone back to Laurel. "This is all we can do. The ball is in their court now."

"It's going to be all right," Joann observed while looking at the clock. "We still have thirty minutes before the Board calls the meeting to order."

Laurel walked to the coffee station again for more hot water. After making some fresh tea she took a few sips, then taking the stack of proposals to the long table, she began removing the staples on the proposals, making ready for the addition of the new signed sheet they hoped to receive.

Laurel walked the floor, one eye on the fax machine, the other on the wall clock.

Joann spoke up, "Laurel sit down and relax. Drink your tea and calm yourself. I'll head down to the Board room and keep them busy with something, while you two stay here and get that fax."

They were twenty minutes late when Laurel and Alex hurriedly entered the Board room. The members were standing around with plates of food enjoying a surprise lunch. Some were mingling about looking at the pictures Joann was sharing of her grandchildren's Easter visit. She looked up and saw the two walking toward her. She whispered, "Did you get your fax?"

Laurel replied, "We are ready."

Alex raised his coffee mug toward Joann as if to compliment her quick thinking. "The Board meeting went well. The proposal was approved and everyone left with a better understanding of the project. Joann asked, "What's next on your to do list Laurel?"

"We need to present our proposal to members of the Illinois Historic Preservation Agency. Stephanie has been working on setting this meeting up, while we were busy with the Board here." She pulled out her phone to check on her progress. "Stephanie, we got the go ahead here. Did you set things up with the other board?"

"Hands down!" Start packing your bags. It's set three days from now, at the community room in The Interpretive Center at the Cahokia park."

CHAPTER 37

It wasn't long until they received the approval from the Illinois Historic Preservation Agency which allowed the project to commence.

Laurel and two members of her team, Rosie and Stephanie were to meet up with the two producers and their camera crew at the Cahokia State Park. Pulling into the parking lot Rosie remarked, "The TV Vans are here."

Laurel's phone rang with Nick Kenyon's name showing as the caller. "You see us? Great. . . where are you guys?" Laurel laughed saying, "That's fine–see you soon." Laurel hung up and turned to her team. "Their camera crew is shooting on top of Monks Mound. Nick and Nigel are up there too."

"I hope they don't need us to come up," Stephanie said. "I'm not sure I'm up to all those stairs today."

"Be cool, Stephanie, they are about through and on their way down."

They walked over to the base of the tallest mound in the park and waited until they descended. Laurel cheerfully greeted, "Welcome to the Ancient City of Cahokia."

Nigel remarked, "Happy to be here."

"Why don't you get them to install an elevator?" Charlie said with a winded voice. Everyone laughed and the camera team sat their equipment down on the grassy plaza, while the producers, directors, and Laurel went over the basic narration script and what film and photos they would need to accompany it.

The making of the documentary was now in its third day and as usual after the evening meal, the crew gathered at the motel's recreation facilities and exercise room. Nick caught up with Laurel in the hall of the motel. "It's a beautiful night outside. You should see the moon. It is huge!"

"Is it? I was preoccupied with phone calls and didn't notice."

"Allow me to be your tour guide, Ms. Robertson." Nick motioned her to follow.

The night air had calmed the strong winds that plagued the day at the mounds, making way for a delightful evening. A few drifting clouds periodically drifted across the brilliance of the moonlight cast upon the Earth.

"Wow! Mr. Kenyon, you are so right." She returned his formal name address, with flirtatious overtones.

"I was up on top of Monks Mound one-night last summer, much like tonight, Mr. Kenyon. We were working a dig site by the area we believed to be where the Chiefdom resided. We worked till dark and planned to spend the night, bringing provisions and sleeping bags. We all had an interesting experience."

"I wish I had been with you guys that night," Stephanie stated. Laurel turned with a surprised look, not aware that she, along with Nigel, Rosie and Charlie had walked up within hearing distance.

"I was there," Rosie said. It was an unforgettable experience."

"Laurel, tell us what happened up there," Nick requested.

"Well. . .it's hard to explain, we each had different experiences. We were close by our dig site and after eating the food we prepared ahead of time, the five of us sat around talking about the different sensing equipment and tools we were using. Then I believe it was you, Rosie, that spoke up."

"Yes, I remarked that back when Cahokia was at its prime, there were priests and elders that were sensitive through their religion. They were gifted to know things and they didn't have the tools we have today."

Laurel explained, "We decided to entertain ourselves, to see what the energy of this ancient pyramid would tell us by using just our five senses."

Rosie added, "It was a full moon just like tonight. We scattered away from each other to cover different areas on the surface. We were to return to our starting point, when finished. I went down several feet to the third level surface."

"I was on the fourth level, north west corner," Laurel said. "I sat to meditate. Soon I heard voices of Ancient Indians chanting with drums from the plaza below. Then later in my mind's eye I saw myself as a young maiden princess standing in that very spot, wearing a white dress and holding a large medallion. I was looking up in the night sky, toward a group of clustered stars, talking to my grandfather's Spirit. *Now that my father has been killed, I am left to be the leader of our great nation—we are under immense threat of annihilation!* I remember wiping tears from my face. I took the medallion, held it to reflect the bright moonlight toward the cluster of bright stars."

"Then I recited a prayer." *I beg of you Great Spirit, instill in me your powers to protect and lead our people–to survive this dark force that is now upon us! Great Spirit, I know the Gods will help us if I ask. Tell me the final symbol I need to activate their powerful tool of wisdom and weapon they left behind.* "It was all quite surreal."

"We went looking for Laurel when she didn't return," Rosie related.

Laurel saw Stephanie glance at her when she heard the word symbols and activate the powerful tool mentioned.

Nigel spoke up. "It appears like your consciousness returned you to a dream like state maybe?"

"It's possible, I guess." Trying to get the spotlight off herself, she turned to Rosie. "Tell them what you experienced, Rosie."

"I did some tai chi exercises and then sat lotus style and meditated. Soon I was looking down at a chunkey game that was in progress. Then suddenly, I was down there refereeing this religious rite. Afterward, I saw hundreds of people taking part in a rather large feast in the plaza. It was so strange. I could hear and see the people as they mingled about, smell the meats roasting. And then suddenly I was back."

"Well Rosie, did you bring any of that good smelling roasted pig back with you?" Charlie questioned. There was nervous laughter among the group.

"You two really did have quite an experience," Nick remarked.

Stephanie shoved Charlie's arm stating, "If you bomb out in photography, I know where they could use a good stand-up guy."

"You don't say. I guess I could use an extra job in the evenings since I don't have a female friend to occupy my time."

"Forget that," Nigel mumbled. "Don't we work you hard enough as it is?"

The conversation continued for a while, then Laurel announced she was going to head up to her room.

Nick said, "Wait up." He whispered so the others couldn't hear. "Walk with me over to the lounge, I need to talk with you over a night cap." They turned around and took a short walk across the motel's parking lot to the Collinsville Executive Lounge. "You know, we should finish up tomorrow after we do the interviews with you, your director, and the corporate official."

"They are flying in from Chicago and will be here around eleven."

"Let's shoot your part just after breakfast, then we'll get the other two after they arrive."

He reached for her hand. "Ms. Robinson, you and I have not had a chance to be alone. It seems there is always someone that joins us when I'm about to have a private conversation with you."

"I guess it's because we both are so darn popular," she replied with a bit of laughter.

"Laurel, I haven't had the chance to sit down alone and talk on a personal note. I don't want you to think that I'm not interested in you. . . because, I am. The Corporation had problems in the distant past with production officials having a relationship with the officials they were contracted with. So we don't cross that line if we want to keep our job. It won't be that much longer and our work will be finished, freeing me from that non-fraternizing clause. I can't tell you how hard it's been for me to stay my distance. I have been attracted to you since we danced together at the cocktail party."

"I thought that might be the case when you didn't ask me to dance the other night at Pier 22."

"Laurel, I want to ask you how your relationship is going with you and your new Director. Sorry, that didn't come out right. What I'm really trying to find out is, now that you're spending time together again, are you finding you still have feelings for him?"

"Well Mr. Kenyon." She smiled. "For your information, it is Alex who wants to win my affection back. I have managed to stay out ahead of his advances."

"Laurel, if there are some feelings you still have for him, then I will back off. Therefore, I had to ask. I don't even know if you would even want to see me after we finish here."

"Well Mr. Kenyon, I find your charming character and personality to be most delightful, along with those hazel eyes. I would be most happy to go out with you when that time comes. Besides you owe me another dance."

CHAPTER 38

The fourth day of filming got underway with the promising start of a beautiful sunny morning. Laurel was thankful that the winds had calmed to light breezes since her interview was about to start. The director announced for everyone to be quiet. "Camera roll!"

Producer Nick Kenyon walked over introducing Laurel, giving her background information and her work history.

"It is through Dr. Robertson's efforts to commission Dr. Emily Weston and her team to use her Space Satellite Archaeology Imaging Technology, right here on the vast acres of Cahokia. They are currently doing this scanning while we are taping this documentary. "We will present the results at the air time of the program. Producer Kenyon continued. "Dr. Robertson, can you tell us what you hope the outcome will be from this Satellite Technology?"

"By using this new satellite imagery, what was once invisible will suddenly become visible, by mapping out the exact locations of many new ancient treasures. When this was done in Egypt, they found seventeen new possible pyramids, over a thousand new tombs, and three-thousand new sites. As for the Cahokia Site, I hope to reveal the answers to a lot of mysteries this vast area has been hiding."

Producer Nigel Stewart stepped in to ask, "Some facts revealed this area all started with a small village. In the year 1000, they were the largest village in the Midwest with over one thousand souls. Shortly after 1050, everything at and around the old village changed. Can you explain to our listeners what happened next, Dr. Robertson?"

Laurel took the mic replying, "Through radiocarbon dating, archaeologist have discovered that over a relative short period of time, a small group of planners, maybe even one single person, redesigned Cahokia from a village to a vast, sophisticated, cosmopolitan city."

Producer Kenyon commented, "You are saying these village Indians suddenly changed their mentality of being tribal, to being a Civilization that built a vast city practically overnight.

That in itself is a mystery!" Nigel proclaimed.

"It's like a mysterious leader swooped in and guided them with the knowledge of designing a planned community," Kenyon remarked.

"Implementing this new design meant that hundreds of the village houses had to be torn down. The bottomlands had to be leveled in some areas. Then Cahokia's huge earthen pyramids and plazas were built. Around them new neighborhoods were laid out. They went up fast–built with prefabricated sapling walls topped with a thatched roof. Their new house slept a family of five, stored their possessions, dried food stuffs, cooking wares, and space to build a fire to heat the interior. It grew to be one of the greatest cities of the world. Cahokia was larger than London in AD 1250," Laura declared.

Kenyon asked, "How long did it take to build Monks Mound behind you?" The camera turned upward to show the entire Monks Mound.

"Archaeologists originally thought it took two hundred fifty years. We have new evidence that it was built in just a few decades. Twenty to forty years of continual work."

"Another reason we commissioned Dr. Weston and her team, is the fact that Monks Mound's west and east slopes, have been experiencing slope failures since the 1980's. The west side being problematic, as we have not been able to get our radar to penetrate deep enough. We hoped her imaging technology would reveal why this problem continues and how we can reach it for repairs."

Producer Kenyon spoke, "By 1350 all of this was largely abandoned by its people. No one is sure why. Neither war, disease, nor European conquest drove them from their homes. What do you think they were afraid of and where do think they went?"

"It appears they were fearful of something, yet archaeologists did not find sufficient evidence of arrowheads, to indicate they were ever under any siege from the outside. I am in process of applying for funding to prove a theory of why they left and where they went. I hope to have the answer to this ancient mystery soon."

"Thank you, Dr. Robertson, for your input."

"And cut!" yelled the director.

Nick and Nigel stood talking with the director for a few minutes, so Laurel switched her phone back on to check for messages, noting she missed a few calls while they were taping. One was from Alex, *"Laurel-call as soon as you get this."*

Laurel dialed his number. "We have been detained here at the airport. We had some sort of mechanical problem. They think it can be fixed within a couple of hours."

"The interviews were the last on their list for today's filming. We just finished filming mine and they are checking to see if everything went well. Hold on, I'll step over and talk with them." She then told Alex, "They still have some other shots to get, then they will work on things in their van. Call when you take off."

"Laurel, when do you think you will be able to start your field work there?"

"The rest of my team are driving down later today with our equipment. I want to be sure they are through filming from the center of the plaza, because this is where we will set up first. I want to further the research in and around mound 49."

"Why this area Laurel?"

"Looking at past research they did not go deep enough or span out north toward Monks Mound. I have an intense feeling there is more this site is hiding."

"I know you and those gut feelings. They are usually right. Laurel, with that large of a team, it's not within your budget to stay at the motel, even with their discounts to us."

"Last season I talked to the owner of a nearby house and put a deposit on it for this season. It used to be one inhabited by another archaeology team. I used my own money to do this because there were no more funds for housing at the end of the season. I applied to get reimbursement out of this year's funds."

"You didn't know last year that you would be directed to come back here. Pretty sure of your-self!"

Laurel could feel the sarcasm in that remark. "I did know. At the end of last season, Joann Maury was filling in as Director. She knew I put in for funding to have Dr. Weston use her satellite technology on Monks Mound. She gave permission for my return before I submitted the proposal."

She could feel he thought he was being finessed. First, she kept the submission of funds for a project from him. Second, he could have assigned her somewhere else. Then she would have to tell him that she was awarded the funds to have the Satellite imaging done. She needed to patch things up, but how?

"Alex, I needed to be here a little while longer. I feel I'm on to something big. I can't know for sure, but I hope the satellite scanning can help uncover the secrets this ancient place is keeping from us."

"I'll call you when they let us take off. . .good bye."

Laurel could tell he was more than displeased. She was not sure how she was going to handle his latest feelings of being played, when he was so used to being in complete control and authority.

Nick and Nigel finished talking to the director and walked back over to where Laurel was standing.

"Everything all right, Laurel?" Nick's brows knitted together.

"Oh. . .it will be okay. Did the taping go all right?"

"Everything turned out great, Laurel. No retakes for you. You could turn professional," Nigel declared in his natural British accent.

Nick explained to Laurel, "Since we are a Mystery program, we are going to have a brief segment about the triangular craft event that happened in the year 2000." Do you think we could interview your young man, Rosie? We could use his input based on the UFO story he told me the night of the cocktail party."

"I think that would be okay." She pulled out her phone and spoke with him about the matter. "He'll be right over," she related. Laurel kept busy with other phone calls while they prepared the set for Rosie's interview.

She made previous arrangements for the house lease to start today and she needed to pick up the keys. She called the owner and arranged to meet him. Laurel walked back close to the set and sat down in one of the comfortable lawn chairs that stretched out into a lounge. She was all to herself with the rest of the crew off in the van planning for Rosie's interview. With her feet propped up she stared up into the beautiful blue sky. The occasional slight breeze was a welcome change from yesterday. The sun was in its mid overhead zone and felt nice and warm. Briefly she closed her eyes, thinking she could use a quick power nap.

CHAPTER 39

Laurel opened her eyes and smiled when she saw Nick's face looking down to hers. She softly breathed the words, "Hey, Handsome."

"Hey, you. Do you know how beautiful you are when you sleep?" Nick replied in his low voice.

Laurel felt herself blush as the camera crew arrived, setting up their equipment. Nigel and the director walked Rosie onto the set and he went over the questions they would be asking for the interview.

Laurel got up from her chair and took a short walk away from the set when she started recalling bits and pieces of the dream she had. *It was those black robe priests again. She saw them walking away from a white church, with a wall around it. Then a lot of people, all walking away from this church and walled place.* None of it made sense.

"Hey sleeping beauty, did you enjoy your power nap?" Nick inquired. His remark brought her swiftly back from the dream recall.

"What? Oh, yes. I guess I must have needed some extra energy, as I haven't been getting much sleep at night."

"Positions everyone!" the director shouted.

Nick said, "Nick Kenyon back again. It has been more than seventeen years since one of the most substantial UFO sightings in the history of the phenomenon has taken place, due almost entirely to the testimonials given by law enforcement officers involved. We have with us one of Ms. Robertson's team members, Mr. Usher Sanders. Your uncle was one of those officers. What did he say happened?"

Rosie replied, "There was a call from the owner of the Highland Miniature Golf reporting the initial sighting. My uncle was one of the officers that investigated the sighting. All the officers saw it, stating it was a triangular object as long as a football field, gliding low over neighboring towns, between four and five a.m. They followed it, radioing to each other, staying in contact with their dispatchers. It's all on tape."

"What towns were involved in this?"

"It started in Highland, Illinois and was reported in Lebanon, Summerfield, Shiloh, Millstadt, and Dupo. It circled back around traveling low over Cahokia. Then one of the officers said it suddenly departed at a high rate of speed."

Producer Kenyon commented, "This is very close to Scotts AFB. Yet, no official investigation was ever conducted. We checked with the US Air Force and they confirmed they were not testing any new aircraft on that night. We asked why no official investigation was ever made. We were told officially, neither the Air Force nor any other government agency has any interest."

Rosie imparted, "There has been speculation for years that something incredibly strange is hidden beneath the Cahokia Mounds. Some even suggest the mounds were built to cover up a UFO, that had been hidden there centuries before."

"Cut!" yelled the director.

It was mid-afternoon when Laurel's phone rang. "Hey Alex."

"Laurel, we are finally in flight. We'll be there shortly."

Laurel was so glad that Joann Maury decided to come with Alex. She was aware of their history, and she had her way of keeping things peaceful. Stephanie walked toward her. "Alex just called. They will be landing soon. Would you run and pick them up at the airport? Also, have you seen Nick or Nigel?"

"They are both inside the long panel truck, going over some film."

Laurel stepped to the open door of the TV production truck. Tapping on the frame she said, "Hello in there. Just wanted you guys to know that Mrs. Maury and Dr. Alex Zuckerman will be here shortly."

"Thanks Laurel. We were just about to leave to set up for that interview."

"You both can't imagine how thankful I am for this documentary. It is a long overdue history lesson about what actually transpired in this country, back when there was an ancient advanced civilization in North America."

"That's precisely why we are here. The mysteries of what existed in ancient times in America is what this network wants to bring to light," Nigel stated.

"We're going to set up over on the west side of Monks Mound, in the Woodhenge area," Nick explained.

Stephanie gave Laurel a call to find out where she needed to meet them. It wasn't long until they were all on set with the producers, director, and crew. The producers took Alex aside and they began preparing what they were going to talk about.

"How was your flight, Joann? " Laurel inquired.

"It was great. We no longer got underway, when the pilot announced we were descending. It sure beats that drive down here. How is your house you rented for the summer?"

Laurel shrugged her shoulders stating, "Haven't been inside yet. Another archaeologist showed me around last season when she told me they would be working another site. I thought it was ideal for my team. The property owner requires a walk through and I have not had time yet. He sounds like a nice man. He's Native American. . . not sure which tribe."

"How many do you have on your team now?"

"I have eleven, counting myself. Three are floaters, so I might have them all season or they could swap out, giving me three different ones, or none. It's up to the Director."

"I would like to see the rental when we finish here," Joann said.

"Will you be talking on camera too?"

"No, it's not my intention anyway. I just came to see how things were progressing. I haven't been here in a long time."

"They brought some fold-up chairs over here. Would you like to sit and watch Alex's interview? It looks like they're about ready to start."

"Positions everyone." Producer Kenyon back again at Cahokia's famous Woodhenge, a half mile to the west of Monks Mound. talking with Dr. Alex Zuckerman, Director of the Archaeology/Anthropology Department of The Field Museum in Chicago. "Dr. Zuckerman can you explain what this area is?"

"This was their Solstice and Equinox calendar. . ." Alex went on explaining in a long drawn out detail of what transpired here, ending his presentation with a final statement.

"The most spectacular sunrises occur at the equinoxes. The post marking these sunrises aligns with the front of Monks Mound, where the leader of this great community resided. A few years ago, my team and I, which included Dr. Robertson, were on a dig right here at Cahokia and privileged to witness a spring equinox. It was an elaborate, visually exciting show. It looked like Monks Mound gave birth to the sun!"

"Thank you, Dr. Zuckerman for your elaborate presentation on Woodhenge," producer Kenyon proclaimed.

"Cut! Let's have a look at what we've got," the director declared.

Alex walked over to where Laurel and Joann sat and talked with them while the director checked his film.

"You gave a good talk, Alex." Laurel commented. "I remember that sunrise. It truly was astonishing! I'll remember it forever."

"You two make me wish I had been there," Joann said.

Laurel's phone showed she had numerous voice messages, all from Dr. Weston. Excusing herself, she got up and walked away to call her. "Dr. Weston, sorry I was on the documentary set when you called."

"Laurel, I have finished the satellite scan with all the settings designed to pick-up and detect the differing densities of materials lying beneath the surface of the terrain. Then I reset my instruments to detect this mysterious unknown material you think might be lying beneath the surface. Laurel, I thought I saw something. But to be sure, I re-adjusted my instruments to do the imaging from a different angle. Plus, I readjusted it to rule out any of our known metals. What I discovered, without doubt, is some strange and unknown material. Two objects mixed in the dirt, one very small, the other large enough to be your hidden craft."

"Wow–where is it?" Laurel squealed, unable to contain her excitement. "I detected the material far and deep inside the west end of Monks Mound. Therefore, you could not pick up anything using your current devices. I will transfer both findings onto two different topical maps and bring them to you tomorrow. I need to walk the grounds to help you understand how this imaging map corresponds to the actual markings, and how to interpret the overlay. I will call you when I arrange for a flight."

"Dr. Weston, we may be able to come and pick you up. Joann Maury, with the McMelton Corporation, along with my Director Alex Zukerman, came here this afternoon in her corporate plane. Let me find out if the plane's schedule is free and I will call you back."

Laurel knew her excitement showed on her face when she approached Joann and Alex. "I just got off the phone with Dr. Weston. You won't believe what she has found with her completed analysis." Laurel related the conversation except for the unknown materials and metals scans.

Joann stated, "We can go get her tomorrow. I will call and cancel my other appointments. Alex and I both need to be here to see all of her results."

The producers and the T.V. crew originally had planned on leaving after the interview with Director Zuckerman, but now decided to stay hoping to get an interview with Dr. Weston on her results of the satellite imaging.

CHAPTER 40

The team members were busy checking out the many rooms of their new living quarters. Some were sitting on the front porch, regardless of the cool evening. Their excitement was building with the news that Dr. Weston would be bringing the satellite results.

Stephanie found Laurel off to herself in her quarters. "Did Dr. Weston say anything about the craft, or the artifact you wanted her to look for?"

"She did," Laurel affirmed. "I'm excited and anxious to see precisely where it is located. Without giving much detail, she said it's on the west side of Monks Mound and would show us tomorrow."

"Holy Mother of God!" Stephanie said just above a whisper. "What time will she get here?"

"We are going after her in the morning. I'll never be able to sleep tonight. She said there was a lot of other buried pyramids, settlements with buildings, and tombs. Lots of hot spots, we could explore on foot." Their conversation was interrupted when her phone rang.

"Laurel, it's Alex, why don't you pick us up at six, we'll go out for breakfast, then on over to the airport, so our pilots can refuel and do their preliminary checks."

"That will be fine," Laurel replied.

"Is everyone getting settled in over there?"

"Oh yes. They're exploring all aspects of their new home."

"I'm anxious to see Dr. Weston's results. I'm not going to be able to sleep tonight. Why don't you meet me over at the Lounge for a drink? Maybe it will help us relax enough to get some shut-eye later."

"Fine, maybe it will. We're all keyed up, also. See you in a few minutes."

As Laurel and Stephanie walked down to the Lounge, she discussed her concern of what would happen when Dr. Weston exposed these strange and mysterious objects lying under Monks Mound.

"I don't see any way around it, since Dr. Weston will show it in her findings," Laurel uttered keeping her voice low.

"Maybe if you cautioned Dr. Weston to not reveal this part of the scan. . ."

"Let's just sit tight about this. I need to think this through a bit longer."

The girls opened the door to a very busy atmosphere of multiple conversations all playing out together above a soft musical background. Laurel knew Nick and Nigel were probably here. She did want to see Nick, but it was Alex who had asked her to have a drink. *Oh, what a tangled web her life had become.*

Both girls looked around, straining to see in the dim lighting when a familiar voice blurted, "Well, good evening Ms. Stephanie Barns and Ms. Laurel Robertson."

Stephanie acknowledged his greeting. "Good Evening to you, Charlie Sorkin!" she said as she reached out and patted his arm. Nick stood up and asked the guys seated to make room for the two. Laurel stared into Nick's hazel eyes. "Would love to join you guys tonight, but I'm here for a meeting with my Director. May I have a rain check?" Laurel turned and looking around the room, noticed Alex standing up in the back-corner waving to her.

"Stephanie, you can stay here if you like, or you're welcome to join Alex and me. In any case, I'm just having one drink with Alex, then we can walk back to our house together."

"I was trying to get your attention." Alex pulled out a chair for her. "I ordered you a margarita. Hope that is what you wanted. If not, we can change it."

"That's fine. I'm so keyed up, it's going to take something to bring me down."

"Me too. Laurel, I wanted to tell you, I finally cleared enough of the bad feeling I had with your grandmother to return her call. When I did, I was surprised at her apology for the remarks and threats she gave me the night of your birthday. I accepted her apology, assuring her I carried no resentment".

"Thank you, Alex, for telling me. It was my hope that you both could put this behind you. I too had some startling revelations during my visit."

"What do you mean?" Alex inquired, as he leaned in closer.

"I found out she had been keeping a lot of secrets from me about my mother and what happened at their last dig site in Arizona."

"Why on earth would she do that?"

Laurel kept sipping on her margarita, she liked the way it drowned some of her emotions. She looked up into Alex's clear blue eyes, searching for the man she used to love. She needed that man to be there for her tonight.

Alex reached across the table and took her hands in his. "Laurel, what did she keep from you?"

Laurel explained, as she returned the grip of Alex's hands. "This story I am about to tell you took several days to unravel and if it weren't for the help of Lawrence, I might not have ever found out what I did. Alex, I'm asking you to hold your judgment on this until you hear all of the story because at the end, you might better understand why she kept this from me." Laurel began the story. At the end of a second drink, she had finished.

"This is an unbelievable story. Do you have the drawing your mother made of the Aztec hieroglyphics?"

"Not the original drawing, but Grams drew what she remembered of my mother's drawing. I have this one. She claims she doesn't have the original drawing, or the artifacts Mother took out of the cave."

"Laurel, these men were willing to kill for these items and they said it wasn't in the wreckage. You know, they had to have put it somewhere before they left to go back to Springfield. Do you believe Barbara?"

"I just don't know Alex. But please listen, there is more. Tomorrow, Dr. Weston is going to present us first the original satellite imaging, the one we commissioned for her to do. This will be phenomenal; as she told me she found a lot of new buried pyramids and treasures."

Laurel continued, "Then Alex, I asked her to do two more image scans. This second one using the same settings as before, geared to pick up our known materials, but scanning inside Monks Mound in the area we couldn't get to with our ground radar and several other devices. The third image scan is where she changed the settings to rule out detecting all known materials, objects, soil composition, bone, anything known to modern humans. Leaving it to detect unknown materials, metals and objects."

"Laurel, what are you saying? What did you ask her to do?"

"With the west side of Monks Mound sinking more every year, and all of our instruments not able to scan far enough inside the west end to see why, I asked her to adjust her imaging to pick up something foreign to anything not known to be of this earth."

"And what did she find?"

"She found sufficient evidence of at least two sizable objects. One large enough that could possibly be a craft of some sort and another smaller object lying not far from the first, that possibly could be the artifact! Then she said there is something more and she will try and explain when she gets here. She charted it onto an overlay, with dimensional readouts."

"Laurel, do you fully understand what this means? The original commissioned scan alone is the find of a lifetime for any archaeologist. If the other imaging turns out to be the craft and artifact depicted with the Aztec hieroglyphics. . . well Laurel, you're going to need some ropes to tie you down to earth." Alex tilted his chair back on its hind legs and broke out into laughter.

Stephanie and Charlie jumped up from their table and came over to inquire what was so funny.

"Just a joke. Our Ms. Laurel here might just need some rope tie-downs, to hold her down to earth after she sees Dr. Weston's imaging report tomorrow," Alex proclaimed patting Laurel's arm with more laughter. Soon his laughter was catching and they all joined in.

Laurel felt better now that she shared with Alex the secrets her grandmother kept from her, along with the cave drawings, and what Dr. Weston discovered with her satellite imaging. Then Laurel remembered she needed to tell Joann before they looked at the results.

"Okay, I had more drinks than I intended. I hear my pillow calling me. It's time for us to head back, Stephanie."

"I most certainly agree. We both need some good ole shut eye." Stephanie turned to Charlie saying, "Good night my sweet, until we meet again!" She smiled and patted his full rosy check with a soft touch, then turned swaying her hips in a bouncy step as she headed towards the entry. Laurel grinned and wondered how many drinks Stephanie had consumed.

CHAPTER 41

A stormy, rainy day, gave way to clear, sunny skies in the University City of Columbia. Laurel held tight to the arms of her seat as Captain Richard brought the Phenom down to a smooth, easy touch on the runway. Laurel was relieved it was not a hard landing and eased her grip on the arms of her seat. As the plane wheeled closer toward the gate, Laurel saw Dr. Weston and her assistant come into view.

Dr. Weston waved her arm at them. Laurel had talked many times to Dr. Emily Weston, but hadn't seen her until now. She was a tall attractive woman, wearing a beige pant suit. Her hair coloring was unique; brunette with a natural white swatch across the bangs, spilling on into the right side, styled in a short cut.

Alex got out and loaded her equipment and luggage in the storage compartment at the rear of the aircraft. After they boarded Dr. Weston introduced her assistant, Jennifer Noor.

"We call her Jenny and I'm proud to call her my favorite niece. She's been working with me for the last three years."

Jenny laughed, explaining, "Actually, I'm her only niece." Jenny wore a smile that accompanied her petite young body of average height, with beautiful long brown hair, heavy with highlights.

Everything went smoothly on the return trip back until they got close to the East St. Louis air space and the stormy weather began creating turbulence for the aircraft. The storm that should have moved on east, was instead now stalled over the East St. Louis area. The Captain's voice came over the speakers, "Everyone in your seats. Keep your seatbelts fastened, ground control has us in a wide circular holding pattern, till this storm can clear enough for us to land."

Everyone became quiet. Jenny pulled the shade down on her window and Joann did the same. Alex and Dr. Weston were deep in conversation. Laurel was just far enough away to not hear any details, but knew it was about the images her satellite technology revealed. Laurel began squirming in her seat.

"Richard is an excellent pilot, Laurel." Joann said. "He was in the Air Force, flying missions in Afghanistan and has taken me and other museum officials over the entire U.S., Mexico, and South America. Both he and his co-pilot, Alan, make a good team, they'll take good care of us," Joann said with a reassuring smile.

The Captain's voice came over the intercom. "Traffic Control has cleared us to land. Stay seated. Seat belts fastened. They advised the severity of the thunderstorms has lessened, but still has heavy rain, so, we may still experience turbulence. We are beginning our descent now, Captain out."

The Phenom 300 was on its final approach lining up with the runway when the plane hit a downburst of air. The aircraft bucked and wobbled and the nose suddenly dropped. Laurel dug her fingers deeper into the arms of the seat and could feel the force against her body when they descended. The engines roared as the captain fought hard to bring the nose back up in a level position. Then there was a very loud bang, accompanied by a bright white light. Joann and Jenny moved in their seats, startled by the loud noise. Alex yelled, "Our right engine has been hit by lightning! It's on fire!"

At that moment, the captain announced, "Brace for impact! Brace! Brace for impact! Bend down and cover your head!"

There was another loud bang and the plane tilted sideways, bouncing from side to side as the captain fought to keep the plane steady.

Thoughts raced through Laurel's head. Is this it? Is this how I'm going to die? In a split second, Bishop Marin's image materialized before her saying, "Remember my child, your path is one of great challenges. It is not your time to parish. Your soul has traveled many incarnations for a single purpose. You are to help in bringing forth the fruits of humankind's labor into new birth. Be consciously aware of this my child. Be one with Jesus." Then just as fast as he appeared, he was gone.

The captain finally managed to get the plane leveled out. Soon the wheels slammed hard against the runway, then the plane bounced back up several feet and slammed down on the runway again. The right wing slid and scraped the runway, leaving a trail of sparks. The Phenom suddenly turned to the right grinding further into the runway, heading in the direction of another small jet waiting in line for take-off. Then the Phenom swirled again, just in time to miss the other jet, bringing itself to a stop in the grassy field.

Fire and smoke bellowed from the right engine and wing. Fire trucks immediately caught up to the plane and were spraying foam onto the right engine and side of the plane. Alex unfastened his seatbelt while shouting, "Everyone prepare to disembark. I will try to get the door open!" He made his way up the steep incline on the left side, grabbing and pulling on the fixtures until he reached the entrance hatch. He shoved up the lever and pushed the door open. The steps, now angled upwards, would not be any help for getting to the ground.

In the meantime Joann held her hand over her right thigh trying to get to the cockpit. Laurel took hold of Joann's arm to steady her and could see the captain leaning over his co-pilot, who appeared to be unconscious. Looking up he shouted, "Anyone hurt back there?"

"Jenny's got an arm injury. I have something wrong with my leg. Everyone else seems to be all right except for minor injuries," Joann reported.

The captain stood up and stepped through the door giving the command, "Deport the plane now!" He then made his way to assist them in debarking onto the fire truck that had jockeyed itself under the door. The EMT's climbed aboard, quickly strapped the co-pilot in a basket and lowered it down to one of the ambulances. The heavy rains and lightning had subsided, but the danger was growing as the fire crew were still combating the electrical fires caused by the extreme heat of lightning.

Joann and Jenny were loaded in the other ambulance and both left swiftly for the nearby Centreville Hospital.

The captain was last to leave with his logbook in hand, he turned back, quickly looking around, as if to say goodbye to the Brazilian built Phenom for the last time.

"We've got to save my Satellite scans. . .my instruments! My computers in the storage hold!" yelled Dr. Weston, as she grabbed Alex's arm.

"I'm on it." But Alex couldn't get close enough to the storage because of the heat. Two firefighters came to his aid. They pried the doors open, managing to get the luggage, computers, and the equipment out. Alex was helped aboard the fire truck, while the firefighters quickly loaded the equipment from the storage, except the long storage tubes that remained on the pavement. The firemen drug the hose closer toward the tubes. When Dr. Weston saw this, she screamed and yelled out, "No! No! Don't spray the storage tubes. You will ruin them!"

Dr. Weston, attempted to climb down off the truck, only to be stopped by a fireman pushing her back into her seat. "Stay seated. We are preparing to leave. We will take care of the tubes and bring them to the hanger."

The fire truck had just gotten halfway between the hanger and the crippled Phenom 300, when a horrific blast shook the ground. Everyone turned to see the remains of the once beautiful, highly proficient jet, spread over the runway.

CHAPTER 42

At the Terminal Building the captain and remaining passengers were provided with dry towels and first aid was administered by the extra EMT's.

Alex shook the captain's hand. "You are an excellent pilot, sir. You handled the aircraft superbly. I just wanted you to know Captain, I would fly with you anywhere, anytime. Then he wrapped his other arm around the captain's back embracing him.

Dr. Weston said, "That goes for me too." She kissed him on the cheek. Then she asked him, "Why on earth did Traffic Control clear us to land, when it was clearly not safe for us to do so?"

"That is an issue I will be taking up with the officials. I am going to request the official weather report prior to the time they instructed me to start my descent to land. The NTSB will run an investigation, but I want to rule out some irresponsible flight controller who just wanted to get all his planes on the ground."

"The terminal officials and police are coming into the room," Alex announced.

Laurel took a seat off by herself while they acquired statements from the captain, Alex, and Dr. Weston. Glad she was last in line, Laurel needed time to reflect on the events. *I hate landings! Now, more than ever– I really hate landings.*

What happened up there? Did I really see and hear Bishop Marin talking to me? It looked like him! Maybe, Laurel surmised, it was the stress of it all. She decided to call Joann and check on her and Jenny.

"Hello," Joann answered.

"Joann, it's Laurel. We have been detained at the terminal. They're taking our statements. I wanted to find out how everyone is."

"I'm here in the room with Jenny. They just finished taking x-rays of her right forearm and confirmed a minor break, just bad enough they want to put a cast on it. As for me, I have a bad puncture wound. I'll be all right."

"What about the co-pilot?" Laurel inquired.

"Doctor said he had a concussion and a nasty knot on his head. He was awake and talking when I last checked on him. But the doctor is keeping him overnight for observation. Jenny and I will be dismissed after they get done with her. Tell them the doctors and nurses are taking real good care of them, not to worry."

"I will tell them. We will leave here as soon as we can to come and get you two."

"Joann, I am so sorry, but thankful that everyone survived the ordeal with the plane. I know you guys left ahead of us and you probably are not aware of what transpired after you left."

"What do you mean? Is everything all right?"

"Joann, we were all aboard the fire truck and before we ever reached the terminal the Phenom blew up."

"Oh my God! I thought they had a handle on the fire when we left for the hospital. I bet Richard is distraught."

"There's more, Joann. The firefighters had to pry open the baggage storage doors. We don't know yet if Dr. Weston's computers and equipment will still work. They sprayed the storage tubes that housed our satellite images. They were starting to melt from the intense heat. The tubes are waterproof, but the end caps were swiveled somewhat, so moisture probably got in. We don't know yet if any of it is any good."

It was early afternoon when they were finally back at the house in Collinsville. Dr. Weston was busy checking her computers and the other equipment, while the rest turned their attention to the best method of retrieving the wet rolled up pages in one piece. Working in the office, Laurel carefully eased the inner pages out of one of the tubes while leaving the others. Alex went with Rosie and Aaron to the storage building, gathering some tools and long wooden stakes.

Working from the opposite end of the long table, Alex said, "Let me try and cut the tube loose, then we can see and cut around the part that is melted." Laurel continued the tedious plight of separating the wet pages.

"It's a good thing the paper is heavy enough to be lifted apart," Laurel proclaimed.

Dr. Weston remarked, "There are a total of four pages in one tube and two pages in the other."

Laurel, with Stephanie's help, lifted off the first wet page and draped it over the long stake, positioning it between the table and the file cabinet so it could dry. Three wet pages remained on the table. Next, they carefully draped the second page over another stake.

"Alex, you should have two pages left in that tube," Laurel said. "Yes, that's what we have discovered. Alex stopped momentarily to wipe sweat from his forehead. "I'm going slow, trying not to cut the paper."

"Could one of you guys round up a fan or two? I believe I saw one around here yesterday," Laurel said. "We sure need to have some air flow going in here."

"I've got one right here," Christina announced, bringing it into the room.

Alex and Rosie cut away the melted plastic storage container from the wet imaging paper and laid it out on one end of the work table. "Dr. Weston, could you decipher what this page is supposed to represent?"

"This is the imaging sheet of the unidentified metals that showed up in the central Cahokia area. Only it's missing some of the vital imaging I wanted to show you–another smaller piece of the same unidentified metal."

Alex turned and looked over to Laurel with an astonished look on his face, like he couldn't believe it, even though Laurel alerted him last night that Dr. Weston was bringing these images.

Rosie said, "Excuse me, Dr. Weston, did you say this was a chart on unidentified metals? Meaning metals not known to earth?"

"That is correct." Dr. Weston offered no further explanation as she glanced at Laurel. Laurel squirmed knowing Dr. Weston had thrown the ball back over in her court. Different explanations ran through her head.

"All right, listen up everyone! Through undisclosed sources, I had reason to suspect there was an unidentified flying craft, or ship that landed in the Cahokia area, sometime back in their early development. That's why I asked Dr. Weston to add this to her scans. As it turned out, this scan sheet does show there is something large enough to be a craft. We will be looking into this, but for right now, I caution you not to disclose this to anyone.

"Our main project is what showed up on the other scans. All the new possible pyramids and sites we need to investigate. We all need to be very thankful that most of the maps have been salvaged. We will know more when the paper has dried and Dr. Weston explains how to read these satellite images." The room erupted with noisy chatter as the young archaeologists' excitement spread.

"Quiet please! May I have your undivided attention. As your Director, I share in all the excitement you are feeling. I want to again caution everyone here to keep this knowledge you have just learned—under wraps. Do not discuss this project with anyone outside the team. Do not discuss this out in public, where it could be overheard. This means you cannot discuss this with your parents, siblings, or your significant other. If you do discuss it among yourselves, keep your voices low, making sure no one overhears you. We don't want the media to come swarming in, or the UFO investigators, and we certainly don't need the NSA to take over our project either. There will be strong penalties for those who do not comply."

Alex continued, "I'm sure you all want to be part of the findings. Your team captain, Ms. Robertson, has put so much of her time and knowledge to secure the approval for this high-tech project with Dr. Weston. Let's give both a round of applause to show our appreciation." After the applause died down, Laurel was bombarded with questions, some she could answer and others she would not.

"What about us three floaters? I for one, sure don't want to leave after a few weeks and go somewhere else."

Laurel turned to Alex. "Can't you make an exception for these three? This has become a security situation now, and they should be able to share in all the discoveries as well."

"Yes, due to the circumstances, they will be made permanent members, excluded from rotation," Director Zuckerman declared.

"Several members of the production crew are at the front door," Stephanie announced. "Are you able to talk with them now?"

Laurel replied, "Please tell them I will come out in just a few moments."

"I will go with you, Laurel," Alex said. "They may want something more than just to see how we are. Remember they are reporters, too. It's best they not know about the unidentified metal just yet." They both stepped outside to talk with the production members.

"Wow, we just heard about your ordeal with the jet," Nick blurted out.

"We hear you're lucky to be alive," Nigel added.

Charlie remarked, "You two look pretty good, despite your brush with the infinite."

"Well, I for one, am glad to be on the ground," Laurel reflected giving way to a big smile.

"I'll never complain again about driving taking too long," Alex said. "So how did you guys hear about our near disaster?"

"We were working in the van when one of our tech's picked it up through our news network," Nick replied. "We remembered you guys were going after Dr. Weston and her NASA satellite results and hoped this wasn't your plane. Later, when they showed the wreckage, we noticed the corporate logo on what was left."

Laurel could feel Nick's desire to be close to her, but she was standing beside Alex. This would not be the right time to show his concern.

"Did you get the Satellite results?" Nigel asked.

Laurel answered, "We had a problem with the scanned printout getting wet and some scorched areas, but we are working on salvaging them."

"Have you spoken with any news reporters about the crash landing yet?" Nigel asked.

Alex answered. "No, we drove straight here." Joann Maury drove up in her rental car, along with Jennifer. They joined Laurel and Alex on the porch and Alex whispered in her ear about giving a statement on the plane crash to their TV associates. Mrs. Maury turned and faced the crew.

"Mrs. Maury, may we have an exclusive on this interview?"

"All right, if you promise to report the truth of this entire mishap." The producers agreed and the cameras were set and rolling.

Nigel started the interview "Did you all see the lightning hit the engine? Could you see flames from the engine? Where were you when the plane exploded?"

Nick asked, "How long have the pilots flown this particular jet?"

"They have flown this jet for the past six years with no problems. Before this they flew another type of small business jet for the McMelton Corporation. These two pilots are experienced with impeccable records," Mrs. Maury affirmed. They answered each question in turn, then Mrs. Maury raised her hand stating, "This is all for now. I think we all need to rest."

"Please," Nick said. "I have just one final question. When can you tell us what was discovered with the high-tech NASA Space Satellite Scans.

Alex came forward. "We don't know anything about the results yet, as we previously stated, the printed sheets received water damage and in some places are even scorched."

Laurel stepped up beside Alex adding, "We are working on restoring the material as fast as we can. We will let you know as soon as possible." With the interview over they were again busy working in the office. Dr. Emily was consulting with her assistant Jenny about the problems she discovered with the special computer they brought with them. Laurel knew she still needed to explain to Joann why she asked Dr. Weston to run the extra scans.

"Joann, I need to speak with you privately about a new development. Is this a good time for you?"

"Sure, I have time right now. What have you got?" Joann inquired.

CHAPTER 43

Laurel led the way through her bedroom to a sliding door that opened out to a small private balcony. "Joann, I wanted to bring you up to date on some new developments away from the team members. I feel they don't need to know as much detail that I am about to share with you." Laurel explained some of what she learned when she went home over the break.

"Laurel, what was your source of information on this UFO Craft and why do you think it is reliable?"

"My grandmother told of some secrets she kept from me all of my life." Laurel continued with most of the story. When she finished she stepped inside her room, returning with the drawing her grandmother gave her, handing it to Joann. Laurel let her study the drawing for a few moments.

Joann looked up from the drawing and stated, "This appears to be an actual map of three crafts landing in three different geographical areas."

"Yes, that's right. Do you recognize the location of the one in the middle?" Laurel asked.

"Well, it looks like the Aztec Temples in Central Mexico. But what about the small group of people who are moving away from this empire, heading some distance toward that cave?"

"This is the priest and two children with four warrior guards accompanying them. This is the Aztec Cave that my mother found and this drawing was on the wall, less some of my mothers detail." Laurel went on explaining about the artifacts her mother took from the cave, and how powerful and dangerous one of them was.

"Laurel, how is the clothing, jewelry, and this artifact relevant to this third ship on the drawing that looks to be landing in the Cahokia area?"

"Since there was a powerful artifact found with the ship that landed in the Aztec area, it is likely one accompanied the other ships also."

"Laurel, your mother finding the hieroglyphs on the wall and the actual artifact device that went with the ship that landed there in Central Mexico is proof that the map is a true rendition of the actual phenomenal event. I would guess told by an Aztec priest. Where are the items your mother found? What museum are they displayed in?"

"Joann, my grandmother claims my mother took them somewhere while she was busy packing all our things, getting ready to go to Springfield. She claims she does not know where my mother hid them."

"But Laurel, we still don't know if it is in the Cahokia area, or even where in the park it could even be. All of this is just speculation. There have been archaeologists digging for years around here and have not found anything relating to what you are telling me."

"But Joann, you just said this map and the artifact my mother found was proof that this is all true."

"This is not the actual map and the artifact your mother took out of the cave. It can't be produced. Therefore, it can't be proved."

"But Joann, there is a purpose I am telling you all of this. We soon will have proof." Laurel smiled as she stood from her chair.

"What do you mean?" Joann looked up with a puzzled expression on her face.

"I asked Dr. Weston to run a scan to pick up on unidentified metal in the Cahokia area. It worked. We have two actual satellite scans–both showing an object large enough to be a space craft. It also showed a smaller object, very close by, that could be the Artifact device. This part of the scan got seared to the plastic storage container, but they remembered which direction it was from the craft."

"My heavens! An actual scan showing where the craft is located? I must admit I never really believed in the UFO phenomenon until now–it looks like we are going to provide some proof."

"Yes, isn't it exciting?" Laurel exclaimed.

A special meeting was called with the officials only. The Vice-President, Director, Team Leader and Dr. Weston and her assistant. Decisions and changes needed to be made. One of which, was how to make their office and house more secure. Laurel got on the computer and ordered a locked file cabinet large enough for the scan sheets, then called their property owner Coleton Cloud, to see about changing the office door and all outside entry doors, to more secure ones with better locks.

Bars needed to go on the lower windows. Some negotiating with the cost was agreed upon.

"I have called in some computer geeks out of St. Louis, a branch of the firm I use in Columbia. Hopefully they can see what's wrong with my equipment. They will be here within two hours," Dr. Weston stated.

Laurel stood gazing at the unidentified metal scan lying on the table, wondering how this would read out when it was fully dry and placed with their corresponding topographic sheet. Jenny came and stood beside her. "I can almost see it from my memory, even without the topographic sheet, I am almost as excited as you are. It's this waiting that is the hardest to do."

"Jenny, just how far away is the smaller spot of metal from the larger one?"

"Not very far. We will measure it tomorrow, placing the two sheets together will give you a better understanding as to the angles."

Evening came and the office door remained closed and off limits, while Dr. Weston and the Geek crew worked on her computers and other machines. After several hours, and some consulting with the technicians in Columbia, they left to acquire replacement parts. It was getting late and the four staying in the motel left for the night. Laurel changed into her night shirt and stretched out on her bed when her phone rang. "Hey Grams," Laurel answered.

"I just heard on the news there was a plane crash near where you are working. Surely you were not in this were you?" Barbara's voice had a nervous tone.

"I was, Grams. But don't worry, I'm all right. Everyone managed to get off although some suffered minor injuries. I was scared beyond words, but I'm okay. Our satellite scans Dr. Weston made for us got wet and slightly damaged, along with her computers and equipment. We have spent the day retrieving the scans and have them drying on racks in the office."

"Oh Laurel, I am so glad you and your associates are okay! Was Alex there with you? Why on Gods earth were you traveling in that storm?"

"Alex was one of the passengers. It was sunny in Columbia when we left to head back to East St. Louis. Laurel went on explaining the details of what happened.

Laurel and her grandmother talked for a while longer then Laurel confessed, " It's been an ordeal and a long day, I'm a bit-tired Grams. How about I call you tomorrow evening? We should know what the scans picked up by then."

"That would be fine, I'm so glad you are all right. You crawl in bed and get some sleep for now. Love you."

Laurel turned out her light and surrendered her stressful body to that of relaxing sleep. But she was soon engaged in a night of dreams filled with action and fearful events.

The morning came early for her; she awoke with the dream still alive, projecting through to her reality. She did not move. She kept her breathing shallow. . . inviting, allowing, then she began to see more. *Walking, lots of people around me. . .we're all walking.* Suddenly the scene changed– *we are running now. . . people hiding behind boulders. We are under attack by Indians! I took cover behind a wagon. A soldier falls by me. . . an arrow in his chest. I take his gun, and I'm shooting at the Indians!* Laurel's phone rang–jarring her back to this reality.

"Hello?" Laurel answered in a raspy voice.

CHAPTER 44

"Good morning Ms. Laurel, this is Colton Cloud. I hope I didn't awaken you, but just wanted you to have a heads up. My carpenters will be at your house in a few minutes."

"Yes Colton, I'm just getting up, that will be fine," Laurel related, pushing herself to get dressed while thoughts of last night's Indian attack from another dimension was still lingering with her.

Everything became busy from this point forward. They installed the new secure office door and were busily taking care of the rest on the list. Dr. Emily Weston and Jennifer spoke to Laurel, Alex, and Joann Maury, explaining how they arrived at some of their conclusions.

"When this technology was used in Egypt, using the street plans of Tanis, once the Capital of Ancient Egypt, the satellite scan found the scale was four times greater than previously imagined." Dr. Weston further explained, "Using this same principal, but with changes, due to your material composition, we found something just as astonishing. We found shifts in the frequency of high-magnitude floods corresponds to the emergence and decline of Cahokia."

"Wow," Laurel gasped. "That must have been a huge surprise."

"But all the archaeological excavations have shown direct evidence of flooding is rare in the Cahokia area." Dr. Alex Zuckerman commented.

"We studied the layout of the Mississippi River as it might have existed at Antient Cahokia at the time of their largest changes, around A.D. 1050. The river was then a great distance away from where it is today." By now, the rest of the team was up and gathered around the table listening with amazement showing in their faces.

Dr. Weston picked up the first image sheet from the rack, laying it over the topographical sheet. "This image scan will show you there is a lot more to your Ancient Cahokia that has eluded you." She pointed to the sheet. "The red color is the field. These marks in blue indicate settlements that were previously invisible to you." She continued to point out how to read the graph. "This different kind of mark in green indicates buried pyramids. You will note there are four on this sheet alone. This swirl mark here in pink, designates a tomb of some sort, lying just beneath this area. Then we have these scattered yellow pock marks believed to be various artifacts."

"Now that you have seen what the different imaging marks and colors mean, I will change the bottom topographical area and place the corresponding satellite imaging with it. Waa la! Just like magic, suddenly this invisible world becomes visible. Your next step will be to go into the field with a GPS receiver along with your map to pinpoint your dig sites."

The chatter in the room began to escalate as Dr. Weston changed out all four sheets, going over each to explain the NASA satellite imaging.

"Jennifer, you have the summary totals. Would you read them for us, please?"

"Certainly. We found two new possible settlements; eight new pyramids; fifty new tombs; over fifteen hundred new artifact sites!" The room was filled with cheers and applauding, everyone was overwhelmed with excitement and chatter about all the new discoveries. The archaeologists, beaming with wonderment, took their new satellite results and plans to the field to begin marking the different sites. Dr. Emily Weston and Jenny went with the group to give further instructions. They worked until darkness set in, marking the settlements and pyramids first, with plans to start marking the tombs in the morning.

Dr. Zuckerman called a meeting with Joann Maury and Laurel. "Now that we have made a good start marking our dig sites, I feel we need to call in more help and establish several dig sites, instead of just one at a time. Also, I want to see what's on this mysterious unidentified metal sheet."

Joann stated, "I like the idea of bringing in more teams, but this is Laurel's project. Laurel, how do you feel about all this?"

"I will agree to bringing in no more than three other teams of experienced archaeologists and pulling in some students from the colleges to help us for this summer. I want to keep this project in my name, with all findings accredited to me, and no one besides myself to write papers on these findings."

Alex replied, "I understand what you are wanting, but Laurel, I don't think you see the scope of this. We haven't even looked at the mystery metal and material scans yet. Depending on what we find, this site alone could take all of your attention."

Joann interjected, "All right, let's not decide on anything yet until after we see the mystery scan. Dr. Weston will be back here in the morning and we can consult with her. In the meantime, Laurel, you can appoint one of your team to oversee the field work."

That evening, after dinner, Laurel took out for a walk wanting to be alone to clear her head. She needed to see the big picture. Alex may have been right about the size this project was escalating into. Even when she was on his team, he never had any project equivalent to this one, and he had an assistant to help him. She felt Alex's original intentions were to win her back but power, authority, and fame are part of his basic underlying character.

If I don't watch out, Laurel thought, he will worm his way into my project and take it over, with me along with it. Laurel knew how he liked to run things. Could she trust him? She knew what she had to do. Her walk took her close to the Motel Bar. Wondering if Nick was inside, she called his cell.

"Well hello, Ms. Laurel. I was just thinking of you. How are you this fine evening?"

"Where are you Nick?"

"I just walked inside our friendly neighborhood watering hole. Why not come and join me?"

"I was out for a walk and I'm just outside the door."

Nick went out to greet her, walking her to a table away from the other group so they could have some privacy. "I have been thinking about you and your crew all day. I was walking to our van and noticed you across the plaza marking several spots."

"We have been interpreting our results from the NASA Satellite scans. Nick, there are over fifteen hundred new sites!"

"Laurel, that's fantastic, I know you worked extremely hard on this project. Did you have any idea there would be this many?"

"I knew when they used this process in Egypt they found an unbelievable number of new sites, but in comparison, I never thought the scans would show this many undiscovered sites here at Cahokia."

Nick reached over to give Laurel a hug. "I'm so excited for you." He kissed her on the cheek. Then he backed away. Laurel clasped his hands in hers as she talked.

"Nick, I've been walking around just trying to clear my head." She went on explaining the problems and conflicts she faced with her ex-boyfriend. "This is my first big discovery and Alex is trying to convince me that it's too big to work by myself."

"So, are you saying he wants to work this with you? How would this even be possible, since he has to oversee the other teams in various locations?"

"He has not come out and said that yet, and Joann tabled everything until tomorrow. You see, Nick, there is another satellite scan I asked Dr. Weston to run in addition to the first one. We will be looking at it tomorrow morning. This one scan may take all of my time, depending what it shows."

"Laurel, what kind of scan are you talking about? How is it different than the others?

"Nick, I can't disclose that right now, for we need to keep the media out of this one for a while. But even not adding any more to what we already have, it looks like I will need help." Laurel began to relax sipping on her nightcap. She enjoyed being around Nick. She felt his nature was genuine and sincere, and his keen since of humor always kept her feeling joyful.

Laurel was up early with anticipation for what Dr. Weston was going to reveal. Only Laurel, Alex, and Joann would be permitted to attend. Laurel unlocked their new secure file cabinet and pulled out the wide sheet marked Un-ID Metals Scan. Dr. Weston laid the scan over its corresponding topographical sheet and started her presentation. "As you can see this scan takes in the Monks Mound area and it shows the location and the size of this particular unknown metal object. It is large enough to compare to an unidentified flying craft, or at least what some of the UFO people have reported. Now I couldn't be sure of its exact shape, so I changed my instruments around to come into this place from another angle. It took some work on my part, but it eventually paid off." They watched as Dr. Weston changed the scan sheet to the second sheet, revealing the exact shape of a triangular craft.

"Wow!" Laurel proclaimed, giving a big smile to the rest of the group.

"That is astonishing!" Joann said as she stared at the scan,

"Laurel, you tried to tell me something totally amazing was going to show up, but I couldn't wrap my mind around it until now," Alex declared.

"There is believed to be an artifact which is no longer on this scan because it seared into its protective container," Laurel proclaimed. "But Jennifer said she remembers approximately where it was on the scan."

"It was about three feet to the northeast of this tip of the craft." Jennifer pointed on the sheet. They took measurements so they would know just where on Monks Mound this craft laid.

"We still don't know why the west side keeps slipping down," Alex said.

"It appears they built over the top of this craft on the west side of Monks Mound," Joann remarked.

"We are going to have to consult a good engineer and geologist to see if we can tunnel over to this," Laurel stated. "Actually, it's the artifact that interests me most."

"Why does the artifact hold your interest more that this craft?" Alex asked.

Joann said, "Yes, why Laurel?"

"It's that dream I had, the night we stayed on top of Monks Mound. The Cahokia Princess pleading to her grandfather to tell her the code of symbols, to open the artifact the gods left behind, so she could save her people. This artifact must be a device to communicate with the gods, or whoever these unidentified beings are. If we can tunnel over to get this device, maybe we could talk to them."

"We may not be able to take the craft out without causing a collapse of the whole Mound, and this can't be allowed to happen," Alex said. "But we might be able to go inside. Think about that and what discoveries we might make."

"All right," Joann said. "Let's get a reputable Engineer-Geologist, then we will find out what can be done."

CHAPTER 45

Three days later, they met with an engineer in the office. Explaining they needed him to be secretive, he agreed and studied their plans. Laurel asked, "Do you think it's possible to tunnel over to these unidentified objects?"

The engineer explained, "It all depends on several factors. We take into consideration the length, depth, soil, and geological conditions, along with the topography and structures that surround it. First my team and I will do testing with our instruments then do computer analysis to see if it is even possible."

"Can you trust your team to be discreet?" Alex questioned.

"Yes, we have worked on other secretive operations in the past, including government projects. My men value their reputations and their jobs. They will keep their mouths shut."

After the engineer left, Joann asked Laurel, "Have you reached a decision on what we talked about in regards to bringing in more help?"

"First, Alex, what were your thoughts and intentions when you said I needed a lot more help?" Laurel wanted Alex to spell out his intentions, not leaving any doubt in her mind.

"Well, as you know from working on some of my teams, a team captain can only do so much and still do a good job."

"Alex, you had at least two assistants on the large jobs, of which I was one."

"But, Laurel, this job is much larger than any of mine in the past. Please don't misunderstand me. I realize you gained valuable on-the-job training, but you still don't have enough experience to run an operation of this magnitude. Yes, you need to bring in more teams, an experienced partner, and several assistants to work some of the new satellite areas. This is a massive production." Joann then asked to speak to Laurel alone and Alex left the office.

"Laurel, you seem to be getting along with Alex in these past few weeks, but I want to hear it from you. Has he quit attempting to win you back, or is he still trying?"

"Joann, we are getting along fairly well. He seems more content with the work here. It's keeping him busy enough that I think he has accepted being just friends, at least for now."

"This is what I hoped for, Laurel. I have watched you both over the past few weeks and noticed you two do work well together, when you put your minds to it. Alex has the experience we are looking for. Do you think you could accept him if he would consent to be your new partner?"

"Joann, Alex's character and personality is that of being in authority. He could never be told what to do. He would be constantly telling me what to do."

"If we laid out in writing the ground rules that this project is yours, with you getting credit for being the initiator, along with credit for any published papers, do you think you could work with this?"

"In the past, he left my name off any papers he published, even though I helped him."

"I understand, Laurel. You two will have to leave your past in the past. Think of the big picture here. Even if we find there is no way to get to the craft and artifact, the fifteen hundred new discoveries are the prize here. The extraterrestrials are a bonus."

"I doubt if he will ever consent to leave his new director position to do this,"

"First, I must have your consent before I talk with him. What do you say, Laurel?"

"Can you give me thirty minutes to myself?"

"Sure, take more if you need to," Joann said. "Just text me when you're ready."

Laurel had to get away from the house to be alone with her thoughts. She got in her FJ and drove over to the park. Getting out, she walked the path, strolling past some tourists. All the while, going over the pros and cons of whether she should work with Alex again. Would they get along? Would he try to completely take over?

She climbed up the steps of Monks Mound, continuing to hash out why she left him to start with. She was trying to be honest with herself. She loved him, but this thing lacking in their relationship. . .what was it? Was it his lack of commitment to her? Did she want to get married and he never asked? Would she have said yes to his proposal? Was this an emotional feeling within her that was lacking? Perhaps his shallowness in his spirituality? She knew he didn't share her exact spiritual beliefs, but even she had changed some of hers in the last several years.

She went to the Northeast corner and sat, continuing to meditate for guidance, paying no mind to the time. For some mysterious reason, this site felt peaceful to her. The energies seemed to swirl around Laurel's body, the deeper she went within. She allowed herself to go further into her consciousness, seeking an answer of what she should do.

Laurel began to see the princess in white forming in front of her. She spoke with her, giving comfort and advice. *"My spirit lives within you. At one time, we were sisters traveling through this universe together, separating only momentarily, when I spent a life as a Cahokia Princess. While being human I found a way to interact with our gods, leading my people to safety through the underground caverns, deep within the earth."*

Laurel's phone rang pulling her back into reality. It took her a few moments to get her bearings. "Hello," Laurel answered in a draggy voice.

"Laurel, it's Stephanie. We dug down around three feet and we are already starting to find things. Where are you? Do you want to come and have a look?"

"I'll be right there." On the way down the steps, she went over in her mind what had taken place in her meditation. The princess said her spirit lives on in me. She said she was able to converse with our gods. Just who are these gods? Are they the ones that created us? She used the plural of God. Is there more than one? This drove Laurel's desire to obtain that artifact more than ever. Laurel reached the dig site and went down in the trench where they were working. Stephanie brushed aside the fine sandy fill to reveal a portion of the first find of a new pyramid the satellite imaging program disclosed for them.

"Good work! " Laurel proclaimed. The team took measures to put up more secure barriers to keep out any curious tourists.

She then called Joann Maury, Dr. Weston, and Alex to come and meet them. Within minutes everyone gathered at the site. Then Laurel called Nick.

"We made our first discovery. You may want to put this in your documentary."

"Where are you?"

"We are just east of Monks Mound." Nick and Nigel took photos of the team working the new pyramid site and had a brief interview with

Laurel and Dr. Weston. After all the excitement simmered down, Laurel told Joann she'd reached a decision.

Back at the office, Laurel and Joann sat discussing what was needed for her project. Laurel gave her consent to partner with Alex if he abided by the contract rules, with her putting down what those rules would be. Joann met with Alex explaining her new offer.

Alex said, "I will temporarily give up my position as director to partner with Laurel on this project, until most of the new sites are worked. Then I'll assume the Director position again." They agreed on the contract and both signed the agreement.

By the second week the engineers and geologists had devised a tunneling plan to reach the unidentified image that lay underneath Monks Mound, one that was safe and would not harm the ten-story prehistoric earthwork. The process was well underway when Laurel commented to Alex, "Our black-out fence installed around the parameters of their work area is only hiding some of the work. The tourists are watching up on top of Monks Mound, taking photos of the engineer's tunneling equipment."

"Our information signs we put up explaining the work being done as restoration of the damage done by the sinking west side may be enough information to appease tourists, but this is not fooling some of the tribes. More and more are starting to congregate out by the building and parking area," Alex stated. "Their gathering is causing too much attention; the media are starting to ask questions. I averted one news team this morning."

"Now for our friends with the World Wonders and Mystery T.V., that continue to be camped on the park perimeters, we can't fool them any." Alex shook his head.

"Just a reminder, we are under contract with them," Laurel said.

"But when is this contract supposed to end?"

"Originally, they announced they would be showing the results of Dr. Weston's satellite findings."

"Laurel, I know you are good friends with Nick Kenyon. I have to ask; Did you tell him what we were drilling for?"

"Alex, a few weeks ago, I told Nick there was another part of the satellite imaging scan. I told him I would disclose it later, only after, and if, we found anything. That's all he knows. Their airing date for the documentary is only eight days away, so they will be pulling out soon."

"Maybe not, because they are doing a lot of the work in that large technician van of theirs."

"I will go and have a talk with him, but first why don't we go over to the parking area and try to reason with the protesters."

"I'll get the security guards to go with us," Alex stated.

The two climbed upon the rock ledge at the Interpretive Center, overlooking the parking area to address the crowd of protesters. Alex raised his arms in the air as he shouted to get their attention over their chanting.

"Please, may we have your attention," Alex shouted trying to override their noisy chants. He introduced themselves stating, "We would like to hear all of your concerns."

Laurel joined in. "At the same, time we want to assure you, that as archaeologists, we want to preserve this historical monument that has slowly, but surely, been listing on the west side. Many attempts have been made in the past with no results."

"We have hired one of the best engineers and geologist to oversee this problem. They are tunneling over to this area to place stabilizers far beneath so it does not collapse in the future."

The crowd toned down, listening, then asking questions of their own. Various news reporters joined in with more questions. Nick and Nigel were there also. Laurel caught Nick's eyes, locking in on hers. She shook her head back and forth attempting to signal him not to ask any questions. Laurel called Nick that evening, asking if he would meet with her. They met at the back table in the lounge.

"Thank you, Nick, for not blowing our cover out there this afternoon."

"Laurel, I think the two of you really did some good, talking to those demonstrators this afternoon, as most went home. Our technicians are going to take the mobile units back to Chicago tomorrow to finish up at the studio."

Nick paused. "Laurel, I had my phone in my hands, about to punch your number, when you called." Nick lowered his voice, and leaning closer to her, he placed his hands with hers. "My part of our contract is fulfilled, as far as the corporation is concerned. I have been patient, waiting until this time to be with you, without the threat of being fired."

He slid closer to her, touching her, stealing a kiss. "I have the three-day weekend off. Come go away with me. Both of us need to get away from our work for a few days," he whispered in her ear.

Nick's passion was getting to Laurel. "I would like to get away for a few days." Laurel sighed.

"Go back to you house, make arrangements to be gone and pack a small bag, throw in your swim suit. I'll get my things and pick you up in thirty minutes." Nick escorted Laurel to her vehicle and gave her a passionate kiss. "I'll see you in thirty minutes. I'll park right by your bedroom."

Laurel made arrangements for her three-day getaway, leaving her new partner, Alex in full charge.

"Just where are you going?" Alex asked.

"I'm going on a three-day cruise with Kourtney, and a few other of my Springfield friends," Laurel replied.

"I bet I can guess one of those friends might be Professor Vaughn," Alex mumbled.

"Why Alex, you sound a bit jealous. But I don't know that he's coming." Laurel couldn't hide the joyfulness in her voice.

"Be sure and keep your phone on. Better yet, give me an alternative number where I can reach you. You never know what could happen around here."

Laurel packed her bag, then knocked on Stephanie's bedroom door to inform her about her secret weekend with Nick.

"Stephanie, please do not tell Alex where I'm going, or who I'm going with. I told him I would be with Kourtney and some other friends from Springfield. If he knows who I'm with, he could make trouble."

"Hey girl, you go and have fun! It's about time. You've been working hard, and you deserve a vacation."

CHAPTER 46

The team had the weather station on while they were eating breakfast. "That line of thunderstorms looks pretty big coming down from the northwest," Alex said. "You guys better get those tents up before it gets here."

"But look down here, out of Oklahoma, this is moving northeast. We may end up getting a double whammy," Aaron remarked.

It was mid Friday morning when the team received a weather update on their cell phones. The line of storms coming in from the northwest was traveling faster than originally reported.

"Let's hurry up, Aaron. Get this equipment loaded and get it over to the site," Alex ordered. Around 11:00 am, Alex received a call from the lead engineer with the progress of the tunneling.

"We've got excellent news Dr. Zuckerman. We just broke through to the Alien Space Craft! Do you want to meet me at the entrance so we can guide you through?"

"Wow, so soon? I'm over at the house in Collinsville. I am leaving right now. See you shortly." Alex arrived at the entrance site within minutes where he found the engineers waiting for him.

"We made a ninety-degree angle straight up," the engineer explained. "We then started clearing out all the debris around the front part of the craft. She's a beauty, Dr. Zuckerman!"

Alex put on protective gear and followed the engineers into the tunneling system until they reached the smaller upward shaft.

"Our probe turned out to be exactly where we needed it to be. So we made it larger, bracing it with strong reinforcements," the engineer explained. "We will build some sturdy stairs here, but for now our ladder will do. I wanted to show you what is here first."

Alex climbed upward on the twelve-foot ladder into the clearing they had made. Crawling around on his hands and knees he gazed at the shiny metal-like craft that was only partly uncovered. He reached over with his hand to touch, then hesitated. But then he went ahead and felt the exterior of the alien craft, running his hand along it, brushing off some of the soil.

"I always wondered what an alien ship felt like." Alex's voice vibrated with excitement. "It looks like metal, but it feels different. There are these small circular protrusions on the underside of this lower section. Did you notice that?"

"Yes, we wondered if this was part of their propulsion system. We are just as curious as you are. It looks as if they buried it, building this whole mound over it."

"The question is, what was the reason for concealing it?" Alex remarked.

"Can you tell how long it's been here, using some of your testing equipment?"

"I believe we might be able to date it by taking a few samples." Alex took a small roll of plastic bags from his tool belt. He filled one with soil that was still stuck next to the craft, untouched by human hands. Then he took another knife tool and tried to scrape off some of the ship material from the upper section. Not getting anything, he pulled a file from his tool belt. Working on the small protruding circular part, he was able to get a small sample.

"This side to the right looks to be part of a wing edge, maybe." Alex pointed.

"So far, we haven't discovered an entrance, but we have only begun. It's hard to tell just yet how big she is." the engineer declared.

"Will you be able to dig all the way around it? It probably will be too large to even consider trying to remove it. We can better assess that when you uncover more, but first, we need a strong gate across the entrance and I will get more security guards for tonight. Then go ahead with building a better stairway where you have the ladder."

"We'll get right to work on that steel security gate. We need to stabilize the area around the craft as we go, making sure it doesn't cave in while we remove more of the soil and debris. All of our stabilizers will help stop the listing on this west side also."

"You go ahead, call me later. I've got to get over to help them tie down a couple of tents at our dig site. We got an update that the line of storms is going to be here sooner than expected." Alex hurried out the tunnel entrance.

When Alex made it to the dig site, they had one tent well anchored, with Stephanie and Gideon putting on the finishing holds. But the other one, they were about to lose. Rosie was busy trying to anchor down his corner, with Christina holding tight on the other end of the long rectangular tent. Justin drove his corner in hard with the sledge hammer.

"Hang on, Christina, I'm coming over to help you!" Alex shouted above the popping noise of the canvas. The gusts of wind were strong. Then came the rain, but the team kept on working. Aaron returned from his trip to their storage building, backing the truck in close to where they were.

"You guys look like you could use a hand," Aaron remarked. "I found better tie down stakes than you are using. Bet they could hold in a hurricane," he laughed. No one joined in with his laughter. They were already experiencing thirty mile an hour wind gusts.

Additional noise could be heard over the wind and popping canvas when a Black Hawk Chopper from Fort Leonard Wood touched down in the spacious Grand Plaza. The archaeologists finished securing their tents then rushed towards the chopper.

"Dr. Alex Zuckerman, I am commissioned to bring you back to the base to be interviewed concerning your activities here, along with the tunnel engineer, Dr. Laurel Robertson, Dr. Emily Weston and Mrs. Joann Maury."

"What do you mean? Are you arresting us? What are we being charged with? What authority do you have to take us anywhere?" Dr. Zuckerman demanded. The others joined in with their questions and protests of the military's actions.

"You are not under arrest. Homeland Security wants an interview with the five of you. We are escorting you to Scotts Air base, then on to Fort Meade where you will meet up with our investigators. Where is Dr. Laurel Robertson, Dr. Weston and Mrs. Maury?" the captain inquired. "We need to talk to all of you."

"There may be a long wait for Dr. Robertson, as she took off on a Caribbean Cruise." Alex said, then turned to Rosie. "You're in charge until I get back. Get hold of Dr. Robertson. There are phone numbers for her on the office bulletin board."

The soldiers got out and started placing a wide perimeter of barricades blocking off the tunneling area in the state park. Alex approached the captain. "Why are you doing this? My team has complete authority and we are under a contract with the Chicago Museum to work this ground. Tell me why you shut the tunneling down. This is how we plan to shore up the west side of Monks Mound."

"This is for your own safety. You are not permitted to cross this barricade. No one is." He instructed his troops to stand guard around the barricades, then the captain sent a ground unit to retrieve Dr. Weston and Mrs. Maury to the awaiting Black Hawk.

CHAPTER 47

Nick and Laurel were the only sunbathers on the upper deck of the Majestic Yacht not long after the helicopter landed.

"This is so wonderful that one of your Mystery Channel sponsors invited you and a guest to come along on this little outing on his beautiful yacht," Laurel said. "And I'm thankful you reminded me to bring a bathing suit."

"Would you like another one of these Majestic specials?" Nick asked.

"Thank you, I believe I could manage another one of those." Laurel smiled. Nick raised his hand getting the bar attendant's attention, and he promptly came over to get their order.

"I was needing to go somewhere for some fun and recreation." Laurel looked out over the relative calm waters, noting an island in the far distance. "Do you know what that is?"

"That should be the island of Bimini," Nick replied. "Have you ever been there?"

"No, but I have heard some archaeologists talking about the large stones and paths that were discovered underwater on the far side of the island, believed to be some remains of Atlantis." Laurel applied more lotion and turned to Nick. "Would you be so kind, Mr. Kenyon, to help me out?" Turning her back to him, she unbuckled the straps to her top.

Nick took the lotion. "I would be more than happy to accommodate your wishes Ms. Robertson." Nick applied the lotion, moving his hands in strokes that extended past her back, touching softly on the sides of her breast, massaging lightly, teasing her with his strokes, then sliding his hands gently toward her back again. He leaned against her, softly kissing her ear, then whispering, "Have I told you how stunningly beautiful you look in that suit, Ms. Robertson?" Before she could reply, the bar attendant appeared with another round of Majestic specials, along with a tray of cheeses, grapes and other tropical delights.

Laurel, still holding the front of her suit with her hands, turned toward Nick. "Thank you, Mr. Kenyon, I enjoyed your application, plus your compliments." She then took one hand away from her suit, reaching to the tray for the small wedge of pineapple. Tasting it, she licked her lips. "Oh, so good. Would you like a taste?" She placed it close to his lips.

Nick took a taste of the pineapple. "So sweet." Nick placed his arms around her and gave her a passionate kiss. Laurel returned his kiss, with her hands moving to the nape of his head, gently stroking her fingers through his thick dark hair. Her desire had built over the past few weeks. It had been a long wait just to be alone, away from co-workers' prying eyes.

Their embrace ended when they heard voices from a group of people coming up from the lower portion of the vast yacht. Separating, Nick's eyes became larger as he smiled in admiration at her bare breast with the orchid tattoo. "My Laurel, you are just full of surprises."

"Oops!" Laurel shrieked, quickly grabbing her top that had fallen to the deck.

Nick, still sporting a capacious and appreciable smile inquired, "How long have you had the orchid 'tat'?"

Laurel blushed. "Oh, this was one of those whims I had when I was in France several years ago. It was all the craze and very fashionable."

Nick, still smiling, moved his gaze toward her lower half. "Got any more surprises, I might be interested in?"

"Why Mr. Kenyon!" Laurel gave him a teasing smile, as she fluttered her lashes at him, then looked away.

"But, you see Ms. Robertson, I only got a glance, but from what I saw it appeared to be very artistic. I do have an eye for fine art, I think it only enhances a woman's beauty to have a little embellishment! Perhaps you'll allow me to have a better viewing sometime," Nick teased.

"Why Mr. Kenyon, if I didn't know better, I believe you just solicited me for a private viewing. I don't know—with all the other activities filling up the day." Laurel teased him back.

"Perhaps we could pencil it in just after the submarine tour of Bimini," he reached out and pulled her up tight, gazing into her blue-green eyes.

"Maybe, we might be able to work that in," she teased him back.

Later that evening, Laurel and Nick were enjoying dinner conversation with their hosts, Martin and Elizabeth Miramonti and one other couple at their table, when Martin was approached by his Chief Steward.

"Excuse me, sir, there is a very important satellite call for a Dr. Laurel Robertson."

Excusing herself, Laurel went with the Chief Steward away from the noise of the dining room.

"Laurel, Stephanie here. Can you hear me?"

"Yes Stephanie, I can hear you fine. Is there a problem?"

"Do not come back here! We have a situation. But Rosie and I are handling it till Alex and Dr. Weston are released by the investigators, if they ever are released."

"Stephanie! You're not making any sense. Slow down, take a breath. Now tell me–what investigators and where were they taken?"

"Homeland Security came. A Blackhawk Helicopter took them away. Even the tunnel engineer. Soldiers are guarding the entrance to the tunnel. They have even closed off part of the park."

"Sounds like they got wind of the space craft we were trying to tunnel to."

"Laurel, the engineers found it this morning. They called Alex to go over and have a look. It was right where the satellite scan marked it."

"But I thought it would take longer to get to. Damn, I should not have left. I should have been the first to see it!" Laurel was glad they found it, but at the same time she regretted not being there.

"They wanted you too, for questioning. We told them you couldn't be reached until after Monday, that you were on a Caribbean Cruise. But that's not all Laurel. . ."

"What do you mean that's not all?" The sound of static filled her ear. "Stephanie? Where did you go? Stephanie?" Static was all Laurel heard. She hung up the satellite phone and franticly went looking for the Chief Steward.

"Can I help you, Ms. Robertson?" a voice declared from behind her. She spun around to see it was the Chief Steward.

Laurel replied, "We got cut off!"

"It happens out here a lot. You did the right thing by hanging up, keeping the line open so they can call back. It may be awhile, so if you want to rejoin your party, I will contact you again when they call back."

Laurel was overwhelmed by the situation Stephanie told her about, plus there was even more? She decided to go back to the dining room and talk to Nick about her phone call. When returning, she found the dinner was over and the guests had left. Laurel scanned the area looking for Nick. Elizabeth approached her.

"I hope your call wasn't any bad news?" Elizabeth stated.

"One of my team members called. She was telling me about a bad situation that occurred there, and she said there was more, then I lost her."

"I'm sorry to hear that your weekend has been interrupted by bad news. If your party doesn't try to call you back. . .say another fifteen minutes, then let me know. We may be able to do something to get hold of them. I saw your friend Nick and Martin go out on the deck. Do you need for me to go get him?"

"Not yet, thank you. I will wait to hear the rest of her message when she calls back."

"Waiting around is the hardest thing to do. Can I get you something? A drink maybe, or even some water perhaps?"

"I think I could use a Margarita, no salt on rim. Thank you." Laurel tried recalling everything that Stephanie told her. *Investigators, military soldiers, helicopters taking them away! I'm glad they found the space craft. She never said anything about finding the artifact. Maybe they haven't got that far yet–of course they haven't!*

"Here you are, one for each of us. You know, I have been in your shoes a few times myself. I used to head a team of researchers before Martin and I got married. I remember having to make quick decisions, and sometimes very difficult ones." They talked another ten minutes when the Chief Steward came for her again.

"Ms. Robertson, they were able to call back." He handed her the satellite phone.

"Hello–Stephanie?"

"Laurel, let me quickly tell you the rest, in case we get cut off again. "We had bad storms across Missouri today. That detective girl– Kourtney, has been trying to reach you, calling here three times. Laurel, you had better sit down for this. Springfield was hit by a tornado! Your grandparent's property was hit. It's pretty bad, Laurel."

"What? Why didn't you tell me this to start with? Were they hurt?"

"Your grandparents' caretakers, Ralph and Maria, called here first, wanting to talk to you. I told them I would try to contact you, not knowing for sure if I could get through. Laurel, they wouldn't tell me how bad it was. I hope they are all right."

"Thanks, Stephanie, you did good. I pray they are unharmed too. I will call and get hold of them. Are they letting you work in the new spots?"

"Yes, but there are guards posted in front of the tunnel entrance, and they have sealed off Monks Mound, blocking any visitors from that area. There are guards around this area, too."

"You tell Rosie to continue to be in charge for now, then Stephanie, you're next in line, should anything happen to him. Don't do anything to provoke the guards, comply with their barricades. We don't want to be kicked out of there. I will be in contact with both of you when I can. Thank you, Steph." Laurel went looking for Elizabeth, stating she had an emergency. "I need to get hold of Detective Kourtney Reed, of Springfield, Missouri Greene County Sherriff's Department. These are the numbers for her. How do I do this?" Elizabeth took the phone and placed the call, explaining the procedure. When she got Detective Reed on the line, she handed Laurel the phone.

"Kourtney, this is Laurel. Please tell me everything is all right back there."

"I have been trying to reach you for a long time. Where are you?" Kourtney inquired.

"I'm on a much-needed holiday. I heard there was a storm. Is everything okay there?"

"Laurel, do you have someone with you? I'm afraid I have some very bad news. The southwest edge, around Springfield Lake was hit the hardest. We had tornado watches, but no warnings. Your grandparent's area was hit bad with a confirmed twister. Laurel, I am so sorry to have to tell you over the phone this way. Neither of them survived."

"My Beloved Mary! That can't be true. Kourtney, please tell me there is some mistake. They had a safe room. Did you check there?" Laurel argued with her to go check. Finally, overwhelmed with emotion, tears filled her eyes.

"They were not in the safe room. Both Ralph and Maria came over afterward and found them. I'm so sorry Laurel, to have to tell you like this. A crew went out to spread tarps over the missing roof line. Ralph is helping all he can. How far out are you, so we can estimate your arrival?"

"I don't know just where, somewhere in the Atlantic. I'm making plans to leave here now. Talk to you later." Laurel hung up their connection and slowly slumped to the hall floor, tears running down her face. Multiple thoughts poured through her mind. *Why weren't they in that blasted safe room? Were they not aware there was a storm coming before going to bed? Damn-what's the point of having a shelter, if you don't use it?*

Elizabeth stepped back in the area to find her sitting on the floor. She helped her to a chair, placing a cold wet towel to the back of her neck.

"Laurel, I can see your message was very bad. Tell me what happened." Elizabeth put her arms around her.

"My grandparents– both gone!" she blurted. "There was a bad storm. A tornado hit their area. They were not in their safe room." Laurel shook her head back and forth. "They had that blame thing built several months ago. Why didn't they go to it?" Laurel ranted with anger, then cried some more. All the while, Elizabeth stayed, arms wrapped around her, holding her. Suddenly Nick was there." Elizabeth released Laurel into Nick's arms. She told him the news of her grandparent's death. Nick held her close while she cried some more.

CHAPTER 48

Laurel finally drifted off to sleep, just a few minutes at a time, resting her head against Nick's shoulder. The hum of the private jet provided by the Miramonti Corporation, lured her into moments of relief, then back to the harsh reality of what her Grams and Lawrence must have endured during the storm. She hoped they didn't suffer. So many questions—were they together when it happened? She hoped they were, for their love for each other was phenomenal. Laurel was glad they had each other, she could only wish she could one day find a love as great as theirs.

Nick was asleep beside her. Their plans were for the jet to take her to Springfield, then to take Nick on to East St. Louis. He had learned his Mystery TV team was back there, covering the news of the soldier's barricading and guarding the tunnel entrance and most of Monks Mound. It seems Nigel gave orders, in his absence, to have this included in the Documentary. Now that the filming had been extended, it was important that no one knew they were together on this little holiday. It might mean him losing his job.

Nick didn't want to leave Laurel under the circumstances, but she insisted she would be all right. She would have her friends in Springfield she could lean on.

A few hours had passed, then the Captain made an announcement over the intercom. "Keep your seatbelts fastened, we will be landing shortly in Springfield. It looks like sunny, to partly cloudy skies with a high of sixty-eight degrees.

Nick awoke and stretched his arms,. Looking at Laurel he asked, "Did you get any sleep at all?"

"I dosed off a few times. Nick, I'm thankful your sponsor provided the ride back here." Laurel began to feel the jet making the landing. She grabbed the arms of her seat as a rush of bad memories from the Phenom 300, came swiftly pouring over her.

"It's okay Laurel, I'm here with you. Just breathe through it. See, the captain's bringing her down easy." Nick gave Laurel a big smile. "I'm going to miss you."

Laurel and Nick said their good byes on the aircraft while it was being refueled. She departed, going inside the terminal where she waited for her ride.

Chris arrived greeting her with a compassionate embrace saying how sorry he was. "She was like a mother to me, too. Both were so kind to me," Chris said, while fighting back the tears welling up in his eyes. "Laurel let's sit here for a while," he said, pointing to a quiet area in the terminal. "I don't know how much Kourtney told you last night when the two of you talked or, if she even knew all the facts at that time."

"What do you mean Chris—our pets? Were they killed in the storm too?"

"Hold on—when Ralph and Maria exited their basement, they came right over to check on Barbara and Lawrence. The electricity was off, but they had their flashlights. They moved enough accumulation of debris to get inside where they found Barbara under a pile of ceiling rubbish on the kitchen floor. Ralph removed enough to see she was tied to a chair."

"Grams was tied to a chair?"

"That's right, Laurel, with tape. That's when he called the Greene County Sheriff's Department! They were told not to touch anything."

"What about Lawrence?"

"They stayed inside, looking for him, calling out his name, but no reply. Then they heard whimpering sounds. They made their way across the foyer, shinning their lights around the fallen and broken remains, making their way toward the whimper and whining sounds. They found his body inside the elevator. Our two dogs were close by. Lizzie was lying by Issie, moaning and licking on her. After checking he found Issie to be dead and Lizzie had a bad leg problem. Ralph was able to coax Lizzie out before the deputies arrived, placing her in the backyard pen."

"Kourtney never told me any of this. Just that there was this terrible storm that hit their house, and both were found dead."

"Laurel, I rushed over after Ralph called. Lizzie needed a vet's help. I found a dart in Issie's neck that killed her. One of the detectives took it for evidence. Doc said Lizzie will eventfully be all right. He wants to keep her for a few days to treat the gashes in her leg and observe her for any signs that she might have been hit by one of those poisons darts. She is in mourning over losing Issie and Lawrence. Doc said we will need to give her lots of love and attention."

Laurel had time to process all Chris told her on the drive back from the airport. She didn't have all the facts, but she could guess the same men looking for that artifact were involved. *They tied Grams to a chair. Were they interrogating her? Trying to get the information as to where the artifact was hidden?*

Chris stated, "They've put yellow tape around the main house, designating no entry. They are investigating it as a major crime scene. Ralph said there was minor damage to the cottage and he had not checked the log cabin yet. Laurel, you are welcome to stay at my apartment above the store if you like."

"Thank you, Chris, for now I want to see Grams and Lawrence. Where are they keeping their bodies?" Laurel asked with a sob.

"They probably still have them at the coroner's office. . . would be my guess?"

Laurel took out her phone and dialed Kourtney, it rang several times before she answered. "Detective Reed with Greene County."

"Hi Kourtney, I'm with Chris here in Springfield now and want to see my grandparents' bodies, can you tell me where to go?"

"Laurel, first I must explain, I'm not allowed to be on this case, because of conflict of interest. But, you should be able to see them at the coroner's office after they complete their investigation." Kourtney gave her directions where to go. "You will need to talk to Detectives Teague and Carter, they have been assigned to the case."

Arriving at the coroner's office, Laurel and Chris were told that the bodies were not released yet. They turned to leave when they were met by the two detectives, Teague and Carter.

"Ms. Robertson, we are so sorry for your loss." I'm Sergeant Luke Teague and meet Detective Rene Carter, we would like to talk with you about your grandparents," Lead Detective Teague stated. "We hope Forensics will be completed with their investigation soon, so we can determine the exact cause of Barbara and Lawrence's death. Mr. Lincoln, we already have your statement, unless you have something more to add, we ask you to excuse us while we speak to Ms. Robertson." They walked down the hall to another room.

Laurel sat across the table from the two detectives. The Sergeant was a muscular guy and looked tough, wearing a black patch over his left eye saying, "You understand your grandparents' house is off limits until the investigations are completed? We know this might be of some inconvenience to you, as we understand you live there when you are not away at your work. Is this correct Ms. Robertson?"

"Yes, as you probably know my grandmother practically raised me, along with my father until his death."

"So, were you away at your work location when this storm hit last night?" Sergeant Teague asked.

"No sir, I was away from my work, on a much-needed holiday," Laurel replied. She was aware the two detectives were just warming up to her, making pleasant talk, when all the while they really were in the preliminary stages of investigating her. After all, they probably think I am the sole heir to the Crawford estate. Which I'm not.

"So, Ms. Robertson you were away from your work, which would have been in Chicago or would you have been, as you archaeologists call it, on a dig somewhere?"

"My group is working in East St. Louis at the State Park of Ancient Cahokia."

"So, tell me Ms. Robertson, where did you get away to on your little holiday?" Sergeant Teague asked.

"I was on a yacht in the Bahamas."

Detective Carter spoke up, "That sounds very nice. Is this owned by the Crawford's?" Carter a pleasant looking, medium height woman wore her blond hair tied back and remained quiet until now.

"No, it is owned by the Miramonti Corporation. I was only a guest for the weekend. What is the procedure here?" Laurel asked. "I will be overseeing the funeral arrangements. I can't get into the house to get my grandmother's address book, or any other records, such as insurance, names and phone numbers. I need those to notify friends and relatives of this terrible disaster. How long will I be shut out of the house? Plus, I haven't seen the damage. I will need to get contractors out there soon." Laurel pressed the two for answers.

"We are truly sorry, but this is a criminal investigation and until the scene is thoroughly investigated, no one enters until we release it. We need the information as to where you will be staying and we need to confirm your phone numbers. After Laurel gave them the information, Sergeant Teague said, "Do not leave town, this is all for now."

Chris drove Laurel out to the Crawford estate where they visited with Ralph and Maria. "I discovered Barbara underneath some ceiling debris and boards. She had been tied to the chair with tape." Ralph choked up telling about finding the bodies. Laurel wrapped her arms around him until he could cope again with the harsh reality. We never went past the elevator after finding Lawrence's body with the two dogs nearby. This part of the house seemed all right. There was some ceiling debris scattered about the foyer, and the kitchen had boards and ceiling debris that had fallen everywhere." Then he committed further about the garage roof and walls that had fallen in on the vehicles, indicating the family room must be damaged, also.

"Have you checked the log cabin yet?" Laurel asked.

"We went over, and it seems to be all right, except for trees uprooted and small limbs and branches covering the roof. But I don't think there is any damage. We had a big tree blocking our front door at the cottage, but we went out another way. We'll have to get a tree service out here to clean up the place," Ralph commented.

"We'll make due till they let us back in the big house. Is the electricity still out?"

"The generator is working in the cottage and may be working over at the log cabin too."

"Fine, I'll stay in the log cabin for the time being."

Laurel gave them a loving hug of gratitude, assuring them she would be financially providing for them until the estate was settled. Laurel explained she knew they were in her grandparents' will.

Maria made a grocery and supply list and Laurel gave her one of her credit cards. After arranging for a rental car, Laurel went shopping for more clothing until she was allowed into the house. *Thank God, she had her make-up bag.* After the shopping was completed, they called Ralph to help get the grocery supplies over to the cottage. He had cleared the major path of some of the storm debris, even the one to the log cabin. Chris had made plans with Laurel for mid-afternoon, to go over and check on Lizzie.

"I'm about ready to leave the shop–where are you?" Chris asked.

"I'm helping Maria over at the cottage. Pull into the Wellness Center parking. It is where I left my rental car. There is not so much tree debris over there."

Dr. Holman greeted them when they arrived. "She's resting now, I gave her antibiotics for the leg wounds and a mild sedative. She was grieving badly over the ordeal of losing both Issie and Lawrence. After examination, I found those leg wounds were caused by knife stabs. She must have pined that intruder down, with him repeatedly stabbing her leg until she let loose enough for him to get away. But you can bet he is bad off, even needing a doctor if he is not lying dead somewhere up on the property," Dr. Holman declared.

Laurel opened the cage door and crawled inside the large kennel with Lizzie, petting her as she talked to her, giving her lots of love and attention. She opened those steel gray eyes of hers, raising her head slightly and made a few whining sounds. Then she looked over to Chris and whined until he reached over and ran his hands through her long white coat.

"That's what she needs, lots of love and attention. It will be wise to keep her off that leg for a while. I want to keep her here a few days for observation," Dr. Holman advised.

The two stayed and talked to Lizzie, stroking her beautiful coat. "If only Lizzie could talk, she could tell us who did this horrendous deed," Chris said.

"What the doc said about her fighting the intruder, we need to tell the two detectives." Laurel called the number on the card they gave her, explaining what Dr. Holman told them. They dispatched an officer to take the doctor's statement, putting out an alert to the hospitals and clinics for anyone coming in with dog bites, scratches, or even in the morgue.

Officers were sent back to the Crawford estate to search the outlying property for any bodies, alive or dead, anywhere around the vast wooded property. With only a few hours of daylight left, they called in help from the National Guard, already in the area. They were just about ready to call off the search because of the darkness, when they found someone close to the water's edge. He was barely alive. There was no identification on him. He had bad bites to his left arm, shoulder and left leg area. They flew him by helicopter to the nearest hospital where he was taken to surgery and put under guard, until he could be questioned.

CHAPTER 49

Laurel went in to meet with the detectives for the second time. Thoughts were busy running through her head. Why were they still focusing on her, when they had the man Lizzie attacked?

"Ms. Robertson, can you provide us the exact place you were last night, May 5th, between 5:00 and 6:00 PM?" Sergeant Teague requested, a harsh tone in his voice.

"Yes, as I told you when I was here earlier, I was a guest aboard a yacht owned by the Miramonti Corporation," Laurel replied.

"Ms. Robertson, we need to speak to the owners or someone who can vouch for you being with them at that time. Can you provide us names and the number for us to confirm this?" Detective Carter asked.

"Certainly." Laurel opened her phone up and found the number for the Miramonti's Yacht. "Their names are Martin and Elizabeth Miramonti." Then she provided them the satellite number for the yacht. Detective Carter left the room to make the call. While she was gone, Sergeant Teague continued with the questioning.

"I need your cell phone," Detective Teague ordered.

"Detective Teague, I must tell you my grandparents had some trouble with some men in the past couple of months. One of which can be confirmed by the Amarillo Police Department." Laurel went on explaining the details of the car break-in and of Lawrence shooting one or more of them. "I'm betting this is the same group. They must have been trying to get my grandmother to tell them where an artifact was hidden."

"When was this? What did they think she hid?" Detective Teague asked.

"Let's see, this would have been two or three days before Easter. They were wanting this Spiritual Artifact they thought my grandmother, or mother hid away."

"Did she tell you where it was hidden?"

"No. I asked her, but she said she didn't know where it was. Their house has been broken into and searched in the past. It was ransacked, but they took nothing. My apartment in Chicago was done the same way. Detective Teague, they could have taken a lot of valuable stuff at both places, but they didn't. It's plain they were looking for one thing, the Spiritual Artifact." Laurel explained the incident in Phoenix while parked at the antique store. "The description of these guys sounds about the same as in Amarillo," Laurel stated.

"Detective Teague, I have a good friend who has known me all my life, Detective Kourtney Reed. She can vouch for me and my relationship with my grandparents. Detective Teague, stood, said he would be back, and left Laurel alone in the room.

She looked around, nothing here but a dark window. *This is how they watch and listen to all your actions.* She sat still with only her thoughts– and she had plenty of those. Why is it they always think the closest relative is the guilty one? *Don't they know, I loved them both. . .they were my closest relatives, since losing both my mom and then my dad!* Tears streamed down her face, thinking of them.

Laurel wondered if the man they found would pull through. Would he talk? She didn't think he was alone in this horrendous plot. Probably the same group in the Amarillo and Phoenix situation. Who are they? What do they want with this artifact? It's much more than a valuable ancient piece of art they could sell on the black market for a few measly million dollars. This is an extraterrestrial priceless device. Are they aware of this? Her thoughts were interrupted when Detective Carter came back into the room.

"I managed to get hold of Elizabeth Miramonti. She confirmed you were aboard their yacht at that time. You are free to go now. But, do not leave the area, or even this state, as we may have more questions for you."

"Are they through with their examinations of my grandparents' bodies yet?"

"No, sorry these things take time."

"My phone. May I have my phone back please."

"Sorry, we need to keep it for a while longer."

"But all my phone numbers are in the phone! I need to call my work team, my boss. I need to let them know where I am. They know nothing of what happened here with my grandparents. You can't take that from me! I need to contact the people I work with. They will be worried about me," Laurel pleaded with her.

"Sorry for your inconvenience. We will get it back to you as soon as possible," Carter told her.

Laurel left their office and wondered inside the Greene County building looking for Kourtney Reed's office. After one of the officers told her Detective Reed left the building, she left and drove over to Chris's apartment.

She rang the bell outside the stair door. "It's Laurel, can you open the door?"

"I've been trying to reach you." Chris buzzed her in, waiting in his doorway at the top of the stairs.

"They brought me in for more questioning. Then they took my phone! Chris, I need that phone, it has all my work contact numbers. They don't know where I'm at, or even the situation here in Springfield. Stephanie called me while I was still on the yacht, telling me about Homeland Security taking Alex and some others in for questioning. Chris, everything is a complete mess."

"Wait a minute, back up. Why on earth would Homeland Security care about your archaeology business?"

"It's a long story and I promise I will explain later, but I need to get hold of your brother Ray. I need to talk to him." Chris dialed his private phone.

"Andrew Lincoln here."

"Ray, it's Chris. I have Laurel Robertson here with me and she desperately needs to talk with you."

"All right, put our little detector champ on."

"Hi Ray. I guess you heard about my grandparents being murdered. Well, the police are investigating me. They took my phone from me a while ago. Can they do this? I have all my work contact numbers in that phone. My boss and co-workers do not know I am in Springfield. I'm in a bit of a predicament here. What can I do?"

"Laurel, I'm here in Springfield attending a state function dinner this evening. I will help you get that phone back first thing in the morning. Can you hold on till then?"

"Yes, where shall we meet?" Laurel asked.

"Come to my Springfield office at 8:00 AM. Chris will give directions. Laurel, I'm so sorry about your grandparents. We'll talk more in the morning."

Laurel let out a sigh of relief after talking to Ray. She then filled Chris in on the story about the artifact and the UFO craft they had the engineers tunneling to. She needed to reach someone of her team, and Stephanie was the only number she knew from memory, so she dialed her.

"Hello, Stephanie Barnes here."

"Stephanie, I'm in Springfield. Something horrific has happened. It was more than a storm and twister that hit my grandparents property–my grandparents were murdered."

"Laurel, how awful! You must be devastated."

"They killed 'Issie' too. Lizzie's leg got all stabbed up, apparently while she was trying to maul one of them. Doc says she will pull through." She filled Stephanie in about everything that was going on there.

Is Alex back yet?"

"Yes, they returned everyone a few minutes ago. I'm going to load up and come down there. You can't go through that all alone."

"I need some clothes. Pack up some of my things in the FJ, you know where I keep the keys. I'm staying in the log cabin until they let me in the house."

"Do you think you are their only suspect?"

"They have the one that Lizzie attacked. He's in the hospital, just came out of surgery and still unconscious. They don't know if he will pull through, but they're standing by to question him. We'll talk more when I see you. Bye for now."

"Laurel, I'm concerned that there might be more of those men and they might think you know something about that artifact and where it's hidden? Do you think they might come back and try and get into that cabin?" Chris asked.

"No Chris, I'll be all right," she replied in a fearless tone, but was not completely sure of what she attested to. Do you want to go with me to see Ray in the morning?"

"Sure, come by here and pick me up."

It was late when Laurel arrived at the log cabin. Accompanied by her mace gun she punched in the security code and entered with caution. Making sure there were no surprises she crawled into one of the loft beds. Her mind was still racing with thoughts of all that transpired. With her mace gun under her pillow, she eventually drifted off to a night of restless sleep.

Laurel awakened early the next morning with thoughts of a dream she had. It was the Jesuits this time, on a Spanish warship experiencing much sickness, dying, and praying. It, too, started to fade away like the others.

CHAPTER 50

Laurel and Chris walked into the outer office of Andrew Ray Lincoln, once her childhood friend and the oldest son of her dad's business partner. Ray was now with the State Attorney's Office. Laurel looked around the room at the interesting pictures hanging on the walls, stating to Chris, "These three photos look very familiar. This looks like scenes from the trip we all took in South Dakota."

"You are so right. I took those with my new Nikon D1x, I received on my birthday that year," Ray affirmed, as he stepped into the room. "Come on in." Ray shut the door behind them. He put his arm around Laurel, giving her a warm embrace. "It's good to see you again but the circumstance could be better. I'm so sorry about your grandparents."

"Now tell me what's been going on with you and Greene County?" Ray asked.

She began by telling Ray everything about the detectives questioning her both times, all the conversations transpiring between them, then taking her phone! How Detective Carter confirmed her alibi, then released her, stating she was to remain in the area. She went further explaining the story her grandmother told her about the "Artifact" these men were looking for, and how they were convinced Barbara knew where it was hidden! "Ray, I am betting these same men are the guilty ones! There is more–"

"Whoa, slow down!" Ray exclaimed. I need to clarify a few things first." After further explanations, Laurel went on with her story.

"I found out while I was on the yacht, DHS took my partner, Dr. Zuckerman, along with my boss Joann Maury, Dr. Weston and the tunnel engineer, away for questioning. I'm told they are looking for me, also."

"Laurel, you were always a handful when we were kids. I remember having to rescue you more times than not, especially on our trips. You were always curious to what lay just beyond your reach. Looks like you continued on that same path, Little Ms. Laurel." Ray shook his head from side to side. "Let's start with me talking to the Greene County Prosecuting Attorney about what you have told me, seeing if we can't get you cleared off their suspect list, and get your phone returned."

"What about the other problem with the DHS looking for her?" Chris asked his brother.

"First things first. I need to get Laurel off the suspect list. We need to find out the exact cause of death from forensics, if they are through with the examination. After that, you can then proceed to make funeral arrangements. Are the DHS still holding those associates you spoke of?"

"I spoke briefly with Stephanie last night. She indicated they were brought back to our camp late last night. I don't know any of the details yet."

They spent the next few hours in and out of various offices, with Ray doing his legal procedures to see if he couldn't help expedite getting Laurel released from their suspect list.

After consulting with the Greene County Prosecuting Attorney, Ray found that Detective Teague questioned the man Lizzie attacked, but he told them nothing. They learned the suspect spoke with an Italian accent, he also had a tattoo on his right arm, mid-way between his shoulder and elbow. A red eight-pointed Maltese Cross inside a circle. The man wore a ring with a similar design. Ray also found out they took his prints to see if they matched any on file. They matched some of the mansion prints and got hits from Amarillo and Phoenix.

The detectives told Ray they consulted with the Amarillo Police Department and learned they found the man Lawrence had shot. He ended up going to an outlying clinic for a bad infection from the wound. They caught him just two days ago. He also has the same tattoo. They were still questioning him. Both suspects seemed to be part of the same group, whoever they are?

"This puts their suspect, that's in the hospital, at the top of the list. There is another thing Laurel, they have no proof you are connected." Ray handed her phone to her.

"It could be these are the same guys that broke into my apartment in Chicago." Laurel interjected. "The police dusted for prints. They will be on file."

"I will have them check that out." Ray made a note on his pad.

"Laurel, they found more evidence inside the mansion after sifting through the debris around the kitchen area where Barbara was found. There was a syringe and two different vials on the floor. The detectives said his prints were on all three items plus there were some different prints on the tape. So the evidence shows that this man was not alone. They are still trying to determine just how many men were in the house and they have tested the drug residue left in the syringe and the two vials. There was a type of sodium thiopental, mixed with an unknown substance. It was a strong dosage, which was what she eventually died from. They found two puncture marks on Barbara's body. They determined her death to be at 5:55 p.m."

Adrenaline filled Laurel's body when Ray said her death was 5:55. *These are the numbers I kept seeing on the clock! Not only was this the time of her grandmother's death, but it also happened on May 5th. The 5th month, the 5th day. Why didn't I put that together? All those 5's.*

"Sodium thiopental, mixed with another substance? Isn't this a truth serum drug?" Chris asked.

"Yes, the sodium thiopental by itself won't kill a person. And if there is a strong resistance, the person won't reveal the truth the administrator of the drug is seeking. But they said a mixture of another substance was used in conjunction with it, which they found in the second vile. This is what caused her death," Ray stated.

"Have they determined how Lawrence was killed?" Laurel asked.

"They determined his body contained the poison delivered in the darts. They found a puncture mark on his neck. He must have pulled out the dart, as they found it near his body. They placed Lawrence's death at around 5:00 p.m. and the wolf dog shortly before him.

Laurel thanked Ray, her big brother savior, for once again helping to pull her out of one more mess. Now that she was off the top of their suspect list, with her phone back, she needed to make some calls. First on the list was Stephanie.

"Hi Laurel, how's things going down there? Bless your heart. Such an ordeal you're having to go through."

"I'm doing better, now that Ray helped get me off the suspect list and got my phone back. Where are you?"

"We are taking turns driving, Christina is with me. We should be there in another three hours. Packed up some warm clothes for you." Stephanie answered.

"Hi Christina, I'm glad you came with her. What did Alex say happened when they took all of them in for questioning?"

"You'll have to talk to him. All I know is he and Mrs. Maury were doubly upset when they got back last night." Christina replied.

"What about you, Stephanie, what do you know?"

"I never spoke to Alex. He got a report from Rosie on the progress of where they were digging in the new pyramid location. Then Alex went back to the motel with the others."

Laurel called Joann next. She wanted information of what was happening at her site, plus she wanted to tell her the circumstances of her grandparent's death.

"Laurel, I am so sorry about your grandparents. I know what you are going through is a dreadful experience. Just take one step at a time and know they loved you very deeply. Rely on your friends there; they will help you get through this. We will give you a leave of absence from your work here. The DHS may have shut down our tunneling to the spacecraft, but we still can work most of the other sites picked up with the satellite imaging."

"Where did they take you and the others? What did they ask you?"

"They took us to Fort Meade, Maryland, the NSA headquarters. There were two investigators, a man and a woman. They heard information there could be an unidentified space craft that we were digging to, they wanted all information concerning this. Alex told us on the helicopter, the engineers had reached it and called him in to look at the small portion they had uncovered. He told us that NSA would go in and see for themselves while we were gone. Our story is- "We were tunneling to get over to repair Monks Mound when we discovered it.""

"Joann, do they have the legal right to take over, keeping us out? This is our project; besides they might try and take it out of the mound, causing a colossus collapse of Monks Mound."

"Both the engineers and Alex explained all of this to them. The investigators proclaimed that this space craft was under the jurisdiction of Homeland Security, and for the safety of the Nation, this project must be under their scientific team, along with NASA. The barricades would remain and our archaeologists could work in other areas of the state park."

"I heard they initially wanted to talk to me also. I wonder if they still do?"

"You can bet they will find you if they think you can shed more light on the situation. On second thought, Laurel, I should come down to help you with those arrangements. I know from my own experience, you will need some help. Do you plan on having both services together?"

"Yes, I think they would have wanted it that way."

"I will make plans to leave right now. I'll call you as soon as I arrive," Joann told her.

Laurel called Alex next to let him know what was happening in Springfield.

"I feel so bad for you, Laurel, having to go through such a horrendous ordeal. But at least you're not their prime suspect any longer. Do you have anyone there for support? I'm so worried about you." Alex's voice cracked.

Laurel explained, "Stephanie and Christina will be arriving in a few hours and Joann is coming to help with the funeral arrangements. Chris, and his older brother Ray, have been helping. I have Ralph and Maria, but bless them, they are grieving also. I probably will see more of Kourtney now. You remember she is a detective with Greene County also. She had to keep her distance because of our close relationship."

"Yes, I met her at your birthday party. Sharp girl, I liked her. Thinking about that party has brought up some bad memories about my last contact with your grandparents. But I realize Barbara was just being overly protective of you. I'm so sorry, Laurel. Even with our differences, I never wished her any harm. I liked and respected Lawrence too, he was a good man."

"Alex, when the NASA questioned you about the Spacecraft, what specifically did you tell them?"

"Had to explain why we hired the engineers to tunnel over to the base of Monks Mound to add supports to shore up the west side to keep it from collapsing. Then they discovered the ship."

"Alex, we need to clean up our office, get rid of any scan sheets we don't need. Nothing like having a clean and tidy office, if you know what I mean."

"I'll take care of that. Oh Laurel, I saw part of the ship! She was a real beauty. I reached out and touched her! I wished you could have seen her."

"Maybe I will, eventually." Laurel's voice shook. "Alex, I trust you will take good care of our project. I'll get back up there, soon as all is settled here."

CHAPTER 51

It was almost three weeks from the time of their deaths that the bodies were released and Laurel was permitted to go inside the house to gather Barbara's address book with the phone numbers she needed to call friends and the few distant relatives they had. Lawrence's partners at the law firm provided the needed information for completing his part. They succeeded in locating his only grandson, Daniel Crawford. They planned to try and get him here for the services. She remembered Lawrence talking about him. After finishing high school, he wanted to study art in Paris. Lawrence financed his trip and enough for him to live on. He never spoke of him very much.

She went through her grandmother's closet to find something for her to wear for the service, selecting a lavender dress with matching jacket. For Lawrence she selected a Beige suit. Laurel gathered up the framed photo of them together, taken by a professional at their last anniversary. They looked so good and Laurel loved this one the best. She went through many past photo's, making selections to give to the director for their making a video memory collage of their lives.

An enormous crowd of people filed through the doors at St. Elizabeth Ann Seton Church, despite the cool dreary, overcast day. A light drizzle, all morning long, continued to bring forth the promise of cleansing.

She knew the regular Catholic Priest would be officiating but hadn't planned on seeing Bishop Marin here also. Laurel wondered if he was going to speak too. Laurel, dressed in a dark Navy dress, wearing a matching hat with a veil over her face, sat in her seat listening as the services started, wishing it to be over.

She began to feel that strange electrical energy swirling, drifting throughout her body, with an overwhelming lightness. She was compelled to stare at a soft glow of light stationed over her grandmothers coffin, lifting the veil and placing it back on top so she could see it better. It kept pulling her into it. Within the glow, an inscription started forming, until a pristine 5:5:5 appeared–then instantly the numbers swirled into a fast-moving black hole sucking the numbers inside. The light disappeared and the remainder of the service was a blur to her.

The women of the church served a wonderful lunch, with relatives and friends scattered about the room seated at the round tables. All her team members were there. She couldn't help but cry, seeing they cared deeply enough to come, some had not even met them. Lawrence's partners of the law firm were seated with their wives. Laurel looked around but didn't see Daniel Crawford and wondered where he was.

She had asked everyone not to send flowers, but to send any contributions to the Wellness Center of the Ozarks, Grams favorite project. After lunch, friends and relatives came over to Laurel, giving hugs and expressing well wishes. Gram's dearest friend, Nina June Morrison came up to visit–they both cried, promising to call each other. Alex appeared, expressing his condolences as well. At the far end of the long line was Nick. Leaning in close, he spoke a tender message of love and comfort, then he turned and left.

On the other side of the room, the Bishop was talking to Professor Vaughn. She glanced up as she spoke to another friend, seeing they were walking toward her. This would be the first time seeing Matthew since their last encounter in the Crawford driveway. Laurel, still somewhat embarrassed, didn't want to look Matthew in the eyes, instead she turned her attention to the Bishop.

Matthew said, "You remember Bishop Marin when he was a guest at the Easter dinner at your grandparent's home."

"Yes, so kind of you to attend the services, Bishop Marin." Laurel wondered if he was going to speak more words of wisdom, hoping he wouldn't.

The Bishop took her hands in his once again, his eyes viewed into hers, piercing deeply into her soul. Then he spoke, "You carry within, aspects from other dimensions. Listen in your quietness, as they speak to you. One carries the wisdom of inner Earth. The other carries a lust for power to rule. Please be consciously aware of this, my child. Be one with Jesus." He kissed her on her cheek. "I am here for you."

Laurel's grandmother wasn't physically present to hear the Bishop's second prophecy, *but perhaps she may have been in spirit. What would she make of this?* Laurel stumbled over the words to say back to the Bishop, but what? Then managed to say, "It is with my wounded heart, in my time of need, Father, I humbly give my thanks for your continued guidance."

Matthew reached out and patted her arm. "Please give me a call, as I am also here for your support. Call me any time—I can help."

Laurel was glad this day was finally over. She never dreamed it would be so hard. Hoping the pain in her heart would subside, she stretched out across her bed and slept well into the next day.

Time was spent the next few days with Laurel concentrating on making repairs to her grandparent's estate. Taking care of their affairs kept her busy and the healing came in slowly. The next week she sat in the office of Attorney Victor Benson, the executor of the estate and he preceded to read the will.

Ralph and Maria were provided for with adequate funding for their retirement with a request that they stay if Laurel requested them to. Daniel Crawford, not present, being Lawrence's only relative, would receive an inheritance of five hundred thousand dollars. The Ozark Wellness Center were deeded the building and property and a fund set aside to operate for the next five years. Victor Benson then looked up from his papers and said, "Laurel, all remainder of both Barbara and Lawrence's estate is willed to you." He proceeded to list all assets and property in detail. Enough for Laurel to retire comfortably, had she wished to. But she had other passions she needed to address and retirement was not on that list.

The damage to the mansion had been severe and would take a good deal of time to complete. The garage, family room and kitchen would need to be replaced. The contractors found that Laurel's bedroom and the bedroom next to hers were unaffected, but the rest of the upstairs on this wing would need some reconstruction. The first thing Laurel wanted done was the replacement of the security system, then she hired a security guard firm to patrol the property while construction was taking place.

The tree service removed all the fallen trees from the yard and the damaged fence was repaired. Lizzie could now be allowed to roam and get some exercise, running free in the big back yard. Laurel knew she still needed to treat her leg and give her lots of attention, so she brought her into her bedroom every night. They gave each other much needed support during their grieving period.

Laurel was making due with the space she had. She made a makeshift kitchen with her refrigerator at the far edge of the foyer, along with her table and chairs she acquired at a used furniture store. Her double door kitchen pantry took care of storage of some dishes and food supply. On one end of the table sat her convection oven, induction cooktop and the coffee machine. She placed a screen up close to the front entry so no one could see inside the spacious windows on each side of the front door, with shades installed across the back-dining room windows.

Chris came over often to check on both her and Lizzie. Kourtney dropped by twice a week and they practiced self-defense maneuvers.

Laurel spent part of her day at the Wellness Center, where Barbra still had appointments on the books that needed to be taken care of. She became friends with one of her grandmother's clientele, Sandra Orman, who was there for a follow-up treatment and asked a favor of her.

"My husband, Tom, received a call from his sister last night about an accidental death of one of his twin nephews. Tom has been suffering pain from an old sciatic nerve problem and he needs to fly down to Flagstaff to help his sister cope with her son's terrible death and help make the funeral arrangements. Could you see if you can help him get some relief?" Laura could hear the worry in Sandra's voice.

Tom Orman was introduced by his wife, then she went out and waited in the reception area. Laurel found Tom was sensitive to the energies, even more than Sandra.

"Sandy probably told you, my nephew, Michael, was killed in a freakish type of accident in Arizona."

"She did, and that you plan to fly down to help your sister."

"I understand, all too well, just going through my own grandparent's death.

"Michael is a twin and he and Daniel both were digging high up on a mountaintop in Arizona in their dad's mining operation. Their dad and his partner had previously been there with them but left to go back to work in Tucson. The boys were doing fine when suddenly, the ground where they were digging, started imploding. So much that it covered them both. Daniel could slowly dig himself out, all the while yelling to his brother Michael, but got no response. When he was able, he started uncovering his brother, but it was too late. He had suffocated. There was no phone reception on the mountain, so he left him, running down the mountain to the house at the bottom where they left their vehicle, calling the sheriff and his dad."

"This must have been a terrible experience for the one twin that survived. How old are they?"

"They were barely twenty-two. My sister, Mallory, was worried about them doing this mining thing with their dad and had asked them not to go. But they are boys, it sounded like adventure to them, with the prospect of finding that large treasure their dad had a map to."

"That sounds interesting. Sandra probably told you I'm a professional archaeologist on leave from my job. My grandmother, who recently was killed, also was an archaeologist along with my mother. They once worked in Arizona in the Tubac area, near the Presidio State Historic Park. Is this close to where the twins father had his claim?"

"I have not been there, but Joseph Mendoza, their father, told me it had something to do with the old Tumacacori Mission and was on one of mountains north of there," Tom explained.

"That's interesting, I think that's pretty close to where my mother and grandmother were working." *What's the chances of meeting someone with relatives working the same area?* Laurel thought.

She worked a long time on Tom until he stopped pulling the energies. He stood up, walked around, and said, "I feel a lot better, enough I can leave for Flagstaff."

Laurel's thoughts lingered with the tragic story she had just heard about the twins and the mining operation. How the earth just imploded where they were digging, covering them both up, smothering the life from the one boy. It was the mention of one thing that kept gnawing at her. The old Tumacacori Mission. But why?

Her thoughts switched to the dreams she was having; mountains, priests in black robes, small horse carrying numerous bulky sacks. Then there was this box, being lowered in the ground, too small to be a body. There was this stormy day, dark clouds, lightning and thunder, an explosion, rocks flying and tumbling, this feeling of great sadness–and the 5:5:5!

Laurel started doing some research in Lawrence's library on the priests that wore the black robes. They were Jesuit Priests. She found the connection to the missions and especially some of them who occupied the Tumacacori Mission back in Pimeria Alta of New Spain–at least until they were expelled in June, 1767. *Are my dreams connected to this Tumacacori Mission? I was drawn to this mission for some reason.*

Reading on she discovered this mission was quite large, almost like a fort with a Spanish population and some Mexicans, as well as Pima Indians all living within or just outside the perimeters. A large portion oversaw the mining operations for the Spanish Government, using the Indian population for the mining labor. They processed both silver and gold to be shipped to Spain. *Those mines were mostly in the same area the twins were digging. Isn't that a coincidence. What were they hoping to find in an already worked mine?*

Laurel's thoughts were all over the place. She started thinking about the Bishop's last words to her. "You carry aspects of other dimensions. Listen in your quietness, as they speak to you. One carries the wisdom of inner earth–the other carries a lust for power to rule." She recited his words to herself over and over.

They have been speaking to me, through my dreams. The men in black robes, the Jesuit Priests. They are trying to get my attention. . .but, why? What happened two hundred and fifty years ago, that could have anything to do with me

Laura's thoughts went to the current Pope. He is a Jesuit, he's the first Jesuit to ever be elected to Pope. That's a big difference, from where the Society of Jesus started from, doing mostly missionary work, expanding into the New Country and supervising the mining operations for the country of Spain, two hundred fifty years ago, to one of them now ruling over the entire Catholic body. *Could this be the aspect that carries the lust for power? If this is true, then who is the other aspect that speaks to me from the inner earth?*

CHAPTER 52

Ocean Voyage Destination: Italian Port of Civitavecchia – 1767

Father Vega and the other Jesuits were aboard the Magnanimo 74, a Spanish, three decks, ninety-four-gun battleship, that had been restructured to accommodate housing the many Jesuit prisoners. There were rows of bunks, four beds high, hammocks, or net swings within the isle, leaving little room for movement.

It was dark, cold, and damp in the belly of the Spanish ship. The only light was the glow from the oil lanterns. Sickness spread among the prisoners as the Jesuit priests and the others tended to their care, praying to God for their recovery. They sang songs to lift their spirits. Many died on the long voyage. Pregnant women gave birth to new life and the cries of the newborn brought smiles and happiness, lifting their spirits,

Father Vega lay on the lower bunk, his thoughts drifting back to the vow he made with God. He renewed that vow often on the long voyage, reminding himself what he must do. *"I will return to New Spain. Our work is just getting started. I will remember the route to the hidden Guadalupe mine, where we stored the vast treasure of gold and silver, along with the maps to all the other mines to help finance our new Papal State, severing all ties from the Vatican."*

When Father Vega slept he would often dream, seeing a woman working near some dirt filled pyramids. She wore tight fitting pants and a shirt. It was a mystery why he kept seeing her. Then Father Vega's thoughts went to the Spiritual Artifact. He desperately wanted the wisdom to be the one to open it and use it. He prayed the Biblical version of "Ask and you shall receive".

"All things that you ask straightly, directly...
from inside My name–
you will be given. So far you haven't done this...
So, ask without hidden motive and
be surrounded by your answer–
Be enveloped by what you desire, that your gladness be full."

Father Vega put all his feelings, amplified with compassion, into the asking of his –prayer, placing himself into a spiraling higher state of consciousness. So much so, that his wishes started to materialize. His body swirled fast, traveling through a tunnel of multiple firing lights and when he came out of the experience he found himself disoriented. He was in a different body, wearing jeans, boots and an undershirt. Upon his head he wore a western straw hat, digging in the earth along with three others, one of which, was his twin brother. His Father and another friend said their good-byes and departed leaving the twin boys to continue digging for lost treasure.

CHAPTER 53

Springfield, Missouri–Present Time

No matter how hard Laurel tried she couldn't come up with the right answers. She walked back to the kitchen area just as the construction crew was locking everything up in preparation of leaving for the night.

"We have everything fully closed in, as far as the outside perimeter goes. She's all sealed up tight, Ms. Robertson, we wanted to get you to where you could be safe once again," the contractor said.

"Thank you, I really appreciate that. See you in the morning." Laurel went inside to the new security panel on the wall, now equipped with all new codes, and closed the front gate.

Laurel went back to the library to try and find more information on the Jesuits and their mining operation. It was a good thing she hired the high school librarian, who was off for the summer, to help her put things back in order. The perpetrators made a complete shamble of the large multi-level library in their search for the artifact. Laurel didn't know if they found it hidden somewhere in this house or not. Grams could have told them where it was hidden, with them using that truth serum. Or maybe she didn't?

As she searched, she remembered Matthew Vaughn told of how he went to a Jesuit high school and studied Religious History at the university. She needed to speak with him, then she asked herself if she had overcome the embarrassing experience of the last time they were together. *But he told me at the funeral to call him saying, he could help. Did I misread his intentions that night on the patio–like Stephanie thought I could have?* Maybe if we start over and keep our distance, it will work out better. Laurel bit the bullet and called him.

"Matthew, this is Laurel are you busy this evening?"

"Why Laurel, I was just thinking about you. How are you getting along?"

"I am making some progress trying to clean up this place. Some more things have come to light recently, and I could use your help, with your background on the Jesuits and Religious History. When can we get together?"

"I'm free this evening. Shall I come over, or would you like to come to my place?"

"I'm in Lawrence's library. Maybe it would be better if you came here, as there might be some books here that could help with my dilemma." Matthew arrived at the front gate and Laurel opened it from inside. Putting a leash on Lizzie, she answered the front door. She told Lizzie to sit, but she didn't. Instead she started growling. Laurel remembered she had not met Matthew before and due to what she recently experienced, she wasn't going to trust him. Laurel gave the command again. Laurel explained to Lizzie that it's all right, that Matthew was a good guy and after a while she stopped growling.

Laurel and Matthew walked back to the library with Lizzie following. She proceeded to explain meeting one of Barbara's clients and how the death of one twin was in the same area where her Grams and mother were doing their dig, twenty-eight years ago.

Laurel explained how her thoughts kept jumping around. She then went to the Bishop, with his last words to her.

"Do you remember what those exact words were?" Matthew asked.

Laurel repeated the best she could recall what the Bishop said.

"Matthew, this has been happening all along–the dreams! The visions!"

"So, Laurel, you said they have been speaking to you in your dreams and visions. Does anything resonate with what he said?" Matthew inquired.

"The men in black robes, I believe are Jesuit priests. When my client stated this mine the twins were digging in was north of Tumacacori Mission, all kinds of bells went off. So far, I found out in my research some of Jesuits oversaw mining for the country of Spain, processing it, getting it ready to be shipped back to Spain."

"This is true. Did you come across any information that they kept some for themselves?"

"Don't you think this was for their compensation?"

"They were rumored to have taken and hid quite a lot more than their meager compensation," Matthew stated.

"No, I had not come across that yet, but it makes sense now. Why else would they get a permit to mine in an area where the Jesuits had already mined centuries ago."

They talked a while about the Jesuits back before their expulsion. Matthew had been around a lot of Jesuit teachers, plus this was part of his Religious History studies.

"I think one of the Jesuit priests is trying to tell me something," Laurel said.

"Do you think this could be one of the aspects the Bishop is referring to?" Matthew asked.

"It very well could be. One of them tried to warn me about the 5:55. I was directed to look at the digital clock most of the time, just after having the dream. The medical examiner ruled this was the time of my grandmother's death." Laurel's voice broke.

"That is pretty phenomenal you can receive what is happening in their dimension. As far as them sending a warning about something going to happen in your reality, that is beyond comprehension. Laurel, how were you to know what that 5:55 was supposed to mean? I know you are feeling regretful that you didn't know what it stood for, but that's something that only experience can teach you. and you had nothing to go by. Don't beat yourself up, you have nothing to be guilty about. It's not your fault."

"But I still feel I should have tried harder. I was so busy with my archaeology work; my attention was taken from this. I made a list of what I saw in these dreams, trying to come up with what they were doing. One showed me something bad happening the day of the storm. Dark clouds moving overhead, lightning and thunder. I saw hands holding coral beads, then something blew up, causing rocks flying and tumbling everywhere. Great sadness swept over me from what happened on that day. Then I saw the 5:55."

"Laurel, I don't know if you realize it yet, but as you were telling me these happenings, they sounded very familiar. Almost equal to what happened here in Springfield. That blowing up would be the twister, causing debris to fly and tumble everywhere. There was great sadness that happened here on this day, also. The time of your grandmother's death being at 5:55. And it happened on the 5th of May, the fifth month and fifth day. It's like what's happening in this other dimension—something similar is happening here too!"

Laurel's phone rang. She saw it was from Greene County and answered.

"This is Sergeant Teague, Ms. Robertson. I'm calling to let you know the prisoner we had in the double homicide has escaped. Are you alone at your house?"

"No, I have a friend here with me. I also have two security guards posted outside and my gates are locked, with the alarm system on."

"Sounds like you have a 'little Fort Knox' there. Wanted you to know, this prisoner escaped with some help. We don't know if they got what they were looking for, or if they will come back there to look for it again. Just be very cautious and alert your security guards," Teague advised. "We'll keep you informed."

Laurel turned to Matthew, "That was Greene County. Their prisoner escaped!" She dialed the lead security guard and notified him to be on the alert.

"I'm not leaving you here alone tonight, either you come and spend the night at my place, or I'm going to stay here with you," Matthew asserted.

"Lawrence used to keep some weapons in that safe room he built. Let's check it out." Laurel stated as she walked toward the hallway then opened the door that concealed the entrance to the safe room. She punched in the new codes and the door opened with all three entering before she closed it again. "They're gone. I should have known; Greene County must have taken them."

"Let's look around, we might find something we could use," Matthew remarked. After searching, they found nothing that would work for a weapon. They sat down in the recliners by the sanctuary.

"Let's stay in here for the night, we have everything we might need," Laurel said. Lizzie lay down, placing herself between Laurel and the door.

Matthew agreed as he stood in front of the sanctuary admiring it. He reached out, running his hand across the detailed craftsmanship.

"Grams said she found it on the church auction block. It came from an estate in Phoenix and had been in their family since the mid 1700's."

"She had an eye for prestige antiques. The workmanship and detail are exquisite," Matthew said.

"The morning she showed me this sanctuary and explained the details of where it came from, I was taken with this life size Immaculate Heart of Mary statue."

"It is very beautiful, too." Matthew reached out and touched it.

"She said they told her it was authentic from Spain."

"How does one know it's authentic? Does the craftsman sign his name somewhere?" Matthew ran his fingers down around the lower part on the front of the statue, not finding anything, he went around to the back side and did the same. "Oh!" Matthew yelled.

"What happened?"

"I snagged my fingers on something down there." He held his hand up to reveal a bloody finger.

Laurel grabbed a tissue from a box sitting on the table and handed it to him. "Is it very deep? Let me have a look." She took his hand and gently unwrapped the tissue revealing a superficial wound. She glanced up to his face. "I think you'll live," she smiled.

He looked at his finger, then frowned. "I believe your right," he whined.

"I'll get you some antibiotics and a band-aid." Laurel walked over to the storage shelves for the first aid kit and a large flashlight. She dressed his finger. With a sheepish grin he said, "Thank you."

Matthew took the flashlight over to the statue, shining it down to where he sliced his finger. "There is an authenticity plaque, but it's loose. Would you hold the light while I lean it over to see it better?" Laurel held the light as Matthew checked it out. "I see something by the edge of the loose plaque." Matthew took out his knife and pried the plaque off to reveal a folded paper tucked into a hollowed part of the statue. "There is some writing on one side." he announced while unfolding the paper.

CHAPTER 54

Laurel looked at the handwritten letter that was in Spanish, recognizing it was addressed to Father Eusebio Francisco Kino. But her Spanish was rusty and she couldn't make out much. She handed the letter back to Matthew.

"How's your Spanish?" Laurel asked.

He took the letter and started to read. "The date is June 3, 1737."

"It is my wish that you, your Mission and the surrounding village be blessed with my gift of the Immaculate Heart of Mary statue. Hopefully you have procured the hiding place of the Spiritual Artifact in the safest location possible, taking care of your obligations of being the New Guardian. The Vatican's soldiers were getting too close, repeatedly walking in the vicinity near its hiding location, in the Estremadura Mountains. I feel it will be safer in New Spain.

As you know I work very closely with the Society of Jesus and I am aware of the Order's wish to open a new Papacy, one to supersede that of the Vatican. We feel the stockpiling of the riches from the mines will aid the financing of the New World Order in the new country. It is hoped that the enlightened one will soon appear and claim his rightful place in activating the Spiritual Artifact, bringing forth wisdom and truth for our new order.

May the peace of Christ Jesus which surpasses all understanding be with you.

Duchess of Aveiro y Arcos, of Madrid"

"Wow, I wonder if Father Kino found the letter?" Laurel questioned.

"Maybe he did but saved it by placing it back into its secret hiding place. We learned through some of my studies that they never found the letters the Duchess wrote to Kino, but they found several that Kino wrote to her. and it scripted as if he was answering her questions," Matthew explained.

"This was two hundred and eighty years ago! Grams said this statue was on the auction block, coming from an Estate in Phoenix. What's the odds of Grams buying it?" Laurel looked at Matthew. "This may be the only letter found that the Duchess wrote to him, making it pretty valuable."

"Does any of this letter resonate with your dreams?"

Laurel nodded. "The Jesuits, the mining, the mules loaded with the bulky sacks– probably the heavy sacks of gold and silver they were taking up to the mine to hide away. Another thing, I saw a box being lowered in the ground. This may have been the Spiritual Artifact the Duchess sent to Father Kino, making him the new Guardian."

Matthew added, "This letter coincides with your mother seeing three separate areas on the cave wall with three ships, with possibly each having at least one artifact."

"This one must be from the European Country," Laurel said. "The Duchess referred to an Enlightened one, that will come forth to activate this Spiritual Artifact. Claiming it will bring forth a kind of wisdom and truth, supposedly for their new order. Matthew, this sounds like one of the aspects the Bishop spoke about. The one that carries the lust for power to rule. I'm sorry, I know you were raised in the Jesuit school system, I really don't know if you became one of them in your way of thinking."

"Remember, I went to part of the seminary school, but I left because I disagreed in some of their teachings," Matthew reassured her.

"Laurel, would you follow along with me for a while, sit back in the recliner, close your eyes, take a deep breath, try and relax. Remember what you saw in the past dreams and visions, go over them again, telling me what you have seen."

She told him what she saw and heard, listing one thing after another.

"Oh my!" Laurel blurted.

"What?" Matthew questioned.

"That stormy day with the lightning and thunder and the sounds like something blew up. The Jesuits blew up the entrance to the mine. I saw them, I heard some of them crying out for help. Matthew, all their Indian helpers were still inside that mine when they blew up the entrance. I saw the rocks flying and tumbling, then this great sadness came over me. Afterward, I saw the hands holding these coral beads. When I awoke, I looked to the clock on the dresser, it read 5:55." Laurel explained, with tears in her eyes.

"It sounds like most of your dreams have been accounted for, and I'm sorry you had to go through that rough part," Matthew said, patting her arm.

"Maybe something to drink will settle my nerves and emotions." She got up from her seat. "Surely Lawrence stashed something to drink besides water in here." She opened several cabinet doors before finding his wine supply. Matthew opened the bottle, filling the glasses half full. They sat by the sanctuary sipping their wine, continuing in conversation. Their glasses were almost empty when the alarm on the security panel went off, blaring in their ears. Lizzie's barking added to the noise.

"What does that mean?" Matthew hurried to the panel to see what it indicated.

"The security's breached!" Laurel declared as she switched on the visual scan of rooms. The new system went directly to the area that was intruded. "This should alert the Security Agency, and Greene County will be called."

"Does that system show what room they are in right now?"

Laurel flipped on the inside motion detector and the system showed the frame where they were, indicating five people in the house, making their way up the stairs. Now that they were in the upstairs hall, they started to split up. Two headed for Laurel's bedroom wing; the other three went toward the master suite.

Laurel's phone rang. "This is the Security System. We have been alerted to an unlawful entry and have called the Greene County Sherriff's Department"

"This is Laurel Robertson. I'm in the safe room with a friend, Matthew Vaughn, and my dog. There are five men on the camera and have made their way upstairs, with three going to the west wing and two going toward the east."

"They obviously didn't get that blasted artifact when they were here last. This means they couldn't get Barbara to tell them with that truth drug, or maybe left because Lizzie was chewing the one up, or it could be because of the twister that hit. Anyway, they still are determined that it's here in this house and won't hesitate to kill to get it," Matthew declared.

"They might be able to get in here if they hack the code," Laurel said.

"Let's search again, there must be something we could use to defend ourselves." Matthew went searching and grabbed a long screwdriver and the fire extinguisher.

Laurel pulled a knife from the drawer. "If they get in, maybe we've got a fighting chance." She looked to Matthew. "I'm so sorry I dragged you into this bad situation."

"No apologies, remember I volunteered to help." Matthew bent down and talked to Lizzie. "Remember Lizzie, I'm a good guy, if there is any fighting going on in this room." He gave a nervous chuckle, while he continued to stroke her plush white and silver coat.

Laurel looked at the security monitor, noticing the Sherriff's Deputy's vehicles were out front. There was gun fire, then nothing for a while. There was movement again, she counted a total of five bodies in motion, none of them together.

"I can't tell if the deputies are still alive," Laurel said. "Maybe if I switch over to the room cameras. . .There, I can see the two deputies, so two of the intruders must be down."

Lizzie went to the door, growling and pawing. Laurel flipped the camera to the safe room entrance, revealing three men in black hoodies and dark pants. "They're punching in codes to this door!" Laurel shouted.

"Let's get in our positions now!" Matthew tucked the screwdriver into his boot and got his fire extinguisher and moved to the area by the door, just out of view. Suddenly the safe room door opened and Lizzie lunged for the first guy's neck, bringing him down. Matthew stepped out and shot the next guy in the eyes with the foam from the fire extinguisher, then hit him over the head with it. A third guy rushed inside coming straight for Laurel. He reached out to punch her in the face. She deflected his arm, moved forward, stepping hard on his foot, then she jabbed her fist into his face. He fell to his knees, Laurel swiftly pulled the knife from her boot and stabbed him in his thigh twice. All three were down when the deputies rushed inside.

Laurel secured Lizzie with her commands so she wouldn't harm the deputies. The deputies quickly slapped cuffs on them. The one Laurel stabbed was bleeding badly. They took his belt and tied his leg off and called for an ambulance.

"I see the three of you did all right for yourselves," the deputy remarked.

"What about the other two guys?" Laurel asked.

"Those two managed to flee, leaving these three."

Laurel wanted to see if these intruders had the same tattoo as the last two that were arrested. Taking her knife, she slit the upper right arm sleeves of their black hoodies, revealing the same red eight-pointed Maltese cross inside a circle.

Laurel was saddened when she learned the two security guards were shot with the same type of poisonous darts as Lawrence and Issie.

Matthew stayed the remainder of the night with Laurel, neither one getting much sleep with all the excitement. When morning came he left to get ready for his class. Laurel, unable to sleep, tried to keep her mind busy by returning to the task of going through her grandmother's things, getting them ready for donations to one of her charity organizations.

Later on she received a call from the attorney's office concerning the additional assets of her grandmother's estate. Laurel got cleaned up and went to his office.

"In addition to this asset summary report, there is a safety deposit box left for you." The attorney handed her the key saying, "This concludes all of the estate of Barbara and Lawrence Crawford. Should you have any other questions, please let me know." Attorney Benson rose to shake her hand.

Laurel drove over to the bank and went in to get the contents that awaited her in the safety deposit box. Laurel opened a black box, reveling a diamond necklace and earring set. Underneath were the deeds and documents the attorney spoke of, plus a sealed white envelope with her name on the outside. Laurel opened the envelope where she found a letter, along with a key.

My Dear Laurel,

If you are reading this letter you know I have gone on to join your mother and your father. Please know in your heart we loved you very much. I have made the decision to pass on to you the Guardianship of the Spiritual Artifact. It has been concealed from view since the Aztec Priest hid it in the cave your mother uncovered when you were four years old.

My intuition told me to keep it concealed until an enlightened person came forth. I protected it from those that would harbor the dark energies, and keep the truth from humankind. This device can only be opened and used by a special soul. Because of the words spoken by the bishop to you, I believe, Laurel, are that person. Meditate and use your discernment always concerning this powerful Artifact device. AVF Mountain Vault– Queen Isabella and Elizabeth.

Love you! Remember, I am always with you on earth and into eternity.

Laurel became emotional with tears filling her eyes. Her Grams was a Guardian, appointed to safe keep and hide this other worldly device. Now she is turning it over to her. An enormous weight of responsibility swept over her. After regaining her composure, Laurel slipped the contents of the box into her purse, putting the key into a small, center pocket with a zipper. Leaving the bank, all she could think about was the letter her Grams had left for her. She had so many unanswered questions. She called Matthew. She needed to talk to him again.

"Hello, Laurel," Matthew answered.

"Matthew, the attorney called and gave me a key to Barbara's safety deposit box. One of the items was. . .well, I can't say over the phone." Laurel voice vibrated with wonder and excitement.

"Where are you?" Matthew asked.

"I am on West Battlefield, shall I come to your place, or do you want to meet me somewhere?"

"I'm just leaving my office at the university. Can you meet me at the Mexican Restaurant on South Campbell?" Matthew asked.

CHAPTER 55

Laurel arrived before Matthew, parking out front. She read through the letter once again thinking, *what's this AVF Mountain Vault?* Taking out her cell phone she looked it up, finding the facility was in Phoenix, she pulled up the web site and read about the facility. Matthew arrived and they went inside finding a quiet booth off to the side.

After ordering, Laurel handed the letter to Matthew and sat patiently while he read it. Then his eyes peered over the top edge of the paper staring at her for a moment in silence. "Well Laurel, seems your grandmother knew all along where that artifact device was. What do you think about the part where she says, *only a special soul can open and use the artifact!* Because of the words spoken by the Bishop, she thinks that person might be you?"

"At this point, I don't know. Another thing, this tattoo symbol that was on the arms of the captured, the red Maltese Cross inside this white circle, do you know what organization this is?"

"Part of this symbol was the old red eight-pointed cross which belongs to the Knights of Malta. A very old organization as far back as 1099 and I think they are still active today. One of my Professors, Dr. Franco Grasso, is more of an expert on their past and could tell us what their activities are today. He teaches at Arizona State University. Do you want to go to that AVF Mountain Vault?" Matthew asked. "If you do, I would like to go along. We could arrange to meet with Dr. Grasso while we're down there. He might be of some help of who these men are who wear this similar tattoo."

"Yes, I would like to see all the contents she put into that vault. I'm hoping my mother's original drawing will be with the artifact. We could fly, but if I want to bring that artifact and the other contents back here, it wouldn't pass through the security check. So let's take my FJ. I need to make a few arrangements, but could leave tomorrow morning. Will that give you enough time? Plus, I think we need some protection. We'll have no dog or fire extinguisher with us." Laurel smiled.

"Hey, I did pretty well. Don't make fun of my choice of weapons,." Matthew commented returning her smile.

Laurel gave Kourtney a call. "Did you hear about the intruders that broke into the Crawford place last night?

"Laurel, I just learned. I'm glad you are all right."

"I'm glad we brushed up on those self-defense exercises." She informed her about her grandmother leaving something for her in a Phoenix vault and how she and Matthew were going to leave in the morning to pick it up. She gave no more details.

"Kourtney, I would feel safer with a gun."

"We still have the weapons in lock-up that belonged to Lawrence and one that belonged to Barbara. Technically, they now belong to you. You can apply for a firearms license, but there is a waiting period for a background check. Those guys you have been dealing with, their weapon of choice is that blasted poisonous dart gun. Plus knifes. That's as deadly as a bullet."

"Well, I will apply for that license so I can have protection in the future. Any other weapon suggestions?" Laurel asked.

"Do you have a Mace pepper gun? It will shoot up to twenty-five feet, or a taser gun, it's range is fifteen feet. Both will disable enough for you to get away. You can purchase both in the Self Defense Store here in Springfield."

"Thanks Kourtney, I'll call when I get back about the guns." Laurel went straight to the self-defense store and purchased both types, returning to her place to get ready for the trip.

That night Laurel and Lizzie spent the night in her bedroom and awoke early the next morning with the birds chirping. She lay still, thinking about her recent dream about the Cahokia Princess. She saw her with the alien artifact pushing the symbols on top. The vision was starting to become blurry, now that she was awaking. Needing some hot tea, she went into her dressing room and started the coffee brewer for the hot water.

As she sipped the hot green tea, she thought about the long drive ahead of them, knowing the trip would be close to twenty hours with both driving. Then she had a revelation. She had the money now, she could charter a plane and easily bring those items back.

Laurel and Matthew took a comfortable seat aboard the Cessna Citation Encore after meeting with their two pilots. The weather report was sunny all the way to Scottsdale. Laurel had both the Mace pepper gun and the taser in her large handbag and planed on giving one to Matthew when they landed.

"I got hold of Dr. Grasso last night. After briefly explaining your situation, he said he certainly would make time to see us. We could come to his home in the suburbs of Scottsdale. We'll need to call him before going out."

"I want to go to the Vault facility first after we lease a car."

Laurel's thoughts about the letter her Grams left in the box at the bank still brought a few tears. Wiping them aside, she looked at Matthew, he was sleeping peacefully. After a while the humming of the jet lulled her asleep awaking when the Captain announced, "We will be landing soon, stay seated, seatbelts on."

Laurel could feel the plane descending and the memories of the crash landing, came flooding through. She grabbed the arms of her chair, her back stiffened, bracing herself.

Matthew noticed her actions and reached over to pat her arm, talking to her with some calming words.

Laurel felt the wheels touch the runway. It was a smooth landing, and slowly she began to feel relieved. Turning to Matthew she smiled. "Glad I made it through that. Thank you."

"You did good, next time it will be much better!" Matthew assured her with a smile.

The pilots brought the plane around to the Charter Building and opened the door for their departure. Matthew shook their hands, complimenting them for such a smooth ride.

"Our business should take us around four hours, we will call if it is longer," Laurel told the pilots.

Matthew sat in the driver's seat of the leased SUV, while Laurel checked the directions, guiding him south to West Thunderbird Road. Laurel asked him to pull in at one of the restaurants, so they could grab a bite before going to the vault facility. She showed him the two guns she purchased, explaining maybe having some protection is better than no protection. She gave him the Taser M26C Police Stun Gun, with laser and holster. She planned to carry the Mace Pepper Gun in the inside pocket of her light suit jacket.

After lunch, they were back in route to the vault facility, instructing him to turn south on Cave Creek Road. They continued driving south till they noticed the drive turned off the road and headed straight into the side of a mountain. All they could see was an office window, door, and overhead door, all flush with the side of a mountain.

"The sign above the door says "AVF Mountain Vault." This must be the right place," Laurel remarked. They parked the SUV and walked toward the office door when two-armed security guards approached them, asking the nature of their business.

"I am here to access my security vault," Laurel told them.

"Please step inside the office," one of guards politely said, escorting them inside the plush reception area. "You must leave all weapons with us until your business is completed and you are ready to leave this building."

Laurel reached inside her jacket and handed the mace gun to them and Matthew unsnapped the holster giving them the taser. They were escorted further to an elaborate, but comfortable, waiting area with an unoccupied and unusual desk in the adjoining room. Abruptly, the door to the back opened and a very little man, dressed in a nice suit and tie, walked forward to the desk and asked, "How may I assist you?" The attendant spoke with a heavy French accent.

"I would like to access my vault please," Laurel stated. The attendant pushed a button on the panel on his desk closing the door of his office from the waiting room. Two more guards entered the room from the back and stood at attention by this door.

"Place your key in the tray please." Laurel watched as an overhead camera instrument lowered and scanned the key. "Please lean forward, placing you face into the privacy computer mask, speaking your password firm and precise."

Laurel stepped up, placed her face inside the mask, and spoke, "Isabella and Elizabeth," then stepped back. The attendant cleared his throat, then said, "I'm sorry, the computer did not approve. It could be you misspoke, or maybe left off a word, or not in the right sequence. Perhaps, you did not speak precise enough. Our rules allow two more tries. Would you like to try again?"

"Let me check my passwords again please, just one moment." Laurel unfolded the letter checking the words. After the "AVF Mountain Vault," there was a hyphen, then word "Queen." Realizing she had omitted this word, Laurel announced she was ready try again.

The attendant motioned her to step up to the face mask for her second try. Laurel leaned forward to speak the four words into the computer. She backed away when finished, waiting for the attendant to acknowledge what the computer determined.

"Sorry, it was not accepted. Reason was volume failure." The attendant said.

"I don't understand. Am I supposed to shout my password into that computer? I was talking normal, and they didn't pass me."

"Please step away, I will run a test to make sure it's working properly." The attendant ran the test and found nothing wrong, explaining this would be her third try if she wished to try again.

Laurel took a breath and thought about it–*they didn't say wrong password, they said volume failure.* Taking a few moments, she addressed the attendant once more.

"I would like to try again, sir." Laurel stepped up, leaned forward, placing her face in position for the third and final time. This time she slowed down, stating each word loud, precise, and distinctive. Stepping back, she waited for the attendant to inform her of the results.

The attendant rose from his seat affirming, "The computer recognizes your password; would you please follow me to your vault."

Laurel let out a big sigh of relief and followed the little attendant as he led the way, with the two security guards walking behind her. On each side of the long aisle were numbered cage vaults. They took the elevator down seven levels, stepping out into a hall with large walk-in cage vaults on both sides. *Surely Grams didn't need one of these large vaults for the artifact and the few other things that she described finding in the cave.* Taking a few more steps he stopped at vault number 755, unlocking the mid-size walk-in vault, he handed the key back to Laurel.

"These two guards will remain outside this door. If you decide to take any or all the contents out of the vault, inform the guards. They will notify transport for removal to the loading zone, where you will be authorized to drive through to pick them up," the attendant instructed, then left the area.

CHAPTER 56

Laurel went inside and pulled some gloves from the inside pocket of her jacket. Placing them on, she started going through the boxes. Wrapped in a special paper that archaeologists often use for preservation she uncovered an Aztec blanket. Another box contained the clothing and the jewelry the Royal Children wore. Laurel opened the box that held the medallion, with a rather large disk and examined it thoroughly. The next container held several marked plastic specimen sacks. Laurel read one marked campfire contents inside Aztec cave, dated 1989, making it twenty-eight years ago.

There was one box left. Laurel anxiously peeled back the top paper, reveling her mother's sketch tablet laying on top of another packed bundle. She flipped through the pages of notes and past drawings until she came to the drawing of the three ships from the cave wall. Here, in her mother's own handwriting were notes about her detailed drawing. She took a moment to study one of the notes by the mound pyramids and long river. Here she noted the river was the Mississippi. She closed the tablet and held it close to her heart, an emotional feeling of love spun gently through her body. Somehow it brought them closer.

Laurel knew the last package wrapped in more tissue had to contain the artifact. Using close attentiveness, she slowly unwrapped the item revealing a pouch container that looked like leather. Peering inside she discovered the rounded cap her grandmother spoke of. She cautiously placed her fingers around it–nothing happened–she carefully slid it out of the container. Here it lay where she could view it better–still it presented no problem. Laurel thought, *so this is one of the artifacts that all these*

236

Guardians have hidden for hundreds, maybe thousands of years to protect it from falling into the hands of the dark side. Laurel ran her fingers over the bottom portion, thinking the minute bumpy surface was familiar, then noticing the slight grip indentations. Wondering how it might feel, she carefully picked it up. Surprisingly it fit her hand and felt good–not too heavy.

She examined the end cap with the different colored symbols, thinking she had seen them before, but where? *Why was this feeling so familiar? Was it because I heard about it during Grams regression? Or, was it something else?* Laurel lightly ran her fingertips over the symbols causing it to tweet. She lifted her hand away and it stopped. She put her fingers back on the surface–again she heard another tweet, even louder. She wanted to start pressing the symbols, to see what it could do. Yet– *this was not the place–too many guards, they might think it was a weapon, and commandeer it. I need to take everything out of here to a safe place where I can examine it in privacy.*

Laurel packed it all back into the box placing her mother's tablet on top. She told the security guards she wished to transport everything. Soon she was back with Matthew, driving the SUV to the front of the overhead door, where three-armed security guards stood prompting her to drive in. The door swiftly closed behind their vehicle.

After loading her boxes, the guard gave instructions, "Just follow the overhead arrows that will guide you out of the facility."

"We need our weapons returned to us!" Laurel voiced in a powerful tone.

"They are waiting at the end of the tunnel for you, please advance forward." Laurel drove on finally reaching the exit door where the guards stood waiting with their weapons. The door raised slowly allowing the brilliance of the Arizona sunlight to spill onto the front of the SUV, blinding them when the door lifted. "Where are my sunglasses!" Laurel declared, squinting to see.

"Wow, this place is heavily guarded," Matthew remarked.

"Boy, I had a rough time just getting through the check-in," Laurel remarked.

Looking at his watch he noted it was 3:00 o'clock. "Shall we call Dr. Grasso to ask if he can see us now?"

"Yes, go ahead and place the call."

Matthew dialed his number. "Hello Dr. Grasso, this is Matthew Vaughn. Dr. Robertson and I have finished our business here and wondered what time you are free to visit with us about the matter we discussed last night."

"I will be another hour with my work at the university. Where are you at right now?" Dr. Grasso inquired.

"We are on South Cave Creek Road," Matthew replied.

"Could you meet me at my house at 4:30? I will have my housekeeper prepare some food for us. It would be good to see you again Matthew, and I'm anxious to meet your friend."

Matthew agreed on the time and got directions. Turning to Laurel he asked, "What would you like to do, we have an hour and a half wait time?"

"I could use something to drink and a rest room, how about you?" Spying a drive-in just up ahead, she pulled into the parking. They pulled up google maps and located the street near where Dr. Grasso lived. Checking the route, they estimated it would be a thirty-minute drive to his house.

Laurel sipped her drink, while telling Matthew about the difficult time she endured with turning in her key and password. A black van with darkened windows, circled around behind them while they sat and talked. When they made their second pass, both Laurel and Matthew took notice, fearing they could be the same tattooed group they fought with back at the Crawford mansion, and were fixing to block them in. Laurel quickly pushed the door locks and backed out of the stall before the van circled around again.

Driving around the end of the building and up the other side, she whipped off the lot turning north on Cave Creek Road.

"They turned north too," Matthew announced, while he kept an eye toward the back. "At the next intersection hang a right and go around the block. Let's see if they really are following us."

Laurel made the right turn, quickly making a sharp right again heading back to Cave Creek Road. "Are they still there?" Laurel inquired.

"Yes, they are trying not to let us see them, but they are definitely following us."

Laurel turned back north on Cave Creek Road. With heavier traffic, she had to travel with the flow. Matthew kept a watch on the black van reporting, "They're gaining on us." Laurel was actively looking for a good place to hide before they got too close. When she topped the next steep hill, she spied a large business building on the right. Double-quick, Laurel decided to turn into the drive. Yelling, "Hang tight!" she whipped a sharp turn and sped the SUV around behind the back side, parking flush next to the building.

CHAPTER 57

Matthew got out of the vehicle and watched for the black van to come rushing over the hill, making sure it continued going north. He jumped back in the car, directing Laurel to speed out back the way they came on Cave Creek road and take the first left that she could, to get out of view. He directed her down to a major street going east.

Matthew kept watch to make sure they were not seen and Laurel began to relax some knowing they may have lost them.

"That black van sounds like the same MO Grams and Lawrence described. How did they even know where we were?" Laurel questioned

"They probably were watching your house and followed your car all the way to the airport, somehow they got hold of our destination, phoned ahead to have us tailed."

Matthew checked their location and how to get over to North Scottsdale Road., knowing they were early for the appointment, but they could find something to do after locating the street they needed to turn on. Laurel pulled into a shopping mall and found a fast food with a restroom.

"Let's take turns going in, with someone staying with the valuables," Laurel suggested.

Matthew agreed, "I'll stay with the car first."

When Laurel returned she moved the box containing the artifact and tablet up front and moved to the passenger seat. Taking the tablet, she turned to her mother's drawing of the cave wall. Here was a thorough depiction of the hieroglyphs. The Aztec priest told of his visions by the pictures he drew. Starting on the left side it showed one of the ships coming down by an Islamic Temple with three pyramids in the background, indicating Egypt may have been first, then Israel, then a mountain area. Next showing the artifact being in a boat crossing a large body of water, coming to rest by a cave with three priests in black robes. Above the cave was a small drawing of what looked to be Our Lady of Guadalupe."

Another ship landed in the Aztec Kingdom, with movement of the Priest, two children, and several Aztec warriors, leaving that area going northward to a cave. Laurel thought, *this must be the cave her mother was in.* The drawing on the right showed a ship coming down by the tallest flat top Mound Pyramid, surrounded by numerous other pyramids all next to a very long river. *I am sure this is Cahokia.* Laurel ran her hands over the pages trying to pick up her mother's energy. She began to feel it, along with a visual of her young, but mature mother. She felt loving arms wrapping around her. Her emotional response became heightened with her tender love.

Matthew returned, pecking on the window to let him in. Laurel continued to go through the tablet looking at the other drawings her mother made, turning back to the final drawing to show Matthew.

"That's a very interesting story that Priest was trying to record. This mountain range to the right of the Temple, must be the Estremadura Mountain where the Duchess hid the artifact.

Matthew continued to read the hieroglyphs, while Laurel pulled back the tissue uncovering the artifact in its case. She noticed a strange clip on the back side of the case. This was probably how they attached it to themselves to carry. Taking it out of the box, she slipped it over the waist band of her leggings, it fastened in place. It was lightweight and felt comfortable. Deciding to remove the two-page drawing, she easily tore them from the tablet, folded them, and placed the papers in her inside concealed pocket of her jacket.

"There was no drawing on the cave wall to indicate what the extra terrestrial's appearance was, just the ships. I wonder what the ET's looked like?" Laurel remarked.

"I wonder if they were human like us?" Matthew imparted.

"I am anxious to try and open the device. We might get some of those answers."

They sat for a while talking, and Matthew wondering what this area of the mall contained, started driving around just to kill some time, all the while being vigilant for the men in the black van.

It was getting closer to their appointment time with Dr. Grasso, so Matthew left the mall pulling out on Scottsdale Road again, stating they needed to watch for their next turn on E. Mountain View Road, then drive a short distance to 113 Haydon Rd.

They turned into a long blacktop drive flanked by large beautiful pines. The driveway ended with a circular drive in front. Another drive that went around the side of the house was gated. He lived in an older, brick, two-story, basement home. They locked up the car and went to the door. They were greeted by the housekeeper who invited them inside, informing them Dr. Grasso would see them in his study, and led the way down the hall. Laurel was feeling an uneasiness, but didn't know why, she didn't discern anything to be wrong.

Dr. Grasso rose from his seat behind a massive desk to welcome them to his home. The two professors shook hands and got reacquainted.

"Dr., I would like you to meet a dear friend, Ms.– excuse me – it's now Dr. Laurel Robertson, an archaeologist. Laurel, meet Dr. Franco Grasso, one of my college senior advisors." The two shook hands. Dr. Grasso was a nice-looking man in his latter fifties, who still spoke with a Italian accent, even though he had been teaching in this country for the past fifteen years. Dr. Grasso asked a lot of questions concerning her work. Knowing they were here because Laurel had requested more information on the Knights of Malta, he seemed happy to give her more insights into the organization.

He began by explaining, "They were originally The Knights of the Order of St. John of Jerusalem, which was formed long before their reign on Malta. Established around 1048, they were a community of monks responsible for looking after the sick in Jerusalem. Their motto was 'Defense of the Catholic faith and assistance to the poor'."

Dr. Grasso gave a complete history of their activities as being mostly a charitable organization. "Currently, they have approximately 120,000 members operating across six continents. These people have 1,500 hospitals and assist refugees, migrants asylum seekers and carry out medical an humanitarian projects in 120 countries. Ruled over by a Grand Master, who answers only to the Pope."

"You say they have a Grand Master?" Laurel questioned.

"Yes. He is called 'His Most Eminent Highness' and is accorded a precedence in the Roman Catholic hierarchy immediately following that of the most junior Cardinal. They have ambassadors or diplomatic representatives in more than eighty nations and have permanent observer status at the United Nations General Assembly."

"That's all very interesting Dr. Grasso," Laurel said.

"Now Dr. Robertson, I need to know from you why you are so interested in learning more about the Knights of Malta?" Dr. Grasso asked with a firm tone in his voice.

Laurel picked up on the change in Dr. Grasso voice, along with a different energy flowing around him. She kept this in mind as she went on to explain the situation of the murder of her grandparents, and how the men in custody each had a tattoo on their upper arm. A red and white symbol of the Maltese Cross, with a circle around it. Isn't this the symbol of the Knights of Malta?" Laurel questioned.

"Basically. There have been variations over the years. Was the cross white in color?

"Yes!" She took out her cell phone and showed him a photo she took of the one in the hospital. He looked it over, acknowledging it was one of the forms.

"They wanted something very badly," Dr. Grasso alleged as he moved closer to her. His eyes pierced directly into Laurel's when he asked, "Do you know what they were after Ms. Robertson?" Dr. Grasso pressed her for the answer.

Laurel felt leery about trusting him, even though Matthew seemed to. "Could you tell me what my grandparents could possibly have these Knights would be interested in–enough to kill them for, since they are supposed to be a charitable group?"

Dr. Grasso turned his hard look into a smile then laughed, as he backed away from Laurel. "It would be impossible for me to even presume, since I don't know what your grandparents were up to?"

He walked close to the kitchen door and checked the status of dinner with his housekeeper. With the smile still on his face he clasped his hands together stating, "Dinner is ready. Please come and join me in the dining room. My housekeeper is a fine preparer of Italian foods." He began filling their glasses with red wine. Matthew pulled out a seat for Laurel and they all sat around a beautiful set table with a centerpiece in a southwest theme. The housekeeper brought out several dishes of food that were passed around. The conversation switched to other topics, more in tune to dining conversations.

"Thank you for having us as your dinner guests and our compliments to your cook," Matthew remarked.

Dr. Grasso's received a call and he listened for a moment, then he got up. "Sorry I need to see to something, it won't take long. You two stay right here for my housekeeper will be serving a scrumptious dessert I know we all will enjoy." Laurel watched him leave, then she excused herself, leaving in search of a restroom.

Laurel walked down the hall going past the study where they had been earlier, noticing that Dr. Grasso was not in this room. The hall turned into another hall to the right, *Laurel thought maybe there is a restroom down this way.* Then she heard voices. Dr. Grasso was talking to another person. Laurel stopped and listened to detect if they were coming her way. They were not, so she stood still and listened. She heard a man say in a heavy Italian accent, "We had them for a while, but then they gave us the slip. We have already searched their car and we didn't find any artifact device."

Laurel reached inside her jacket and grasped her mace gun. Lifting it out, she flipped the safety off. She was ready if they started walking her way. She could still hear them talking, so she quietly, but rapidly reversed her path rushing back to Matthew who stood by the dining table. Grabbing hold of his arm she blurted, "We have to leave–right now!"

"What! Why, what's going on?"

"I overheard Grasso talking to one of those tattoo guys that chased us–I'll explain in the car."

"Don't let them see your weapon," Matthew declared, as they both hurried toward the front door. Laurel had the door open and was half-way out with Matthew right behind her when Dr. Grasso yelled, "Where do you two think you're going?"

CHAPTER 58

Matthew and Laurel kept right on going, with Laurel pushing the key unlocking the doors as she ran toward the passenger side of the SUV. Matthew was attempting to get inside the driver's side, but one of the men caught up to him pulling him from the seat onto the pavement.

Matthew rolled over trying to get away from the man's boot that was constantly kicking his leg while struggling to lift the taser gun from its holster. He pointed it at his attacker and squeezed the trigger, but nothing happened! Realizing the safety was still on, he fumbled around until it released, firing the load just in time, knocking the man backward. He fell, jerking profusely from the shock of the electrical current.

While Matthew continued his battle with another, Laurel was confronted by one of the men at the rear of the vehicle. He lunged at her with a knife. She twisted her body avoiding the blade, pulled the mace gun from her pocket and squeezed the trigger delivering a spray onto his upper body. The man yelled in pain and was partially blinded, but still came at her swiftly lurching the blade as Laurel kept moving backwards to avoid his jabbing. Again, she quickly stretched out her arm, thinking *it's now or never* and pulled the trigger, turning her head away so not to get any on herself. The man dropped to the pavement rolling and screaming with his hands to his face, yelling some words in Italian.

Another one of the men quickly came at her knocking the mace gun from her hand. He threw a punch at her, but she slapped his arm aside. Then he surprised her with a fast-left punch. Laurel went down; things were spinning for a while until she passed out. When she came to she managed to crawl over to the grass and roll to her side. She saw the same man slowly coming her way again, knowing she was at a disadvantage with his greater size and weight. She desperately needed help and intensely wished she had some sort of weapon in her hand. Miraculously the memory of how the artifact felt in her right hand came flooding through to her.

The artifact device that was once resting in the case at her waist was now resting in the grip of her outstretched hand. The man was getting closer, more memory came through–the coded keys on the end panel–one lit up making a beeping tone. Then she remembered more, she quickly depressed the key on the panel and out came a blue laser. She delivered the shot hitting the brick planter that stood six feet away. Laurel took better aim at the approaching fighter, hitting his hand that held a dart gun. He dropped to the ground in pain and holding his bloody hand.

Laurel turned to check on Matthew, finding him holding the taser gun pointing to Dr. Grasso with his arms raised in the air. Sirens could be heard blaring. Laurel said, "Leave him–come on let's get out of here!"

As Matthew was climbing back in the driver's seat, another man came rushing toward him. He pointed the gun saying, "You want a shot of this? The man kept on coming, so Matthew delivered another shot sending the tattooed man sprawling on the pavement.

Matthew immediately pulled himself all the way in the seat and leaned out the window shouting to Grasso–"Call your dog's off!" He then sped off. Matthew slowed down a few blocks after leaving, pulling into another resident's drive, they ducked down low in the seats until the patrol cars with their sirens sped on by. Then they backed out and left.

"Boy, am I glad to get away from there! Your expert on the Knights of Malta turned out to be with a group of Black Knights that split off from the original, working for the dark side," Laurel declared.

"I'm sorry, Laurel, I didn't know he had connections to the tattooed guys. They are tough and well trained and scattered everywhere. I wonder just how many of them there are."

"Are you hurt?" Laurel noticed the scrapes on his left arm.

"I'm all right but can't say the same for those back there lying on the pavement." He smiled at her when he spoke in his sexy southern accent. "Sure glad you gave me this 'mini-lightning thrower'. How about you? Looks like you'll have a nasty bruise on you check?"

"It smarts a little, but you can bet we are not out of the woods yet." Laurel thoughts went to the artifact device and the experience she just had. Matthew must not have seen her use it, or else he would have been surprised. She wondered what all it could do, with so many different codes?

"Do you remember the route to the airport? Laurel asked.

"I'm pretty sure we're on the right road."

"I'll call ahead and tell them to get that Cessna ready." Laurel laid her seat back as far as it would go and climbed in the back to check her cargo. It had been thrown around while they were looking for the artifact, but it looked like everything was still there. Laurel bundled everything back into two boxes, moving them to the floor behind her seat and climbed back into the front.

"Everything all right back there?" Matthew inquired.

"I think it's all there. I won't know if they damaged anything until I inspect it better." They both felt more relaxed just to get some distance away from Grasso and his bad minions–the Black Knights of Malta.

Matthew looked over and grinned at Laurel, "I can say this about you Laurel–Life is never dull around you." Laurel tilted her head slightly and smiled back at him.

Matthew turned onto East Cactus Road, a four-lane highway, and had only been on it a short distance when he noticed a black van weaving in and out of the traffic behind them.

"We've got company again," he announced as he speeded up.

"Are we ever going to get rid of these guys?" Laurel thought about where in Springfield she could keep this device safe from the hands of the Black Knights, *if we ever make it to Springfield, I should have thought this through better.* Matthew weaved in and out of traffic trying to stay ahead of the black van.

Laurel felt a vibration from the artifact clipped to her waistband. Then she heard a single beep. Her hand reached for the device. Pulling it out of the case, she looked down at the rounded top panel of code symbols. It beeped again along with one of the symbols flashing, then it was gone.

Matthew blurted, "They're closing in on us, just two cars back now." Sirens began to blare, traffic was backing up and slowing down. Suddenly the beeping and flashing on the device panel was going strong.

Matthew remarked, "What's going on over there?"

"The artifact. It's beeping and flashing a symbol." Laurel exclaimed. "It's trying to tell me something." Laurel remembered her Grams words, *"Meditate and always use your discernment concerning this device."*

"That van is gaining on us, we are going to need some help." Laurel placed her finger over the top of the flashing symbol.

Matthew looked over at Laurel. "What are you going to do? No Laurel–don't push that button!" In a split-second Laurel's finger came down on the flashing light. The action created a large light flash and Laurel felt a fast projection, revolving and spinning through a turning vortex at lightning speed. Then she was firmly settled into a different location, a different reality. Somewhat dazed, she tried to adjust to her new surroundings. Then she saw Matthew.

He was gasping, holding his hands to his head, he turned and looked around, observing his new and different surroundings. His hands went to his stomach. He bent over and threw up.

"Are you all right," Laurel asked.

Once he caught his breath he said, "Oh, I'm sick. What happened? Where in the world are we?" Mathew, still looking around at his strange surroundings, turned to Laurel saying, "What did you do Laurel? I told you–*Not* to press that button! But you went ahead and pressed it anyway–didn't you!"

"We were in trouble and I felt compelled to push the symbol that was flashing and beeping," she replied, noticing it had stopped. She placed the device back in its case clipped to her waistband.

"Did you even know what that symbol stood for?" He growled at her.

"Keep your cool–Man Up Professor! What's done is done! We'll just have to figure things out," Laurel declared as she reached out with both hands to feel the glass-like wall that felt smooth and hard. "I think we are in some sort of tunnel."

Suddenly they heard a noise from behind. Turning around, they were startled to see these rather tall feline-like beings standing there. Matthew grabbed hold of Laurel's arm, pulling her close to him. They stood still, gazing at the strange beings. Their skin was smooth with a color tone of soft teal blue and large almond shaped eyes. They were thin and wore shimmering silver-gray, tight-fitting suits.

CHAPTER 59

The one being in front pointed to the artifact on Laurel's waist-band. While speaking in a telepathic capacity, he conveyed a message. "We wish you no harm. We have been watching you and detected you were being chased by an audacious group who belong to a secretive society of a cabal that have political and religious ambitions to rule over all the surface of Earth. These people stem from an old demonic reptilian race. They would have killed both of you to take the CTD transponder that you are wearing. This device was missing from one of our ships that crashed near the Aztec Empire during the time Earth was bombarded with massive solar flares that disabled several of our ships."

"Who are you beings? Where are we?" Laurel questioned.

"You are safe with us. We are the Lemurians, a race that are the descendants of the Alta-Ra, Scientist-Priests of Atlantis. I am known as Aśtika. You are in the tunnels just outside our vast city, deep inside the Earth's caverns, under the area you call Arkansas. Our group on top-side picked up your emotional vibrations, Laurel Robertson, because you are connected to our people."

Matthew looked at Laurel with questions written all over his face.

"We enacted the CTD transponder, emitting those tones and flashing light, which triggered a deep memory within your subconscious of the time when you once used a device like this one. You pressed the symbol, having no fear in doing so."

The Lemurian pointed his CTD at the tunnel wall in front of them, transforming the wall into a doorway, revealing a whole new world. Before them was a very high bridge, spanning fifty feet across a body of water, leading to a massive crystal looking city, that could be viewed for miles.

Laurel and Matthew looked below to some purple dolphins in the water. The sky above them filled with beautiful cumulus clouds, drifting in a glorious sunlit day. Except, there was no sun to be seen. The colors were spectacular, more pronounced, than the ones on Earth's surface. Laurel's attention followed a wondrous, unusual looking blue bird with long tail feathers as it flew in front of her, swooping down and landing on some shoreline flowering shrubs. There, a group of orange and teal butterflies had flocked to partake of its nectar.

After crossing the bridge, they climbed aboard a long bullet shaped shuttle craft, designed for six. A glass domed roof instantly rolled over their heads. The craft raised up and took flight. Laurel looked down over the buildings. They were different types and styles, but all crystal in appearance. They had trees, some were green, others were blue in appearance.

The craft landed by a group of buildings that resembled old ancient temples, spread out in a large semi-circle. As they deported the craft, they noticed others were walking around in the area that had stopped to look them over. The Lemurian's led them up the steps of the center temple, into a large auditorium. They went down front to the stage platform where they stood by a large fifteen-foot circular pool of water that flowed over the top like a waterfall.

Laurel and Matthew watched as a massive six-sided clear quartz crystal, started rising slowly from the pool until it stood eight feet above the surface of the water. The Lemurian Priest named Aśtika said a prayer, calling forth the Supreme High Leader to meet their visitors. A few moments passed then suddenly a being appeared on a platform above the crystal. To their surprise, he appeared to be more human looking around thirty-five years in age, with a short beard and skin tone with a hint of blue color. His hair was long and pure white, wearing a diamond inserted in a gold band across his forehead. Then he spoke with a deep voice that echoed across the auditorium.

"Welcome! I am Alt, Supreme Leader of this city of Atlan. Time, space, and matter as you know it, does not exist here in 5D. We temporally altered your consciousness so you could exist and interact with us. I appear to you in this state of being because I have spiritually advanced to a higher dimension and can only exist here for short periods of time." They listened and watched his movements– his appearance was more like that of a Hologram.

"We came to earth more than 200,000 years ago, originating from Lumania and Mu, descendants of the Alta-Ra, who were trained by the spiritual Pleiadians. They were initiates of a great wisdom school with disciplines of scared science and spiritual proficiency in the Law of One. We interacted with the Alta-Ra and assisted in coding the vast fields of crystals that lie deep in the earth under Arkansas and Brazil. Our home is under the Arkansas region. Our skin tone is teal blue in color, mainly because of the mineral content of the water we consume here.

Your Native Americans knew of these caverns, we have even interacted with the group you are now studying that you call Cahokia. These crystalline regions of Earth are playing the most prominent role in the shifts and upgrades in dimensional frequency as part of your ascension process you may be feeling on the Earth's surface."

"You have been rescued from one of Earth's most powerful enemies, the Illuminati, that infiltrated The Knights of Malta and formed their own branch of a Secret Society within their ranks. This enemy is vast and has infiltrated many of Earth's organizations, such as another very old group, The Priory of Sion. All with one goal, to take control of everything. Creating One World Government and One Universal Religion, so they can present their Anti-Christ to the people on earth's surface. They have tried to do this in the past by causing and manifesting wars. But this didn't work, it was taking too long.

"They are in pursuit of our CTD devices, which would allow them entry to the Inner Earth, where they would try to destroy us, making it easier for them to go forward with their plans. This conspiracy is so large it is hard for your people to grasp, or even believe that it exists, but it has been growing inside these organizations since the mid-thirteenth century."

Alt, went on explaining. . .

"We work closely with Earth and the benevolent beings of the Star Nation. There is a New Earth being made ready. As its frequency continues to increase, so does the vibratory rate of our crystals. The major crystal fields of the planet play an important role in the dissemination of the crystalline pattern. Our region of the Earth is playing a most prominent role in the shifts and upgrades in dimensional frequency by stimulating the pineal gland. We assure you there is a divinely orchestrated and meaningful call within the crystalline members of the conscious mineral kingdom to increase the flow of vital life force and coded geo-energy that it receives from the Earth and the Central Sun.

"There is an event coming that will counteract all that this demonic society has planned for earth, but this is not yet the time for this to come about."

"We have been watching our CTD Devices that some of the earth people have labeled a 'Spiritual Artifact'. We knew where these were located, hidden away by the Guardians. The one you have was safely hidden by an Aztec Priest in a cave until your mother removed it. We know that you have discovered another of our craft, hidden halfway inside the largest mound of the North America continent, that you called 'Monks Mound'. This was built by an ancient race that is traced back to the Hopewell Culture, calling themselves the Tallegwi. In time, you will find evidence that this is true. The CTD that accompanied our pilot is there too. It is in immediate danger of falling into the wrong hands.

"You, Laurel Robertson, by being a multi-dimensional human with the Sirian-Pleiadian-Arcturian Alliance, were tasked to find and return the Lemurian CTD when it became apparent they were in danger of being found. Your fellow humans would term this as a "Universal Spy.

"The NSA, a part of your Government, has taken over the uncovering of this craft. But no new technology will be gained, as we rendered everything inoperable. If they try to remove the craft it will cause the Ancient Mound to collapse. We will not allow this to happen.

"These CTD's that are missing once accompanied the pilots of our downed crafts when Earth was attacked from space. Not by aliens, but by a natural event. This solar event of 993 A.D. came about after the sun generated and stored vast magnetic fields of energy in its interior, then released it, sending out intense coronal mass ejections that are far more powerful than solar flares.

"This powerful radioactive field hit Earth and three of our crafts that were already on Earth's surface. Many of the people went underground and survived, but thousands were not close to shelters and perished. This direct hit rendered the navigation system from working properly. They were stranded on Earth's surface. It was the pilot that taught the Ancients their planed city, and the hiding of our craft."

"Laurel, it is not until this lifetime that you started receiving the information, coming to you through your dreams, and visions. The device hidden in the abandoned Guadalupe mine is safe for now, even though there are ones searching with maps to find the massive treasure.

"I was an aspect of the Duchess of Aveiro y Arcos, of Madrid," Laurel affirmed.

"You were also an aspect of the Guardian recipient, when Father Kino became seriously ill and you were called to his bedside. Do you remember who you were then?"

Laurel momentarily thought. "I have been dreaming about a Jesuit Priest for the last several months," Laurel suddenly recalled. "I was an aspect of Father Giovanni Vega, of the Tumacacori Mission." Then she realized where she, or him in this case, hid the CTD–lowering it down into the old abandoned shafts of the Guadalupe mine.

The Supreme Leader allowed Laurel enough time to connect with these individuals that she carried an aspect of before declaring, "There is another Guardian that you may remember. Do you recall who this was?" Alt asked her.

Laurel's consciousness took her to the Aztec cave where she viewed all that was inside, knowing they had spent some time to rest before continuing their journey.

"We had taken the prince and princess, children of King Moctezuma II and Queen Teotlalco, his second wife, and fled. We purposely left the artifact, the children's royal clothing and the painting on the cave wall. We then buried the entrance with heavy rocks. We journeyed north to our other cave, where the subterranean tunnels were. This is where our ancestors arrived long before, explaining the tunnels were already in existence. Our Aztec people, just weeks before us, journeyed to hide our vast storage of gold, silver, and other treasures, in these tunnels, knowing that Cortez's army would be back to plunder and ravage all they could."

Matthew spoke up, "You placed the device in the cave, hiding it from the invading conquistadors. It's like you came full circle and have possession of the device once again."

"There is another aspect you may remember," Alt added. "The Cahokia princess that guided her people to safety. Listen for her messages, as she continues to be a part of your human experience. It is time for both of you to return to your dimension on the Earth's surface as the temporary heighten of your consciousness will be wearing off soon."

"I am Alt, Supreme Leader of Inner Earth and crystalline service. You are always loved, continue to shine your light all around you, as you walk your path. Until we meet again." Then spontaneously he was gone, with the giant crystal receding back into the pool.

They boarded the flying shuttle to the bridge where they walked across, then both turned around to view the city one last time before departing through the gate of the tunnel. The Lemurian Priest alerted them that he was ready to activate the transport symbol on the CTD. Laurel latched onto Matthew's hand, nodding that they were ready. Then there was a large flash!

CHAPTER 60

Laurel and Matthew were lifted and spun into an energy vortex that would soon place them back on the Earth's surface. Laurel could feel the changes going through her body as she spiraled inside the vortex, seeing and feeling the energy of the colors as she passed through them. They returned to their seats in the SUV, now parked on the shoulder of the road.

Both were temporally dazed and trying to regain their bearings, wondering what had happened to them and where they were, seeing strobe lights bouncing all around them.

Matthew grabbed his stomach again. Then there was loud knocking on the windows, on both sides of the car. Their first thoughts were the Black Knights again. Laurel reacted with a quick reflex, sending her hand to the mace gun. Soon they were looking at badges–flush to the windows.

"We are the NSA–roll down your windows!" They loudly shouted. Again, they banged on the windows shouting, "Roll down the windows– Now! Or we are coming in!" The agents commanded, still holding their badges up.

Matthew rolled down his window and quickly hung out his head, releasing the remaining stomach contents. "Look out!" The agent declared, as he dodged the projectile. Laurel removed her hand off the mace gun and slowly rolled down her window. She was slow in being coherent, but it appeared they were pulled over by two black vans with strobe lights.

Agents surrounded their vehicle. Laurel and Matthew, still dazed from the transport they had just gone through, were beginning to comprehend.

"What can. . . we do. . . for you. . . officer?" Laurel managed to speak first, still trying to bring her speech into balance.

"Are you two all right?" The NSA agent asked, shining his flashlight around in their vehicle, while the others did the same.

"Yes. . . of course," Laurel remarked, knowing her speech was not normal she limited herself to saying as little as possible, until it caught up to her vibrations.

"We saw a dark van chasing the two of you. We intercepted just as they were trying to run you off the road. You managed to keep it on the shoulder, but then we saw two flashes of light inside your vehicle."

"What happened inside–what caused those flashes?" The NSA agent pressed for an answer.

Laurel looked to Matthew with unspoken words. They both surmised they must have seen the flash of light when they were transported through the gate. Even though their visit with the Lemurians was roughly three hours, since there is no time in the higher dimensions, the NSA agents only caught the flash of light when they left here and another when they returned.

Matthew said, "Sorry about my suddenly throwing-up–must be motion sickness." Shaking his head, "As far as a light, I have no idea what that could be officer. I had my cell phone out, attempting to dial 911, when suddenly your team appeared." His words were slow, but distinct and precise.

The one NSA agent stepped aside talking on his phone, then returned stating, "Laurel Robertson you are wanted for questioning. Both you and Matthew Vaughn need to step out of this vehicle."

"First officer, we need to disclose we both have weapons on us," Matthew said.

The Agents drew their guns. "Both of you, raise your hands high." They opened their doors. "Now slide out and stand in front of the vehicle. The agents patted them down removing the mace and taser guns. Cuffs were put on both. "You both will come with us for questioning."

"Officer, I have valuable's in my vehicle. I can't leave them here."

"We are searching right now, all will be accounted for." Laurel and Matthew stood in front of the vehicle until the search was completed. They were taken to the Scottsdale airport where they boarded a private jet for Lackland Air Force Base in San Antonio, Texas.

Laurel was taken into a room where she met two NSA agents, Collier and Parks. They wanted to know why these men were chasing them. What did this group want from them?

Laurel explained these men had killed her grandparents over something they thought they had. Then followed her and Matthew down to Phoenix and Scottsdale thinking that she might have this item since they didn't find it with her grandparents.

"Ms. Robertson what item is it they thought you had?" Agent Collier asked.

"Well, what they seek is nothing but a myth. It doesn't exist," Laurel commented.

"Ms. Robertson, tell us about it?" Agent Collier pushed for the answer.

"They are looking for a device they call a 'Spiritual Artifact', believed to be a powerful extraterrestrial device of some sorts."

Agent Collier looked to Agent Parks and smiled.

"So they killed your grandparents and were chasing you two because they thought you were in possession of this ET device?" Agent Colliers tone was depicting non-belief.

"You can check with Greene County in Missouri, where they now have three of these men in custody after they broke into my house several nights ago. All had the same tattoos on their arm. We found out they were members of a secret society within the Knights of Malta! They also have one in custody in Amarillo, which makes four."

Both agents left the room leaving Laurel alone. Her thoughts went to their recent experience with the blue beings, the Lemurians. *It's starting to feel like everything I experienced was like a dream. I need to firmly plant in my conscious mind what I learned from them, before it starts to drift away. . .fading from my mind completely. I wish I could write it down, but that's impossible, while I'm stranded in this interrogation room.*

Laurel started to repeat the most important parts of what she learned, over and over, firmly planting the information in her conscious mind.

The interrogation door opened with the same two agents returning with more questions. They started with the contents of the boxes found in the SUV, then to all she knew about the Craft she and her archaeology team discovered at Cahokia.

Several hours passed by. Finally, Agent Collier straightened up in his chair and announced, "Ms. Robertson this concludes our investigation. We are releasing both you and your friend, Professor Vaughn, back to Scottsdale."

When they deported the plane, they were given the two boxes of valuables taken from the SUV. Laurel checked, everything was still there. Then the agents handed back their mace and taser guns, just before they turned and boarded their agency's jet.

"Let's go over and see if our charter jet is still here," Laurel said, with a hint of hope.

The desk agent picked up his phone and was talking to the hanger manager, when they heard him say, "Tell them to hold up. Their two passengers are standing here, ready to go. Man, you two are lucky, another five minutes they would have been on the runway. I'll walk you over."

"Welcome back Ms. Robertson, I have already filed our flight plan to Springfield. Are there any changes to be made on this?"

"No, thank God! Springfield sounds pretty good to me." They both got settled in their seats and Laurel made her apology, "Matthew, I am so sorry. I hope they weren't too hard on you? Did they question you as long as they did me?"

"No, there wasn't very much I could say. They wanted to know how I knew Dr. Franco Grasso, and why we were meeting with him. It seems they have been watching him and his activities for a long time. They questioned me extensively about those flashes of light. I was questioned about forty-five minutes about various things. The rest of the time I just sat there until they finished questioning you. Laurel, I never disclosed you ever had possession of the ET device, just that those men from the secret Knights organization were chasing us, thinking we might have it."

"Did you disclose any information we learned from the inner Earth? "Laurel asked.

"No. No way! You know, everything I saw and learned from them was very interesting, especially this Leader–Alt, he put forth some serious information. But, you know, it's starting to fade somewhat." Matthew shook his head. "Did that really happen? Did we actually get transported to Inner Earth?" Matthew smiled, and his smiling turned into nervous laughter.

When he stopped, Laurel explained, "It will continue to fade much like a dream until you repeat the parts you want to retain, anchoring it firmly in this consciousness." They leaned back and went to sleep.

When the flight was over they walked back toward her vehicle. Matthew faced Laurel. Putting his hands on her shoulders, he began to smile as he stared into her eyes.

"You know Dr. Robertson, I finally figured out why I'm so attracted to you."

"And how's that, Professor?" Laurel inquired as she returned the smile.

"It's that winning personality of yours. It simply takes me out of this world sometimes." They both broke out in laughter, his hands remained in place.

Laurel leaned in and kissed him in a most loving manner. Matthew returned the kiss and stepped back. Smiling, with a glow surrounding him he asked "Since we're starting all over, do we consider that our first kiss?"

"I would say yes–but watch yourself, Professor, things get a little too hot when we get close!" Laurel reflected with a smile.

"What are your plans next, Dr. Robertson?"

"Get some food and more sleep. Those guys didn't offer me anything but coffee or water. I thanked God they had some tea bags. I didn't care what kind it was at that point." They both started laughing, finding it hard to stop as they got into the FJ cruiser.

"I think we're suffering from jet lag," Matthew declared.

"Also, you can add dimensional lag." Laurel's statement caused more laughing. "It's sort of like a marijuana high. . .everything is funny!"

"I'm starved too," Matthew said. "I know of an all-night restaurant not far from here."

The early morning dampness and humidity reminded them they were back in Missouri as they walked to the restaurant.

They made themselves comfortable, sprawling out on each side of the booth, waiting for their order.

"Those blue beings will stick in my mind for a while. . .and that Crystal City was amazing!" Matthew affirmed.

"Weren't those colors beautiful down there? Did you see that large blue bird with the long tail feathers, the blues were variegated and looked like velvet."

"No, I missed that one, but saw a strange looking green and black bee with almond shaped eyes, hovering over a tall purple flower."

"I wished we could have stayed longer, I wanted to walk around and explore more of their world, "Laurel said.

"Something tells me you have been there before. That transport– that energy vortex– it didn't bother your stomach like it did mine."

"But you recovered in time. It probably will get easier every time you do it. Do you have the whole summer off?" Laurel inquired, trying to steer him away from her energy abilities.

"Mostly," Matthew answered. "I want to take Sophie to a museum. I'm hoping the new Wonders of Wildlife will be opening soon. I hear it's going to be right up there with the rest of the world class museums." He smiled. "What's turning over there in that pretty head of yours?"

"I'm going to take these ancient Aztec articles and put them in Lawrence's climate-controlled room temporally, until my next trip back to the Chicago Museum. But first, I'm going to pay a visit to our dig site in East St. Louis."

"You're going to try to recover that CTD Artifact aren't you, but how? Didn't you say there were guards posted in front of the tunnel, and other parts of the park blocked off completely?"

"I'm not sure until I get there. Things may have changed, depending on if there is a crew working inside that ship. Or there is a possibility they might be stupid enough to try and dig it out. Alt alleged they would not allow this to happen."

"How would they stop them?" Matthew asked.

"I don't know how, but I'm betting they could do it."

"Laurel, trying to recover that one at your work site, still sounds like too big of a task for you, with all those guards. I hope you don't get yourself in trouble again with the NSA, or fool around and get yourself killed!"

Laurel smiled and inwardly thought, *we'll see. . .that's the one I need to get to first, before the NSA does.*

Laurel parked in front of Matthew's place and he reached over to her shoulder gently pulling her toward him. With a smile he said, "We're still good about starting over, aren't we?"

"I'm looking forward to it. Thank you for going with me on that little adventure. I'll call you when I return."

Matthew leaned over giving her a most passionate kiss. "Just play it safe and make sure you do get back. I'm going to miss you," Matthew declared, still smiling as she pulled away.

Laurel met the chartered craft and boarded for East St. Louis, knowing Rosie would be there to pick her up.

CHAPTER 61

"Morning Rosie." Laurel greeted her co-worker. "How are things going?"

"We're doing fine here. It's so nice to have you back." On the drive to the rental house in Collinsville he caught her up on their activities.

"What's going on inside the tunnel?" Laurel asked trying to get a feel for what the NSA was doing.

"We have been seeing a lot of activity, people going in and out. Several days ago, they backed a truck up close to the entrance."

"That sounds like they may be ready to load up something big. Have they widened the tunnel any?"

"No, we haven't heard those big heavy machines the engineers used when they were digging the tunnel out."

"They may be planning on bringing out parts of the interior. Have they put up a security gate across the entrance?" Laurel asked.

"Can't tell from our angle. The soldiers are still guarding out front."

Laurel took the binoculars from the drawer stating, "Lets climb the mound across from the tunnel and watch them for a while. I need to know more of what they are doing."

Rosie parked his jeep at the Cahokia parking and the two weaved their way around so none of the guards saw them. Then they started climbing on the back side of the mound across from the tunnel entrance, making their way to the top side, hovering close to the ground, thankful enough shrubbery stubbles remained to hide behind.

There was an open gate and they watched as some men got out of another vehicle and went inside. After three hours they came out wheeling a cart carrying something wrapped and loaded it inside the truck. They watched them all morning. After loading a total of four wrapped items, they locked the gate and both vehicles left. Laurel could see the lock using the binoculars. It looked like a combination lock. The two guards were still out front.

Laurel whispered to Rosie, "We can leave now." The two crawled back out the way they came.

"What's your plan, Ms. Laurel?" Rosie asked on their walk back to his jeep.

"I don't know yet. I need to get to that artifact, somehow, before they do. Got any suggestions, Rosie?"

"I've been inside while they took everyone to be investigated; I know how far back the tunnel goes and what it was like inside where they dug out only a portion of the craft. They probably dug all the way around, by now. I heard the engineers were planning on shoring up around the craft to stabilize the earth and soil so it wouldn't collapse."

"I need to talk to Jennifer Noor again. Is she still around with Dr. Weston?"

Rosie looked at his watch. "They usually run in to Collinsville for lunch at that sandwich and salad place. Want to surprise them?"

Laurel and Rosie walked into the sandwich shop finding Dr. Weston and her niece Jennifer sitting at a table with Joann Maury.

"Anything good on the menu today?" Laurel questioned with a big smile.

Joann jumped up and said, "Where did you come from?" She reached out to greet her.

"I thought I would just drop in and surprise everyone. I was getting homesick and hitched a ride up here, calling Rosie to pick me up." Looking around she saw several more of her team, and went over to say hello, then returned to Joann's table.

"After lunch can you three meet me back at the office, I need to go over a few details with you. Does anyone know where Alex is?"

Joann replied, "He took Stephanie and Aaron and went in to St. Louis to get one of the radar instruments repaired."

The three met back at the office and Laurel drew a diagram of the west end of Monks Mound and the tunneling. Rosie gave the approximate dimensions back to the craft. She asked Jennifer to tell her once again, how far off the east wing tip, and the angle she remembered seeing the artifact device.

"If they dug around the craft far enough past that wing, which we can guess they probably would to get accurate dimensions," Laurel commented. "And if they went out two, maybe three feet to leave a walkway, then we could figure that in. Right here is where the artifact should be." Laurel pin pointed on the drawing.

"How do you propose to get past those guards?" Joann asked.

"And that new gate with a combination lock on it we discovered this morning?" Rosie inquired. "Do you plan on sneaking in when the gates open? There will be workers inside."

Just then Alex walked through the door with Stephanie and Aaron. They were surprised to see Laurel standing at the office table. Stephanie rushed over to give her a hug. "I didn't know you were coming back so soon."

Alex smiled and reached out his hand. "Glad to have you back." His hand clinched hers very tightly, as his other hand reached around her shoulder for a hug. Laurel explained the diagram she drew and asked Alex if he thought these were the correct measurements.

"The tunnel length back to the craft is a few feet shorter. Other than that, it looks about right. We saw trucks taking soil away and depositing it away from the restricted area. It was enough soil we could determine they dug around it.

"What about our engineers? Did they leave and go to another job?" Laurel asked.

Alex and Joann laughed, with Alex explaining, "Same job site, new employer. The NSA told them they would no longer be working for the McMelton Corporation. They were rehired to finish digging out around the craft and to build the supporting soil stabilizers. It seems we had hired the best tunnel company around."

Laurel put her diagram away for now and went with the crew to the new pyramid site. Their progress was slowed with the malfunction of their ground penetrating radar, but now that it was repaired their perimeter work could resume.

"I bought this new piece of tech equipment while we were gone," Alex related. "It's an SIR 4000, a hand held GPR Controller, for processing and imaging. We can run this along the edge of the pyramid and get a read out of what's directly underneath, appearing on the LED display."

Laurel tried it out, learning what it would do. This is exactly what she needed to run on the wall inside the tunnel. This could find the right location, measuring how deep to dig, and not be cumbersome like the other radar instruments! That evening Laurel spoke with Alex again, making sure no one else was listening.

"Alex, do you know if the engineers installed any air vents back in the tunnel?"

"There is one in the cave ceiling close to where I was standing, about six to nine feet away from the front of the Alien Craft." Alex looked at Laurel in a curious manner. "What are you thinking, Laurel? If you're thinking, what I'm thinking. . .then yes, it's big enough. I know just where that vent is on the first level surface."

"Yes, I'm thinking the same thing." Laurel smiled. "How far of a drop would you estimate it would be?"

"Oh, it's about twelve feet from the tunnel ceiling to the floor, but the length of that ventilation shaft is what I'm uncertain about," Alex disclosed.

"We need to tie off our ropes to something, and we can't go banging on a steel stake, announcing to the guards what we're about to do."

"Laurel, I need to ask you something." Alex had an intense look about him.

"Yes?" Laurel awaited his question.

"Were you thinking I would be going with you?"

"Why not, after digging out the artifact, we can have a look inside the craft. They probably have that door opened by now."

"I know it's large enough for you, Laurel. My concern is, is it large enough for me?"

"Only one way to find out. Let's change into some dark clothes and go measure it," Laurel replied.

"It's a good thing we have a full moon to help light our way." Alex remarked keeping his voice low as they made their way up the west side of the mound. They crossed the first terrace over to the place where the surface extended southward in a position that aligned with the center of the third and fourth terrace. "It should be somewhere in this area," Alex whispered to Laurel, as they crawled around on their hands and knees. After a few moments Laurel felt the grid, with a rain deflector on top. Barely able to reach Alex's foot, she shook it to let him know she found the vent. Alex crawled back to meet her while Laurel changed her position to shield the light from her phone.

Alex took one of the tools from his bag and commenced prying the grid off. Then suddenly, the scrape of the tool against the metal let out a screech. They paused for a few moments, hoping the guards didn't hear. He proceeded again, working slower and more careful he managed to remove the grid. Taking his measuring tape, he measured the opening and placed the tape back on his belt.

"Well?" Laurel whispered in his ear, anticipating his answer.

Alex whispered back to her, "Laurel, don't you know by now, I was always a good fit with you," he snickered.

Laurel gave him a stern shove backwards whispering, "This is no time to play around."

Alex took some steel repelling stakes from his tool bag. He unwrapped the padding he had placed around them to insure their quietness and pushed them with all his strength into the ground, about two feet apart. Laurel set the top of the grid loosely in place, and the two quietly crawled out the way they came, making their way back to Alex's Hummer.

Alex drove to the neighborhood lounge. "I think I could use a night cap after our recent prowl." The two walked in to a relatively quiet night crowd. The Mystery T.V. people had left the area now that most of the demonstrations had died down. Alex found a table off to the side, away from the other group so they could talk. "Now that we're all set, we need to decide when the best time would be to drop in, so to speak"

Laurel explained what she and Rosie saw this morning. Those large devices they loaded up in the truck may have been some of our NASA electronics to try and access the ET's controls. Or maybe they took out some of the ET's instruments. I think we should get a few hours' sleep, set our alarms for three, and return with all our repelling equipment."

"We need a strong third person up on top, so who do you want to recruit?" Alex questioned.

"Finish your nightcap, we're going back to talk with Rosie," Laurel remarked as she downed hers.

CHAPTER 62

The three unloaded their equipment and took the same route quietly up the side of Monks Mound over to the air vent. Alex and Rosie fastened the ropes to the steel repelling post. By hand, they pushed them in deep and at an angle so they would hold the weight. Laurel descended first, kicking off the ceiling grid, then Alex followed. They came down right by the ET craft, finding the door partly open. Alex stuck his head inside to look around, then he stepped inside to have a better look, with Laurel following him. She thought, *this is going to be a mistake; it's going to be difficult to get Alex out of here.* Laurel grabbed his arm saying, "You promised me we would dig the artifact out first, so come on out of there– We'll come back later."

"Hold on–don't get your thong in a knot," Alex uttered while he shined his flashlight across the interior.

Laurel followed the light as he continued to shine it around. Somehow this was beginning to look familiar, but Laurel didn't know why. She grabbed his arm again, but he stayed, not paying any mind to her. Laurel needed to get to the artifact before their time ran out. She knew there was only one thing that would tear Alex away from here. Oh, she thought, *what we Alliance people must do– all in the line of duty! I'll see if I can work up a touch of magic. I know just what will turn this one on.* She got up close to him and started softly kissing around his right ear, while she ran her fingers through the hair on the nape of his neck. She started slowly kissing his cheek, teasing ever so lightly. Laurel could tell by his reactions; the mysterious ET Craft was starting to take a back seat to her playing around.

"Well, if I knew you were going to get so turned on by an alien ship, I would have dropped you down here a whole lot sooner." Alex breathed into a little playful laughter as he started to return her advances.

Laurel chuckled and continued her seductive kissing. easing toward his lips, teased him some more. Taking his hand, she led him through the door hatch and around by the side of the craft. "I promise to bring you right back inside that craft for more fun and games, and afterwards you may be the only human who could actually boast they joined the 'Stranded Alien Air Craft Club'."

"All right! Where is my new SIR 4000? Let's get that baby found and dug out. . . so we can get back inside to our alien craft inspection and those fun and games!"

Laurel ran the new infield GPR device slowly on the tunnel wall, while Alex got the tools and bags ready for digging. She was being patient, as she thought this was the right spot. After a while, she stopped and looked at the LED and settings to make sure the sound was on.

Alex said, "Let me try. Maybe it's a little higher than your short arms can reach." He ran the device up high then sweeping back and forth. Nothing was happening. He started sweeping more behind the craft, when abruptly he let out a cry."

"Alex! What happened?" Laurel asked while she shined the light in the direction he was standing, discovering he had fallen in a deep hole. "Are you hurt?"

Alex managed to stand back up. "I'm okay, I think. It appears they didn't finish their walk-way because of this sink hole pocket."

"Hang tight. I saw some boards stacked over there." Laurel found one that might work and returned to help Alex. He managed to climb out with Laurel's help.

"That was unanticipated," he said as he brushed himself off. Alex unzipped his sweatshirt and reached in for the GPR he had placed inside, commenting, "she is good to go."

"How about you? Anything broken?" Laurel inquired, taking the GPR from his hands.

Alex shook his head and smiled at her saying, "You'll be glad to know, all the important parts are undamaged and ready to go."

"That's good, Alex, now let's try that SIR right above the wing tip," Laurel suggested. She moved it around slowly sweeping the whole area, then heard a beep. Moving the device back she pin-pointed it.

"All right!" Alex declared. "Let's have a look at what she reads."

"It's showing an object lying twenty-two inches inside. Our first discovery, Alex!" Laurel was so excited; she grabbed Alex and hugged him tight.

"Oh, that was sore," Alex related. "I think I bruised a shoulder muscle."

"Sorry about that." Laurel spread out a plastic sheet to catch the dirt. Taking her hand trowel, she started digging out the object. Alex took turns helping her. When they finally reached the object, it appeared to be sitting on a shelf. Laurel very carefully took her brush and dusted all around it. "Yes, it is sitting on a shelf–a rock shelf. Alex, what do you make of this? There were never any rocks found in any of the other mounds. Why was it used here?" She had brushed around the artifact enough to lift it out.

"That's right." He took his brush and continued to dust around the shelf.

Laurel kept cleaning up the artifact, being very careful not to press any of the symbols. She thought this looked just like the other one, belonging to the Lemurians. So this confirms the alien ship is Lemurian. Also, her mother's drawing by the Aztec priest was right. *Which was really me, I guess?* It's a shame she couldn't tell Alex this craft, that has him spell bound, is a Lemurian craft from the Inner Earth."

"I have discovered this rock shelf goes all the way down several feet," Alex disclosed. "I think they placed that artifact device here for a reason, but why? Let me see it."

Suddenly they heard voices down in the tunnel coming toward them. Laurel pushed the button on her cell phone, plunging them into total darkness, and clipped the artifact to her belt. They both slipped around the right wing, sliding the plastic sheet containing the dugout soil, behind the craft. The voices became louder as they walked inside the cleared area and went inside the craft. Laurel and Alex continued to hear them talking, with one complaining of getting up so early. It sounded like they were setting up to run some sort of test.

Laurel wondered if they could sneak past the open door without them noticing. Laurel moved up to the door first. With the technicians' backs to the door, she very quietly slipped on over to the area under the vent. Rosie saw her and dropped one of the ropes. Laurel climbed as quickly and quietly as she could. Alex gave her a head start, then he went past the doorway.

Rosie was watching for him and slid the other rope down and Alex started his climb. They were making progress, when abruptly Laurel's rope started slipping. Rosie grabbed it, pulling tight, but it was slick up on top after the morning shower, and he too started sliding. Laurel came crashing down onto Alex, and their bodies clanged against the metal sides of the ventilation shaft, making enough noise the two men hurried out of the craft to see what made the noise.

The men looked around seeing nothing, then one looked up and saw the two hanging inside the ventilation shaft and called the guards. Laurel was partially resting on top of Alex, still holding to her rope when she heard beeping coming from the CDT transponder. She took one hand and pressed the symbol. There was a flash and Laurel felt the spiraling energy flow through her again as she traveled in the vortex, knowing she would be joined by Alex this time.

Laurel and Alex were transported to the same space as last time inside the tunnel system, just outside the Lemurian City of Atlan. They landed in the same position they were in when she pressed the beeping symbol, with Laurel's legs wrapped over Alex's shoulder and body. Laurel crawled off Alex and stood up, adjusting to the change to higher energies much faster than Alex.

Alex sat on the tunnel floor, looking around at his strange new environment. "Where are we?" he uttered as he managed to stand up. Soon a small group of the Blue Beings entered the transport area speaking in their telepathic communication to Laurel.

Laurel raised her hand greeting them, asking, "Where is the one called Aśtika? May I speak to him?"

"He is expecting you. We will escort you to him," one of the Lemurians answered.

"Laurel, what is going on here? Am I dreaming?" Alex asked.

"How do you feel?"

"Strange as hell." Alex stared at the blue beings.

"Alex, these beings are the Lemurians. They are good people from the Inner Earth. I can vouch for them."

Soon they were through the tunnel, walking across the bridge and sitting in the long shuttle. This time they flew over the city to one of the crystal mines. Alex was amazed seeing the giant crystals that stood on the outside of the mine.

"Laurel, look, I bet you never saw a crystal that big before."

"Aśtika will meet you on the third level," the Lemurian said, as he opened the door to the elevator. Laurel and Alex followed him through a maze of amethyst crystals to where they met Aśtika.

"Welcome, Laurel. I see you brought along another visitor, and I see you recovered another of our CTD devices. You have been 'busy', as you surface humans say."

"This visitor is Dr. Alex Zuckerman, he is an archaeologist that I work with on the surface." Laurel went into another area with Aśtika, leaving Alex to look around at the mining operation. Laurel unclipped the CTD and handed it over to him, explaining where she found it.

Laurel rejoined Alex to find him holding his head. "My head is starting to hurt pretty bad," he moaned.

"The energy from the crystals are too strong down here for us," Laurel announced.

"Of course," Aśtika said, we ourselves must limit our stay until our tolerance is built up."

They were ushered into a nearby elevator and taken to the topside where they said their farewell.

"Boy, my head was hurting so bad, I'm glad we got the heck out of there. There were so many of them," Alex remarked.

They rode the shuttle back and crossed the bridge to their arrival point within the tunnel. Laurel took his hand when the blue being pointed the CTD at them. Soon they were back on the Earth's surface, laying on the grassy Monks Mound, next to the air vent, alongside Rosie. Laurel quickly removed the ropes and placed the vent back. "Let's hurry and get out of here." Laurel grabbed Alex's arm. "Come on–get moving, they will be after us. Laurel knew he was still dazed from the experience, but if she could get him moving, he would eventually adjust to this reality. They heard the guards shouting as they searched for intruders that the technicians had reported. They managed to get away in Rosie's Jeep, not using any lights as they left.

On the drive back to the rental house, Alex asked, "I'm confused, what happened back there?"

"We nearly got caught, that's what happened. Don't you remember? My rope slipped, I fell into you making some noise, then they saw us inside the air vent. It's a good thing Rosie grabbed my rope and I was able to climb out, with you scrambling right behind me," Laurel replied.

"Man, it all happened so fast," Alex uttered.

"Thanks, Rosie, for being there," Laurel declared, adding, "We saw the inside of the ET's Craft."

Alex stated, "I wouldn't have traded that experience for anything, all those high-tech instruments plus gadgets I have never seen before. It was amazing!"

"Did you find the artifact, Ms. Laurel?" Rosie asked.

"We did find it using Alex's new detecting tool, but unfortunately, it bumped off me when I fell into Alex." Laurel knew they both would not remember the true version of the story, as it would fade away, more so with her planting a new version to take its place.

The next morning, Laurel said her goodbye's until she could return after overseeing the renovation of the Crawford Estate. Alex drove her over to the airport car leasing agency.

"Laurel, I would be more than happy to drive you back to Springfield," Alex declared. He had a longing look that she knew was the result of her teasing him inside the E.T. craft.

"Thank you, Alex, but you are needed here more than ever, since I will be gone. Besides, I will be back in a few short weeks." She got out saying, "I trust you to take care of our project and uncover as many of the new sites as you can. Until next time." She smiled as she waved good-bye, watching him pull away in his Hummer.

On the drive back to Springfield, Laurel's thoughts returned to her experiences with the CTD Transponder, aka 'the Spiritual Artifact!' When she was in trouble fighting those Black Knights, the CTD mysteriously appeared in her hand. She didn't have one on her waist band any longer, after returning it to the Lemurians, but she sure wished she did. She remembered what it looked like, all the minute details, the rounded panel with the raised symbols. How it called to her with the beeping and flashing light when she was in danger. Her memory of it was keen. Her connection to it was heightened. So much was her desire to have one in her hand again–it began to feel like it was there. With her left hand on the wheel, she lifted her right hand–"It's actually there!" Laurel proclaimed with excitement.

Laurel was happily surprised that she was able to call up her own personal CTD when she wanted to. Her agenda; She wanted to finish the reconstruction of her grandparents mansion, it would be hers now to use as her home base when she was between jobs. Her following task– Arizona, to retrieve the CTD that Father Vega called a 'Spiritual Artifact'.

Then her thoughts went to her friend, Professor Matthew Vaughn. He did ask her if we were still good about starting over. He is so hot! And, that kiss. . . Humm. She replayed that memory, savoring how he smelled and felt with his hard body next to hers. Feeling his lips against hers. Yes, he bothers me very much when he starts touching me. I will have to watch that if we are going to have a new and different relationship. I think he understands me better now, who I am and where I'm coming from. He's definitely attracted to the human part of me, no longer fearing the extra-terrestrial energies he once picked up around me.

I wonder if he's up for any new adventures.

ABOUT THE AUTHOR

Linda S. Gleason: The power of the word has always been a key fascination while I worked in Real Estate and later carried into my Past Life Regressions with the writings of many Trance Induction Scripts and CD's.

I have had many fine teachers during my path that have guided and positively influenced me to reach my goals. I believe that I am good at reflecting this on to others with my writings. Linda resides just outside Springfield, MO.

www.ingramcontent.com/pod-product-compliance
Lightning Source LLC
Chambersburg PA
CBHW071124170626
46809CB00002B/489